THE COIN

1/23

Marissa -
Hope you enjoy the read.
May God bless you!
Freedom over tyranny!
W.T.

THE COIN

W. T. EARLEY

LIBERTY HILL PUBLISHING

Liberty Hill Publishing
2301 Lucien Way #415
Maitland, FL 32751
407.339.4217
www.libertyhillpublishing.com

Unless otherwise indicated, Scripture quotations taken from the King James Version (KJV)–*public domain.*

Paperback ISBN-13: 978-1-66286-328-8
Ebook ISBN-13: 978-1-66286-329-5

Dedication

To my loves, G 'n' E.
May the world found in these pages never come to pass.
Freedom over tyranny, always.

Cast of Main Characters

Jeanette "Jeannie" W Garcia, M.D. – OB/GYN; wife of Rolando Garcia

Rolando Rafael Garcia, J.D. – Lawyer and columnist; husband of Dr. Jeannie Garcia

Stefan Ertz, Ph.D. – Director, Living Legacy; husband of Anjali Gowda

Anjali Gowda, Ph.D. – Wife of Stefan Ertz

Cassandra "Cassie" Bowles – Communications Director, Province House

Boris "Bo" Berko – Senior Advisor, The Legacy

Eleanor Uhegwu, M.D. – OB/GYN; colleague of Dr. Garcia

J. Edward Klein – Author and columnist

Henry "Hank" Hatua – Inventor and entrepreneur

Simon Bowles – Father of Cassandra Bowles

Analia Garcia – Oldest daughter of Dr. Jeannie and Rolando Garcia

Julieta Garcia – Youngest daughter of Dr. Jeannie and Rolando Garcia

General Anthony Briggs – Commanding officer, *Molon Labe*

General Warren Wright – Commanding officer, The Legacy

Supreme General Janice Cafferty – Top military commander, The Legacy

Alondra Garcia – Mother of Rolando Garcia

Eve – *Molon Labe* patriot

Klaus Markus "Zim" Zimmer – Team leader, *Molon Labe*

Mitchell Iron Falcon – Commanding officer, *Molon Labe*

Shontae Lewis – Commanding officer, *Molon Labe*

Frank Gies – Co-owner, Che Bakery

Bhavna Gowda Ertz – Oldest daughter of Anjali Gowda and Stefan Ertz

Nyra Karin Ertz – Youngest daughter of Anjali Gowda and Stefan Ertz

Headmaster Rice – Principal, Revolution Elementary

Anthony "Tony" P. Bowles – Great grandfather of Cassandra Bowles

Emily Bowles – Mother of Cassandra Bowles

Hannah Klein – Granddaughter of J. Edward Klein

Dianne Hutchinson Bowles – Wife of Simon Bowles

Alexandria Aquino – Team leader, *Molon Labe*

Martín – *Maître d', Casa de Flor*

Zach – Team member, *Molon Labe*

Marvin Cruickshank – Farmer; husband of Betty Cruickshank

Betty Cruickshank – Farmer; wife of Marvin Cruickshank

Disung Lee – Director, Global Population Longevity Center, People's Republic of China

Katrina Wisniewski – Cousin of Zim Zimmer

Chuck Wisniewski – Husband of Katrina Wisniewski

Everett – Chief of staff to Boris Berko

General Zhang – Commanding officer, People's Liberation Army, People's Republic of China

Margo Gies – Co-owner, Che Bakery

CHAPTER I

"Push. Push!"

Another wave of excruciating pain enveloped the mother-to-be. Sweat streamed down her face. She pushed so hard that the nurse busily worked to keep everything clean and sterile.

"You can do it, Audrey. Focus and prepare to push as hard as you can for as long as you can. Ready?"

Audrey nodded and muttered something inaudible under her breath. She was spent, yet not done.

"In three, two, one. Breathe, Audrey . . . and push!"

A shriek pierced through the delivery room and beyond. The crown began to show. The baby's head appeared. Then, nothing more.

"Push, Audrey! Almost there. Push!"

No movement. The baby's head was fully exposed. The baby's body was not moving.

"Audrey, we need you to breathe and bear down. One final push. Give it everything you have. In three, two, one. Push! Push! Push!"

The lithe young woman's face was scrunched, blotchy, and exhibited a vibrant shade of red. Sweat emptied out of every pore. Her deep guttural scream belied her demure stature. It was her final, draining push to the finish line. She braced herself, then pushed with everything she had left.

Nothing moved.

The baby's left shoulder was stuck behind the pelvic bone. Without getting the body through, the baby could not begin breathing.

In stark contrast to the animated and encouraging coach she was seconds earlier, the doctor calmly yet sternly directed her staff. "Prepare for McRoberts," she ordered. "Ready? Now."

The two nurses immediately began flexing Audrey's hips to her abdomen, each succeeding flexion designed to create more space to loosen the baby's stuck shoulder.

Still, nothing.

Audrey sensed something terribly wrong. She felt like a helpless onlooker to her own child's birth. And she was becoming so anxious that physical pain was a dull afterthought.

"Prep for Gaskin."

"Audrey, I am going to need your help now. Everything is going to be okay," the doctor said with reassuring eyes. "One of the baby's shoulders is stuck. So, we're going to need to get you on all fours to help free the baby. Do you understand?"

Audrey nodded.

"The nurses are going to help move you into the all-fours position. Ready?"

Audrey nodded again.

"Let's do it, in three, two, one. Move into Gaskin."

The nurses on either side of Audrey helped to move her while the baby's head still protruded out. Time was of the essence.

Audrey was now on all fours. The doctor hoped that the act of rotating the mother to the all-fours position would set the impacted shoulder free.

Nothing.

Audrey was clearly panicked. Tears mixed with sweat running like a small river down her face.

If this was another time, before socialized medicine and the rationing of healthcare, an emergency C-section would have been performed. That used to be the go-to answer for most birthing complications. However, in the post-war and post-regime change era, this was not an option, at least not for someone like Audrey in this particular hospital. Such luxuries were reserved for the privileged few and only available at party-affiliated healthcare facilities.

Turning to her staff, the doctor simply said, "Woods."

"Audrey. I'm going to help move the shoulder manually. It will feel a little tight and may cause pain and cramping. Please do everything that you can to remain still and focused. It will be over very soon. Everything will be okay, but I really need you to keep as still as possible. Understand? Okay?"

Audrey breathed in deeply to steel herself. She then nodded an emphatic yes.

Without wasting a second, the doctor carefully and deftly entered the birthing canal. Her hand immediately found the non-impacted shoulder and began to slowly rotate it. She began to move it like an expert sommelier uses a corkscrew.

Audrey gasped but stayed as still and quiet as she could as she began to mouth something akin to a prayer.

The doctor twisted her arm again. She closed her eyes in focus as she continued twisting.

"Got it!"

The baby's cry was as welcome a sound as could be for mother and delivery team.

Audrey cried tears of mixed joy and residual pain. The attending staff smiled while collectively sighing relief. For the doctor, she was pleased. Not overly so, though. This was her job. She was well trained to do this . . . even more, if needed.

As Audrey handled her newborn baby for the first time, the doctor approached her with a golden box. About the size of a large hand, it was quite ornate in design. On all sides of the box, save one, were gold inlays in a woven floral design. On one side of the box, there was an opening with what looked like the petals of a flower in gold on the perimeter with a circular hole in the middle.

The doctor presented the box to Audrey. Just like she had said hundreds of times before, but with emphasis as if the script was newly minted just for this occasion, the doctor pronounced, "Congratulations. On behalf of The Legacy, with her first breath, we welcome your baby girl into the Book of Life. Thanks be to The Legacy."

On cue, Audrey pulled out a gold coin from her gown's pocket. Consistent with established ritual, she placed it carefully into the circular hole in the box. A perfect fit.

The gold coin illuminated.

CHAPTER II

Rolando kept pushing his body harder. Finding the most streamlined position while working his arms with precision and a faster and stronger pull, he increased his pace ever so slightly. He passed the halfway mark; no time to give in to the inner voice now, that voice suggesting that today could be an off day. A day of easy rest. A day to coast. Funny, he heard that voice every day. Good thing for him, he rarely listened.

The salt water kept pace with him, increasing its flow. Rolando, or "Double," as his family and friends have called him for many years on account of his middle name being Rafael, was lost in his effort to beat his 2K time. Finishing strong with a negative split was his daily goal. This time was different. He felt the effects of aging. His shoulders ached. His arms felt the burn. It was harder and harder to keep an efficient stroke, especially considering the additional twenty pounds added from his college days. But his will was stronger now. Much stronger. Something about "experience" he thought would carry the day—never admitting the "A" word and its impact on his efforts: Age.

As a kid, he was a junior swimmer. His parents thought young "Roly" would benefit from the social interaction—and exercise. He hated it. As a twelve-year-old, he was a bit pudgy. Not fat, but Rolando Rafael Garcia was a well-fed boy since birth. In a world where resources were scarce, having enough food for your kid was viewed as loving and sacrificial, no more so than in the Garcia family's neighborhood of Upper Guevara. Set among a series of high rises, reminiscent in "style" to those rows of monoliths found in Stalin-era eastern bloc countries, there was little to bring pride to those families occupying the concrete monstrosities except the pride in devoting every last available resource to their children. It brought a sense of hope to the hopeless. For decades, hope was a word rarely used, especially for those outside The Legacy's inner circle.

Rolando loved being in the water. It was his safe place, a place where he could be alone with his thoughts and feelings. A place where he had laughed and even cried while stroking away with nobody the wiser. There was something refreshing and renewing each time he stepped into his pool. Each swim session, he thought of two people. One, his paternal grandmother, who could not swim and had an intense fear of the water. Second, his uncle. His uncle was a successful collegiate swimmer who went on to great success in the military. He was on the fast track to senior leadership, but his "politics" got in the way. By politics, Rolando's uncle did not play politics. He did his job. He did it well. He was loyal. Loyal to his country. Loyal to a fault. Loyal to his death.

Rolando felt gentle pressure, two separate taps on his left wrist. Two hundred meters to go. He kept pushing through his workout. He had settled into a good pace. Soon, it'd be time to turn it up a notch.

Every now and again, he'd get a good mouthful of water. It was a minor annoyance, certainly not more annoying when he swallowed what seemed to be a gallon of pool water when he first tried out for the Guevara Junior Swim Team. What he did at that time could barely be called swimming. His body position was all wrong. He dragged his legs along as if they were anchors. He consistently crossed the centerline of his stroke, making his body look like a coiling snake with each movement. His poor mechanics, body weight, and lack of self-confidence led to a miserable experience, an experience made only worse by having ingested so much water that he grabbed the lane buoys and began to heave. Fortunately for the swimmers in other lanes, they had an intuitive sense to steer clear of him as they smoothly went on their way. But for Roly Poly, the retching seemed as if it wouldn't stop. The only fortunate part of all of this was that the pool's water covered the tears he was unsuccessfully fighting back. It was his worst day ever.

Yet, there was no quit in young Rolando.. He went from Roly Poly at age thirteen, to province champion at sixteen, and off to college at nineteen with all expenses paid. These were the days before everyone got a free ride. It didn't bother him that he had to earn it as he believed having done so set him up for his future.

Never quit. Never ever quit. That was the motto he lived by. It was the motto he repeatedly recited to his two young girls. But these were times of many mottos. Many of the contemporary mottos competed directly with those of his upbringing. He had to file those older teachings away, perhaps never to revisit. They were now considered too dangerous to think . . . and certainly too dangerous to utter aloud.

He thought about his grandparents. Both sets. What their lives must've been like at his age. How different. What could they have predicted? Would it have changed any of their decisions? Would they have had children knowing what he knew now? Then, he laughed. Face straight down in the water between bi-lateral breathing strokes, he laughed aloud. It just sounded like a muted howl in the water. What a silly thought, he considered. After all, he had two kids of his own, and he clearly knew now what he knew now, maybe not enough oxygen getting to his brain. He chuckled again.

A single tap on his wrist—one hundred meters to go. It was time to start moving harder, faster, and yet maintain his stroke's integrity. Turnover rate increasing. Breathing accelerating. He'd grab an extra pull out of his breath every second or third turn. The water was having a hard time keeping up with him. He stretched his body out further as if he could simply extend his spine when his mind desired.

The aches turned to burn, the burn with which he was very familiar. That burn was a comfortable friend, one that gave him discomfort, but one that gave him so much success. Over the years, he had learned to push into the burn. The burn wouldn't go away, but if he swam faster, it would end sooner. So, why not go all out?

He was in the zone. Nothing was in his mind now except stroke, breath, body lengthening, and pushing into the burn. It was his escape. Other than his family, this is what he lived for. Sheer focus. Complete the goal. Get that negative split.

A loud buzzing sound disrupted and enveloped Rolando during his final twenty meters. As much as he wanted to continue and finish what he started, he knew he couldn't. This wasn't quitting. This was surviving.

He stood up, hit the off switch, and composed himself. His pool was not much longer than he was. It was an inside pool, with just enough depth and length for Rolando to swim without touching bottom or edges. It pushed a current, which adjusted with his stroke and pace.

Trying to regain his breathing and not sound so winded, he closed his eyes and gathered himself. He then simultaneously touched a button and opened his eyes. He looked at the camera lens attached to the wall adjacent to his pool. He spoke first.

"Wéi, nǐ hǎo."

Chapter III

Province House was as non-descript of a building that there was. Located on *Avenida de la Victoria*, it was as immense as it was drab. There was no signage. It wasn't necessary. Everyone knew what the building was. They might have also suspected what went on there. For most, except for a select few, that's where the clarity became quite hazy.

Most warehouses had more personality than Province House. That was by design. The sheer size of the building was intended to show power—in an absolute sense—and strike fear into those who might attempt to challenge that power. The massive proportion was combined with selective archways at every block. It may have been the architect's effort to avoid the mind-numbing work of lining block by block of symmetrical, rigid, gray, and imposing structures. Province House took up an area of seven city blocks by five. Not all thirty-five square city blocks were built out. There were gardens, a small lake (really a large pond), and a military parade staging area.

On the east side, an elementary school field trip entrance exhibited the most ornate welcoming. An extension from the building to Avenida de la Victoria provided protection from the elements for disembarking children. The extension was externally adorned with an inlay of silhouetted historical political figures from The Legacy. While the inside quasi-tunnel used a mixture of light and sound to create an exciting, welcoming, and educational atmosphere for the children, all by design, nothing went without a thought in the regime.

The inside area accessible to the children and other guests resembled a mixture of multi-media showrooms and political campaign offices, along with related games to play, all focused on educating the attendees on the benefits brought to them and their fellow neighbors by The Legacy's varied programs: free schooling, including college; free health, dental, and vision care; food subsidies (even free food in many cases) and distribution into previously neglected areas; free or subsidized entertainment; free or subsidized housing; quality communications with free network access; and free or subsidized transportation. Noticeably missing was mention of an aged population.

Older residents, meaning those sixty or older, were a rarity. They just weren't seen—or talked about. A series of global pandemics decimated the older, chronically ill, and disabled populations to such a great extent that to see or know of someone in that group was an oddity. Medical science had progressed yet, notwithstanding The Legacy's claimed efforts to the contrary, there seemed to be a substantial failing in protecting those vulnerable persons.

Dr. Stefan Ertz raised his left wrist, showing his watch. It was more than a watch. It was a combination of watch, wallet, geo-locator, and passport. It also contained access to his health records, bank account, family heritage, familial associations, and, if needed, data on his temperature, brain wave function, and more. Some surmised that it also was a recording device that could pick up even the slightest whisper.

The solid, metal door opened. He always entered on Province House's northwest side. Not by choice. That was the sole access point for him.

As director of Living Legacy, Dr. Ertz led a team of researchers, technologists, futurists, and ethicists. Their mission was simple: manage and match anticipated population growth with projected available resources. On the job for over eighteen months, Dr. Ertz felt like he was finally fitting into The Legacy's framework. His transition wasn't particularly smooth.

As a young boy growing up in Borgsdorf, a smallish rural area approximately thirty kilometers NNW from Berlin, Stefan Ertz enjoyed science over *Fußball*. He knew he wanted something more than to work in the brewery alongside his father, uncles, and, no doubt, cousins in the future. For ages, they were brewery men, perhaps better described as brewery men for the ages. As far as he knew, his family worked in the brewery business for hundreds of years, even predating the reign of Kaiser Wilhelm. At least that's what he was told many times by elder family members, who, after having sampled some of their professional output, were keen to revisit old family stories and potential exaggerations. He didn't mind. He enjoyed their enthusiastic storytelling . . . notwithstanding how loud it became with each passing *Schlucken*.

He did well in school. Not the top student, but close. He studied at the prestigious Marie-Curie-Gymnasium before he matriculated to ETH Zurich (Swiss Federal Institute of Technology). His family was shocked. Although he was considered smart enough by his parents, never could they have imagined that he would be accepted into one of the world's highest-ranked universities. At the time, ETH Zurich was right up there alongside Massachusetts Institute of Technology

(MIT), Stanford, University of Cambridge, and Nanyang Technology University (NTU) as the top universities for science and technology. Perhaps excelling in his *Abitur* exams helped. It might have also helped that his middle name was Einstein, who just so happened to be the most notable ETH Zurich alumnus of all time.

At ETH Zurich, Stefan dabbled in several areas of studies. He had interests in so many things, including medicine (fundamental research, technological advancement in diagnostics, prognostics, and therapy, along with building infrastructure to advance these studies), sustainability (food security, energy supply and climate change, and habitat and natural resources management), and even manufacturing (future-oriented production and manufacturing processes brought to scale).

Although he had interest in those separate areas and took some classes to explore that interest while at ETH Zurich, his love was saved for just one topic and one topic only: big data. He loved data. The bigger, the better. At ETH Zurich, Stefan was exposed to all aspects of the data science world. He took classes in data management, engineering, statistics, machine learning, algorithms, data optimization, and data visualization. The more he learned, the more he wanted to learn. He especially found compelling the interface between data management (big data management) and engineering. How those disciplines, working in tandem, impacted social, economic, medical, and environmental sciences kept him up late into the night almost every night.

He was hooked by his studies, so hooked that the thought of having a social life while at the university was never a thought. Or, at least, he never admitted having thought about it, that is, until he met a graduate student from India, Anjali Gowda.

Anjali Gowda hailed from the state of Karnataka, located in southwestern India. A beautiful and diverse state, and an economic powerhouse within the country given Bangalore's (as it was referred to in past times) location therein, Anjali's family wasn't part of the elite or even middle class. She grew up on the family farm outside Gulbarga City, near Gulbarga Fort. And she grew up poor.

Her economic position did not seem to slow her down. Anjali was smart, wicked smart. She took advantage of every opportunity presented to her, no matter how slim her chances were to succeed. Anjali started reading at three years and never stopped. She'd read anything. She'd even read signs, packaging, cartons, and more in all languages. It didn't matter to her. She'd just read. If she didn't know the language, she'd try to figure it out . . . or, at least, make believe in her own mind that she knew what it was saying.

In school, she always sat up front. Anjali did her homework and even more studying beyond her assignments each day. She still had chores to do on her family's black cotton farm. But she would squeeze in extra reading time whenever she could. To do that, she'd always have a book with her. She would always travel with at least two books. One, a technical book to advance her technical understanding. The other, a guilty pleasure book—what was then referred to as a romance novel. Her favorite author was the American Catherine Bybee. She read all her books. It was Anjali's escape, her fantasy. Her drive to achieve that fantasy life was found in the technical books.

Her intellect and drive gained her admission to the prestigious Dayananda Sagar College of Engineering in Bengaluru (Bangalore). She almost didn't accept the invitation to attend given the distance from her family. Although they shared a state, the drive from Gulbarga to Bengaluru (Bangalore) was long. At almost 600 km, it would take at least eleven plus hours to make that trek by auto—even longer by bus, and even longer yet if traffic was an issue. And it was almost always an issue.

However, the cheapest and fastest way to make that trek was via Indian Railways. Anjali's Uncle Raadhik, who became an accountant for the government in Bengaluru, promised to sponsor her travel and other necessary expenses. Her immediate family could not afford to assist in any way. After all, there were six other mouths to feed (not including her parents), bodies to clothe, and educations to consider. Plus, farm expenses usually commanded every last resource the family could muster.

Anjali accepted her place at Dayananda Sagar College of Engineering, and it quickly became home for her. She threw herself into both her studies and social activities. She was an outgoing young woman. Quick to laugh, quick to smile, and quick-witted herself, her innate ability to connect with people was one of her greatest strengths. Plus, it didn't hurt that she was easy on the eyes.

Anjali embraced the Bachelor of Engineering program with an emphasis in Artificial Intelligence and Machine Learning. She was one of only three females with that focus. Tough program. Tough ladies to confront the studies and historical bias. Anjali Gowda stood above all of them, male and female alike.

She graduated first in her class. The world of AI was available to her anywhere in the world. ETH Zurich offered her not only a place in the master's program, but it also offered her a job and housing. It was an easy choice for her. Although her family would be even farther away, she had grown accustomed to being at a significant distance. She couldn't make it home more than twice in any one year. In her final year at Dayananda, it was only once. She figured that she could most probably meet that same number no matter where in the world she was, especially since her future job prospects and income potential looked very bright.

At ETH Zurich, Anjali worked on her master's degree while also serving as a teaching assistant in certain AI/Machine Learning classes. And that's where Cupid's arrow struck right between the eyes.

Anjali was a student teacher for an introductory "AI Meets Big Data: Past, Present, and Future" class. Sitting in the lecture was a first-year student from Borgsdorf, Stefan Ertz. Unlike his teacher, Stefan liked to sit in the back. It gave him a better overall view of what was happening. Plus, he had an intense dislike of having anyone sit behind him. He would've felt comfortable in the Old West, just like James Butler Hickok, better known as Wild Bill, who had an affinity for sitting with his back to the wall.

As a front-row devotee all her academic life, it was frustrating for Anjali to see habitual backbenchers. So, she decided to make it her sport to save all the tough questions for members of the notorious backrow bunch. That included Stefan.

Although the classes were conducted in English, there were many sidebar comments in German. Anjali's English was akin to a native speaker, while her *Deutsch* was only a hair better than basic. But she had an uncanny dexterity with language, an exceptional ear for it. That was truer for accents—she could divine location within one hundred kilometers or less. She knew that Mr. Ertz, or *Herr Ertz*, was not a Swiss German. Nor was he Austrian. Not Bavarian either. He sounded like he could be a Prussian from Berlin. The giveaway? He'd greet her before class with a shy *Juten Tach* as opposed to the *Hoch Deutsch* morning greeting of *Guten Tag*.

She thought she'd test her hypothesis. One day, when discussing the properties associated with Hadoop, she asked, "What are the common input formats in Hadoop?" Customary silence followed her question. Many times, it seemed like these were rhetorical exercises. However, in this case, she focused her eyes firmly on Stefan and asked, "*Piepel*?" In Berliner slang, *Piepel* means "young man." The standard German equivalent (*Hoch Deutsch*) was *kleiner Junge*. In English, it sounded like an invitation for "people" to answer.

Stefan, thinking he was being called on and referred to as young man, straightened himself up in his chair and felt his face turning warm. He knew the answer. He just felt all eyes on him, especially the TA's.

"Er, ahem, the common input formats in Hadoop are text, sequence file, and key value. I can discuss them further if you wish."

"No, thank you. That is correct. Thank you, *Piepel*." She smiled as she said *Piepel* slowly with emphasis.

Stefan knew at that moment he'd been set up. He was part bemused and amused. Above all else, he was intrigued.

What followed was a twist on the classic tale. Boy meets girl. Girl embarrasses boy. Boy gets interested. Boy embarrasses himself . . . over and over and over. Girl finally says yes. Then, they marry and live happily ever after. That's how they described it to friends over the years.

They repeated this story hundreds of times without any appreciation of changes to come. How would they have known to do otherwise? How would anyone?

Chapter IV

Dr. Jeanette "Jeannie" W Garcia poured herself a half-glass of red wine. Then she thought better of it. Instead, she filled her glass to the top. One of those days . . . again. She removed the clip that was straining to hold her flowing, curly hair together behind her face. She slowly combed her fingers through her hair; in part, to detangle and, in part, to emphasize that this day was coming to an end. Tomorrow could wait. But first, wine. And quiet.

The stillness lasted less than five minutes as the front door to the high-rise living quarters flew open, and two screaming girls called for her running full speed, oblivious to the wine in hand.

"Mommy, Mommy!"

"Hey, Dad, Mom's home! Hey, Mom!"

Two girls, aged eight and six, found a spot on their mom's lap. Thankfully, not a drop of red spilled.

"Hi, hon. Tough day, I see." Rolando bent down to kiss his wife.

"Gross," said the youngest.

"Yuck. Do you mind? There are children present!" emphasized the oldest with an over-the-top dramatic flair.

The parents smiled that parent smile. They briefly kissed again.

"Let's go, J girl. You don't need to see this." With that, the older of the two girls took her younger sister's hand, and they ran together down the hall giggling. A door shut.

"Can't say it was any better or worse than any other recent days," Jeannie sighed as she took another sip.

Rolando poured himself a small splash of red wine. Trying to get back in shape wouldn't be easier if he gave into temptations like wine very often, he thought.

"Care to share?"

"I'm not sure where to begin or how to tell you what's troubling me. It's weird. I get the feeling that something's wrong."

"I see. I can cut back on my workouts and do more with the girls—"

Jeannie interrupted, "That's not—"

"Okay. Sorry. I'll just listen."

"Thanks. I can't shake this feeling that's been growing inside me. Something is terribly wrong at work. I can't place it. I had a very disturbing dream a few nights ago. It seemed so real. I was doing my job, delivering babies. Then, I had blood all over my hands. It was all over me. I could smell it. It was a strong smell. But it didn't feel like life. It felt like, felt like . . . death."

"I'm sorry."

"Here's the thing. It had nothing to do with me. It had something to do with something else. I had blood on me, but there was no source for it. What made it even stranger, I got the feeling that I was just a cog in the machine. Something. Somewhere. Something was not right. Something wasn't working the way it was supposed to."

She took a breath. And another.

"See, I can't put my finger on it. It just doesn't make sense. But, Rol, it was so real. It was as real as me touching you now."

She reached out and grabbed his hand. She wouldn't let go.

"My life has been about life. That's why I do what I do. I know there are times of death. But I know I can save lives. In fact, just today, I know that I saved one, maybe two lives. I'm good at what I do."

"Yep, you are. Just don't dislocate your shoulder patting yourself on the back."

They both chuckled.

"Seriously," Rolando continued softly, "you're so talented. I don't quite understand your dream, but I do know this. It was only a dream. Things are crazy now. They have been crazy, unsettling, even nightmarish. Nothing seems right, so your dream, at some level, makes sense to me."

She managed a smiled. Rol, as she called him, always knew how to soothe her nerves. "You're right. It was only a dream. Strange how some dreams stick to us . . . and with us."

"Yep. Strange indeed." Rolando drifted somewhere else.

Chapter V

It was one of those still nights. Not a breeze. No noise. No babies crying. No transportation moving. No dogs barking. That wasn't strange, as there were hardly any dogs left in the city. It was as if everything had come to a complete standstill.

A small group of commandoes decked out in all-black technical suits slipped softly into one of the high-rise apartment buildings. They made their way up a stairwell without making a sound.

The seven of them stopped in front of a non-descript door. Using hand signals only, they assumed their positions.

One of the commandoes raised his left wrist. The door unlocked. Again, no sound to be heard. The commandoes entered. No lights, just wearing glasses, allowing for perfect nighttime vision.

Inside, a family was sleeping soundly. A man and woman slept with a little girl between them. She was clutching a small stuffy friend while also clinging to the woman's arm.

Three commandoes entered the sleeping room. Two others scoured the home, looking for something. Another two entered a child's bedroom, where another child was sleeping on the top level of a bunkbed.

One of the commandoes leaned in toward the sleeping man. He got right up to the man's face. He whispered in the man's ear.

"Don't make a sound. Do not make a sound."

The man stirred. His eyes opened.

"Don't move. Don't make a sound. Blink if you understand."

The man blinked, although he could have been blinking to get his bearings.

"Do as I say, or your family won't survive. Understand? Blink twice."

The man complied.

"Now, slowly, get out of bed and follow me into the other room."

The man slowly and carefully rose and slipped out of bed. He was as quiet as could be. While rising, he stole a glimpse of his wife and youngest daughter. He took a mental picture. As he walked down the hall, the man looked at his sleeping older daughter. All he saw was the back of her head. He longed to see her face. That was not to be. He closed his eyes and took another mental picture. Something in his gut told him that this would be the last time he would see them.

The commando leader signaled the man to follow him out the front door. The other commandoes followed. The door was closed. Not one person stirred. Not one person heard anything. Not one person knew they had been there except for four important items that were missing.

A bookcase near the window in the front room had a thoughtful mixture of family pictures and books. All books were technical in nature, save for a few language dictionaries and kids' books too. On the top two shelves were four, ornate golden boxes. The circular hole in the middle of each of those boxes was empty.

Chapter VI

The governing business portion of Province House was mostly conducted in multiple subterranean floors. While the reception and meeting rooms, along with senior official offices, were above ground, the real heartbeat of day-to-day activity was below street level.

Cassandra Bowles had worked at Province House for over a decade. Hailing from London's West End, she started as a kindergarten tour guide and made her way up the ladder (or down the elevator) in successive moves every eighteen to twenty-four months. There was usually an opportunity that opened if you were patient enough.

Cassandra worked on the B-3 level in the communications department. Her job was simple enough. Find creative ways to connect the regime's goals with its citizens. The main points of repetition were based upon the foundational principles of the three Ls:

- Liberalism
- Loyalty
- Legacy

Each story, billboard, banner, and more that Cassandra and her team produced had to answer one question: How does this tie into one of the three Ls?

Cassandra wasn't a true believer, but she was a true operator. She had a keen political sense. She had an eye for talent and hired the best available talent to work on her team. She also had a mysterious way of extracting the best work product and then making changes to her team.

"Keep it fresh and keep it on point!" was her consistent direction to her team. She also received direction. And it was always delivered sternly and clearly.

Boris "Bo" Berko was a humorless bureaucrat who struck fear into all who crossed his path or even heard his name uttered. Raised in the former Ukraine, he was the eldest son of a tradesman. He was as smart as he was vicious. He was also shrouded in mystery. Yet, he had unfettered access to and undue influence on The Legacy. He was described by some, in hushed terms, as being the reincarnation of Rasputin. Curiously, those who made such statements disappeared.

Cassandra was engaging with her team when Berko walked in.

"Bowles, a moment." Berko routinely called Cassandra by her family name. It was as if each time he uttered "Bowles," he wanted to stress to her that her place in the regime was tenuous and that she served at his pleasure.

Cassandra immediately shut down her presentation and followed Berko into an adjoining room. He closed the door.

"New orders from The Legacy," he said matter-of-factly.

Cassandra had her tablet in front of her.

"Shall I use voice dictate or take notes, sir?"

"Neither. Put that aside. This is of the highest security."

Cassandra complied and put her tablet down on the table. They both stood. Although she stood a half-head taller than Berko, his presence consumed the room in a way that made him seem much taller than anyone else.

Berko spoke deliberately and calmly. "The Legacy has decided to recall all Legacy Coins. Someone in technology has discovered a glitch in a batch of coins manufactured and distributed in the past several years. As a result, and to avoid needless panic, we need to develop a comms strategy to have the public return all Legacy Coins. Of course, they will be replaced with newly minted Legacy Coins that do not contain the defect. The replacement coins are ready to be distributed upon return of the defective coins."

"Timing of comms strategy, sir?" asked Cassandra.

"Immediate attention. This is your number-one priority. Number one. There is no second. We need to present the comms strategy to The Legacy's Leadership Council tomorrow. By the end of the day today, you will provide me with alternatives. I know this is a short timeline." Berko reached out and touched her arm. "I have faith in you, Bowles."

She didn't know whether to feel flattered or fear. Perhaps both. His touch caused her to feel a sense of cold coupled with dread . . . and a hint of nausea. She shivered ever so slightly and hoped he wouldn't notice.

Bo Berko had an extremely high emotional intelligence level. He didn't use it in a traditional way. He used his high EQ level in a way to increase his influence. He also used it to control people.

"We won't let you or The Legacy down, sir."

"Good."

Berko headed toward the door. He turned back to Cassandra.

"How's your father doing? I hope his recovery is going well."

Managing a small smile, Cassandra responded. "Thank you for asking, sir. He's improving."

"Good. Very good. Hope that continues. Thanks be to The Legacy." Berko smiled. His smile wasn't sincere. It was more of a message. Everything he said aloud or used his body language, it was all intended to communicate on multiple levels. As a seasoned communicator, Cassandra understood. His message was clear.

After Berko left and was gone to at least a count of ten, she shivered again. This time, anyone walking by would have noticed.

Chapter VII

Jeannie felt much better. She got a good night's sleep for the first time in a long time. Her nerves had calmed. The day was sunny and bright. It matched her mood.

No matter how much rest she got the night before, Jeannie was always up early. She was regularly first to her office. She'd use the time to quietly enjoy her coffee and prep for the day. She reviewed her schedule. No surgeries. Nothing planned, at least. Somehow, babies *in utero* had their own timing and agenda, so the written schedule didn't always match the day's actual schedule.

Dr. Eleanor "Ellie" Uhegwu peeked her head into Jeannie's office. "Ready?"

"Yep. Let's do this."

The two colleagues headed to a nearby examination room. Jeannie disrobed and changed into a gown.

"Okay, you know the drill," Ellie said as she began a physical exam. Blood draw. Urine test. Breast and pelvic exam. They joked and smiled throughout.

"Well, as you already suspected and probably knew, I am proud to tell you," Ellie said as she took on a more formal tone, "on behalf of The Legacy, we welcome your pregnancy. May your baby be entered into The Legacy's Book of Life."

The two colleagues, in actuality, good friends, embraced.

"Does Rolando know?" asked Ellie.

"Nope. Not yet. Didn't want to get his hopes up."

"He's looking for a mini-me, huh?"

Jeannie laughed. "I'd say so. Don't get me wrong. He loves our girls. He loves being their daddy. To his core, he does. But I know deep down he'd love to have a son too, someone to share what being a man is, someone to carry on his legacy, in a different way. You know what I mean?"

"I see." Ellie suddenly lowered her voice, spoke slowly, and chose her words wisely. "Jeannie, I totally understand. I love you, Rolando, and the girls. Please tread carefully about why this pregnancy is important to you." She paused, "You know what I mean."

"Oh Ellie, I do. Thank you, my dear friend. And know I love you too."

The two embraced again.

"Okay, guessing you'd prefer your muscle versus direct injection. Am I right?" Ellie asked.

"Yep, you got it"

"Right or left?"

Jeannie pointed to her left. "This one, if you please."

"Just a quick prick." Ellie administered a shot. Quick in and out. Jeannie winced slightly.

"Guess I ought to get back to helping others." Jeannie chuckled, "But not dressed like this."

As she started to change out of the examination gown and put her clothes back on, Ellie interrupted her.

"Can you believe this? I almost let you get away without this."

With that, Ellie extended her hand. In it was a gold coin.

"Your Legacy Coin for this one. Congratulations again." Ellie left.

Jeannie looked at the Legacy Coin. Without another thought, she placed it in her pocket.

CHAPTER VIII

"Here, take this. It's soup. Chicken and rice. Your favorite." An older man craned his neck up to meet the soup. It was good.

"Take it slowly. Just a little bit at a time."

The voice reassured the man. It was a young woman, his youngest granddaughter. She always found ways to make him feel better. This time proved no different.

"You'll start to feel better in a few days. You need to get your strength back. The doctor said the surgery went well." She smiled. "She got it. It was all intact." Her demeanor promptly changed. "Opa, you ended up with an infection. That's what's zapped your strength. You'll get your voice back soon. She had to intubate you, so your throat will be sore for a while"

He nodded slightly.

"Just one more spoonful." He took it. Then relaxed his head back onto the pillow.

"Please get some rest. I love you, Opa."

He closed his eyes. His granddaughter continued to hold his hand until he began to breathe deeply. He was resting and looked to be resting comfortably.

His sleep was not so comfortable, though. He dreamt he was a kid again. He knew he was wearing his finest clothes as he looked down at his shoes. They were polished black, with a few scuff marks. He must've been a young kid as his family kept calling him Jimmy. They spoke to him in the way you speak to small children or dogs you love. He held a basket. It had some eggs and a few chocolates in it. It must've been Easter. He was encouraged by his mother to keep looking for more Easter eggs.

"Come on, Jimmy. There's more out there, honey. Don't give up. Keep looking."

In his dream, his mother's words were just like he remembered her voice. Her face, though, was not his mother's face. It was something else. But her voice kept encouraging him.

"Jimmy, go to your left. Farther left. You're getting closer."

Instead of finding an Easter egg, he found a box hidden behind a tree. It wasn't hidden particularly well, just enough so the box wasn't in plain view. In his dream, young Jimmy picked up the box. It was a beautiful box. He looked at it with amazement. He had never seen anything like it in his life, at least he thought so in his dream.

"Look, Mommy, look what I found. A box. A beautiful box. I love it, Mommy. It's so pretty. Just like you."

He always told his mom that she was pretty. It made her so happy.

"Bring it here Jimmy. Mommy wants to see it."

He walked toward her. He still recognized her voice. And he called her Mommy. But something didn't seem right. He couldn't see her face. No matter how hard he tried or where he moved in relation to her, he could never get a glimpse of her face. He recognized her hair. It was reddish brown. And the voice was clearly hers. Jimmy thought, *Why is she hiding her face from me?*

"Mommy, can I keep the pretty box? Can I?"

"Give it to Mommy, Jimmy."

"Mommy, I really love this box. Can I please have it?"

Jimmy looked at the box again. It was glowing on the opposite side.

"Jimmy, give that box to me now. I need it." Jimmy's mother's voice turned from sweet and loving to agitated and anxious.

"James Edward, give me the box at once." This was no longer his mother's voice. This voice scared him.

"Okay, Mommy, I'll give you my pretty box."

As he prepared to hand the box to his mother, he flipped the box over. In the split second of turning the box over, he saw an illuminated coin in the middle. His mother snatched the box from him. She laughed. It was an ugly and scary laugh. He could then see her face. He recognized the face. It wasn't his mother's face at all. In fact, it wasn't the face of anyone he knew as a child. It was the face of someone he's seen many times but never met.

The light emanating from the coin disappeared. So did the coin. He saw it clear as day in his dream. He also recognized the person holding the box.

It was the public face of The Legacy.

The man woke up in a sweat. His granddaughter was still holding his hand. He was clutching hers with all his strength. She looked at him lovingly and whispered, "Opa, that must've been some dream."

The pain in his abdomen began to worsen. He grimaced and reached for his belly. His granddaughter caught his hand and pulled it back.

"You'll have to leave that alone. The doctor said that you'd have some discomfort for days—maybe up to a few weeks. This wasn't an easy surgery, especially out here. I'll see if they have anything to help with the pain. Be right back. And don't touch that belly."

He nodded and watched her walk away. His eyelids heavy, he drifted back to sleep.

Chapter IX

Rolando Garcia loved his job. He always enjoyed writing. He was talented and creative. For years, all he wanted to do was write. However, growing up with scarce resources led him into a career that was more practical than it was exciting for him. Rolando became a lawyer.

Like many people who practiced law, he quickly learned that the law was a jealous mistress. He had no time for anything other than his cases. He excelled at his practice. But it was wholly unfulfilling. It further led to a lack of sleep, poor eating habits, and a general sense of stress and irritability.

When they were newlyweds, with both a doctor and a lawyer in the house, Rolando and Jeannie came to the conclusion that one of them would need to find a job allowing for more flexibility, less stress, and the ability to be available for the children they were planning on having. In reality, the *planning* stage had already morphed into the *working on it* stage.

Jeannie loved her job. She couldn't see herself doing anything else. So, the decision was quite easy. Rolando would look for another career path. Luckily for them, another career path found him before he set out to find it.

He and his firm represented The Daily Herald, a long-running and well-respected news outlet. It still published an actual newspaper, but times had changed so much that very few folks consumed their news that way. It was mostly digital and online. Rolando handled a defamation case for The Daily Herald. The Herald and senior management were all named defendants in that case brought by a vocal, conservative adversary against the building liberal regime. Rolando's excellent brief writing skills and creative legal arguments caught Herald management's eye.

Once the case was concluded—a defense victory on all causes of action via summary judgment—Willy Weintraub, the Herald's editor-in-chief, set up a meeting with Rolando. The young lawyer thought the purpose was to review the case, and perhaps the bill as principle was an expensive proposition. He was accurate, in at least one respect. Weintraub did want to congratulate him. Although he remarked about how expensive the process was, Weintraub quickly pivoted to the real reason for the meeting. He offered Rolando a job.

"Young man, I've been in this business for a long time, and I know people," remarked Weintraub. "I see how talented you are; excellent writer, strong work ethic, devoted to the truth, yet creative in approach."

"Thank you, Mr. Weintraub. That means a lot to me coming from you."

"Rolando, I'll get straight to the matter. I think you are not as happy as you can be in your current job. I'm prepared to help fix that. I am offering you a job here at the Herald as a columnist. I like your take on things. As we've shared so many stories and life views over the past several months, it dawned on me that you have a voice, a perspective, if you will, that needs to be heard and shared."

"Wow, that's very kind, sir."

"Here's the deal. We are offering you a job as columnist. Your focus will be mostly sports, entertainment, and some general interest topics. You know we have Ed as our lead political columnist. My thinking is to have you work closely with Ed to help develop your voice, your style, with an eye toward how it fits with the Herald way."

Rolando was bordering between shock and giddiness. He kept his professional composure, though. After all, he was a lawyer, and that's what lawyers do.

"I'll be truthful. It will be probably half the pay for you, but I can promise you this, it will be at least twice the fun."

Rolando chuckled. "At least twice is probably an understatement."

"Well boy, what say you?"

Rolando paused. Should he think about it? Discuss it with Jeannie? They had already gone over this scenario many times, just not this specific one. Rolando felt confident that he knew his wife well and knew of her support for this type of opportunity.

"Sir, Mr. Weintraub," said Rolando with confidence, "it would be my distinct honor and pleasure to join you and The Daily Herald team as columnist."

"Grand, boy! Simply grand! We'll get the paperwork all drawn up. Go easy on us, though. Don't go all lawyer on us, got it?" Weintraub winked.

"Got it. Oh, just to clarify. You do know that I'm saying yes to you now subject to there not being any veto by the boss. Right?"

Weintraub laughed heartily. "My boy, I've been married for thirty-seven years and happily married for at least twenty-one of them. I get who the CEO of the family is. A little hint," he leaned in for emphasis. "It ain't us!"

They shook on the deal. Rolando left Weintraub's office, his feet seemingly walking on clouds.

The future looked brighter than ever for Rolando and his family-to-be.

Chapter X

It all went to hell. Everything. Hell. No matter the language, it was hell. Kuzimu. 지옥. Impeyerno. Ад. Hel. জাহান্নাম. Infernua. الجحيم. Địa ngục. Gehena. 地狱. Peklo. Hölle. جهنم. Infierno. לעזאזל. Hell.

If there was a hell, everyone sharing the planet was living in it. Perhaps, if there was an actual hell, it would be an improvement over what they were going through on the earth's face. Dante's Inferno looked like an all-inclusive resort when compared to the events of 2049.

Post-2049 scholars, the ones who survived subsequent purges, at least, saw the events leading to the 2049 tumult as being a set of dominoes falling in exactly the precise order. They also called 2049 "The Year of a Thousand Cuts Finally Bleeding Out."

For each country and each region within a country, there was a story to tell. For example, the patchwork of Spain finally caught up with it: Basques, Catalonians, Galicians, Muslims. Roman Catholics, Jews, Gypsies; each with some grudge against another, a historical grudge; in some cases, dating back centuries. Powder kegs had more stability than some of these countries.

The leading powers at the time, China, the United States, Russia, Germany, and the United Kingdom, were having an increasingly difficult time sharing power and influence on the worldwide stage. They began to fatigue of proxy battles. Some elements in each country itched for a full-blown war to settle things once and for all.

They got what they wanted. And they got it in 2049.

It started as innocuously as it could have. A low-level Chinese Embassy staffer in Washington, DC had her credentials revoked and was expelled from the United States. The administration had no clarifying remarks, but it was generally understood that she was caught engaging in espionage. As expected, China responded in kind. A low-level US staffer had his credentials revoked and was expelled from his posting in Xi City.

Then, an escalation began, a slow ratcheting of tit-for-tat. The UK expelled two Chinese agents. Again, the charge was spying. China expelled two UK. agents. China further cracked down hard in Tibet, cutting off communications and trade routes. Tibetans ambushed a Chinese patrol, killing six Chinese soldiers. Chinese agents then seized His Holiness, the 16th Dalai Lama, who was in Germany giving a speech and meeting with students at the University of Rostock. Germany responded by expelling a cadre Chinese businessman. It further cut off negotiations with both Huawei and ZTE for expansion and upgrade of Germany's wireless network infrastructure. China expelled executives from BASF, BMW, and Allianz.

The former EU countries, along with the UK, USA, Japan, Australia, New Zealand, and South Korea, met to discuss a coordinated response. The result was a suspension of any further trading of Chinese companies on stock markets in those countries. These countries also agreed to send formidable naval resources into the South China Sea. Not intending to pick a fight, it was meant to send a message.

China sent its significant navy to meet the multi-national fleet. It, too, had no keen interest in picking a fight at that time, but it had to save face by meeting the "invading Imperial force" in its claimed territorial waters. China had developed several naval bases and installation in and along the South China Sea in the preceding decades. It looked to be a prescient decision on the CCP's part.

Although Russia was noticeably silent on picking a side, it, nonetheless, sent an observational force into the region.

What happened next was viewed through the ideological lens of the person recounting events. There were conflicting accounts. There were conflicting testimonies. There was no conflicting outcome. Conflict began, which quickly escalated and got out of control.

The day was July 4, 2049.

Chinese officials claimed that a French *Suffren*-class submarine intentionally collided with a Chinese Type-09VI submarine. There were substantial injuries claimed by both sides. Three Chinese submariners and one French *Sous-Marinier* perished.

Contrariwise, the French claimed that China's submarine made an unsafe ballast blow move, causing the accident to occur. The French made no claim of whether the collision was intentional or not. They simply held firm with characterizing the event as an accident.

Conspiracy theorists claimed, with some evidence to support, that Russians in the area interfered with navigational instruments on both the Chinese and French subs. The Russians intended to create a collision. The claim is that Russians stood to gain a handsome prize for holding out for the best offer in picking a side. It wanted to increase the tension. Conspiracy theorists also pointed to the date of the battle, July 4, as further evidence that the Russians sparked the conflict. The date chosen, it was claimed, was no coincidence. Neither was it coincidental that the year of the battle was 2049. After all, China celebrated the centennial of the People's Republic of China in 2049. It was also the sixtieth anniversary of the Tiananmen massacre. Except nobody appeared to recall that bit of history anymore.

If conspiracy theorists were, in fact, right, Moscow could not have known what they were about to unleash. For if they did, they would have stood down.

July 4, 2049—the most calamitous and deadly naval battle the world had ever known. It would also be known as the day World War III started, the free world ended, and the formation of The Legacy began.

Conservative pundits in the United States, including J. Edward Klein in The Daily Herald, had consistently raised concerns about the country's direction. For instance, these commentators and military scholars noted that for years—decades—leading up to 2049, the United States had systematically begun the process of defunding and dismantling its military readiness in the name of social justice. It started with the "defund the police" movements of the 2020s. Those dollars were redirected to social programs *du jour*. When the "defund the police" movement was met with feeble resistance, those in power and those who funded them and their instrumentalities decided to go after the big budget item: the United States Department of Defense.

As a graduate student in 2048 Klein wrote his thesis entitled *Precipitous Decline: America's Face Plant*. In his thesis, which was ultimately published along with several of Klein's more notable and controversial columns, he shared insightful analysis which proved to be prophetic. Among other things, Klein wrote:

> Under the guise of "build smarter, not bigger," liberals and their media enablers focused on efforts to create a technology-based defense, including that for Homeland Security. The hushed comments in halls of power in DC, coupled with budgets beginning in the 2020s and well into the 2040s, exposed the true meaning of "build smarter, not bigger." It might have been better stated as "build needy voters, national security be-damned."
>
> The failure to devote necessary resources to the Defense Department to improve upon the then-existing technological advantage and ways to protect those advantages from being stolen caused many in the Pentagon to raise warnings. Those warnings fell on deaf ears. As a result, many experienced military leaders retired as opposed to suffering further congressional emasculation.
>
> Alliances changed over the years. Many Asian countries acquiesced to China's insatiable hunger for power, and they were rewarded handsomely for it. A new convergence of alliances in the region emerged; those countries bordering on the South China Sea on the one hand (aligned with their Western backers), and

> all others standing with China. China's spending spree for friends may box in the other outliers. Who knows whether, when confronted with China's robust military and economic power, the Western powers of the past will honor their commitments and stand with China's holdout neighbors?

Klein didn't spare his ridicule for those who "canceled" what it was to be American and what made the USA special in history.

> To destroy history, our shared experience, and replace it with a watered-down version of truth—with a heavy dose of politically-correct fantasy—will leave us in disagreement at best, and at one another's throats at worse. Perhaps there is little need to fear a foreign enemy. With sincere apologies to Master Commandant Oliver Perry and arranging his words to better fit our current times, "We have seen the enemy, and it is most-definitely us."

Klein was persecuted for his writings. The liberal left harassed him at every turn. Before long, Klein was gone. Retired. Rumor was that he and his wife moved to a beach home somewhere in Baja California, Mexico. Nobody ever saw him or heard from him again.

July 4, 2049 saw a barrage of ballistic missiles never previously seen. In a weird way, the sky show above, and explosions below, was eerily reminiscent of US Independence Day fireworks. But these fireworks didn't bring oohs and aahs. They brought pain, destruction, and death.

In 1944, in the Battle of Leyte Gulf, the United States and Australia fought against Japan on the high seas for four, long days. It was, at the time and for more than a century to follow, the biggest naval battle ever fought. The battle raged near the Philippine islands of Leyte, Samar, and Luzon. Along with being famous for being the largest naval battle of all time, it also gained infamy for the first known use of organized kamikaze attacks. The Americans and Aussies commanded approximately 300 ships, while the Japanese Imperial Navy had 67 ships under its command. The casualties were significant. Over 15,000 combatants perished, roughly 80 percent of those on the Japanese side.

The July 4, 2049 battle was termed the Battle of Brunei, given the proximity of the deadly exchange to Brunei off the north coast of Borneo in Southeast Asia. The US and her allies had approximately 325 ships deployed, while China had over 450 under her flag. The Western ships were outdated. The Chinese ships had the most advanced technology and systems integration, much of it stolen from the US and then improved upon in secrecy.

In shortly over four hours of intense combat, nearly one-third of the US-led coalition ships was sunk. Another third was damaged to the extent of being inoperable. Of the remaining third, almost half of those weren't functional due to technical problems caused by Chinese cyber warriors. The Chinese lost less than 10 percent of its fleet.

The death toll was as horrific as it was uneven. The US and its coalition members suffered 20,289 dead or missing. An excess of 47,000 were wounded. The Chinese, according to unverified reports, tallied 1,303 dead or missing, and another 2,500 or more wounded.

Not only was the nautical battle lopsided, so was the corresponding cyber battle. Simultaneous with the Battle of Brunei, the Chinese unleashed modern warfare to its maximum effect. The Chinese were able to effectively disable, and in many cases, fully incapacitate energy grids, water purification and delivery systems, and financial markets throughout the United States, Oceana, portions of Asia, and western Europe.

The US and her allies, within less than ten hours, were brought to their knees. And it didn't stop there.

Chinese submarines cut off enemy ports. Chinese cyber warfare successfully shut down energy transmission, including natural gas pipelines. People panicked. The panic was worse than the global pandemics of 2020, 2026, and 2037. People cleared out food and related supplies within days. The have nots began to take by force what they could not otherwise acquire. Martial law was declared throughout the lands. The social compact, which had kept the relative peace over many centuries, crumbled into unrecognizable bits.

The war, dubbed WWIII, morphed quickly from international to intranational conflict on a grand scale. In the United States, states fought with states over resources like food, potable water, energy, and other staples. Within and among adjacent states, counties fought with counties, regions fought with regions, urbanites fought with rural dwellers, and neighbors fought with neighbors. Most distressing of all, families fought within families.

As most guns and ammunition had been confiscated in the early 2030s, the battles were up close and savage. Anything would do for a weapon. People unscrewed chair legs to beat others with. Bows and arrows became popular, so dodging flying arrows became an artform. Blow darts. Poison. Homemade weapons, many of which were developed through 3D printers. Ordinary household chemicals were employed to create explosives. You name it, it was used. Desperate people did desperate things.

As Edward Klein opined post-2049:

> There appeared to be nothing to hold our country together any longer. Not shared values; they were gone long ago. Not a shared vision for the future; there were too many competing factions for that. Not a shared sense of religious faith; that was essentially quashed decades prior. Within countries like ours, any semblance of loving your neighbor was nonexistent. It was fending for yourself and your family—and do so to the death, if required. In many cases, sadly, it was indeed required and remains so to this day.

Chapter XI

Rolando loved to read. He loved to study, especially history. He had interest in learning about China. He fashioned himself a quasi-expert in modern Chinese history. He also dabbled in learning Mandarin Chinese. By this time, only small segments in China spoke Cantonese. That language had been outlawed by decree of the CCP after Hong Kong was officially and completely annexed into the PRC without any further autonomous or semi-autonomous rights. Hong Kong was renamed to honor the man who successfully reintegrated Hong Kong back fully into Chinese control. It was renamed Xi City.

China intrigued Rolando. From the era of "insult and humiliation," as Mao Zedong referenced in his inaugural speech to the First Plenary Session of the Chinese People's Political Consultative Conference on September 21, 1949, to preeminent global power, no country in the history of the world had achieved such meteoric success. China transformed itself almost overnight. The CCP's stranglehold on every aspect of society no doubt facilitated that swift success. Rolando didn't agree with the methods used, nor was he a fan of socialism (he didn't dare express that thought out loud, not even in his own home), yet he admired the industry, planning, and dedication it took to achieve such lofty national goals.

He wondered how China was able to keep it all together. Although the Han Chinese made up over 90 percent of China's population, there were some fifty-five separate ethnic groups in the country. The outside world saw China as monolithic. Internally, the CCP knew it was not so. It took steps, sometime very harsh steps, to keep those minority ethnic groups in check. It saw what happened to the former Soviet Union. It saw what happened in eastern Europe, including the fall of the Berlin Wall in 1989. It would not allow such an outcome to occur on its soil.

China's rise to power was fueled by opening markets, the United Nations, Richard Nixon, Henry Kissinger, World Bank, International Monetary Fund, and membership in other global organizations. None was bigger or more impactful than China's entry into the World Trade Organization. Having well over one billion people at its disposal didn't hurt China either.

Rolando dug deeper but kept coming up with dead ends. He had to be cautious in his approach. All research was monitored. Every query archived. He knew as much. Under the guise of his interest in researching the history of ascendant China, he was looking for clues.

He carefully searched terms like:

China top trading partners

China United Nations Population Vaccines

China birth control population planning

United Nations population planning

Africa population planning Sanger

He typed five additional letters to his last search, then stopped. The next search could flag him, or worse. He had his family to think of. One column wasn't worth his life, neither was his intellectual curiosity. He deleted the five-letter name from his last search.

Chapter XII

Dr. Stefan Ertz was bewildered. He didn't understand. What was he doing here? He wasn't exactly sure where "here" was, but he had a clue. What did he do? It had to be a mistake. Right?

He was in a holding area by himself; the only company he had was a sink and toilet. He was given a jumpsuit to wear. It was no doubt the geo-tracking variety. Not as if he was the James Bond type. He knew he wasn't going anywhere unless they let him.

Stefan heard voices outside the cell door. He couldn't make out what was being said. The voices sounded calm. Was that a good sign? He could answer that both ways.

Berko entered. Probably not good then, as Stefan settled on that answer.

"Dr. Ertz, do you know why you're here?" Berko wasn't known for small talk.

"No, sir. I don't, sir." As much as Stefan wanted to sound calm, he was scared more than he had ever been in his life. His voice cracked consistent with his fear.

"Dr. Ertz, The Legacy is quite concerned about your projections and how those projections may cause panic. Does that help?"

"You mean the five-year agricultural projections and unit valuations?"

"Yes."

"My team and I took all available data, modeled it, and came up with our projections. We have all meta data contained therein if you'd like to review it. We took all available datasets from the provinces just like we always do."

"Is that right? Like you always do? Nothing different this time?"

"No, sir, nothing different at all."

"Oh, I see." Berko managed a slight smile. Stefan felt a sense of relief for a moment.

"So," Berko continued, "why were you visiting with Dr. Webb in nanotechnology? You were there for almost forty-five minutes. What was the purpose of your meeting?"

Berko caught Stefan off guard. The initial questioning had nothing to do with why he was being held. He must be in B5, he thought. Not good.

"Dr. Ertz?"

"Yes, I met with Dr. Webb to discuss ways in which we might, just possibly might, not for certain, how we might, um, consider a collaboration," Stefan replied.

"In what way," Berko added with emphasis, "specifically?

Stefan's heart sank. He felt hollow. He longed to see his wife's face. He imagined holding her and their children, in one long, last, loving embrace.

"Dr. Ertz, you should know that Dr. Webb has already been interviewed. So, please share all details of your conversation."

Berko's face looked like he was trying to hold back pure happiness. He was enjoying this like a junkie enjoys a fix. His background in special services made him a master inquisitor.

He rarely needed an audible answer to his questions. Facial expressions and body language told stories too. One just needed to know how to read them. And there was none better than Berko at that discipline.

"Please, my wife doesn't know anything about this."

"We know."

"I will sign whatever document you want. Please do not harm my family."

"We will take that into consideration, Dr. Ertz. Your statement has been prepared. In ten minutes, you will be escorted to sign your written statement, record your oral statement, and be transported to your next destination from there."

Stefan barely heard what Berko said. He made a mistake. He dared to think beyond his charge. Even worse, he dared to discuss aloud his suspicions, no matter how cleverly he thought he couched them. He knew better. He endangered his colleague. He put his family in danger. He was careless. He was reckless. He was soon-to-be dead.

Berko walked to the door. He knocked once, and the door opened. Berko stepped through the portal, then turned back to face Stefan.

Smiling now, without attempting to hold it back, he said, "Goodbye, Dr. Ertz."

The door shut.

Chapter XIII

Henry "Hank" Hatua was the world's richest man. He inherited a good deal of his fortune. Unlike others who had done the same, he multiplied that fortune many times over. He was innately intelligent. Not one for the confines of the classroom, and much to the chagrin of his parents, Hatua dropped out of the University of Cambridge before the conclusion of his sophomore year.

Hatua's father, Dr. Henry W. "HW" Hatua Sr., was a renowned heart surgeon, entrepreneur, and philanthropist. His mother, Madeleine "Maddy" Hatua, was formerly a pharmaceutical sales representative. They met while HW was working in cardiology at the Mayo Clinic in Rochester, Minnesota. After falling in love and getting married, they moved to New York City, where HW became chief of cardiology at Mount Sinai Hospital.

HW and Maddy had three children, Hope, Hank, and Harmony, in that order. Hank was only briefly known as Junior. Although they shared the same name, including middle name (William), HW wanted his son to forge his own path and have his own identity. He only came to that conclusion after his son was named. Thus, Hank did not have "Jr." attached to his name.

While his sisters excelled in their studies and athletics, Hank preferred playing video games. He was competitive and participated in video game tournaments. But his size—lack of—and chronic asthma put him squarely at a physical disadvantage growing up. He was teased but not bullied. His family name helped keep him from that fate.

Dr. Hatua gained substantial notoriety and wealth by designing a tissue-based heart valve replacement that lasted between thirty to forty years. This was a substantial breakthrough as most other valves of that nature lasted only ten to fifteen years due to tearing and leaking. This development was huge as it reduced the number of heart surgeries needed, especially for younger patients. Dr. Hatua licensed the rights to his tissue valve innovation to Medtronic and other top biomedical companies. For this, he was richly rewarded. The residual income streams propelled his family into the top half of 1 percent of total net worth in the US.

After graduating from The Dalton School, Hank headed off to the UK to attend Cambridge. He selected Cambridge, given its perceived slight edge in science over the University of Oxford. He also thought it was "cool" to study at the same institution as Stephen Hawking, Robert Oppenheimer, and Charles Darwin. At least that was what he told his parents and their society friends. Truth be told, the deciding factor for Hank was one of his favorite actors/comedians of all time, Sacha Baron Cohen, was also a Cantabrigian.

It was curious how Hank went from Junior to no Jr. to a young man with high expectations to follow in his father's footsteps as a medical doctor. It was interesting to Hank at a low level. His true passion was computers and computer technology. He especially focused his interest in the intersection between technology and medical science. He was a huge proponent of using science to help control global overpopulation while creating a sustainable world food supply to meet global needs.

After an inauspicious two years at Cambridge, Hank started his own company with two friends. Their company, Global Genomics, Ltd., was founded in the UK and initially located in the burgeoning science and technology hub on London's South Bank.

It moved shortly thereafter to the "golden triangle" between Oxford, Cambridge, and London. It used this new location to be closer to other potential co-collaborators. It also gave young Hank an upfront seat to evaluate other start-ups in the area for potential investment. It proved to be a wise decision.

Global Genomics quickly grew. Its team received critical acclaim for having advanced the use of big data to support safe and reliable birth control. Initially, that also included effective, safe, and implantable birth control.

Hank was invited to give a TED talk on the interplay between global population growth, poverty, and climate change with agricultural practices, sustainability, and access to global food supplies. His presentation and conclusions were met with high praise; his call to action even more so.

Hank's call to action was quite simple; access to reproductive health services for all was a basic human right in addition to a global imperative. In his opinion, the world's future depended on it.

Without dispute, Hank believed, to his core, that this was the right direction for the planet. It was also without dispute that his company, Global Genomics, stood to gain handsomely if this call to action were adopted.

Global Genomics was the new corporate darling. It was privately held. Its value soared as its profile increased. At least on paper, Hank was about to surpass his father, HW, in terms of net worth. And Hank would not look back as Global Genomics began to acquire other companies in its space and beyond.

The United Nations Conference on Population Control invited Global Genomics to attend and present. The UN had been growing increasingly concerned that birth control methods, be they pills, condoms, intrauterine devices, implants, injectables, and cycle beads, were not effective in stemming a continued rise in population and concomitant increase in demand for resources. The UN voiced its concern about religious and political objections to some or all of these methods. Certainly, the UN never discussed abortion as a form of birth control. It was too hot a topic to confront, at least not directly.

The UN also had multi-tracked studies and related conferences on vaccines to prevent or mitigate the effects of disease, including diphtheria, chickenpox, measles, Hepatitis B, tetanus, influenza, and polio. Malaria, which had been the source of much research and experimentation, was gaining ground toward a vaccine. For the United Nations, having a vaccine that helped meet multiple goals and objectives was tantamount to a golden goal, an instant winner.

That's where Hank Hatua and Global Genomics came in. Hatua, through his wealth, connections, and notoriety, had the ear of UN leadership. His pitch: Combine shots or jabs to allow for multiple positive outcomes, birth control included.

The UN embarked upon a study. It chose eastern Africa as its targeted locale and contracted with Global Genomics to come up with the injectable birth control device.

Hank had an idea to make an even bigger impact, a game changer. Only his closest and most-trusted advisors were let in on his plan. It was risky. However, in Hank's mind, it was well worth the risks, he was excited to move forward with this initiative, and he knew it could be done.

Global Genomics would develop a cross-placental pregnancy termination implantable controlled by an outside source. Simply put, Global Genomics would create an abortion on-demand implant.

Chapter XIV

Dr. Garcia felt wretched. Her morning sickness had taken ahold of her like never before. She brushed her teeth and gargled to get the hint of bile taste out of her mouth.

Perhaps her strong reaction to her pregnancy was because she was older. Perhaps it was because she had more stress than during the times of her earlier pregnancies. Perhaps, just perhaps, it was because this pregnancy was different in biological ways.

Yet, she was as happy as she ever was. She loved Rolando, loved him with all her heart. She loved their girls, loved them with everything she had. Their girls were special, kind, considerate, joyful, smart, and respectful, yet with a fun, playful, and sassy side. They were strong young ladies in the making.

She was deep in thought about her pregnancy. To bring a child, another child, into this world currently in its history wasn't something to take lightly. She knew what it would mean, the work it would entail, the sacrifices, but the love, yes, the love.

She knew the potential to give her husband a gift. Another child to love, to adore . . . to hear his bad dad jokes. The potential for new life and further potential for a boy made her decision quite easy.

She weighed the pros; there were many. When first engaged, before these times, she and Rolando had agreed on three children. They had two thus far. They had room in their home and hearts. They had resources. They had established roots in the community. They both were established in their careers. They loved giggles and laughter. Age timing might be good, as that window would likely close soon. She was in good health, and the girls had been increasingly vocal in their desire for a baby sibling. She knew better than to give this too much weight, but she included it on the plus side in her analysis anyway.

She weighed the cons. Additional stress, at least in the short term, and upsetting the family routine, which seemed to be going smoothly. Would adding a third be the tipping point—going from man to man to zone defense? As a former athlete and basketball player, that point caused her to chuckle. Finally, given society's current views on family size, how would she deal with any blowback? After all, she was a frontline player in that effort. She counseled hundreds of families on this exact issue. Was she a hypocrite? Or, rather, was she just a loving mother who loved her family more than doctrine?

She looked at the Legacy Coin. Why had she not cared or dared to study it like this before? It was part of her daily routine. For years, she had handed out Legacy Coins. She had discussed what they meant, how they could or if they should be used.

Another thought crossed her mind. The thought grabbed her and rocked her hard. Her hands started to sweat. She put the Legacy Coin down gently on the bathroom counter. She felt a bit dizzy and clutched the counter with both hands. When the dizziness passed, she looked in the mirror. She saw a look of primal fear on her face. Her hands trembled as she covered her mouth. Tears began to well in her eyes.

The Legacy. What would The Legacy think about her pregnancy? Would they pressure her to adhere to their wishes? What if she refused to do so?

A wave of nausea hit her. She threw up again. This time, it might not have been related to the baby growing inside her.

Chapter XV

J. Edward Klein, known as Jimmy back in his childhood, was now resting comfortably. It had been hours since his surgery. It wasn't elective surgery, per se, but it did save his life. He only had days, maybe hours, to live. The doctor in this rural area was magnificent, given what few surgical instruments and meds were available to her.

Klein was over sixty years old. Given what he knew and who knew what he knew, he had no alternative but to proceed. The surgeon deftly entered his abdomen area and rooted around for the smallest of the small. Good thing for Klein she knew what she was looking for.

Klein was someone who balanced his role as public watchdog with surviving. That balance became more difficult with each passing year. During his lifetime, he saw the world fundamentally shift in a seismic way.

What was the country of his birth, the United States of America, was effectively no more. China was the ultimate world power. The globalists took control and began to carve up the world into provinces. For them, it was a game, a sick game, but a game, nonetheless. For Klein, and people like Klein, the globalists' game was no game at all. They destroyed basics like freedom, liberty, and justice. The few benefitted. The many suffered.

When The Legacy first crept into power, nobody took them too seriously. Some even dismissed them as a joke. Although clearly backed by China, at first, The Legacy's regime was more of an idea than a powerful political force. The Legacy's point of view was to focus on the future, to create a better tomorrow than today. To create, in essence, a legacy. The Legacy argued that looking backward was only helpful to the extent of clearly seeing collective errors, to admit that the prior legacy, the country's past, was replete with discrimination, retaliation, war, racism, fascism, sexism, and all sorts of other 'isms and 'obias.

The Legacy went so far as to discredit those who had built the country, who made it what it was, to attack and vilify their contributions, and to demean them at the basest levels possible as people. To make a better future, according to The Legacy's doctrine, the country had to not only admit to these wrongs, but its people also had to apologize, sacrifice, and repair relations. The only 'ism to survive? Wokeism.

Wokeism was akin to a new religious faith with attendant fervor. It stepped into the place formerly occupied by Western Christianity, one religion replacing another (or others). The notion of traditional religion was gone, swept away in the tide of devotion to the idea of collectivism, power, and critical race theory. Anything or anyone associated with prior power structures were viewed as suspect. There was no more love, fellowship, or fairness, just destruction, dismantlement, and death.

Beyond that, everyone was a cog. The masses became replaceable. Everyone was a candle burning brightly if only for a brief moment of time.

Post-WWIII, there were serious shortages of many staples. Food production was low due to the destruction of farmable land. Healthcare was rationed as there were too few healthcare professionals and related support staff to meet demand.

The Legacy took advantage of world events and fortuitus timing to step into the gaps caused by world hate, destruction, and xenophobia. Peoples of all regions desired many of the same things: a family to love, a job to provide for that family, a sense of meaning and community, and some distractions, something to fill the void created by time. The Legacy knew this and more.

Slowly, the peoples of the world took stability as the most important quality in a society; stability, predictability, safety, and security, all more important than freedom, personal rights, and privacy. In exchange for security and peace, people gladly deposited their freedoms as payment for that need. They also willingly, in most cases, turned in their arms too. In the former US, what was the Second Amendment to the Constitution became a symbol of selfishness and a bygone era.

Not everyone agreed with the globalists' approach and actions. Vocal opponents were summarily and harshly dealt with. People disappeared—for good. People were sent away, only to return "changed" and in favor of what they previously protested.

In an odd alignment, both Abraham Lincoln and Nikita Khrushchev similarly predicted America's future, a future that became reality. Klein recalled both historical points with a level of clarity. Both leaders opined that the greatest danger to America was from within. Although, in Khrushchev's case, he liked to attach the USSR's participation in that demise while Lincoln discounted interference from abroad.

Lincoln and Khrushchev could not have been more prescient. America, and what was then called the West, did indeed consume itself from within. *Strange bedfellows with symmetrical views*, Klein mused.

Klein considered these historical points often. He couldn't fathom how those who came before him didn't heed the warning signs. Those signs seemed so clear to him. He appreciated what advantage he had in looking back. Yet he could not comprehend how his compatriots during preceding years didn't sense what was happening to them. They must've been the real-life example of the decades-long political allegory of the boiled frog.

Klein's wound started to throb in pain. It must be time for a pain killer. He tried to go as long as he could before taking another pain-cutting pill. He knew they were low in supply. If he could tolerate the pain just a little longer, perhaps it would subside, and someone more in need would get relief. He closed his eyes. He thought of Khrushchev again. This time, more of a myth about Khrushchev—perhaps his pain was causing him to focus on myths. He chuckled to himself, then winced. Chuckling, albeit ever so gingerly, was not advised post-op.

It had been debated for many years whether Nikita Khrushchev actually uttered what had been known as the eight levels of control. Whether true or based on a well-distributed fable, they were worth Klein's mental time in reconstructing how he, how they, got to this state of being.

Klein didn't care if Khrushchev, Saul Alinsky, or some conservative ghostwriter penned the eight levels of control. It didn't matter. What mattered was the outcome. It had happened.

The globalists learned from how others took control of their respective societies. Klein studied this and wrote several columns about the dangers associated with this approach.

First, preach that your country was bad. Evil. Fill schools at all levels of instruction with liberal globalists. Check.

Preach that the military and police were bad, that they acted in self-interest, that they unfairly and without provocation caused harm and death to others in a discriminatory and racist way. Defund them to the greatest extent possible and marginalize them. Check.

Preach (strange word Klein thought as to this point) that churches were evil, that there was no God, that the notion God created the heavens and earth was a fairytale used to subjugate others, that it was a form of fascism and had been born of a desire to subjugate the least powerful in societies. Replace religion with a combination of government and science. That would be the new form of worship. Government and science together would take care of people, not an amorphous deity. Check.

Preach about the inherent inequities in society. Divide people by race, religion, color, ancestry, national origin, age, sex/gender, disability, and class. Foment discord and division in all things. Frequently and consistently promote historical grievances while arguing little to no progress has been made to rectify unfairness. Preach this loud. March in the streets. Do battle as needed. Check.

Preach about all these issues and more via media. Infiltrate media of all types, including new uses of technology to share information, to preach the globalist agenda. Use opinionmakers to preach about the agenda. Shut down and shut out those with opposing views. Silence and marginalize critics. If need be, create alternative narratives about those with opposing views, whether there is evidence to support it or not. Check.

Preach about the judicial system and the need for significant reforms. Fill the judiciary with globalists. Prepare future jurists and lawyers through packing law schools to look for opportunities to advance the agenda while condemning and imprisoning opponents under the guise of public safety and security. Check.

Preach about changing history written by oppressors. Rewrite history books. Tear down statues and other public displays of those unworthy of acclaim. Rename schools. Rename buildings. Expedite the dawning of a new normal where people (dead or alive), ideas, historical events, and more would be destroyed to such an extent that it would be as if they never existed. They would, in effect, be canceled. Embrace the cancel culture aligning exclusively with globalist thoughts, ideas, and goals. Check.

Klein sighed deeply. He winced. It caused some abdominal pain, but that pain was nothing compared with the emotional pain he was feeling. It was more than discomforting. It was disheartening at the deepest level imaginable.

One of the greatest countries the world had ever known, if not the greatest, was gone. Cause of death? Assisted suicide.

He paused to contemplate this reality. How did he not see the convergence of all these factors before it was too late?

He closed his eyes. He closed his eyelids tight. Then he prayed. He hadn't prayed in a very long time. It was so long ago that he forgot how to do it, but he just prayed, nonetheless. He asked God for help, for guidance, for intervention. He thought of Christ on the cross and the pain He must've suffered. He thought of Jesus crying out to His Father, asking why He had forsaken Him. Klein kept repeating his prayer.

A sense of calm rushed over Klein. It was as if an ocean wave totally enveloped his body, heart, and mind. He felt a warmth of spirit he had not felt in decades. He was at peace.

Then, as if through the peace and strength he now possessed, the fighter in Klein woke up. He asked himself this question: Was the greatest country in the world gone for good? He answered his own question: Not without a fight, it wasn't. Not without a fight.

Chapter XVI

Global Genomics got it done. Within its injectable birth control device, it was able to include an imperceptible piece of nanotechnology that could cause a pregnancy to abort.

Hank Hatua could not have been more pleased. He and his company would be able to influence the world for the better. It could help those impoverished and without much hope to reinstate a scintilla of opportunity for their future lives.

In the run up to Global Genomics' meeting with the United Nations, Hatua began to do some additional research on his own. His topic? Eugenics.

Hatua was smart enough to foresee that there could be an outcry against his program of birth control coupled with abortion on demand. He felt that, given the location of the proposed UN study, he could be accused of some form of genocide or creating a program of eugenics. He expected the program to achieve such success that it would be rolled out worldwide. He needed to be prepared for claims that he and other global elites were simply trying to stack the deck in favor of reproducing more people like themselves, that their traits were desirable and improved humanity. Those with differing traits were undesirables and should, by reasonable means available, be prevented from procreating.

Hatua read up on eugenics and related topics as much as he could. He was surprised to learn about the United States' ignominious past with eugenics. He was especially surprised to learn that the heart of eugenics was found in California. *California*? he thought at the time. His research discovered the use of government power to force sterilization on people who were deemed *unfit* or *undesirable*.

The US was not alone in its shameful history with eugenics. The United Kingdom, Australia, Brazil, Canada, Japan, Korea, China, Singapore, Sweden, and others all engaged in some form of eugenics at some time. Of course, the most infamous of all was Nazi Germany.

Hatua was especially interested in the history of Margaret Sanger. Sanger was one of the most well-known proponents of eugenics. It seemed to Hatua through his research and anecdotal observations that recasting Global Genomics and the UN's effort as "reproductive health" might solve the issue. After all, he had almost limitless resources to cultivate public opinion is his favor.

Hatua was keenly interested in protecting Global Genomics in this effort. He was focused on protecting his status and wealth even more so.

Global Genomics presented its research and technological findings to the United Nations, including its prototype. The UN was so impressed that it greenlighted "The United Nations Programme of Reproductive Rights and Health" to commence as soon as product scale was achieved.

The UN linked the new reproductive health program with its sustainable development goals to reduce poverty. It was a blueprint for global peace and prosperity to meet present needs without compromising the needs of future generations. The

UN plans, put together, was known as the UNRHSD (United Nations Reproductive Health and Sustainable Development Programme).

The Global Genomics plan was more simply named. Hatua dubbed it, The Coin.

Chapter XVII

Rolando Garcia was hitting his stride. He loved his job as a columnist. It offered him the freedom to do many things. Writing what he wanted to write, unfortunately for Rolando, was not one of them.

What he loved about his job was the flexibility to spend time with his family. He was available to be with the girls when they finished school each day. He helped with homework. He helped with family errands. He helped to keep the home tidy. He dabbled in the kitchen, dabbled and failed mostly, but dabbled, nonetheless.

With the advent of The Legacy's ascension to power and the tight controls on media they asserted, he dared not write what he wanted. His opinions were The Legacy's approved opinions. His facts were The Legacy's approved facts. His public comments on his writings were The Legacy's approved comments. Consistent with most everyone else, The Legacy owned Rolando Rafael Garcia.

One guilty and dangerous pleasure he had was to study the writings of J. Edward Klein. There was something authentic, raw, and real about Klein's writings, especially those penned in his final months.

Rolando noticed a subtle shift in Klein's writings over the years. If you just read him daily, you probably wouldn't have noticed much if anything. If you compared his writings several years apart, the difference was clear. Klein evolved from fanciful and verbose to strident and damning. His later pieces had a melancholy tone to them. Klein also had some clever takes on The Legacy and related political-social changes. Perhaps they were too clever or not obtuse enough.

Why did he take those risks? Such a shame to lose such an extraordinary man and commentator, Rolando thought to himself. *He didn't need to die. He could've continued to find the gap between permissible and problematic. It was as if he was asking to be a martyr.*

Rolando began to read and reread Klein's works. He started to see the writings in a different way. He started to notice patterns. Mondays and Fridays were more general interest, like what was going on in entertainment, his family, the past or upcoming weekend, special personal profiles, things of that nature. Tuesdays and Thursdays were current political and social commentary. These were usually muted, benign, and at least mostly consistent with The Legacy's stated and ever-evolving positions. It was Wednesdays that was reserved for the most biting and acerbic of his opinions. Rolando concluded that reserving Wednesdays for his hardest-hitting columns was no accident.

The Legacy's official Count of Progress was released each Tuesday late afternoon/early evening. The Count of Progress was a running tally of metrics against goals. The myriad categories included agriculture, manufacturing, raw materials, labor, service, and consumption. Importantly, the Count of Progress was adjusted for inflation and population. It was the latter—population—that earned Klein's attention during many of his final Wednesday columns.

For those in the know, with access to real data, it was understood that these numbers were fudged. That is, the production numbers were brought in at a range, not a definite or absolute term. There were so many people involved in building those output numbers that to get away with recasting them was a tough task. Inflation was understood to be stable, as stable as inflation can be over time. It was the population number that was the variable most clearly under The Legacy's control.

Klein figured this out. He as much as admitted so in his ultimate Wednesday column. He wrote:

> A society that cannot trust information provided to it creates not so much of a utopia as it creates a prison. So, who are the imprisoned, and who are the guards? What benefits inure to inmates who are only provided three squares and a place to sleep? Are the guards more of the outside or an inside portion of the prison? Stated another way, are they simply instrumentalities of the warden and have no greater rights than those they are tasked with confining?
>
> We are fed information from the media. The media receives the information or direction about how to characterize the information from others. My friends, who are we in this scenario? Who is the media? And, finally, who is our ultimate keeper?
>
> I cannot in good conscience any longer turn away from an inescapable truth. Life matters.

All life matters. Yours. Mine. Our neighbors. People we don't even know matter. Don't they strive for many of the same things we pursue? Life. Love. Liberty. Truth. Freedom.

What about the most vulnerable among us? The old. The disabled. The infirm. And the unborn. Aren't we, as a society, claiming to have the moral high ground, to be judged by how we hold dear and protect those who need us, rely on us, and put their full faith and trust in us?

Have you ever considered why so many of our older citizens rarely if ever make it much beyond age sixty? Have you ever considered why the birth rate in many of our lower-income regions and communities is so low? Have you ever considered why we don't see as many of our disabled neighbors as we used to—or at least as I used to many years ago? Have you ever considered who or what has an incentive to rid our society of these vulnerable lives?

I implore you to think for yourselves. Don't just willfully accept all that you are being force-fed. If you have safe and secure access to do so, research Margaret Sanger, Hank Hatua, Global Genomics, and United Nations Reproductive Health and Sustainable Development Programme. Compare their stated goals with unstated outcomes.

> There appears to be nothing to hold our country together any longer. Not shared values; they were gone long ago. Not a shared vision for the future; there are too many competing factions for that. Not a shared sense of religious faith; that was essentially quashed decades prior. Within countries like ours, any semblance of loving your neighbor is nonexistent. Beginning in the 2030s, it was fend for yourself and your family—and do so to the death, if required. In many cases, sadly, it was indeed required and remains so to this day.
>
> The sad truth is that we are all guilty of allowing the holocaust of our times to proceed without mounting any opposition. We have been content to survive on three squares and a place to sleep. Inmates and guards alike.
>
> May God have mercy on our souls.

Rolando sat there. Stillness encased him. He thought to himself, *Klein took on The Legacy . . . and lost. He's gone. Dead, most probably. What did Sanger, Hatua, and Global Genomics have to do with this?*

Klein risked everything to make his points. He knew what the outcome would be for him for having done so. What was Rolando willing to risk?

Chapter XVIII

Berko eyed Bowles carefully. There was a silence that would have been uncomfortable save for its frequent use. Berko liked silence for two reasons. One, he liked to think but not aloud. His quick mind sped through options at the pace of many computers. Two, he used silence as a tool to keep others off guard. Allow them to fill the space. If they spoke and spoke rapidly with lots of animated details, what were they hiding? What were they afraid of? What were they trying to convince him of? And why?

Cassandra Bowles was too experienced in her dealings with Berko to make the mistake of stepping into the silence. So, she waited.

Berko thought about the proposed alternatives. Bowles presented three. It was remarkable that she and her team could come up with three separate and quasi-complete campaigns in just a few hours. Understandably, they followed the strict dictates of the three Ls: Liberalism, Loyalty, Legacy.

The first campaign proposal focused on being excellent stewards of the environment. The campaign claimed raw materials were at a premium. That claim, and the passion it evoked, fit squarely into the liberal environmental agenda. The concept was based on limiting the need to mine and develop additional natural resources and the need for the materials found in Legacy

Coins for other critical projects. To do otherwise would cause needless pollution and wasting of environmental assets. It was also easy enough to utilize school-aged children to achieve this end as they were consistently fed plentiful doses of environment over the individual. They'd be allies within homes to be sure.

The next campaign concept was a straight loyalty play combined with social credit. The basics were: The Legacy needs you to do this. You love The Legacy. You support The Legacy. Similar in style and verbiage to the old *Uncle Sam Needs You* campaign in the United States back in the previous century, it played on patriotism, duty, and allegiance. Stated otherwise, it appealed to unquestioned loyalty and how an individual could exhibit an outward manifestation of that loyalty. Plus, if you did the right thing, your social credit account would be boosted. Loyalty is one thing. Increasing your social credit account could be a familial game changer for generations.

The final concept was based on a basic human need—safety and security for oneself and loved ones. Following Abraham Maslov and his "Hierarchy of Needs," after basics like food and water are met, safety and security follows as the next primal need. We are hardwired to seek this need. In this case, The Legacy was providing it, subject to the individual taking one small step to assist with that effort. This campaign admitted that there was a glitch in Legacy Coins, which could lead to calamitous results. There was no mention of the exact nature of the glitch. The transparency (albeit minimal transparency at best) was also a selling point. "Trust us. We are here to protect you. And we are being transparent about why we are doing this. All good?"

Berko assessed the options presented. He migrated toward the safety and security message. He thought that such a message would bring about a higher percentage of compliance, and that was the singular goal. He thought that omitting the specific malfunction was brilliant. It was better to allow people's particularized fears to fill that void. Different people were motivated by different things. Different people feared different things at a different level. Use that to our advantage, he believed.

"Cassie, I have decided that we will present the safety and security campaign to The Legacy for final approval," said Berko. "In addition, I want to incorporate the social credit component of the loyalty campaign into the safety and security campaign. Can you have this updated proposal ready for me within the hour?"

Cassie replied, "Yes, sir. We'll add the social credit component, and you'll have a clean proposal in less than an hour. Anything else, sir?"

"Yes," said Berko. Again, a long pause. "I would like for you to provide me with an updated report on all communications by and between *Molon Labe* and those within our media comms, both internal and external. Please have that to me by morning."

Bowles understood what this meant. Another purge was forthcoming. The only question she had was when the purge would include her.

"On second thought," said Berko. "I'll come by your unit later to review the results with you there. 8 p.m."

Bowles's body turned numb. Her body responded to Berko's words before her brain did. She knew what was in store for her. Periodically, Berko took advantage of their wholly unequal power position. Bowles knew that to object would be catastrophic for her family, and her.

Perhaps, Bowles thought, being caught up in the purge would be a welcome outcome after all. She smiled. Her smile was genuine, but not for the reasons Berko suspected.

Chapter XIX

Everything was perfect. Jeannie couldn't have been more pleased. She was able to switch shifts with Dr. Ellie and took the day off. Jeannie wanted everything to be perfect for their tenth anniversary. She also wanted everything perfect for the sharing of her—their—news.

The house had the sweet aroma of simmering ossobuco, Rolando's favorite and one of Jeannie's signature dishes. The mixture of gremolata (fresh parsley, garlic, and orange zest), plus onions, celery, carrots, and white wine, made for an arousing scent. She prepared risotto alla Milanese as a complimentary side. For starters, stuffed mushrooms and caprese salad stood ready. And for dessert, a from-scratch homemade cheesecake with fresh fruit. Having substantial social credits had its perks.

Prior to medical school and marriage, Jeanette Washington, as she was named then, worked in a restaurant. She started as a hostess. Then she was promoted to server. Then, after taking some culinary classes, became a chef. She wasn't a good chef. She was a great chef. And that's how she came to meet Rolando Rafael Garcia.

Rolando came to her eatery, *Pavlov's Human*, one night. Notwithstanding its curious name, *Pavlov's Human* was considered one of the best eateries in town. Rolando arrived with a date. He left in love . . . with the food. He would return time after time. After having dined several times at the restaurant, he sent his compliments to the chef via his server. The chef that evening was Jeannie. She came out to thank the patron who sent his compliments on her culinary skill.

As she approached the table, she noticed a young dark-haired man dining alone. Rolando made it a habit to eat at *Pavlov's Human* at least twice per week, mostly because he loved the food and had a personal challenge to taste everything on the menu at least once. The other reason was more basic. Rolando could not cook.

"Thank you for sending compliments to the chef. I'm your chef this evening. It was my pleasure to cook for you, sir."

Rolando immediately folded his napkin and placed it down neatly. He stood to shake the chef's hand. As he did, he looked at her chef's jacket. "Chef Jeannie, your work is exquisite." He kissed his left fingers and gestured into the air in a confident, glib, and flamboyant way. They then locked hands in a firm but friendly handshake.

Jeannie was amused. And intrigued. Rolando was handsome. A tall, muscular man with a swimmer's body, his shoulders were broad and his skin a light golden brown. His brown eyes gleamed with the beginnings of laugh lines coming from the corners. He had an easy smile and easier way about him. All in all, Jeannie was smitten. And a bit embarrassed.

Jeannie, on the other hand, had her hair pulled back and collected it with a scrunchie. The kitchen was hot, as most kitchens are, so she had a faint glow to her. It might've been the sweat too. She wore no makeup at work. And why should she? She was a natural beauty. She enjoyed being outdoors when not working. She'd even study outdoors, weather permitting. Her father was a Black American while her mother was first-generation Austrian from Werfen, a town about fifty-five kilometers south of Salzburg. People had a hard time figuring her ethnic background. She stood at five-foot-three and was strong. Her strength belied her small stature. Her blue eyes, combined with her curly brown hair and light-colored skin, made for a beautiful combination. Rolando couldn't keep from staring into her eyes, as if he was looking for the answers to an upcoming contracts law exam.

Jeannie broke the semi-awkward silence. "Do you eat here often, Mister . . ."

"Garcia. Rolando Garcia. But my friends call me Double."

"Good to know, Mr. Garcia," she smiled.

"I come about twice per week."

"Ah, double."

"Clever. But you may not know this . . ." He leaned in to get closer to her and whispered, "This place is sort of pricey."

"Yes, you don't say. Well, I'll have to see if we can get you a punch card or something. You know, buy ten, get one free . . . dessert, that is, one dessert free."

Oh, my goodness, Rolando thought to himself. *She's a chef, is beautiful, and is sneaky funny. The Holy Trinity!*

"Well, I have to get back to the kitchen. Thanks for coming this evening, Mr. Garcia." She flashed that bright smile again.

As she stepped toward the kitchen, he stepped toward her. "Chef, one quick thing. I'm just a simple, humble, and poor law student. Okay, simple and poor law student. We'll go with that. Anyway, just wanted you to know that, as much as I'd like to punch that card you were mentioning as many times as possible, my thin wallet may not support it. Perhaps it'd be better for my financial and palate's well-being, to have you just, I don't know," he looked down and shuffled his feet a bit to look all golly-geewiz'ish, then raised his head, cocked it to the side with the cheesiest of cheesy smiles, "marry me?" She laughed out loud. She snorted even louder. She immediately covered her mouth. Her laugh and related sounds were so loud many patrons sitting tables away stopped mid-bite to see what was happening.

Okay Casanova, Jeannie thought. *Was this getting weird, or was this the start of something very special?* Sometimes you only have a fleeting chance at life and love. One of her favorite quotes she learned from her paternal grandfather was the Yogi Berra classic, "When you come to a fork in the road, take it!"

"How about this idea instead. Why don't we meet for coffee at Jake's Friday at 7:30? I'll be there. Hope to see you too if you care to join me."

"I'll be there. Yes, Jake's, Friday at 7:30. What's your coffee of choice?"

"Espresso," she turned partially, "and make it a . . . double." She twisted as her hair followed in a semi-circle around her neck. Rolando was done. That was the woman for him.

No matter the day, no matter what she was going through at any particular moment, recalling how she and her husband met that evening was always a memory that brought her warmth, a feeling of love, and at times a blurt-out laugh—and even a snort to boot. It was the evening that changed her life.

She thought of her Pop Pop Washington. He was a man of faith and baseball. She looked up, "Thanks, Pop Pop." Jeannie was thankful she took his advice and, providentially, that fork in the road.

Chapter XX

Berko gave the order. It was time to roll out two campaigns. The first campaign hit on all communications channels directly. The message was clear and to the point. It was designed to reach everyone in the province within minutes and have multiple views throughout the next three days.

> Friends, please return all Legacy Coins immediately. There is a serious safety and security concern. Deposit all Legacy Coin(s) in your possession in any Legacy Coin receptacle. Once received, you will be issued a safe and similarly beautiful replacement Legacy Coin. In addition, you will receive fifty social credits for each Legacy Coin returned. If you are aware of outstanding Legacy Coins that have not been timely returned, please contact your designated precinct captain with details. For each confirmed referral, another twenty social credits will be issued to your account. Thanks be to The Legacy!

As planned, the announcements were seen and heard throughout the province within minutes.

The next campaign was not for public consumption. It was time to implement the next purge. Anyone whose name came up as having communicated with *Molon Labe* without it being on official business was guilty. There was no inclination to spend the time to determine if these people were guilty of anything. They were to be purged for their crimes against The Legacy. They could not serve The Legacy and *Molon Labe*. If a person had any communications with known *Molon Labe* members or any of *Molon Labe's* known associates, that person was a traitor. The penalty for treason was death.

Berko studied the list Bowles had provided. He was perversely pleased. On the list were several influential opinion makers. There were intellectuals. There were military leaders. There were entertainers, even a few athletes and media personalities. It was a robust list, one that he was very pleased to pass along with his approval to the Resolution Department.

Before he forwarded the final list, though, he considered making one final change. Berko toggled back and forth. He pondered the best option. He finally settled on his decision.

Berko deleted one name from the list: Bowles, Simon.

Chapter XXI

Rolando pushed through his swim workout. Although he preferred to swim at home in his saltwater swim pod, he knew Jeannie wanted time alone at home to prepare for their special evening. So, he made do swimming at the municipal pool near his office. The muni pool was a relic of the past. A once gleaming and clean locker room was now reduced to a dank, dark, and underutilized space, where it abortively fought back mold, mildew, and the residual smell of athletes of a prior age. He didn't care, especially because he knew it meant a lot to Jeannie to have him out of the way that afternoon and because he'd be willing to do just about anything for his love.

There were plenty of open lanes from which to choose. He selected one near the middle of the eight-lane fifty-meter pool without anyone in either adjacent lane. No doubt fresher water here, he chuckled to himself. Rolando adjusted his goggles and fit his earplugs in tight. He dove in the water without hardly a splash. The first split-seconds of immersion always felt so good to him. In the water, he was in his second home.

He picked up the pace. He didn't want to be late. After all, it was his tenth wedding anniversary. The kids were having a slumber party at their grandmother's. His mother always showed the girls a great time. She'd also never miss a chance to share an embarrassing story from his childhood. The girls loved to tease him about it later. But for this evening, it would be just he and his one, true love. Rolando picked up the pace even more. He couldn't wait to finish, clean up, and head home.

He was particularly pleased with himself that he was able to find such a unique gift for Jeannie for their milestone celebration. It was wrapped and hidden in his dresser drawer at home, along with a special card he wrote several nights earlier. *She'll be so pleased,* he thought. *I'll probably have to explain it a bit, but that'll be meaningful too. She'll love it.*

While he was deep in thoughts about his wife and the family they had created together, he started to feel a little stitch in his side. No big deal. He'd had too much coffee and hadn't hydrated enough, he thought. As an experienced swimmer, he knew to just slow the pace a bit, take some deeper breaths, and lengthen out his stroke to stretch the area. *Glide a bit more. That'll take care of it.*

The stitch didn't improve at all. *Well,* he thought, *maybe I should just call it good and get home.* As soon as he had that thought, he doubled over in pain and took in water. *Maybe this is what an appendicitis feels like,* he thought while his mind raced. He felt his heart racing too. He felt flush. He barely was able to get to the edge of the pool when another, stronger wave of pain shook his entire body.

He lost his grasp of the side of the pool. He slipped into the water. More pain. Then, darkness washed over him. Briefly, he felt the coolness of the water. It was oddly refreshing. The next feeling that washed over him was a sense of peace. He couldn't move his arms or legs anymore. He couldn't get his head out of water. He couldn't reach for the pool's edge. Yet, he didn't panic. Rolando accepted what was happening to him. He knew what it was. He knew there was nothing he could do to reverse the course. He maintained that sense of peace and understanding to the end.

Rolando Rafael Garcia, champion swimmer, was gone. His cause of death was reported as drowning . . . in five feet of water.

Chapter XXII

News of the most-recent purge was allowed to trickle out of Province House in a controlled manner. It was part of the coordinated campaign of one-part fear, one-part security, and one-part secrecy. Keep the masses guessing, keep them off-balance, keep them under control.

The Legacy Coins were collected in scores. Once received, they were mechanically scanned and automatically archived in proper place. Ready for deployment, if ever needed. Additionally, Global Genomics had developed a system whereby The Legacy could determine if an active Legacy Coin was not turned in. A list of offenders was sent to the Resolution Department for, as made sense, resolution.

The Legacy's Resolution Department was an essential part of The Legacy's rise to power in the post-war era. The "Reso," as it was called, was akin to the *Gestapo* of the Third Reich in Nazi Germany, the Soviet *KGB*, and the East German *Stasi*. The *Gestapo* had nothing on the Reso insofar as terrorizing and ruthlessly eliminating any opposition to the ruling political power base. It was The Legacy's preeminent killing machine. It was evil, cruel, and the fear it struck into hearts and minds was well deserved. There was no limit to the malevolent ways in which the Reso was permitted to operate.

All intelligence, counterintelligence, law enforcement, and interrogation aspects of societal security came under the Reso's direction. The Legacy gave the Reso wide latitude to conduct its operations, including the authority to detain, arrest, imprison, torture, and dispose of suspected criminals, including political criminals. There was no evidence needed to be arrested, no appeal rights, no lawyers, only the potential that there might be a better use of keeping someone alive than to kill them. Perhaps turn that person into an intelligence-gathering asset. That wasn't very frequent. It was easier and less time-consuming to just be rid of the problem.

Moderates and conservatives, clergy and faith leaders, vocal proponents of a belief in God, nuclear families, and limited government—and especially those who whispered those views—were all likely to earn the attention of the Reso. As were pro-lifers, advocates for the disabled, and activists for the aged.

Neighbors had economic incentives to turn in other neighbors for crimes against the state. Social credits were the coin of the realm. The potential of mutually assured self-destruction—neighbors turning in one another—didn't exactly slow down the pace of reporting.

Children were taught from an early age to love The Legacy and the opportunities that it and only it could provide. Thanks to their educational indoctrination, children loved The Legacy more than family members, including parents. It was so Orwellian in nature that nobody who had ever read George Orwell's masterpiece, *1984*, could believe this was happening in their actual lives.

People feared the Reso so much that if they ever suspected that they were the target of a Reso investigation or were about to be picked up by the Reso, in some cases, they would prefer to commit suicide. A well-placed word to the right person at the right time was another Reso trick to have the target rid society, and The Legacy, of the problem before it had to do so. Truth be told, the Reso preferred to take care of the problem itself. After all, that's what attracted so many to apply to join the Reso's ranks.

Although word would "seep out" regarding purges, details were never forthcoming. There was never an official pronouncement confirming that a purge occurred. There was never corroboration of who was entangled. The only "evidence" of a purge was an unusual uptick of deaths reported, deaths with myriad underlying causes. Disappearances were attributed to allegations of infidelity to the regime, economic malfeasance, or, in some cases, kidnapping. Reso agents particularly liked playing the kidnapping scenario. They used it for a sick form of fun and sport. They'd spend time creating fake scenarios and put families and loved ones through all forms of unimaginable hell, all to pull the rug out just before what was to be a joyful reunification.

In very limited circumstances, a "kidnapping victim" would be allowed to successfully return home. There was always a cogent reason behind doing so. It usually involved development of an important regime plan. And that plan most often had a singular author, Boris Berko.

Before assuming his role at Province House, Berko was a Reso commanding officer. He rose in ranks to general in record time. He seemingly had no conscience, remorse, or limits to the wickedness he would be willing to perpetrate. His well-earned penchant for evil earned him the nickname, Satan's Spawn. He enjoyed the nickname, attention, and fear he generated within his own colleagues.

Rarely did Berko encounter a situation without a plan. He liked to say that he kept The Legacy's interests first, his second, and everyone else be damned. The truth was that his interests always came first.

As much as The Legacy relied on Global Genomics and Hank Hatua, Berko didn't care much for Hatua. Berko viewed Hatua as a necessity, for the time being, to execute on short-term operations. After that, Berko would not see any reason why Hatua couldn't, shouldn't, or wouldn't be caught up in a purge. Hatua was rich beyond measure. That was a liability in these times.

No matter the century, mankind has had a penchant for jealousy. These times were no different, and Berko himself was no different. He hated Hatua, what he stood for, what he looked like, where he came from, and what he had. That was because Hatua had something that Berko seemingly would never possess, the willing company of Cassandra Bowles.

CHAPTER XXIII

Comply or die. Comply or die. Comply or die. Those three words kept flowing through his head like it was on an infinite loop, akin to an earworm of a song that you couldn't shake. *Comply or die. Comply or die. Comply or die.* Always in threes, set to a little jingle, similar in notes to the 1980's hit "Boys Don't Cry" by The Cure. It had a scientific basis. Referred to as unprompted auditory imagery, an earworm repetition flowed in reaction to an auditory cue or primer. Further considered a spontaneous recall, given it was intentionally implanted to respond to cues, some scientists queried whether it was better described as calculated as opposed to spontaneous.

The door opened unexpectantly. Anjali was overcome with joy. It was Stefan. He was home. She held out the smallest flicker of hope that he would return to her, yet the practical scientist in her knew the odds were not in their family's favor. She hugged Stefan so hard that she may have cracked one or more of his ribs. No matter, Stefan was ecstatic to be in his wife's arms again.

"Where? What? I . . . just . . . Stefan." Anjali broke down sobbing. The weight of having to keep a brave face for her girls now collapsed, and she let it all out. Stefan held her tightly again.

"It's okay my dear. I'm home now. All is good. I'm home now. And I won't leave you again."

Anjali composed herself enough to ask, "Stefan, where were you?" She knew the answer, yet she needed to hear from him.

"The Reso. The Reso took and held me. I'm fine. It was a mistake. They made a mistake. They even admitted it."

Anjali was wiping her tears when she shot him a glance. "They did?"

"Yes," Stefan replied calmly. "They received some bad intel, and they thought I and others in my division were caught up in something against the regime. They must've obtained some further information that proved what I was saying, so they let me go."

Even though it was her husband, her best friend, the father of her children, Anjali knew better than to ask the obvious follow-up question: "Did you do anything wrong?" If she did ask, and he answered yes, she would be under a duty to report him. Spousal communication privilege was a thing of the distant past. If he said no, and he did do something, she would compel him to lie to her. It was better to just go forward with the shared and unspoken understanding between them—she wouldn't ask, and he wouldn't tell.

The girls came running in. "Daddy! Daddy! Daddy's home!" They almost knocked him over. He bent down to embrace and kiss his girls while Anjali looked over them. She couldn't help but to wonder what happened. He seemed shaken but also seemed like himself. But she knew of stories of how some captives were released by the Reso to do their bidding later. Her sharp mind raced so fast it seemed like it might blow a gasket. She looked for any signs of torture, of anything out of the ordinary, of anything to support the rumors of programmed returnees.

Stefan looked up at his wife while his girls showered him with more hugs and kisses. Their eyes met. In a flash of a moment, she knew the answer to the unasked question, and he knew that she knew as well.

Chapter XXIV

The Garcia girls were inconsolable. They held onto each other and buried their heads so their sobbing could not be seen, only heard. They could barely perceive what they were being told. They understood only one thing—the only thing that mattered to them—their *Papi* would never be returning to them.

Analia Garcia was seven years old, soon-to-be eight. A classic older child, she overachieved at everything she set her mind to do. Strong in character and well-behaved, Ana was as reliable as she was controlling. Like her sister, she was a good athlete, although not as naturally gifted in that arena as her younger sibling. Practical and cautious, she was viewed as a natural leader among her peers. She basked in her parents' attention, especially her father's.

Julieta Garcia had recently turned five years of age. She was, in a word, a firecracker. Fun-loving and outgoing, she was highly social with a keen sense at an early age of how to get what she wanted. She was particularly good at problem-solving while excelling at garnering attention for all she did. A performer, she was unafraid of crowds and never considered any shortcomings as a failure—she believed, and rightly so, that everyone loved her. She began swimming at six months and had a natural affinity for the water. Like her father, she was a natural.

Jeannie was in shock. *How could my love be gone? His smile. His laugh.* She kept replaying his laugh over and over. His touch. She'd never touch his skin again, never be held in his strong arms again, never smell his body again. It was too much to accept. She cried yet did so quietly. Her tears flowed symmetrically, in rhythm, as if dripping from a leaky faucet.

"Girls, we have to go soon. Let's take a moment to gather ourselves and be ready to leave in about five minutes. Okay?"

The girls managed a slight nod. She kissed each of them on the head.

Jeannie entered the master bedroom. She was looking for a few extra handkerchiefs to take along to the service. It was best to have some extras, she thought. On top of Rolando's dresser, she saw a collage of pictures of their history. The pictures helped tell their story—dating years, travel adventures, special occasions, the births of their daughters, and more.

How? Why? He was strong, fit, healthy, and no family history of heart disease. He certainly did not drown. He was a champion swimmer. As a physician, she knew that the human body was a uniquely fragile machine in some respects. But for Rolando to die at this young age, something didn't make sense.

As she was opening his top right dresser drawer, out of the corner of her eyes, she saw the girls' Legacy Coin boxes sitting atop her adjacent dresser, the happiest days of their shared lives. And now, what would she do with another child on the way? Their third child, a child who would never know his or her father, a child he never knew was coming.

"Oh no! No!" she gasped aloud.

"Mami, are you okay?" she heard Ana ask from the other room.

"Yes, honey, be out in a moment," She lied. She had no choice.

Chapter XXV

J. Edward Klein authored several books, really more like pamphlets, which became underground triumphs—especially with followers of *Molon Labe*. One, entitled *Big Tech, Big Lie: Censorship's Slippery Slope*, explained how what seemed to be a societal premium on protecting freedom of speech and expression became anathema to desired political ideology and outcomes. Klein wrote:

> Censorship, shaming, and ostracization of conservative and libertarian voices began in earnest in the early 2020s. It was in vogue at that time as much as investment in Apple or Microsoft stock. Intensified demonstrations and retaliation took place in opposition to speech, which violated some obscure notion of personal space.
>
> When the then-largest names in big tech took it upon themselves to decide what speech would or would not be permissible on their platforms, the American ideal of the fair marketplace of ideas and freedom of expression were set aside for partisan political expediency. Outcomes were valued over process. The proponents of

censorship argued that they were merely serving society's need for protection and security in personal and public spaces.

Have we heard that in more recent times? What was then described as quieting voices intent on harming communities or certain groups within communities quickly developed into a much broader silencing—even of those who were initially vocal proponents of these silencing tactics. That is, until those tactics were used on them. It was as if nobody saw that camel's nose exposing itself under the freedom of speech tent.

The then-power triad of media, technology, and political elites consolidated and coordinated their respective influence and control to create a new day in expressive rights. It was called the "Dawn of Truth Speech." It was a clever turn of a phrase while also paying homage to Sojourner Truth's speech, "Ain't I a Woman?" The neo-expressionists combined theories around equal rights, discrimination, and protections against verbal assaults to advance their clamping down on speech with which they disagreed.

Who then became the arbiters of truth? During the early years of the "Dawn of Truth Speech," it was the global technology companies, their employees, and their algorithms that decided whether certain words, put into a particular order, were permissible or impermissible for public consumption. That power was so great that both traditional media and politicians began to angle for their slice of that power pie. The ensuing turf battle over the years, coupled with continuing diminishments of personal rights guaranteed under the United States Constitution and other like-governing documents around the globe, amounted to the perfect storm for what we know today as The Legacy.

If you control what "truth" is, no matter the facts supporting that so-called truth, then you have a firm hold of the society which you seek to control and govern. If conflicting ideas are forbidden, if there are no means to share conflicting ideas, if truthful truths, as opposed to untruthful ones, are killed in embryonic stages, then how would anyone be the wiser?

Importantly, and to continue influencing the power triad's stranglehold on communication and political thought, academia and its institutions were onboarded. This was no shock to anyone paying attention.

In the 2030s and into the 2040s, many important private corporations were nationalized under the guise of national security. This was occurring worldwide. Industries impacted included energy, defense contracting, firearms manufacturing, telecommunications, transportation, water, and natural resource mining. Financial institutions were tougher to nationalize. They were brought under national control in 2048. Noticeably absent were the media and tech media companies. They continued to enjoy greater autonomy. That is, as we all know, until the post-war era.

China's post-war influence on where we currently find ourselves as a culture cannot be overstated. Our newly minted system of social credits is derived almost exclusively on the China model. Instead of creating a culture of "sincerity and social trust," as claimed by social credit proponents, it has instead fostered and cemented a culture of fear. Informants revel at the opportunities to spy on and rat out neighbors, colleagues, and family members. To call the results "chilling" is too weak of a word choice.

Hindsight is always 20/20, or so they say. In retrospect, the diminishment of personal freedoms, including the sanctity of freedoms of religious exercise, speech, assembly, and the like could have been foretold and should have been foreseen. The train should have been destroyed before it left the station. Now, the train is humming down the track at breakneck speed—without any brakes onboard. We should have opened our eyes and engaged our brains.

> The failure of our forefathers to revolt against creeping totalitarianism in our society is, without question, the greatest failure of this twenty-first century.

Klein thought to himself, *How reckless I was then. Yet, here I am. Most of my family is safe and with me. We have found fellowship with like-minded people from all walks of life who aspire to one thing and one thing only—freedom.*

History was full of examples of peoples who would dare rise up against a superior force, a superior power, all in the name of freedom. Klein recalled the words, but not the source, for a quote which had been nagging at him for some time:

> When government fears the people, there is liberty. When the people fear the government, there is tyranny.

No matter the source, it rang true to him. The perplexing question that he could not find a satisfactory answer to remained, how to go back to liberty once tyranny was well-ensconced?

Chapter XXVI

Bo Berko had all the data before him. The dashboard hovering above his desk was opaque, although, off the sides for a few inches, it was completely transparent.

Numbers don't lie, he told himself. He also knew that numbers didn't always tell the full story either. He focused first on the purge report. It was very satisfying. Across the province, over 1,200 deaths, with nearly 250 still under interrogation. Of those, perhaps twenty-five to thirty-five would be released back into the population to act on The Legacy's behalf. Good numbers. He was pleased.

Berko next turned to the Legacy Coin return numbers. In the first three days, over 63 percent of all coins outstanding were returned. That was a good start. He had an internal sense that 80 percent or more for the first week would be satisfactory, 85 percent excellent. After week two of the campaign, over ninety would be satisfactory while ninety-two or higher would be excellent. The rest would be handed over to the Reso for handling. He knew the Reso was wishing for low return rates.

Drilling down, he could see where some pockets of resistance was forming. In Cantalunia County, there was an expected low percentage of returns at 56 percent. This county maintained a generally older population. They typically moved slower than others in compliance. Not because of ideology; it was simply a product of getting organized to do the task. There was also a greater level of sentimentality associated with years gone by. That would include holding onto Legacy Coins to remember loved ones gone before them. Berko understood this ahead of the launch. Cantalunia's return rate was meeting his expectations. Doward County suffered the same results due to an older demographic as well. Doward came in at 57.5 percent. Again, nothing that concerned him there.

However, he saw something that grabbed his attention. Siouxland County, located in the rural areas of what was formerly a combination of parts of Nebraska, South Dakota, Minnesota, and Iowa, came in lower than expected. Much lower. This area encompassed a greater swath of land than what was originally denominated as *Siouxland* in a series of novels authored by Frederick Manfred back in the middle 1900s. Over time, the term *Siouxlander* came to be known more for personality traits found in the peoples occupying the greater upper Midwest region of the former United States.

Siouxlanders were raised and resided in tough surroundings. The summers were oppressively hot and humid, while the winters brought Arctic air masses in for long stretches with lows between minus twenty and minus forty. That did not include allowance for wind chill.

As a result, *Siouxlanders* were known for exceptional toughness—mental, emotional, and physical. They maintained a love of country and a reverence for God. Being "simple" was a positive. That is, enjoying the simple things in life like food, friends, and family. Extroverted, agreeable, conscientious, and respectful were well-known character traits about these people. They also put a premium on something missing from the newly expanding cultural norm of massaging facts. They were truthful and valued those who spoke truth. In fact, they held dear, and oft-repeated to one another as a source of inspiration, language from the King James Version of the Bible's second book of Timothy, chapter 2, verse 15:

> Study to shew thyself approved unto God, a workman that needeth not to be ashamed, rightly dividing the word of truth.

A fiercely loyal and independent thinking bunch, this group was among the final holdouts when The Legacy consolidated its power and rule in the early 2060s. With the help of China and its technology located in the region, The Legacy routed the last vestiges of an independent America that died with those Siouxland patriots at the Battle of the Black Hills.

For forty days, the Battle of the Black Hills raged. Men, women, and children—boys and girls—old enough to fire a weapon (in their case, usually around six or so), gave a fight for the ages. They battled with a ferocity consistent with the region's historical roots. The warriors lived off the land, ate bison, and used their hides for shelter. They hid in caves and the dense forest. They used tactics from the French and Indian wars of centuries past, adopting their Native American ancestral and regional history to inspire them.

"Asymmetrical warfare," as it was called, provided some incredible prowess and success for the patriots. For example, a small cadre of patriots enticed a company of "treasonous traitors," as they were called, to follow them in and around Hill City. The pursuit lasted for hours until the patriots lured the company into a ravine located between Custer and Hill City. Exhausted and spread out, the company stopped to regroup. At that time, the patriots hit the company's flank and wiped it out. There was nobody left to report what happened. The Legacy watched body camera footage of the rout. Also watching, if stone mountain carvings could do so, was the Oglala Lakota warrior, Crazy Horse, who observed the battle's results from his perch carved into the mountain. Given the tactics used, Crazy Horse had to have been pleased.

The patriots continued to wage their best defense. They used the terrain to their advantage. They used "hit and run" fighting methods along with being fiercely independent in their tactics. The patriots confused The Legacy's forces and engaged in small versus large battles as much as they could.

Thursday, November 23, 2062, Thanksgiving Day, the families who had come to Siouxland to engage the enemy in a fight for the soul of a nation paused to give thanks for their blessings. A group that started with over 200,000 was reduced to less than 6,000 in thirty-six days of engagement. They gave thanks for having the opportunity to have lived in the greatest nation on earth as free people, thankful for being able to fight for freedom and the right to worship as they saw fit, and, finally, they gave thanks for their brothers and sisters in arms—those who had lost their lives and the small number who remained. They prayed. They ate what small supplies they had available. To their last collective breaths, they gave thanks to the Great Almighty.

It was total war to the end. The remaining patriots decided to fight to the finish under the memorial dedicated to the founding, expansion, preservation, and unification of the United States of America. They decided to make their final stand below Mount Rushmore.

The patriots, led by General Anthony Briggs of Tecumseh, Oklahoma, broke their makeshift camp near Sylvan Lake on

Sunday, November 26. They marched over thirteen miles in approximately five hours. They set up their defense up the hill from the abandoned Mount Rushmore visitor center. They knew their fate. They awaited the treasonous traitors.

The Legacy's commanding officer, General Warren Wright, had his overwhelming forces stand down at the base of the carved granite sculptures and beyond while a drone was sent up to the area occupied by the patriots. He further ordered that a video be displayed on the rock formations just below the carved figures of George Washington, Thomas Jefferson, Teddy Roosevelt, and Abraham Lincoln. The message, including corresponding audio, was precisely focused below Jefferson's face on what might have been Washington's left arm and shoulder. It was from The Legacy's top military commander, Supreme General Janice Cafferty. In it, she said:

> Friends, it is over. Lay down your arms. There is no need for further bloodshed. Especially, for the children, let them come down to us safely. They will live. They will live a good life. You have my word as an honorable soldier and a mother, no harm will come to them.

She paused to let her words sink in. She added slowly, with emphasis, and with a facial expression of concern mixed with empathy:

> My friends, surrender your weapons.

The response by General Briggs was swift. The patriots had already debated this potential offer in advance. They expected it. They had an answer prepared. They knew the impact of their response on their immediate situation. They unequivocally knew the impact of their response on the future of their land, the people they loved, and the movement for which they were willing to sacrifice all.

The drone moved closer to General Briggs. He looked straight into the camera, which was broadcasting in real time throughout the province and to The Legacy. The Legacy wanted all to see its power while it took final decisive action against the rebel holdouts. It further wanted people to see its merciful offer to let the children survive what was to come.

The mass of patriots moved in tighter and closer together, locking arms as they did. They all looked directly into the drone's camera. General Briggs said, with strength and conviction:

My friends and countrymen, we have a response.

The patriots came even closer together. Parents held their children tightly and gently placed their hands over their kids' eyes. It was time. They shouted in unison:

Molon Labe! Come and get them!

Monday, November 27, 2062, forever remembered as the day that 5,954 patriots perished at the feet of one of the most iconic symbols of freedom and democracy the world had ever known. All patriots assembled, including the children, died. Mount Rushmore itself was reduced to dust and rubble.

The events of November 27, 2062 gave birth to *Molon Labe*. The long-held battle cry of "Remember the Alamo!" was replaced that day by "Remember Mount Rushmore!" It became the battle cry of *Molon Labe* and all those who valued freedom over tyranny.

Berko knew what needed to be done—*Molon Labe* had to be extinguished . . . once and for all.

Chapter XXVII

The room was small. At best, it could hold two dozen people. That wasn't necessary. Rare was the need to accommodate so many people at a Legacy Fulfillment Memorial service, especially when a service came during the time around a purge. People knew better. There was no need to arouse suspicions with the Reso.

Unlike in decades prior, Legacy Fulfillment Memorial services were designed to run no more than fifteen minutes. At the family's election, they could be open or closed casket. After that, all remains were incinerated. There was no choice. Everyone knew that Legacy Fulfillment workers, formerly known as funeral workers or morticians, were either Reso employees or paid informants. So, decorum at these events was imperative for survival.

Attendees would swipe in. They'd raise their personal communication devices (referred to as a PCD; they looked like an ordinary smartwatch) when entering to have their attendance recorded. If a Legacy Fulfillment worker was not present in the room, cameras would monitor and record what was done and said. It was hardly a place where grief could be provided some level of privacy and dignity.

The marque above the door illuminated Rolando Rafael Garcia's name. There was no program. People knew the drill.

Anyone could say whatever they wished, so long as they wished to have the Reso hear it too. They could pray silently to themselves, but to end prayer with crossing oneself was a certain way to attract suspicion . . . and earn social credits for someone well placed to report it.

Jeannie and the girls wore all black, as was customary. Rolando's mother, Alondra, attended, also in black. That was it. Just the four of them. Neither Rolando's siblings nor anyone else on either side of the family attended. They couldn't. It was too risky. Rolando would have understood. He might have made the same decision if the tables—or caskets—were turned.

Jeannie, the girls, and her mother-in-law all sat in the front row together. They looked at Rolando's face. He looked peaceful. The sides of his mouth curled up a bit, as if he was about ready to spring to life and tell them that this was all just a joke. It was no joke.

The girls stared ahead, not really looking at their father. *How could they,* Jeannie thought, *this is too much for them to bear. Yet,* she thought, *they need to say goodbye to their Papi and begin to find a way to move forward from here.*

Alondra stood up, adjusted her dress, and gathered herself. She approached the casket. She spent several minutes quietly looking at her son's face. Jeannie knew what she was doing. She was praying. Although Jeannie was not a believer, her mother-in-law's secret was safe with her. She loved and respected Alondra too much to turn her in.

Alondra leaned forward to kiss her son one last time. As she did so, she lost her balance ever so slightly. She bumped Rolando's left arm in the process. His arms, which were crossed, were now off to the side. His right just a bit. The left moved down straight along his side.

Alondra sat down. Jeannie asked the girls if they wanted to go up. They both shook their heads with an emphatic no. That was fine. That was their choice. They were present. That was enough.

Each Legacy Fulfillment service was not to exceed twenty minutes. That was based on two reasons. One, that limited the potential of emotions getting out of hand. Previous such services and outbursts of emotions—some leading to damage—led to the imposition of the time rule. Second, depending on timing, like after a purge, there could be a group waiting outside for their twenty minutes and so on and so on. The Legacy Fulfillment workers used the ten minutes between services to switch out the bodies. Pride was taken to keep services on schedule at the top and bottom of each hour.

Jeannie saw that time was running down. There were three minutes left. She walked with confidence to Rolando. He didn't look like the man she knew and loved. He had makeup on his face. It was the wrong color. It was not the healthy brown he sported every day. It was a pasty, flaky light beige. No matter. He wasn't there anymore. It was a shell, a shell of his body, his personality, his mind. Just a shell, nothing inside any longer that was the love of her life.

Two minutes to go. Why? Why? *Why did this happen to you, Rolando,* she said to herself. Her eyes started to moisten. She didn't want to cry. Not here. Not now. She wanted to show strength. For the girls. For Alondra. For herself. *I never got to share our news. Our child will never know you. How cruel fates can be.*

One minute until they would be excused and escorted out. She bent over to give him one final kiss. She paused for a moment. They put lipstick on him too. She closed her eyes, took a deep breath, opened her eyes, and kissed his lips one final time. While doing so, she caught a reflection down by his waist. While her lips were still on his, she looked closer. It was his PCD. Normally, these are removed by the Legacy Fulfillment workers. Why was his still on?

As she removed her lips from his, the door opened, and a voice commanded, "Times up. Please come with me."

Jeannie cried out loud. She began to wail and clutched at her husband. Not letting go. She ran her hands over his body, embraced him as much as she could, given how Rolando's body barely fit in the casket he lay in, and cried out loudly, "No! No! Noooooo!"

The worker approached her and said again, in an austere voice, "Ma'am, it is time. Now!" There was no solace, no caring, no compassion in that voice, just a hurried order to get her out so the tight schedule could be met.

She let go of his left hand followed by brushing her right wrist up and along his left arm. She ran her right hand across his abdomen, just below the rib cage. Her final touch. She held it for a count of three. Then let go. Forever.

She turned to the impatient worker, who offered a weak smile then hurriedly moved the casket out of the room. Jeannie extended her hands to Ana and Julieta. Mother and daughters walked out of the room, hand in hand. Alondra followed closely behind, gently touching Jeannie's left shoulder.

Jeannie kept her head low, not wanting to make eye contact with any of the people awaiting the next service. How could she? She didn't want to risk being found out by having her eyes give her away. She may have just gotten away with something big. If she did, she may have begun the hunt to figure out what really happened, why, and who was to account for her family's loss.

Chapter XXVIII

Transportation was a unique challenge for The Legacy. It was a constant source of friction—literally and figuratively. After years of spirited debate in the early and middle 2000s about the proper use and investment in technology to allow for the movement of people, there was no clear winner of this debate. The opposition camps were dug in. On one side were proponents of autonomous electric pods. Built for energy efficiency and safety, these pods were limited in size and range. On the other side were advocates for speed, just speed, and more speed.

In the middle of all of this was Hank Hatua. When The Legacy was in its formative stage, Hatua laid out the plus/minus analysis for both extremes. After careful consideration, the regime announced that it was making autonomous electric pods the focus of its transportation policy. It allowed for people to have some sense of self-sufficiency by traveling to destinations of their choice. It served The Legacy's goals by limiting the available range of such travel, thereby keeping tighter controls on its people.

That wasn't all, though. Hatua's speed projects continued in development. These projects included hypersonic air travel and ground Hyperloops. These would be reserved for the uber-wealthy and regime leaders. It would also benefit The Legacy in terms of the movement of goods and Reso personnel as needed.

Hatua and his team developed a prototype Hyperloop system. Instead of beginning above ground, they went straight to work on a below-ground tube through the Rockies. Relying on an open-source vactrain design, first proposed back in the early 1900s by visionary inventor Robert Goddard, Hatua's team improved upon Elon Musk's joint SpaceX and Tesla design.

Thanks to improvements in boring capabilities, the tunnel through the Rocky Mountains was created in record time. Hyperloop technology had been somewhat simple to describe. It became much more difficult to execute.

Hyperloop was explained as using sleek metal pods with riders or cargo hurtling through a low-pressure vacuum tube at speeds between 500 and 700 miles per hour. The windowless pods used both magnetic levitation and electromagnetic propulsion. The ride was exceptionally smooth.

The Legacy wanted to find a way to connect major cities and regions within the province. Although personal travel was a plus, it was moving goods and security personnel in a fast and efficient way that tipped the scales in favor of this technology being advanced and built at breakneck speed.

With all the advantages involved with Hyperloops, there was one serious and potentially fatal flaw. And that potential failing was a big one, safety.

Engineers had long debated the engineering requirements for the safe and secure operations of Hyperloops. Open questions included:

- Composition of the steel tubes

- Environmental factors impacting the tubes, including thermal expansion

- Impacts of sudden pressure changes on the system's integrity

- Security against tube breaches

Without fully resolving these issues, The Legacy moved Hyperloops forward with alacrity.

Chapter XXIX

Jeannie's PCD was flashing at her. She knew why. She could feel it herself. Her heartrate and blood pressure levels were registering as very dangerous. It made perfect sense, given what she was experiencing and thinking about.

She got the girls set up with a virtual reality math lesson, which was cleverly designed as a game. Her children loved the game. It adapted to the user's skill level. They could play it together. And loved to do so for hours on end. It was a good distraction and a sense of something familiar to help the girls cope with the devastating day and thoughts they had of challenging days ahead.

Jeannie closed the door to what was now her bedroom. She sat on the chair she used for reading medical journals late into the nights. It was also the chair where she nursed her girls. She tried to calm herself using some breathing techniques she learned when she was a teenager regularly attending yoga classes with her girlfriends. It helped, enough at least to keep her PCD from further flashing.

Dr. Jeanette W Garcia had advantages that others did not. Being a trusted physician, she was considered an insider of sorts. Jeannie had always been a practical person. She had her opinions, some very strongly held. She decided at an early age that she'd best reserve developing opinions exclusively about things she could impact. Professional pursuits in medicine and healthcare were one. Family rearing was another. Politics was not. She could not change anything falling into the category of political. As a result, she became wholly apolitical. Similarly, she eschewed religion as a youngster. That opinion stuck with her throughout her adult life.

It served her well. Being an outstanding doctor, especially an obstetrician-gynecologist in the age of The Legacy, provided special benefits and privileges for her and her family. Under The Legacy's social credit system, she consistently earned points, which translated into access to special stores with special goods, travel opportunities, and the best education for her daughters.

Another advantage Jeannie had was access. Her Personal Communication Device was a mobile medical office. Using the latest secure technology, Jeannie could perform extensive patient evaluations using the internal scanning and evaluation capabilities built within her PCD. The results were then shared with The Legacy's Department of Wellbeing. It was not optional; it was required.

The Department of Wellbeing was a bit of a misnomer. People knew that if their diagnosis was dire, they might be denied care except for brief hospice-styled services. Resources were scarce. Not surprisingly, post-war valuable resources found their way to China. It was China's leadership who decided what province would receive what specific resources and support.

With an uneasy combined sense of dread and hope, Jeannie accessed her PCD. She used the display function to bring up a screen with myriad options. She deftly used her fingers as they typed into what appeared to be thin air. Screens appeared and disappeared in a flash as she dove deeper into available data sets.

There it was, the file she was looking for. She held her breath. Before doing anything further, she took a brief moment to consider what might happen to her and, more importantly, her daughters if merely accessing the file was deemed disloyal to The Legacy. Yet, she exhaled with a clear sense of pursuing what was right. This was not a political pursuit. This was a professional and familial pursuit.

Her next action was life-changing. It was dedicated to truth. It was dedicated to love. It was dedicated to Rolando Rafael Garcia. She tapped the screen and entered the file.

Chapter XXX

In the post-WWIII era, China emerged as the singular power. It did not occupy, yet it tightly controlled the provinces that emerged. Former national boundaries were dissolved. The United Nations was dissolved. Related NGOs were dissolved. The leaders of the Chinese Communist Party drew the new world map. It didn't resemble anything seen before.

The CCP took care to create provinces that could be more naturally administered. It was mindful of historical contention among peoples. It considered the need to ultimately maintain order and especially to maintain its power in the process. China allowed great latitude among the provincial leaders to permit intra-provincial fighting. China's thinking was it was best to allow others to rid themselves of potential troublemakers before the respective provincial governments, with China's aid and support, would have to step in.

Taking the original seven continents as a starting-off point, the CCP carved up provinces without input from the provinces themselves. China itself was not a province. It remained a sovereign land. It was THE sovereign land. China annexed Taiwan, realizing the long promise of cross-strait unification. It also had fourteen former neighboring countries with whom it had border disputes. The Philippines, Indonesia, Vietnam, Japan, South Korea, North Korea, Singapore, Brunei, Nepal, Bhutan,

Laos, Mongolia, Myanmar, and Tibet all had historical territorial disputes with China. All were resolved in China's favor, with no exceptions.

The CCP debated whether the provinces should include larger or smaller land masses, former country borders, and related peoples. They settled on a bit of a compromise. The compromise was predominantly based on a need to effectively control the new provinces.

After China assumed control of and established its full presence in the formerly disputed areas, the new provinces were announced. It didn't take long to figure out what provinces would be easier to govern than others. For example, North Asia Province appeared on its face as one of the easier areas to control. It covered a large land mass but relatively few people. North Asia Province was the new name for what was formerly known as Siberia.

West Asia Province combined the Arabian Peninsula with most countries in what was known as the Middle East. West Asia Province included the former independent countries of Armenia, Azerbaijan, Bahrain, Cyprus, Georgia, Iran, Iraq, Israel, Jordan, Kuwait, Lebanon, Oman, Qatar, Saudi Arabia, State of Palestine, Syria, Turkey, United Arab Emirates, and Yemen. Although smaller in land size, this region was expected to be a tough neighborhood.

Central Asia Province covered the region between the Caspian Sea and China. This included the former "stan" countries of Afghanistan, Kazakhstan, Kyrgyzstan, Tajikistan, Turkmenistan, and Uzbekistan.

Before formation, East Asia Province was subject to great debate. Some in the CCP argued for inclusion with what would be the new Southeast Asia Province. Hardliners wanted full absorption into China itself, especially for retaliatory purposes—especially directed at Japan for the atrocities committed by the Japanese invaders while they were in Manchuria. As much as that seemed appealing in a vindictive way, the CCP settled on a smallish province, named the East Asia Province, where it could exert very close and personal control. East Asia Province included the former countries of Japan, North Korea, South Korea, and Mongolia. Both former Special Administrative Regions of Hong Kong, along with Macao, had been subsumed into China many years earlier.

Bounded by the Indian Ocean in the south and the Himalaya mountains in the north, South Asia Province was created along the lines of the southern part of central Asia. Included in this region were the former countries of Bangladesh, Bhutan, India, Maldives, Nepal, Pakistan, and Sri Lanka. South Asia Province contained the largest number of people.

Southeast Asia Province included the maritime area of Southeast Asia plus the Indochinese Peninsula. The former nations included in this new province were Brunei, Cambodia, Indonesia, Lao PDR, Malaysia, Myanmar, Philippines, Singapore, Thailand, Timor-Lest, and Vietnam.

When deciding on a provincial structure for the south Pacific Ocean area, commonly referred to as Oceania, multiple ideas surfaced. Combining Australia and New Zealand was a given. What to do with regional island areas became the issue. Afterall, the CCP was considering how to create a cogent administrative structure for approximately one-fifth of the earth's surface area. Would each of Polynesia, Micronesia, and Melanesia constitute separate provinces? Did it make sense to combine them together? If so, with or without Australia and New Zealand?

Given the difficulties associated with the area being so spread out, it was deemed better (although not much better), to combine all of the regions together. Therefore, the new Pacifica Province was created, populated by the former American Samoa, Australia, Cook Islands, Easter Islands, Fiji, French Polynesia, Guam, Kiribati, Marshall Islands, Micronesia, Nauru, New Caledonia, New Zealand, Niue, Northern Mariana Islands, Palau, Papua New Guinea, Pitcairn, Samoa, Solomon Islands, Tonga, Tuvalu, and Vanuatu.

The inclusion of American Samoa, Guam, and the Northern Marianas was a bitter pill for the former Americans to swallow. What was worse, and caused even more rage, was that the CCP added Hawai'i to Pacifica. It was an intended poke at their former world rival. It was an effective jab.

Africa was divided into five separate provinces. That was a fairly simple task, and the reasoning behind it sound as a supermajority of CCP leaders agreed. North Africa Province comprised the portion of the African coast along the Mediterranean Sea, plus Sudan. Along with Sudan, the former countries included Algeria, Egypt, Libya, Morocco, Tunisia, and Western Sahara.

West Africa Province was created to include that part north of the Gulf of Guinea in the northwestern portion of Africa. The former nations in this region included Benin, Burkina Faso, Cape Verde, Cote d'Ivoire, Gambia, Ghana, Guinea, Guinea-Bissau, Liberia, Mali, Mauritania, Niger, Nigeria, Saint Helena, Senegal, Sierra Leone, and Togo.

Central Africa Province was the area formerly known as Middle Africa or Equatorial Africa. The province included the former countries of Angola, Cameroon, Central African Republic, Chad, Republic of Congo, Democratic Republic of Congo, Equatorial Guinea, Gabon, and the former island nation of Sao Tome & Principe.

East Africa Province included many former British colonial areas. It also included many islands. The former nations included were Burundi, Comoros, Djibouti, Eritrea, Ethiopia, Kenya, Madagascar, Malawi, Mauritius, Mozambique, Reunion, Rwanda, Seychelles, Somalia, South Sudan, Tanzania, Uganda, Zambia, and Zimbabwe.

Southern Africa Province was bounded by the Indian Ocean to the east and the Atlantic Ocean to the west. Former countries included Botswana, Lesotho, Namibia, South Africa, and Swaziland. The naming of this province followed a bit of a different convention as not to overstate the importance of the former Republic of South Africa.

Europe was divided into four distinct provinces. North Europe Province included the former nations or regions of Denmark, Estonia, Faroe Islands, Finland, Greenland, Iceland, Ireland, Latvia, Lithuania, Northern Ireland, Norway, Scotland, Sweden, United Kingdom, and Wales.

West Europe Province encompassed that part of Europe bounded by the Atlantic Ocean to the west, the English Channel and North Sea to the north, and the Alps to the south. Former nations in West Europe Province included Austria, Belgium, France, Germany, Liechtenstein, Luxembourg, Netherlands, and Switzerland. This was the industrial heart of Europe.

East Europe Province included the geographical region east of Germany and west of the Ural Mountains. Former countries included Belarus, Bulgaria, Czech Republic, Hungary, Moldova, Poland, Romania, Russian Federation, Slovakia, and Ukraine. The CCP considered breaking up the territory east of the Ural Mountains, taking it from Eastern Europe Province, and placing it instead in the Central Asia Province. They decided to place it in the East Europe Province pending further review and evaluation of how well the administration went.

South Europe Province was the Mediterranean region along the like-named sea. This province included the former countries of Albania, Andorra, Bosnia & Herzegovina, Croatia, Cyprus, Gibraltar, Greece, Italy, Kosovo, Republic of North Macedonia, Malta, Monaco, Montenegro, Portugal, San Marino, Serbia, Slovenia, Spain, and Vatican City. Importantly, Vatican City was given SAR status, with that status set to expire upon the death of the then-Pope John Paul III. He died a mere thirteen months later. Portions of East Thrace, part of what was called European Turkey or Turkish Thrace, was assimilated into the South Europe Province. The balance remained with West Asia Province.

In the Americas, the newly created South America Province wasn't controversial in its creation—at least not in terms of geography and what former nations were included. This new province comprised the former states of Argentina, Bolivia, Brazil, Chile, Colombia, Ecuador, French Guiana, Guyana, Paraguay, Peru, Suriname, Uruguay, and Venezuela.

Like South America, the islands and archipelagos of the Caribbean region was an easy draw for the CCP and its new world order. Caribbean Province was created with the former countries and locales of Anguilla, Antigua and Barbuda, Aruba, Bahamas, Barbados, Bermuda, British Virgin Islands, Cayman Islands, Cuba, Curacao, Dominica, Dominican Republic, Grenada, Guadeloupe, Haiti, Jamaica, Martinique, Montserrat, Puerto Rico, Saint Kitts and Nevis, Saint Lucia, Saint Vincent and the Grenadines, Trinidad and Tobago, and the US Virgin Islands. There was a brief discussion of including Bermuda with

North America, given its location in the North Atlantic. That idea went nowhere.

The tougher decisions for China's leadership focused on the former United States. Before finalizing the balance of the Americas, from Panama north, the CCP needed to decide how to best govern its American foe and de-risk its population from uprising against provincial leadership and, ultimately, the CCP itself.

There were several potential plans considered. One was to combine all the Americas north from Panama. It would create a super province of sorts. That option was summarily rejected. Another was to combine the US, Canada, and Mexico into one region while establishing a separate region for Central America. That plan made sense at one level, yet there was an even more appealing option advanced by CCP hardliners. And those hardliners held great sway when it came to the former United States.

The hardliners proposed a phased-in series of moves. They would only announce the first structure without disclosing that changes would follow. The initial plan was to establish North America Province. It would indeed rise to a super-province status as it would take Panama from the south and add everything up to Canada and Alaska. The CCP's reasoning was sound. Taking down borders and understanding the fragile dynamics and history of how the peoples of the region had interacted, they might help solve future needs for intervention by fighting amongst themselves. A few years of chaos might be good. It might be smart to arm them—both sides and give them implements to kill one another in as great of numbers as possible—like in a Mad Max movie. They'd beg Beijing to intercede and bring peace.

Thereafter, perhaps in two to four years, and to further isolate the former United States and reduce the chance of the US ever challenging China again, the plan would call for a split. Central America Province would be established to include the former countries of Belize, Costa Rica, El Salvador, Guatemala, Honduras, Nicaragua, and Panama.

North America Province would then include the former nations of Canada, Mexico, and the United States. Depending on the outcome of the first two to four years, this newly established North America Province could last for an additional two to four years, maybe more.

Then, at the most opportune time, Mexico would join Central America Province, Canada and Alaska would form the Canaska Province, while the United States would have a singular province, to be called North America Province.

Great debate within the CCP focused on the idea of splitting the US into five separate provinces. That plan was seriously considered. Yet the leadership's view was it was in the CCP's best interest to maintain a level of friction among the peoples in the former US, thereby negating any potential rebel activity against provincial rule. The idea of incremental changing of provinces within the central and northern Americas created instability and migration of peoples. Keep people unsettled. Trade on historical bias, anger, and division.

Finally, the CCP determined to directly control both Arctic regions. Its position was simple. The natural resources and strategic geo-military locations of both poles mandated China's direct administration. It created the Arctic Province: one province, two polar regions.

The CCP understood the steps involved with establishing its provincial administrative structure, especially in central and northern America, would require a bit of short-term pain. That was not a problem for China. It always played the long game. And, with these moves, China anticipated securing its long-term global dominance for centuries upon centuries to come.

In sum, China created twenty-two provinces out of 194 separate sovereign nations as it realigned the world to fit its needs. China then identified and established leadership to fit its provincial requirements. Unless there was evidence of a perfect fit for future alignment with China's plans and goals, former leaders and potential leaders within a region were visited by the Reso. Every province had its version of the Reso. Those potential leadership challenges were dealt with swiftly and with finality.

Chapter XXXI

Molon Labe needed a win. They had been consistently routed over the past several months. Their numbers were dwindling, not because of death. It was something worse than death. It was discouragement. Their ranks were returning home to live out the rest of their days in peace. Or at least the relative peace of being captive in your own homeland. There was a dearth of supplies, personnel, and morale. And what they did have of those three was evaporating quickly.

Klein saw this firsthand. His surgery was performed in a *Molon Labe* field hospital—if you can call it a hospital—somewhere outside of Chadron in the Nebraska National Forest. As forests go, it wasn't exceptionally large. Nor did it provide a lot of cover. It was a rolling hills and sparsely timbered type of forest, nothing like the Black Hills about 130 miles to the north.

But it did have one thing in its favor. Nobody would think to look for them there. It was almost like hiding in plain sight.

Klein roamed freely in the area. He was getting his strength back. His mind was as sharp as ever, his will even stronger. He was one of the lucky ones. Most people never saw much more than a few days after their sixtieth birthday. At sixty-one plus a few days, he already outlived most of his contemporaries.

There were global pandemics to blame. At least that's what the regime claimed. After the COVID-19 pandemic of the early 2020s, pandemics seemed to be on the rise. Klein had his suspicions. By his thinking, and a bit of digging, global pandemics seemed to occur around the time of food or medicine shortages. Was an actual pandemic unleashed to the population that impacted those aged sixty and above so precisely? How could that be? His body felt the same at sixty-one as it did at fifty-nine, fifty-eight, and so on. It just didn't register with him.

Klein believed that The Legacy and other regimes in their respective provinces used pandemics as an excuse to cull the herd. He realized that was a dangerous thought to have. But how? If he was right, how did the provincial regime do it? They had technology. They had science. They had motive. It might not be such a wild thought after all. It was still a dangerous thought.

When news of his arrival and surgery survival spread within the camp, there was a buzz. It was like a celebrity had been dropped in their midst. Klein was famous—infamous to The Legacy—for his writings and ability to weave his arguments without crossing the line. The Reso never bothered him. Well, there was one time when he mentioned the Khmer Rouge in one of his columns. He wrote a piece to run on May 20, which was the National Day of Remembrance in the former Cambodia. He used it to discuss hate as the day was also referred to as the National Day of Hatred or, as translated by some, either Day of Tying Anger or Day of Maintaining Rage.

He also used May 20's column masterfully to point out the particularized evil of regimes, such as the Khmer Rouge, Nazi Germany, and Hutu power movement in Rwanda. He tied the three together with special focus on tools and methods used to commit genocide, including starvation, overwork, or disease. There were outright executions used as well.

The Reso was not amused. They paid him a visit one day to express The Legacy's displeasure at his piece. Klein was an endearing man, a humble man without airs about him. He could talk to anyone about anything, even those with whom he disagreed, and they would be left feeling better for the time as if they had gained a new friend.

The Reso members who visited him were not immune to Klein's special charms. They decided not to bring him in for questioning at B5. They simply warned him to stay far away from the line. Everyone knew what the line was. Klein agreed. They chatted a bit more about events happening in Chiapas (armed conflict with provincial leaders), and they left. Klein escaped. It was almost like nothing would stick to him until, of course, his column of November 27.

He was asked to join the *Molon Labe* leadership in camp for a meeting. He wasn't a soldier. In fact, he had never shot a weapon in his life. Other than in pictures and video, he had barely seen many weapons. He wondered what he could offer to its leadership.

He entered the camouflaged tent expectantly. When he entered, four people stood—two women, two men. They all shook hands, and each person identified themselves just by first name. Eve, Zimmer, Mitch, and Shontae. There was a table and five chairs in the tent. That was all. No maps. No computers. Just tables, chairs, and some waterskins hanging off to the side. *Siouxlanders.* These folks were the real deal.

Shontae led off. "Mr. Klein, we are pleased to have you with us. You are *with* us, correct?"

"Yes," Klein replied dryly, trying to hold back his affable self to not have them become needlessly suspicious of him, "I am with you, as you say."

"Your granddaughter has been a brave and loyal member. We took her at her word when she arranged to have you join us. We'll take you at your word too," Shontae continued. "You know our plight. You know the odds against us. We here share a fundamental belief in freedom, equality, and liberty. And, above all else, a deep faith in God the Almighty."

"I concur with all of that."

"Ed," Shontae used his first name, which Klein took as a good sign, "We could use your help."

"Anything. You saved my life."

"I will speak plainly. We need a victory, a substantial victory. What I mean is we need to do something to not only seriously damage the regime, but we also need to do something that will spark a fire within our country. This is still *our* country, as we see it. Do you have any thoughts about a potential target or targets we should consider?"

Klein paused for a moment. He looked at each of the four. Clearly, Shontae was in charge. As soon as she said her name, he knew exactly who she was. Having never met her, he had heard plenty about her. He also knew something of Mitch.

Shontae Lewis was a former pharmacist. Born of a Black father from Georgia and a Native American mother of the Ojibwa (Chippewa) tribe from Minnesota, Shontae was a US Army Ranger. She specialized in reconnaissance. She gained notoriety and the unwanted attention of The Legacy and its Resolution Division when she and a small troop of similarly trained special operators destroyed a cache of regime weapons near Pryor, Oklahoma. Klein recalled having read about the raid and the heroism associated with it. Of the two dozen *Molon Labe* forces who took part in the raid, only two survived, Shantae Lewis and Mitch Iron Falcon.

Mitchell Iron Falcon was descended from a long line of leaders of the Oglala Lakota nation. Most especially, he was directly descended from Chayton Taku Skanskan who, alongside the notable warrior and Lakota Chief Red Cloud, famously defeated the United States Army in 1866. Although not as famous as his renowned chief, Chayton Taku Skanskan was similarly skilled as a warrior, tactician, leader, and diplomat. His blood and hereditary characteristics ran strong and were evident in Mitchell Iron Falcon. The 2080's version of Taku Skanskan's lineage saw a man devoted to country. He served in the Army Rangers. He was a fierce warrior and superior military tactician.

Both Zimmer and Eve were unknown to Klein. While in camp, he heard the name "Zim" many times. It mostly had to do with food and provisions. He recognized having seen him as well, as Zim was holding court regaling the assembled group about some story he couldn't hear. He did hear the several bouts of belly laughs, though. *Good for camp morale,* Klein believed at the time.

As for Eve, he heard nothing. He knew nothing. She struck him as young yet intense. She glanced at him while he was thinking. She smiled faintly as her ocean blue eyes cut a hole deep inside him. *Good thing she's on our side,* he thought.

"I have a few ideas," Klein offered. He had their attention. "I'm not a military person, as you know, so please forgive me if you've already considered my thoughts beforehand. Moreover, if it's a stupid idea and can't be pulled off, please just say so."

"Oh, we will," said Zim glibly. Shontae shot Zim a "shut up, or I'll feed you to the Reso myself" look.

Klein continued, "Good to know. Okay, well, I've been thinking about all this for years. What can be done to incrementally take down The Legacy and, ultimately, the CCP's rule over us?"

Klein noticed Mitch slowly closing his eyes. It wasn't in a disrespectful way. It looked more like he was turning to prayer and perhaps channeling his ancestors for guidance and wisdom as he prepared to listen attentively to what Klein was prepared to say.

"I've asked myself over and over, what does The Legacy value? What comes immediately to mind is its relationship with China. The Legacy wants, no, it needs to have excellent relations with the CCP, especially the hardliners. So, how does that translate to our situation and *Molon Labe's* objectives? The word stability comes to mind. The Legacy, after the initial first few years of culling of the most extreme of us in this region, has put a premium on stability."

"What then would cause instability?" Klein stated rhetorically. "Certainly, safety and security issues come to mind. However, I think there is something even more basic here. Food and water. If the people don't have ample food and clean water, The Legacy has a huge problem on its hands."

Zim couldn't hold himself back, "Ed, we have thought of these things before. Do you have new takes on old issues?"

"Maybe. Maybe not," replied Klein. "I do know that the threat of something catastrophic is many times worse than the actual thing itself. With that in mind, I'm sure you have thought about the transportation network, especially the Hyperloop system, as a target. It does, after all, transport most of our agricultural products, especially fresh products to major urban centers."

They nodded. There was a collective sense that more was coming from Klein if they were patient. So, they were patient, even Zim.

"Now, it has been told, broadcasted, papered, and drilled into all of us in so many ways that the Hyperloop system is impenetrable, that nobody and nothing can do anything to disrupt it, that its construction materials and techniques, its engineering, its monitoring systems, and its security and safety protocols are beyond compare. I dare say that the message that they have conveyed to us and which resides in our conscious and subconscious is, 'don't mess with the Hyperloop because you'll fail.' Am I right?"

Again, heads nodded in agreement. They had a sense where he might be going. They sure hoped they were right. Disrupting the Hyperloop would be a game-changer; no more potential Reso movements at their will throughout the province and disrupted food and supply delivery. The Legacy would then face demonstrations calling for the basics to be delivered. Those demonstrations could get violent, and The Legacy's Resolution Department would have a very difficult time mobilizing and moving its forces to regions out of control if the Hyperloops were not available to them.

"What if," Klein paused. He didn't want to give false hope, but he didn't want to take what he knew to his grave either. "What if there was a way to destroy—at least partially—the Hyperloop? And what if we could disrupt water purification and delivery systems and could further pinpoint those disruptions wherever we wanted or needed throughout the province?"

They looked at one another, save for Mitch, who still had his eyes closed. Klein was right. Disrupting or destroying the

Hyperloop system could be the key to their campaign against The Legacy.

"One more thing, if I may." Klein looked for approval. Shontae nodded. "This recent Legacy Coin recall seems quite curious to me. I suspect there's something brewing here. Why would The Legacy's communications team hit all channels so aggressively and frequently with a recall? I know this won't come as a shock to anyone here when I suggest the recall has nothing to do with the people's safety and security. Another option for us is to intercept Legacy Coin collections. Or, on a much bolder and grander scale, repossess Legacy Coins already collected by the regime. Get in. Take 'em back."

Mitch opened his eyes, his gaze fixed squarely on Klein. Mitch wondered if his ancestors spoke directly through Klein. Or were his simple prayers for a miracle being answered? His thoughts were disrupted as Eve spoke.

"Father God, thank You for delivering Ed Klein to be here with us. Lord, we humbly ask that You bless him and keep him safe. If it is Your will, may You please give us the wisdom and strength to successfully advance forward to create again our one nation, under You, forever and forever. We humbly ask in Your Son's holy name. Amen."

Klein then knew what Eve's role was in this group. He was indeed on the right side in this battle, a battle that would soon become war . . . an uncivil war.

Chapter XXXII

Jeannie first immersed herself in Rolando's health scan results. As a doctor, that was her first priority and interest. While saying her goodbyes to Rolando, it occurred to her to scan as much as she could. Seeing his PCD prompted her to do so. So, she took every available second to download his PCD to hers. She then scanned as much of his body as she was able, given time constraints. She focused primarily on his mid-section and vital organs. Her final wailing gave her enough time for that at least. What was not done was a brain scan. That would've been helpful, she thought. She quickly turned to the business at hand—reading and interpreting the results. Hopefully, there was a clue there. He could not have drowned, she kept telling herself.

She first looked at any data to support Rolando having suffered a heart attack, stroke, or pulmonary embolism. She also looked for a potential drug overdose. She knew, or at least thought she knew, he didn't use drugs. But her medical training required her to exhaust all possible causes. Among other things, she scanned the BMP and CBC results. The cardiac values were negative for myocardial infarction, arrythmia, or evidence of cardiomyopathy. Similarly, there was nothing for Rolando having suffered a stroke. His pulmonary arteries were unobstructed. And, as she suspected, nothing suggested a drug overdose.

The scan further revealed no heart disease, cancer, or joint infections. No issues with either thoracic aorta or abdominal aorta. There was no evidence of large or small bowel disease. Appendicitis was ruled out. Liver, pancreas, gall bladder, adrenal glands, spleen, and kidneys all checked out. No internal bleeding was noted. No masses or traumas were found. Neither was there any report of bone fractures, arthritis, or impaired blood supply to the bones. His spine was fine.

Rolando's lungs showed signs of damage. That was expected. He was found face down in the swimming pool. Similarly, Jeannie noted fluids in the paranasal sinuses, mastoid cells, trachea, and main bronchi. A frothy foam was reported in the nasal cavity and pharynx. His stomach and small intestines were distended. These findings were typical. They weren't particularly specific or helpful, Jeannie thought.

What next? What was she missing? It had to be there. She reviewed the test results again. Nothing stood out. She pulled up Rolando's full physical test results from seven months prior and ran a comparison to see if that might give her a hint.

There it was! How could she have missed it, she thought. "Yes!" she blurted out loud quietly as she pulled her tight fist toward her. His choline levels. That was the clue. Still within normal range, but markedly increased from his last test. That's why she missed it. It was within normal range. At least when she scanned him, it was. Choline in and of itself was not the culprit. She had a hunch what was. But she'd need some help to prove it.

Next, she turned to Rolando's Personal Communications Device records. She was able to access his PCD because both she and Rolando exchanged access information. The Legacy forbade such exchanges. Punishment for violating this directive was severe—loss of substantial social credits and a minimum two-rung social demotion. For the Garcias, that would mean loss of their living quarters, access to special stores, and the girls' expulsion from their top-level school. They decided to risk it, especially given Rolando's job. It seemed to be a calculated risk worth taking.

There was so much there; where to start, she asked herself. She knew that all PCDs were set up differently. There were common aspects to all PCDs, such as legal name, nickname, former names, date of birth, place of birth, current residence, lifetime residences, spouse or partner (if any and prior, if applicable), child or children (if any), parents, and siblings. For each spouse, partner, child or children, parents, and siblings, the same background information was included. Also, PCD direct access numbers were included in case those people needed to be contacted, for example, in case of emergency. That's how The Legacy explained the need anyway.

She looked at his calendar, appointment notes, and social credits. She pulled up his daily blog. It was more like a diary. Just random thoughts he dictated as if he were talking to himself . . . like a madman. Lots of column ideas, some musings about this and that, and family gift ideas. She could hear his voice. It was eerie. She wasn't sure what to think. An overwhelming sadness enveloped her. Her eyes welled up. She blinked the tears away. There was no time for this.

There was a subfile entitled DC. That was his nickname for her. Dr. Jeanette W Mensah Garcia. Mensah was her family's last name, although that wasn't always the case. Her grandparents on her father's side were forced to give up their historical family name. They had to give it up if they wanted to survive in the age of cancel culture. So, her family all agreed to change their last name to Mensah. As they viewed it, the M in Mensah was an upside W. In the space for her middle name, her parents gave her W, for Washington—her family's prior surname. No period, just W. The last name Mensah provided them protection. It was a common Ghanaian family name. It seemed every tribe in the former country of Ghana had a Mensah. Interestingly, during the years of cancel culture, the US added many Mensahs too.

Cancel culture took root and wiped out so much and so many, leaving innocent victims and abundant toxicity in its wake. No one was spared. Jeannie would be asked over the years, especially in school, what the W stood for. Her reply was always the same, "W stands for W, that's all." For her, it was a stark reminder of her family's history and racial background. She was bi-racial, Black and White. More White than Black, according to her Black friends and Black-devoted family members. More Black than White, according to her White friends and White-devoted family members. She could never win. It didn't matter. That was a long time ago. Nobody really won during those cancel culture days. Most definitely, nobody won anymore. Everyone was ultimately canceled in some manner or form.

When they were dating, Rolando asked about her name. She explained her family's history and how W became prominent yet subtle in certain ways, a dig at those who sought to cancel her, her family, and their proud history. Rolando immediately latched onto "DC" as a pet name for her. Each time she heard him call her DC, she felt him with her, with her family, that he loved her so much that he would join in the inside jab at those who tried to deny her who she was and where she came from. When he said "DC," she felt warmth, devotion, intimacy, and love.

She opened the DC file. The most recent entry was recorded only two days before his death. His hologram stood before her. That face. That handsome face. She longed for him even more. And his voice. She loved his voice. His tone. How he said certain words. Aloud, she said, "Play." In his message, Rolando spoke calmly and clearly. There was love and purpose, which shone through.

> Hi there, DC. You found me. Well, maybe I should say you found my message to you. This is just for you. DC, I am gone. I'm so sorry, my love. So very sorry. I tried to stay safe. Most of all, I tried to keep you and the girls safe.

Jeannie could hear the emotion in his voice. She saw what looked like tears mixed with strength and resolve.

> You know the old expression, "curiosity killed the cat"? I'm the cat. I was curious. Not just for curiosity's sake, I was curious for our family and our country's future. Not province—our country, the United States of America.
>
> Yep, you now know, I'm one of them. Those people. Please hear me out before you judge and convict me.
>
> How could I deny who I am? Who we are? You understand this all too well. I am an American. My family is American, not some amorphous provincial being bending the knee to a foreign

> power and their local puppets. I just couldn't do it anymore.
>
> You know I grew up in a faith-filled home. I know you didn't. I also know that your family was once full of faith in something greater than The Legacy. I know because I did the research. Your great grandparents were Christian missionaries in Haiti. You probably knew that. Your parents, and grandparents to some degree, wanted to protect you and your brothers. They knew what was happening. They predicted what was to come. They were right. They were right to protect you, DC. I love them for it. And I miss them terribly.

There was a long pause. She wondered if the message was over. He went out of view, but she thought she heard him shuffling around in the background.

> Sorry, thought I heard someone. DC, I didn't mean to lie to you. I'm so sorry and hope you will forgive me. I had to continue my faith journey. So, I did so. In secret. For years.
>
> My disloyalty to you was wrong. Being disloyal to God was also wrong. I couldn't live like that anymore. I had to be true to Him. I knew you wouldn't want to hear about this. I knew you *couldn't* hear about this. I want you to know the reason I didn't tell you before now wasn't

> because of fear that you'd turn me in for social credits. If you were going to turn me in, I figured it would be for something better than that!

She heard him chuckle mildly at his own joke. He liked to do that. It was infectious. She chuckled too.

> I didn't want to have you live knowing that there was something that could cause you to be dishonest to The Legacy or, God forbid, the Reso if they ever started sniffing around. I wanted to keep you pure. Keep you safe.
>
> So, with all that, why am I telling you all this now? Doesn't that directly contradict what I just said? Yes, it does. And here's why. Things are changing, and they're changing fast. It's Legacy Coins. China's CCP wants them. Wants them all. They're exerting pressure on the regime here to gather as many coins as they can as quickly as they can—then turn them over to China. I've been working with an inside source with the CCP. He's credible and extremely brave to share with me. He says the hardliners are about to pull off an inside job within the party. That's why they want the Legacy Coins. What he and I don't know is why. Why would they want the Legacy Coins? How does this fit with the hardliners' internal purge?

> DC, listen, I think this will impact you. Maybe not today or tomorrow, but very soon. I was going to share all of this with you at our dinner. Guess I didn't make it. Hate to miss your osso-buco. Dang!

He chuckled again as she dabbed her eyes.

> Go to my dresser drawer. Upper right. There's something there for you. Go ahead. I'll wait.

She did as instructed. It was as if he was there with her, watching her. He even had a smile while he waited patiently. He knew her so well. She opened the top right dresser drawer: a card and a wrapped present.

> Go ahead, open it. The present. You can read the card later. Go on.

He was enjoying this. How could he be so calm? Jeannie almost asked him aloud, nearly forgetting that he wasn't there with her. She unwrapped the present.

> I hope you like it. Happy Anniversary, DC . . . DC!

The gold necklace and pendant were beautiful. She didn't wear much jewelry. She didn't have much jewelry. It was a luxury many didn't have, even those privileged like they were. And if they had it, many didn't wear it for fear of it being stolen or ostracized as being insensitive to others. Jeanne looked at the gift she held in her hand. She looked at him and told him,

"I love it. I love you. Happy Anniversary . . . Double!" The pendant's decorative design was of two interlocking DCs, one forward looking on top, the other set below looking the opposite direction. Small, encrusted diamonds were strewn vertically along the spine of the Ds while two additional diamonds flared out horizontally—two to the right along the bottom of the top D, and two to the left along the top of the bottom D.

Rolando continued as Jeannie kept looking down at the beautiful pendant in her hand.

> My source tells me that the hardliners plan to do away with Reproductive Health Services. In their words, "won't be needed." What does that mean? "Won't be needed"? Something's not adding up. And Department of Wellbeing's Reproductive Health Services, that's you, DC!

Jeannie looked up. She said, "Rewind fifteen seconds."

> —me that the hardliners plan to do away with Reproductive Health Services. In their words, "won't be needed." What does that mean? "Won't be needed"? Something's not adding up. And Department of Wellbeing's Reproductive Health Services, that's you, DC!

> I've been working on a lead to help. That's why I told you what I did earlier. One of my brothers in Christ believes someone at Province House knows. It isn't just in China. There are apparently plants throughout who know something

> or at least pieces of something. I don't know who that is at Province House. I was getting close. Guess I got too close.

He offered a sheepish smile.

> DC, please forgive me. I know this is a lot to consider. I think you and the others in RHS are expendable. If you hear the CCP's hardliners taking people out in a coup or something like that, go to Frank Gies. He's at the Che Bakery near Province House. He's the brother I just mentioned. He'll help you. Order an almond croissant, plus a coffee with double cream and quad sugar; that'll get you in. Frank's a good man. I trust him with all my soul.

Rolando brought the camera closer. Jeannie could see deep into his misty eyes.

> I love Ana. I love Juli. And I love you, DC, so much. Until we meet again, my love.

He blew a kiss as Jeannie paused the hologram. There he was, standing before her. Rolando Rafael Garcia. Her true love. The father of their children. Her partner. Her best friend. She wanted to climb inside the hologram and hold him, hold him forever. She knew that thought was lunacy, but so was the world around her. Pure lunacy.

Chapter XXXIII

Anjali Gowda stepped aside from her academic and professional pursuits to raise her daughters. It was an easy choice for her. Stefan never asked for her to do so. She always wanted a family of her own. The thought of strangers raising her children was abhorrent to her. Even though she broke tradition and glass ceilings, she was a traditionalist at heart.

It didn't come without repercussions. The Legacy enjoyed complete obedience in all aspects of society. This was no truer than in the school systems. The children were taught—indoctrinated—in every school grade. Songs extolling virtues of The Legacy, teachings about the heroics of The Legacy, and allegiances publicly displayed in support of The Legacy were daily fare.

Anjali was smarter than her husband. Of this, they both agreed. Her test scores were higher. She advanced further, faster than he. To his credit, he was smart enough to not argue the point. So, he had that going for him.

She had better opportunities than he when it came to jobs. Yet, she wanted to be at home with the girls, and that was that.

Anjali and Stefan raised the girls to be independent thinkers. Aligned with that, they would ask the girls, "Does that make sense?" Their plan was to instill in their offspring inquisitive minds. They also preached the orthodoxy of The Legacy of

Liberalism, Loyalty, and Legacy. It seemed a bit counterintuitive on its face, but Anjali and Stefan figured that for their girls to succeed in the world into which they were born, they could just be like all the other blind followers, or they could be trained for more. Someone had to lead. Why not their girls?

Bhavna Gowda Ertz was an eight-year-old second grader going on twenty. Smart as smart could be, Bhavna spoke three languages: English, German, and Hindi. She was social enough with her classmates, although her real love was coding. She had been coding and working with computers since around the time she spoke her first words.

Her younger sister, Nyra Karin Ertz, was three and never met a stranger. She'd say hello to anyone. She had deep brown eyes and long eyelashes. She could get whatever she wanted from anyone . . . and she knew it, especially when it came to her father. Her mother, not so much.

As an eight-year-old, Bhavna and her fellow second-grade classmates across the province were soon to participate in The Legacy Loyalty Pledge. During this special ceremony, all second graders were required to congregate and declare their love for The Legacy by reciting a solemn pledge.

> I pledge my love and devotion
>
> To The Legacy, its founders, and leaders.
>
> I promise always to follow the 3 Ls of
>
> Liberalism, Loyalty, and Legacy.
>
> I vow to protect our enlightened society

> From those who seek to harm it.
>
> I pledge to put The Legacy above all else,
>
> Including the lives of friends, family, and even my own.

For supporters of The Legacy, its regime, and policies, to have their children swear such an oath was no problem. For those with a contrary view, this rite of passage created many difficulties. Families with children who had sworn such an oath had been routinely visited by the Reso for both real and imagined offenses against The Legacy. Children who did not want to do their homework, be disciplined, or otherwise took offense to anything said or done (or not said or not done) at home could find a sympathetic ear at the Resolution Department.

Such outcomes were more than just hypothetical fears. They happened often. The regime took otherwise well-adjusted young people and turned them into a younger version of the Reso. They were commonly referred to as the "Resitos," the little Resos.

Both Anjali and Stefan attended The Legacy Loyalty Pledge ceremony at Bhavna's school, Revolution Elementary. It was the best elementary school in Legacy City. Bhavna took her place on stage in the second of four rows on the riser. In the third row, three children over Bhavna's right shoulder stood one of Bhavna's classmates, Analia Garcia.

All children wore the same uniform. The collared shirts with matching shorts were a blue-grey color. The kids wore matching black socks and black sneakers. It was the same uniform they wore each day, with one exception. Normally, they wore a colored belt and neckerchief corresponding to their grade. For second grade, that color was green, but they didn't wear green on this day. This day, they each wore a bright red neckerchief and matching red belt. Red was reserved for this day and this day only. Going forward, these children would be reminded of their pledge by the addition of prominent red patches to the end of each collar on their shirts.

Anjali and Stefan took their seats in the front row. Stefan was reformed from his prior backbench days. He and his wife learned many years prior that sitting in the front was a show of support for the children and The Legacy. Every move made by parents was being watched. Body language. Facial expressions. Everything. Who knows, perhaps they were being scanned for blood pressure too? Even with all that, there were still those backbenchers who thought nothing of calling attention to themselves.

When Jeannie arrived seats in the back were all occupied. She made her way forward, looking for three seats together. One here, two there. The only place where there were three together was in the front row. Jeannie took her seat in the front row next to an obviously nervous father. Julieta sat next to her, and Alondra sat down between Juli and Anjali.

The ceremony began with the usual musical flourish. Then all stood for The Legacy's anthem. As if people had no sense of history, the ritual required a straight arm salute during the anthem. The anthem itself had a melancholy nature to it, as if it were composed by a Soviet during the mid-1950s. When the anthem finished, the crowd yelled in unison, "Long Live The Legacy!" Then they sat.

Headmaster Rice stood to address the gathering. A humorless and bland woman, she was known for running an excellent school. She was also known for setting "examples" of students and parents alike with little to no provocation. If she felt like embarrassing someone, she did so. In some cases, there were social credit deductions made depending on the severity of the claimed offence.

"Parents, teachers, and administrators, welcome to the highlight of the year, The Legacy Loyalty Pledge ceremony." She led an overly enthusiastic clap for what she just said. "As you know, I'm Headmaster Rice." She awaited applause, which came, finally and sporadically. "These Revolution Elementary second-grade students behind me have proven themselves ready and worthy to take our most solemn pledge, our pledge of loyalty to The Legacy." Again, overtly enthusiastic clapping on her part, as if she was being watched so closely by the Reso that her life hung in the balance between moderate and over-the-top applause.

Jeannie tried to focus. Her mind was alternating between what she was witnessing before her and what she witnessed the day before from her husband's final message to her. "Won't be needed. What does that mean?" She kept trying to decipher what he meant.

Headmaster Rice continued, "Before we hear from the children, let me remind you of your important duty to our dear children, to them as future influentials, and to them as they support our beloved leaders. Your duty is to raise children who love The Legacy. That is your number-one priority and duty. Additionally, The Legacy requires you to raise these children to have great influence over others in support of the 3 Ls. Finally, to remind these children—who are *our* not *your* children—to put our beloved leaders, this regime, The Legacy, before all others." Once again with the clapping. Headmaster Rice looked overwhelmed with emotion. She no longer resembled the humorless and bland bureaucrat she was at most other times.

Headmaster Rice took a moment to calm herself. She then instructed those gathered to "Please rise." The crowd looked to rise in unison, as if they were all part of the same military outfit. "Friends, you are now to respond with 'we will' to each of my questions to you."

Anjali thought to herself, *well this is new. Be careful, who knows who might report anything suspicious here.* She side-glanced at her husband. She still had questions about him and what happened to him, unanswered questions.

"Will you accept your collective duty to raise our children with an abiding love for The Legacy?"

"We will."

"Will you support, encourage, and ensure that our children live a life consistent with the 3 Ls of Liberalism, Loyalty, and Legacy?"

"We will."

"And will you support The Legacy in its mandate to have our children love The Legacy, its leaders, and its regime before all others, including yourselves, your family, friends, and even the children themselves?"

Jeannie's head was spinning. When did we get to this? It was as if Rolando's parting words opened her eyes—and brain—to the reality of their world. She understood and respected him even more (if that was possible) by having lived an authentic life. She understood why he didn't share his re-found beliefs with her. It must've been some silent torture for him to do so. No grudges. Only love and respect for him.

"We will," the crowd said in unison. Jeannie mouthed the words. She wondered if anyone noticed or even cared.

Apparently, someone did. The man next to her walked down the aisle and got the attention of an official-looking person at the end of the row near the stage. Her seat neighbor whispered something in the man's ear. He looked like he worked security. In fact, he looked like he could've been selected right out of Reso central casting, if there was such a thing. Dark and sunken features. Pointed nose. Short, dark hair. Slim build. The security man nodded. Jeannie avoided looking at the security man. She also avoided looking at or otherwise acknowledging the presence of her seat neighbor when he returned.

"You may be seated. Now, the moment we have all been waiting for . . . the children." Headmaster Rice was back to her sober self. "As a reminder, after *our* children have concluded the pledge, they will individually step across The Legacy Line, symbolizing their complete and unequivocal commitment to The Legacy, the 3 Ls, and their place in our enlightened community."

Jeannie could feel eyes on her. She dared not look around. She kept her eyes focused on her child—*her* child—Analia.

Headmaster Rice then said with great gusto, apparently her energy and faux personality returning, "Friends, please stand as I present to you our second graders of Revolution Elementary and The Legacy Loyalty Pledge!"

As she stood, Jeannie began to feel queasy. She felt dizzy. She stood while trying to keep her composure. She felt like she was under surveillance from all sides.

"To lead the class in its pledge, I give you, Natalie Burns, second grade commander in The Legacy's Youth League at Revolution Elementary. Natalie."

A polite level of applause followed. The man next to Jeannie was zealously clapping and whistling. Without doubt, Natalie was his daughter.

Without looking for fear of fainting, Jeannie tried reaching for her youngest daughter standing next to her. If only to provide some stability, she thought. The stage was spinning, or was it her? She couldn't find her daughter's shoulder. Her mouth was dry. She felt her blood pressure rising. She tried bending her knees.

Natalie Burns stood at crisp attention facing the audience. She then pivoted with precision to face the class. "Friends, class, repeat after me. I pledge my love and devotion . . ."

Jeannie caught a brief glimpse of her flashing PCD. She was redlining. It was the last thing she remembered seeing.

Dr. Jeanette W Garcia collapsed in a heap.

Chapter XXXIV

The Hatua Hyperloop was ready for its biggest test yet. There had been a few delays during construction of the loop itself. There had been a few glitches in producing the pods. Now everything was ready. Hatua and his engineers had promised The Legacy that the Hyperloop would be in operational mode by late fall. It was late summer, and it was coming together nicely.

Everything Hank Hatua and his companies did was noteworthy. The Legacy comms team spent an extraordinary amount of time documenting how Hatua was able to bring The Legacy's ideas to life for the betterment of the province. Hatua didn't mind sharing—rather, giving—credit to The Legacy. It was his insurance policy to live lavishly beyond The Legacy's laws and purview.

Hatua invited Cassie Bowles to join him on the final test run of the Hyperloop from Legacy City to Denver. The almost 1,300-mile trek would take them under parts of the Sierra Nevada mountain range north of Lake Tahoe. It would also test the new extension across the continental divide underground through the Rocky Mountains, an exceptional feat for him and his team. Hank wanted Cassie to be there as they celebrated their success. He also had special plans for her.

As they departed the capital city, Cassie felt a sense of excitement mixed with dread. She and Hatua had been dating for almost a year. It wasn't dating like she'd ever known before. Most people didn't have access to food, travel, and all the trappings of wealth that Hatua had. She enjoyed this special access and experiences—to a point. She had a conscience, a heart for others less fortunate. She felt strong pangs of guilt. She was very good at masking these thoughts and feelings.

There were times when she was uncomfortable with the way Hatua referred to his work with The Legacy. She was also quite uncomfortable with how frequently and openly he interacted with the CCP, including those she knew were so-called hardliners. It seemed more than a convenient business relationship. Rather, to her, there was an openness and friendship between Hatua and these ironfisted Chinese leaders who clearly had a visceral disdain for the North America Province, its history, and its people. As a Londoner, she aroused no suspicion that she could detect when engaging with those hardliners. They seemed to revel in her company almost as much as they did with Hatua. Good thing. If they knew about her father or more about him and his personal journey, things might get very dicey for her. Hatua knew some things about her father. Berko knew all there was to know . . . maybe more.

Cassie had mixed feelings for Hatua. She admired his creativity and ability to tackle the world's toughest challenges. He was positive, and he had confidence to match his extreme intelligence. He had a dark side, which she rarely saw. She knew it was there and was unnerved by it. In unprotected moments, she sensed his discomfort with children. He wasn't around them much. Likely his choice, she surmised. He would occasionally make dispiriting comments about families, children, and mothers. It predominantly came up when he was making a point about global resources and "certain people" who either required too many resources or who could not manage their lives well enough to extract themselves from extreme poverty. His comments were often directed at minority groups and those living in different provinces. Whenever he would make a comment like that, it was as if he was stabbing her right in her belly. That's not how she was raised to think or believe.

The Bowles family came into money back in the late 1900s. They were famously early investors in BCM, British Chip Manufacturing. Cassie's paternal great-grandfather, Anthony "Tony" P. Bowles, was an electrical engineer and dabbled with investing in early stage electronics companies throughout Europe. The family wasn't rich, but Tony Bowles' family was certainly upper-middle class. Tony Bowles ascended to a senior management role in the privately held electronics company, FuturElectronics Ltd. Cassie's great-grandfather had the vision to invest in several early-stage semiconductor companies focused on creating faster, smaller, and more powerful semiconductors for use in memory chips, microprocessors, and integrated chips.

As a devotee of Moore's law—number of transistors per silicon chip doubles every year—he knew that a computer chip revolution was forthcoming. He wanted to take advantage of that opportunity of a lifetime. So, instead of saving for retirement or taking extravagant holidays with the family, Tony Bowles put every last penny he and his family had into these speculative investments. His bold vision paid off quite handsomely.

He invested as much as he could cobble together in an early-stage company he had heard about on the west coast of the

United States. That company was founded in the mid-1980s by seven former Linkabit employees, including Irwin Jacobs. These seven had the vision to build quality communications for the masses. That company was Qualcomm. As a result of Tony Bowles' investments in the 1990s and Qualcomm's stock increases plus multiple stock splits, the Bowles family went from upper-middle-class to a secure place in Britain's upper class. Tony Bowles amassed over £100,000,000 by virtue of his initial BCM and Qualcomm investments, while parlaying some of those substantial gains into other tech companies, most notably Elon Musk's Tesla. Great-Grandfather Anthony Bowles was a good engineer. He proved to be an even better investor with exceptional timing. He set his family up for generations.

At least that's what he and his family thought. The world fundamentally shifted after Cassie's great-grandfather passed in 2018. In the ensuing years, class warfare become more pronounced. Notwithstanding the Bowles Family Trust's consistent commitment to numerous charitable causes around food insecurity and infant mortality in the former UK and in many troubled areas around the globe, the Bowles family was subject to continued verbal assaults in the media as well as certain politicians ingratiating themselves with the have-nots. It was unpleasant, but the family continued with its dedicated work on behalf of those in need through its Trust.

After China's military and economic crushing of the Western powers in 2049 and beyond, families like the Bowles became even bigger targets. This time, the threats weren't just verbal. They became physical and dangerous.

Cassie was a post-war baby. Born in 2051 to Simon and Emily Bowles, Cassie spent her first few years living in the family's luxurious West End London home. Just before she turned three, her family began a series of moves in and around London to avoid the roving gangs of socialists, communists, and anti-fascists who threatened harm to all, including children, if they dared not accede to their demands. Their demands included divestment of what they called "ill-gotten gains," including homes, personal possessions, and financial investments. They also demanded cash, lots of cash. In other times, they would have been labeled mobs, thugs, gangs, extortionists, or robbers. Instead, they were termed "justice warriors" and "fair play advocates" while being feted by the liberal elite. It was only a matter of a short time before those same elites who celebrated these lawless bands would themselves suffer dearly at the hands of the JW or FPA.

What Cassie remembered from her early years somewhat contradicted the reality of her situation. She recalled lots of love and laughter, being showered with attention and hugs, feeling safe and secure, and playing games with her parents. She particularly liked the polar bear freeze game to see who best could mimic a polar bear in hibernation by hiding under blankets while being still and quiet. It wasn't until she was older did she understand the game she played with her parents was not, in fact, a game. Cassie still had the stuffed polar bear friend from those days. Artie from the Arctic she'd named him. She kept Artie in her chest of drawers to remind her of her parents, their love for her, and the sacrifices they made. She hoped one day she could pay them back.

The Bowles family was forced by the new North Europe Province regime to divest its wealth. Like others in their position, there were no appeal rights available to them. After all, any appeal would be decided by the sole governing body that issued the edict in the first place. It would have been futile. After years of moving about, Cassie and her parents settled in a small two-bedroom flat in West End Westminster. It was affordable, given the small stipend they received, yet it was a notoriously dodgy area. Cassie honed her street smarts while growing up and going to school in that neighborhood.

Emily Bowles, who always put Cassie's needs above her own, died from breast cancer when Cassie was eleven years old. By all reasonable accounts, Emily Bowles was not only not provided with adequate healthcare, but she was also affirmatively denied basic humane care because of her family's name and her stature as being part of the former elite class. "Punish them!" was a well-understood reality for those who may have had some perceived advantage. To the JW, FPA, and the new North Europe regime, anyone who had accumulated wealth or something of value, must've stolen, misappropriated, or swindled others to advantage themselves. These advantaged souls were considered to be devoid of heart, compassion, and communal caring. They had to be punished. And they were. And the Bowles family felt that punishment and associated loss to their core.

Simon Bowles did his best to fill the void left by the loss of his wife. Raising a preteen daughter by himself seemed a daunting task, even for a man as loving and patient as he was. They had a series of serious sit-down conversations about what would be best for Cassie's future. Namely, to live with her aunt and uncle in the North America Province, if that was possible, or to continue to live in Westminster with him, just the two of them. Her aunt and uncle had two children, aged fifteen and twelve, a boy and girl respectively. Cassie enjoyed her cousins, but she argued for living with her father. In her mind, he needed her as much as she needed him. She was ultimately correct in that assumption.

They struggled mightily. Simon did his best to provide. The meager stipend provided by the regime was insufficient to meet their needs. Perhaps that was the plan for the Bowles family and those like them. Simon was offered work at Feeding London Food Bank & Kitchen, which he accepted. This was the very same charitable organization that the Bowles Family Trust had so generously supported over many, many years. He was hired to work as a bus boy and general duties associate. He'd clear tables and keep the dining area clean. He was charged with keeping the restrooms clean and sanitary as well. The regime placed him in this position to embarrass him, to make him feel somehow less than, to have him feel shame and humiliation; from benefactor to busboy, from being served to serving the poorest, most unhealthy, and downtrodden.

What the regime didn't know, what they miscalculated, and what they failed to consider was that Simon Bowles had an extraordinary heart for all people in all stations in life. Perhaps he had been raised with a silver spoon, but he was born with a golden heart. This was the best job for Simon, his self-worth, and his faith. While his grandfather was a devotee of Gordon Moore, co-founder of Intel and author of Moore's law, Simon was a devotee of the writings and works of Agnes Gonxha Bojaxhiu of Skopje, otherwise known as Mother Teresa of Calcutta. The regime couldn't have placed Simon in a better job.

When Cassie was seventeen, she competed for a coveted spot in an exchange program between provinces. She caught the eye of the committee by virtue of her essay entitled, "Deprogrammed for the Greater Good: One Family's Journey from Privilege to Pardon." Not only did she have her father's blessing to write this piece, but he also helped her craft the idea at inception. More than anything, Simon loved his daughter and wanted her to have opportunities he could not provide. If that meant they would be separated for a year, that was a price worth paying in his opinion.

Cassandra Bowles was offered a place in the next exchange class. Notwithstanding the essay she penned, Cassie was still who she was at her core. She was a beautiful mixture of her parents, her upbringing, and their values. She also learned how to survive, thrive, and play the game. Cassie was on her way. Destination—Legacy City.

"How's the ride been so far? Enjoying it? Smoother than you thought, right Cass?" Hank Hatua startled Cassie with his voice and series of questions. Her trance-like thoughts came to an abrupt halt. From the time they left Legacy City, Hatua had been occupied doing business with other invited guests and dignitaries in their pod. She lost track of him . . . and time. He sat down next to Cassie and squeezed her hand.

Cassie reminded herself where she was and who she was with. Being in the pod wasn't at all what she'd thought it would be. It was smooth and glided along without any perception of the 700-plus miles per hour speed. Before the trip, she was anxious, but at that moment, she was relaxed. At least she was before being startled.

"Hank, it's wonderful. Truly is. You should be proud. A fitting tribute to The Legacy and your commitment to the future."

Hank smiled. He enjoyed hearing about his successes, especially from Cassie. He squeezed her hand a bit harder and said, "I'll be right back."

Cassie looked up and saw their position on the Hyperloop's real-time map in front of and above her eye level. Just about two minutes until the Rocky Mountain tunnel. "On time and under budget," is what she heard Hatua say to the assembled.

She was in the first row. She heard him then say, "A wondrous work and construction marvel. Thanks be to The Legacy!"

"Thanks be to The Legacy!" the group responded.

Hatua continued. "We will be entering The Legacy's Great Divide Tunnel in three . . . two . . . one."

A unified gasp came from the passengers as the lights went out. It was dark in the tunnel. It was also extremely dark inside the pod. No lights were on, save a few small emergency lights near the pod's exit points.

"Ladies and gentlemen, nothing to fear," said Hatua confidently, not a hint of stress in his voice. "I have something very special for you. Here, please take one." Hatua was handing out personal flashlights, which looked more like a sparkler than a flashlight. He started in the back and made his way forward. Everyone was given a flashlight. Everyone except Cassie.

"Friends, you are here for two momentous occasions. One, the final test run of The Legacy's Hyperloop connecting Legacy City and the western plains in Denver. What do you think?" Hatua threw his arms up in the air. The guests knew their next move . . . thunderous applause, which was way more deafening than any noise made by the Hyperloop during the journey.

"Thank you. Thank you. And now, for number two." He grabbed Cassie's hand and guided her up out of her seat. He turned her around to face the passengers. "You all know Cassandra Bowles. She is the most amazing woman I know. As we prepare to cross directly under the Great Divide, I wanted to share with you all another important crossing point in my life. Cassandra Bowles, my dear, Cass," Hatua paused. He stole a glance at the map. Great Divide was coming up in five seconds. Perfect, he thought. He dropped to one knee. He reached into his pocket and pulled out a ring. It was spectacular. He presented it in front of her.

Oh, no! Please Lord, no! Cassie thought to herself. She maintained her smile. All of a sudden, everything slowed down, at least as much as it could while being propelled at 723 miles per hour in a dark hole.

"Cass, will you honor me by becoming my spouse?"

She cried, tears flowing down her face. What could she do? She was being proposed to by one of the wealthiest, most powerful men in the world who had close contacts with leaders in the province and world. To say no might be dangerous for her. However, if she were to say yes, Berko would eventually find out, and not only she but her father would be in grave danger. She didn't have time to think it through. Perhaps Hatua could help protect her and her father if she could trust him enough to do so.

She stood and hugged Hatua. Tears still flowing down her check. He felt those tears and smiled.

"She's overcome with emotions, friends." Hatua quipped, followed by a bit of nervous laughter.

"Well, Hank, what'd she say?" asked one of the guests.

She whispered something in his ear. "My friends," he paused for dramatic impression. "Yes! She said yes!"

Thunderous applause. Hank kissed Cassie. All she could think about was how this was going to play out.

In anticipation of a favorable reply, Hatua had plenty of vintage champagne on ice ready to be liberally served to all guests in each of the pods following their lead pod. There were four pods in all, each carrying twenty-eight passengers sitting in fourteen rows of two per row. An announcement was made celebrating the news. Hatua had someone make a short video of their time together. It also included photos and video snippets from Cassie's early years in London, including some of a very little Cassie with her mother. *Where did he get those?* she wondered to herself.

No matter. She didn't have time to consider any of that as well-wishers bombarded them with hugs, handshakes, and bowing akin to the Indian namaste. Post-pandemics, especially the 2047 version, many people avoided touching others completely.

Their pod approached the Denver Hyperloop station. The doors opened. There was a buzz—literally and figuratively—coming out of the pod as the passengers disembarked. Why not? Perfect ride. Successful final trial. Proposal of marriage and bottomless glasses of 1959 Dom Perignon. Plenty of reasons for fine buzz indeed.

Hatua and Cassie were the last to leave the pod. As Cassie stepped off, she felt a chill in the air. *Must be the Rocky Mountain air at altitude*, she reasoned. She shivered for a brief moment, clutched her jacket tight around her, and tried to shake it off. She couldn't. She felt someone staring at her. *Must be the champagne*, she thought to herself. As she and Hatua walked arm in arm toward the Hyperloop station, she looked up. Cassie immediately caught his eyes. There it was . . . the stare. The Berko stare.

Chapter XXXV

Jeannie had three messages on her PCD. She had only been sleeping for less than two hours. Alondra was watching the girls while Jeannie rested. Jeannie checked them. Two video messages and one voice only. Jeannie played the video messages with holograms. Ellie and Lynne from work. Technically, Ellie was her physician for her pregnancy. Ellie reported that all vitals looked good, just some minor bruising from the fall, no damage to the baby. Lynne passed along her wishes for a speedy recovery. Lynne probably wanted a speedy recovery because she was thoughtful that way. Plus, she didn't want to take on an additional caseload.

The voice message was from someone she didn't recognize. She played the message:

> Hello Doctor Garcia, this is Anjali Gowda. You may recall me from my three pregnancies, two of them successful. My oldest girl attends Revolution Elementary with your oldest. They know one another. I was sitting next to your mother-in-law when you took ill. I'm calling to offer my assistance in case you need anything. Food. Have us watch your girls sometime. Whatever you may need. I know you don't

> know me well, but we'd be most pleased to assist in any manner.

Anjali had a very proper way about her. Her voice sounded kind, thought Jeannie.

> Please forgive me, I don't mean to bring up something painful. I am aware of your husband's passing. For that, please accept my family's heartfelt condolences. You are no doubt a very strong person, Dr. Garcia. I recently went through something very difficult as well. Don't think I handled that as well as you have with your devastating loss. I'm not trying to be forward. I just felt compelled to call and leave you this message. You may reply as you wish. Again, anything you need. It would be my honor to be of assistance to you and your family. Goodbye, Doctor.

How interesting. Jeannie did remember Anjali and her cases. Her first attempt at pregnancy was unsuccessful. A boy, stillborn. There was nothing anyone could do. You never forget those cases, and Jeannie was no exception. She remembered the couple, Anjali from India, and her husband from Germany, such an interesting couple. Very smart, the two of them. She was struck by Anjali's desire to keep trying to have a family.

The two girls Jeannie delivered for Anjali and Stefan were contrasts. The first, a tough delivery, but an even tougher mother. Anjali hung in there and did everything just as Jeannie demanded. Anjali was so pleasant and thankful throughout.

Who did that? *I'd be screaming bloody murder to Ellie if I went through what Anjali did,* thought Jeannie. Ultimately, it was a successful delivery. The next girl was easy by comparison. It happened that way. No muss, no fuss. One, two, three . . . out she came.

Once more, Jeannie recalled how grateful and gracious Anjali was during the whole process. Both pregnancies, different experiences, save for one. Anjali was an amazing patient. Jeannie then recalled how she thought at the time it would be great to get to know this extraordinary woman better; all the best of intentions to do so. Then, life happened and got in the way. Career. Family. Sleep. And yet here, Anjali popped up again at a time of distress and need. *These days, you just never knew who to trust.* Jeannie hated that the thought came to her while she was having such pleasant memories of Anjali. Jeannie didn't have many friends. Most people didn't. It was a luxury, but something about Anjali seemed authentic.

Without wasting another second, Jeannie hit reply.

Chapter XXXVI

Klein felt more invigorated than he had in years, maybe decades. He loved to write. He loved to share ideas. Yet there was something revitalizing to his entire existence by being in nature, breathing fresh air, and engaging in much more physical activity. He lived in his head. It used to be a fun place for him to reside; how to describe a complicated point using plain language, how to turn a clever phrase, and in more recent times, how to push the limits without crossing the imaginary line. Those were noble pursuits. But being in nature, now that was special by itself.

He went on supply gathering walks with his granddaughter. She was excellent company. A young person with so much promise, and what should be a long and fulfilling life in front of her, was forced to join the ranks of freedom fighters. Klein had great respect for his granddaughter. He wished that he and his generation would have left a better world for her.

Shontae and Mitch met Klein when he returned to basecamp. "Ed, a moment of your time please," Shontae said.

"Sure. I'll catch up with you in a while," Klein said to his granddaughter, who smiled in acknowledgment and walked away.

"We'll be breaking camp soon," Shontae said in hushed voice. "We'll be dividing up our group. Tonight, we'll meet with the team leaders and review plans. Ed, we can't thank you enough for your help. Your ideas and encouragement were key in solidifying our approach. We can get you safely to Montana, where you can continue to recover and provide strategic counsel from there."

Klein felt disappointed. *That's odd,* he thought, *why am I feeling disappointed?* He quickly understood.

"That's very kind and generous. I'm recovered. Never felt better. No need for special treatment. I may not have military training, but I'm able and certainly more than willing to help. Assign me to a team. Perhaps with Hannah. I can and want to do my part." Klein looked directly at the two, first Shontae, then Mitch. He held their gaze in an effort to convince them of his strength and readiness.

Mitch really studied Klein and looked him over intensely. Mitch then turned to Shontae and nodded his head.

"Okay, Ed," Shontae replied, "Go get checked out on weapons and how to use them. Now—right now—would be a very good time. See you tonight at 7."

"Thank you. I will." Klein didn't know whether to salute, high-five, or fist bump them. He did none of them. He simply turned and started walking toward the weapons tent. His body felt light. He had a spring in his step. He was grinning from ear to ear.

J. Edward Klein was alive and in the fight.

Chapter XXXVII

Stefan and his team were hard at work evaluating data and cross-checking numbers. Based on the information gathered from multiple sources, the scenario building commenced. Fitting population with resources was an inexact science where exactness was expected. *Perhaps that's why nobody lasts in this job more than two years,* Stefan supposed.

The Living Legacy Division's tasks were, in some ways, impossible. For as long as weather impacted farming production and output, there could be no satisfying the requirements to dial the ratios in tight.

Stefan and his team pored over production numbers for cattle, corn, soybeans, cotton, fruit tree nuts, rice, vegetables, and more. There was a comparison done on both rolling five and ten-year averages to account for weather-related issues like late planting, derecho winds, hurricanes, tornadoes, early freezes, drought, flooding, and hail. Differentials were also caused by soil erosion, biodiversity loss, disease, and destruction caused by pests and insects. Machinery downtime was another factor considered. Access to an ample water supply had always been critical. Technology and yield percentages impacted the equation. Finally, land ownership and related production (or nonproduction) goals were assessed. Foreign, now called "interprovincial," land ownership became a critical component in predictive modeling, especially starting in the 2020s when then-foreign countries purchased sizable agricultural land as family farms were sold without any government restrictions against foreign ownership. The truth was many of those family farms were forced to sell due to oppressive tax burdens, penalizing those who preferred the passing down of farms within a family.

Before the all-hands meeting, Stefan's team was required to reevaluate source data to be certain when they met they had the most relevant and most accurate data available that day. He put pressure on his team to get it right. After all, he was under intense pressure to do the same.

The modeling used was improved upon by Stefan after his arrival. He was able to run multiple what-if and Monte Carlo scenarios to create stunning visual presentations at the press of a button or two—or voice command, whatever his preference. Once finalized, Stefan would take one more pass at the data and related presentation charts and media. He wanted to be certain that what they passed along, ultimately to be viewed by The Legacy, was their absolute best work.

The original model was created to solve for a final ratio of 1.00. That is, when all the inputs on the food production side were compiled and put into mathematical form as the numerator, the corresponding population side represented as the denominator, should line up as 1.00. That would be the exact match required for the population level at any given time.

Stefan ran the numbers. The ratio came to 1.102. There was plenty of food production, in fact, an overabundance, which might point to waste this year or fallowing of farmland next year. He ran the numbers again. Same result, 1.102.

Something stirred deep inside Stefan's brain. It was as if he were hearing a tune. It became more pronounced, following a rhythmic cadence. *Comply or die. Comply or die. Comply or die.*

CHAPTER XXXVIII

The playground was full. The din created by so many children playing was the perfect atmosphere for Jeannie to help clear her mind and get the girls outside for fresh air and exercise. While Ana mostly visited with her friends around the playground set, Juli was out on the soccer field mixing it up with kids twice her age and size. She was holding her own, dishing out as much as she was getting, maybe more.

Jeannie sat on a bench, alone. It was under one of the few shade trees. It was a nice respite from the afternoon's heat.

"Hi Jeannie." It was Anjali. Jeannie stood to greet her. They automatically embraced. For both of them, it seemed the right thing to do.

"Anjali, thanks for meeting me here."

"Of course. My pleasure, truly."

"Where are your girls?"

"Running over there, playing tag, or some made-up game." Anjali pointed just past the playground equipment, where Ana was still chatting with school-aged friends. "Once Bhavi sees Ana, poor little NyNy may be odd girl out."

"Such an awkward time for girls."

"Not likely to get better, will it? Except for us, we were model young ladies growing up," Anjali winked.

"Only if you say so." They both chuckled.

"Thanks for the suggestion, Jeannie. I know my girls need to get outside more. I do too. What a lovely day."

Jeannie looked about. "You know, I was just thinking about that. Something about being outside surrounded by little voices to give perspective."

"Little loud voices, I'd say. Especially that one." Anjali motioned toward NyNy, who was embroiled in an animated and very loud conversation with another child near the swings, something about sharing.

"Gotta love the youngest. Full of confidence," Jeannie said.

"And the oldest, full of opinions, especially about the youngest and how we parents aren't raising them right."

Jeannie sat there quietly.

"Oh Jeannie, I'm so sorry. What an insensitive thing for me to say. Please accept my . . ."

"Not to worry, Anjali. Please don't feel like you need to walk on eggshells. That will make things uncomfortable for both of us."

"Okay, got it." Anjali seemed relieved. "Jeannie, is there anything you or your girls need? Anything we can help with?"

"Not that I can think of at this moment. Just being here is perfect."

"It is perfect, isn't it?" They both just sat there. Neither felt the need to fill the air with chatter. There was enough chatter, laughter, and even some kids crying to fill their senses. What was nice was being. Just being.

"Mommy, can I have a snack?" Juli said while gasping for air.

"Are you done playing soccer?"

"Oh no, Mommy!"

"Honey, how about a drink then? You can have a snack when you're done playing."

"But Mooooom, I'm huuuuungry!"

"Great, when you're done playing soccer, you can have a small snack. And then you'll be hungry for dinner later. Here, here's your water bottle."

Juli took a quick drink and was off again. Quick in and quick out.

"Oh, my goodness, sounds like conversations we have in our family. Over and over and over again." Anjali shook her head while she spoke.

"Yep, it's child comment number three. 'Mooooom, I'm huuuuungry!'"

They both laughed. Jeannie needed this time. It was the first time that she relaxed and laughed since Rolando passed.

Jeannie then asked, "So, before all of this," she pointed to the kids on the playground indiscriminately, "what did you do?"

"Computers," Anjali answered. "I was involved with computers. I spent some time teaching, some time in industry, and some time in government. Then . . ." she pointed to the kids on the playground indiscriminately, "all of this happened."

Jeannie laughed. "Computers. That's interesting."

"Most people don't say that. I thought so."

"Tell me more." So, Anjali filled in details about her experiences. Jeannie was duly impressed with Anjali's background and even more so with her modesty. Anjali was a computer science, engineering, artificial intelligence, and big data rock star. She gave it up to raise her girls. Impressive woman. Very impressive woman. Jeannie liked her even more than she thought she would. She also began to sense that she could trust Anjali Gowda.

Chapter XXXIX

For almost a full week, Cassie had been back at Province House. She had seen Berko several times, but he never mentioned a thing about seeing her at the Denver Hyperloop Station. And he certainly never said anything about her engagement to Hatua. He had to have known. Just a few small interactions around to-do items; nothing major, and nothing lengthy. With each passing day, hour, and minute, she was becoming more uneasy. That was Berko.

Cassie's PCD pressed against her flesh. It was on silent mode. It was a new message . . . from her father. She couldn't play it at Province House, too dangerous. It would have to wait until after work. Even then, she'd have to be very careful where she played it. She couldn't play it at her unit. She figured some time ago listening devices were installed. Probably cameras too, although she wasn't as sure about that. She hadn't heard from her father for months. She missed hearing his voice and seeing his face. *He must've thought things were improving for him to reach out,* she thought.

Berko appeared at the doorway to her office. He just stood there, saying nothing. How long had he been standing there? Cassie wondered. Did he see me looking at my PCD? Did he know a message was coming from my father? Berko's face was expressionless, save for the smallest hint of a smile, not a real smile, a Berko smile.

"Hello, sir. What can I do for you?" Cassie said, as she slowly moved her left arm with PCD—and engagement ring on her left ring finger—down to her lap. No answer. Berko continued to stand there. Looking at her with a Berko stare and Berko smile. Cassie thought for a split second to hit connect Hank Hatua on her PCD. Her thought was interrupted as Berko spoke.

"Tell me, Cassandra, is there anything I should know?"

"About what, sir?" Cassie was dying inside. She was frightened, more frightened than she had ever been. It was getting late, and most co-workers had left. There she was, she and Berko. She rehearsed how this conversation might go many times in her mind, but her mind was blank now. All she could think about was fleeing. Berko had never threatened her with physical harm. He didn't have to. Just being him, with all the power and knowledge at his disposal, was enough.

Berko didn't answer her question. He was playing her, playing her very well. He could see that she was terrified. Good, he thought. That was a good thing.

"Are you asking me about the Hyperloop ride last weekend?"

Berko moved in a few feet, still staring, still with that hideous smile, still silent.

"Are you perhaps asking me about what happened during the Hyperloop ride?"

Berko again moved in closer, still with gaze affixed, no blinking, still smiling, his mouth never moving, not even the slightest, and still silent.

"Sir, what can I tell you? Please help me here. Is it about Hank Hatua?"

"No, dear Cassandra, no. That's not it at all. What I do want to know . . ." he paused. It was a long, painful pause, "is what your father said in the message he just sent you."

Cassie immediately thought about several responses. What message? My father did what? I deleted it. She knew none of these responses would be satisfactory. Odds are that Berko had intercepted and listened to the message already. He probably then approved the message for forwarding to her. That was how Berko operated.

"Go ahead, Cassandra. Play the message." Berko moved in even closer to her. He leaned in and whispered, "How about now?"

Cassie couldn't swallow. She was probably visibly shaking. She'd normally try to hide it, but there was no way to do that in this circumstance. She had no way out. She barely was able to eke out, "play."

It was her father's voice. Upbeat and oblivious to who was listening.

> Hello there, my darling girl. Hope you are doing well. I heard your news. Congratulations. I know how difficult it is for you to communicate, especially given your job and who you're marrying. I just wanted to wish you . . .

Simon Bowles paused. Perhaps he did know that this wasn't a secure message.

> All my best as you begin this new chapter in your life. Dianne and I love you more than you can imagine.

Another pause. This time to regain his composure.

> I'm doing much better. The doctor here thinks my illness has slowed down, at least for now. They still don't have a handle on it. No real diagnosis. That's okay. I'm staying positive and . . .

Again, he paused as if he knew someone was listening. If they were, he wouldn't want to give them any evidence to use against her.

> Getting some sun when I can. My ruddy complexion certainly can use it. Sweetheart, please be well, stay safe, and congratulations again. I love you and always will with everything I am and have.

Throughout the entire message, Berko just stood there. Staring. Smiling.

Berko turned toward the door. He didn't look back as he said, "Good to hear that your father's recovery seems to be going well." After walking a few more steps, he stopped but didn't turn around. "Thanks be to The Legacy." Berko left.

Cassie couldn't control her emotions or her body. She was a mental and emotional wreck. Berko had a way of controlling her. Yet, she did control one thing. Cassie moved her lips to say ever so softly, "Thanks be to God."

Chapter XL

Molon Labe's plans were set. Mitchell Iron Falcon designed a fine series of plans. If they worked, the arc of their fight for freedom might change in *Molon Labe's* favor. There was timing to consider. Timing was key to the plan's potential success, timing to get the plans out to those *Molon Labe* cells throughout the province, and timing, as in coordinated timing, of each aspect of the plan's execution.

As all electronic means of communication were subject to being intercepted or disrupted by The Legacy's Resolution Department or CCP, the only way to effectively communicate the plans without undue risk was via a comprehensive set of signal mirrors. When Klein heard that their hope of success was riding on using a set of mirrors, he was highly skeptical yet intrigued. Hannah explained to her grandfather that Mitch had meticulously designed a series of mirror relays. *Molon Labe* had then painstakingly developed and deployed the comprehensive series of mirrors throughout the province according to Mitch's design.

Communication via the mirrors was based on a dot and dash system, similar to Morse code. Once the message was received and relayed to the next signal mirror, human assets would then spread the word to local *Molon Labe* cells. Hannah shared that Native Americans had used such communication methods with great success for hunting and war parties. However, nothing on this scale had been attempted. After *Molon Labe's* low-level satellite was destroyed by the CCP, the signal mirror system became their safest and most effective communication method.

As a way to further increase message security, Mitch implemented a code talker-based transmission. He borrowed from historical precedent of World Wars I and II by using little-known Native American languages as the basis for transmission. Messages were then encoded or decoded by use of cyphertext. As Mitch assumed that The Legacy might intercept the mirror signaling, he had preestablished a rotating use of various Native American languages to the relay system. For good measure, he also included the Basque language of *Euskara*. Hannah assured her grandfather that Mitch had thoroughly considered all options and that they were prepared and well trained.

In fairness, she did share a few potential downside risks. Use of mirror relays was time-consuming. To communicate to the entire province considering potential weather and other disrupting factors could take several days to be certain all necessary parties were informed. Moreover, the signal mirror system carried an additional risk of being misunderstood or perhaps not wholly understood. These plans were quite involved. A missed word here or there could be calamitous. Hannah ended with a further cautionary note. Although test training went well, *Molon Labe* had never tried to communicate such involved plans via mirror signaling.

The Legacy, on the other hand, didn't share those same concerns. The regime routinely had its communications intercepted. It knew that was happening. At times, it appeared that The Legacy wanted its communications to be intercepted, an easy way to spread some *dezinformatsia.* Yet intercepted comms didn't seem to matter to The Legacy. They had overwhelming force, resources, and confidence on their side. *Molon Labe* hoped that The Legacy's confidence, perhaps in the form of overconfidence, would prove to be their Achilles heel.

Chapter XLI

Jeannie read and reread Rolando's handwritten card so many times she'd lost count. It was as dear to her as the necklace and double DC pendant she wore without exception.

> Dearest DC! So blessed to have taken that "fork in the road" with you ten years ago! Here's to the next ten . . . and beyond! Love you with all my heart and soul, RR

She held the card close. *I love you too, Double,* she said internally to herself. Now, she thought, *Time to figure this out.*

When she initially downloaded Rolando's PCD to hers, Jeannie had no concept that his PCD was so full of complex data. At first blush, it appeared he was a mad man. Garbled letters, numbers, and symbols all mixed together like a twenty-ingredient goulash. What a mess. It initially exasperated her. Then, the more she studied what seemed to be notes from a toddler striking at an old-styled keyboard, she noticed something that caught her eye. There were some repeats. Some of these incoherent garbled words—if they could be called words—had some pattern to them. Or, at least, so she thought. Perhaps it was wishful thinking.

Jeannie studied the mix of letters, numbers, and signs over and over, looking for a pattern. Frustrating. *What was he thinking? My goodness, what was he trying to hide?* She had an idea. She compared the same-day calendar entries with same-day notes. Ah ha! A pattern. In evaluating his calendar and comparing it with his daily notes, she noticed some combinations that repeated. They didn't make sense to her. Jeannie noticed a word written as *golre!!a* several times in both notes and calendar in days preceding his death. "What is *golre!!a,* Double? Come on!" Jeannie blurted out loud. No matter, the girls were at school, and she was home alone on her final day of leave after her fainting spell.

And there was *yoenloocred*. That combination occurred several times. She also saw *scieengu*, *nicogelclay*, and *unhakthaa* more than once over a few days in his notes. And, for the coup de gras, there was this beauty, Jeannie's inner voice said sarcastically: 和子羊羔狮. Jeannie was so pleased that Rolando was too busy to become fluent in Chinese.

Jeannie sat down and looked out over the courtyard below her unit in the sprawling, concrete jungle. *Think. Think.* She kept telling herself. *Rolando didn't want someone to understand what he was doing. He must've known that what he was doing was dangerous. Why would he put himself at such risk? He had us. He had our family. Why would he do this?* Jeannie was fighting back a combination of sadness and anger. *Why? Why? Why, Rol?*

Then it hit her. He was working on something for them, for their future. It had to have been something big, something so much greater than himself and their family. She thought of his hologram message. The only answer that Jeannie could come up with was it had to do with The Legacy and its plans. That's why he took these extra steps at protecting everyone involved. She played his hologram again, this time seeing him and hearing him through a different lens.

> My source tells me that the hardliners plan to do away with Reproductive Health Services. In their words, "won't be needed." What does that mean? "Won't be needed"? Something's not adding up. And Department of Wellbeing's Reproductive Health Services, that's you, DC!
>
> I've been working on a lead to help. That's why I told you what I did earlier. One of my brothers in Christ believes someone at Province House knows. It isn't just in China. There are apparently plants throughout who know something. Or at least pieces of something. I don't know who that is at Province House. I was getting close. Guess I got too close.
>
> DC, please forgive me. I know this is a lot to consider. I think you and the others in RHS are expendable. If you hear the CCP's hardliners taking people out in a coup or something like that, go to Frank Gies. He's at the Che Bakery near Province House. He's the brother I just mentioned. He'll help you. He's a good man, and I trust him with all my soul.

She stopped right there. She knew what came next. She just couldn't right now. She needed to pursue who did this to him, to them. And when she did, she'd likely also find the answers Rolando was seeking.

Chapter XLII

"Is this your best work?" Berko asked without looking up.

"I believe so, sir," responded Dr. Ertz. "My team has devoted itself to providing the best data and analysis given the inputs. They, rather we, have been working night and day to confirm . . ."

Berko looked up and stared. Dr. Ertz lost his place. He just looked at Berko initially, But that didn't last more than a second or two. He then looked around, then back to Berko, as if inviting Berko to say something, to direct him. Berko remained silent.

"We always strive to serve you, *Herr* Berko, and The Legacy, of course."

Berko continued to stare at Dr. Ertz.

"The numbers were off to begin with, so I reran the figures and double-checked our source data. I noticed two input errors, which I fixed. It all has proper backup now." Dr. Ertz then stopped. He noticed Berko getting up out of his chair and coming toward him. Dr. Ertz was bigger than Berko, but Berko was stronger in more ways than one. Dr. Ertz backed up ever so slightly.

Berko stood directly in front of Dr. Ertz. Still staring. Then, something unexpected happened. Berko broke into a laugh.

"Oh, *mein Freund*, Stefan," Berko said while still laughing. "Just a little fun with you today. I'm sure everything is in order.

I trust the numbers are as we expected, *nicht war*?" Berko gave Dr. Ertz a friendly pat on the shoulder.

Stefan had never seen Berko laugh before, nothing even close to a laugh. He'd never seen him truly smile either. This was as unnerving to Stefan as when he got the Berko stare or the visit down in B5.

"Stefan, to confirm, your ratio of .93 can withstand audit. Is that right?"

Dr. Ertz began to answer, but he was distracted for the briefest of moments. He faintly heard the familiar rhythm, the rhythm and associated words that went with that earworm that popped into his head periodically getting louder and faster. *Comply or die. Comply or die. Comply or die.* He tried to shake it off.

"Yes, sir, Herr Berko, we have all the proper source materials ready for your review, if you'd like."

"No need. No need at this time. *Alles in Ordnung.*"

"*Ja*. Yes. Thank you, sir. Will there be anything else, sir?" asked Dr. Ertz.

Berko replied quickly, "No. No thank you, Stefan. Excellent work by you and your team. I will see to it that each of your team members receive fifty social credits."

"That is very generous, sir. Thank you."

"And Stefan, " Berko added, "you will be receiving two hundred and fifty additional social credits for a job very well done."

Dr. Ertz couldn't believe what he was hearing and who he was hearing it from. "Thank you very much sir. Again, it is my pleasure to serve you and The Legacy."

Dr. Ertz shook Berko's hand, probably more enthusiastically than Berko would've preferred, but considering what Stefan did for him—just him—how could he object?

Berko had one more comment before Dr. Ertz was fully out the door. "Dr. Ertz . . ."

"*Ja*, yes, sir."

"Please consider taking your lovely bride out for a nice dinner. Perhaps to *Casa de Flor* on *Revolucion*. I have taken the liberty of making reservations for the two of you for this Friday evening at 7 p.m. You will dine as my guests. All expenses covered, including wine. Just ask for *Martin* when you arrive. Hope you and Anjali enjoy your night out of the house."

"Thank you again, sir. We greatly appreciate your generosity."

The earworm faded as Dr. Ertz walked away. He had an uneasy feeling, worse than before. Dr. Ertz kept mulling over one question in his mind. *How did Berko know Anjali's name?*?

Chapter XLIII

Jeannie was back at work. It seemed odd to be there. So much had changed. Actually, she had changed. Her life had changed. She used to be onboard with the world. How things played out. So long as her space was secure—her family, her job, her immediate surroundings—she just didn't care much for politics and that world. She tried to insulate herself from politics. She knew enough to have a well-mannered conversation if it was possible with that topic. But she shied away from knowing too much. Perhaps she missed something important by taking an ostrich approach.

She also didn't see much benefit with religion. It was good for others. She didn't try to convert others away from their beliefs. She just didn't believe it herself. Now that she knew how much that was an important part of her one true love, her best friend, she wondered if somehow she missed something about that too.

One thing she did know was how much she loved her girls. They were her everything now. And the baby too. The baby. The child growing inside her would be born into a family without a father. There would be love. Plenty of love. But something would be terribly missing. Rolando brought so much joy and laughter, so much teasing and kidding, so much heart and insight. This product of their love would know nothing of it, save for stories shared by her, the girls, and others. There would be his writings. They survived him. Jeannie made a promise to herself to gather Rolando's writings and bind them in some form for posterity's sake. At least the baby would have those to read at a later date.

Another thing she knew was how much she loved her job. It was a safe place for her, a place where she could help others, a place where she could be challenged and excel in meeting those challenges and see new life. New life. She thought back to Rolando. Why didn't he say something about his beliefs? It must've been hard for him to hold back knowing full well that she and her colleagues were part of a system allowing for abortion to become such a normalized part of the culture.

Once The Legacy came to power, abortion was never easier. It was part of The Legacy's narrative, one of The Legacy's key principal points in garnering support from a majority of the public. It was expressed in terms of how best to promote society's collective goals, to protect a woman's right to control all decisions about her body at all times without exception. None. Zero.

The Legacy further contended that society needed to ensure that all who entered our new world, a better world under the new regime's policies, were given proper amounts of food, shelter, clothing, education, and love, especially love. How could society build a strong and vibrant future legacy if we allowed babies to be born of poverty, indifference, crisis, instability, and a lack of love?

When she was a resident, Jeannie recalled several in-service trainings about new health programs for expectant mothers. She and her colleagues would receive the most recent abstracts surrounding reproductive health, birth control, and pregnancy termination options and procedures. One specific in-service training was notable in its use of technology.

She specifically recalled receiving this training shortly before she and Rolando were married. She thought back on how she learned about this new program while thinking about someday, if she was fortunate enough to become pregnant, she herself would be on the receiving end of this program. How would she feel? Was it safe? What if there was an accident or something went wrong with the technology?

Jeannie satisfied her curiosity by educating herself more about the program, science, technology, studies, company, and people involved. Her opinion advanced to the point of not only understanding the program, but she also thought it was brilliant. Dr. Jeanette W Garcia became a vocal and loyal advocate of this new approach to comprehensive reproductive health. So much so that she would be asked to take a lead role in developing and presenting future in-service trainings on the program to doctors and staff.

The program's concept was simple enough. The science and technology behind the program was anything but simple. Once a woman was found to be pregnant, she would be required to receive an injection of a cross-placental pregnancy termination implantable. Using nanotechnology, the implantable was controlled by an outside source. The outside source was referred to as The Coin.

Jeannie thought of the hundreds of Coins—maybe thousands at this point—she had distributed over the years. She explained how The Coin worked to so many women, as well as doctors and their respective teams, for so long that she could recite her basic explanatory session in her sleep.

I have just given you an injection, which is safe. There should be no complications for you or your fetus. Here is your Coin. It is unique to you and your fetus. Please keep it in a safe place throughout your pregnancy. The injection I just gave you includes a piece of technology, which is safe and effective. If you decide to abort your pregnancy at any time prior to birth, all you need to do is deposit your unique Coin in one of the Coin receptacles located throughout the province. We have one here in our office too. Once confirmation takes place, which is for your safety and security, your implant will emit medicine to terminate your pregnancy. It will also emit medicine to allow you to pass the pregnancy tissue naturally. Only in rare cases would you need to come in for assistance. If you have any complications, please call me immediately. If you take the pregnancy to full term and give birth, then the technology is disabled, and you may keep the Coin as a memento. Do you have any questions?

Normally there were questions, especially from first-time expectant mothers, questions such as:

- Does the implant really work?
- When is it too late to use it?
- What happens if the Coin doesn't work?

- Does the implant hurt my baby?
- Does the implant ever kill a baby without turning in a Coin?
- What is the implant made of?
- What is the Coin made of?

The most frequent question asked, by far with no close second, was:

- What happens if my Coin is lost or stolen?

Jeannie had answers for them all. The only question that caused her concern, which she tried not to show, was the last one. The reality was there was nothing she could do if the Coin was either misplaced or taken.

"Welcome back!" Dr. Ellie entered Jeannie's office sporting a friendly smile and arms extended. They hugged. "So wonderful to see your beautiful face, my dear! Missed you so much," Dr. Ellie said enthusiastically.

"Missed you too, E. Nice to be back," Jeannie responded, with less energy than her colleague, yet still with sincerity and warmth.

"You've been through the ringer. Look, if you need more time away, you just say the word. We can make do here. Really, no awards for toughness being given out. We know how difficult this must be for you and your littles."

"Thanks, E., you're the best. I'm fine."

Ellie shot her a look like she wasn't convinced.

"Really, I am," Jeannie said in a more convincing and stronger way.

"Okay, I hear you. If things change, you just say the word, and we'll cover for you. Got it? Okay?"

"Yes, yes, got it. And, thanks Ellie. You're a dear friend."

Dr. Ellie looked at her friend closely, then turned and shut the door to Jeannie's office. Dr. Ellie remained in the office and grabbed a chair and moved it close to where Jeannie was sitting.

"Look, please be careful." Dr. Ellie was barely speaking above a whisper. She leaned in even closer to Jeannie. Dr. Ellie continued, "When you had your little fainting show at the school, I was alerted because you are technically my patient. I immediately tried accessing your PCD health data. I couldn't get it right away. Something was blocking access. I could see that your health data file was there, but that's all I could get to. It was as if someone had denied me full access rights, which is odd because I have rights to that file. Then," Dr. Ellie whispered, "it got stranger. I noticed that there was an adjacent health file. It looked like Rolando's. I couldn't figure how that was. What the heck was Rolando's health file doing on your PCD? It just didn't make sense to me . . . at first."

Jeannie sat there intensely listening to Ellie. She didn't show any emotion, just listening.

Ellie continued in hushed voice, "I finally got in through a workaround. You're good, health wise. Baby's fine too."

Jeannie showed a little emotion and some relief to give Ellie something. Jeannie hated having to act in front of her friend, but she had no choice. It was for Ellie's own protection, she justified.

"Listen, I know Rolando's death is hard. I can't even imagine what you and the girls are suffering. But, listen my friend, please,

please promise me that you will not go snooping around looking for reasons. You know, reasons. I know you know he didn't just drown." Ellie focused her gaze as deeply and as penetrating as she could. "But, please, please, I beg you. Don't, just don't. If only for the girls."

All Jeannie could muster was, "Thanks Ellie. I hear you. Thanks, my dear, dear friend."

Chapter XLIII

Klein, his granddaughter, and eighteen others were on the move. They had their orders and needed to hump it to Chicago as quickly as they could. It was close to a 1,000-mile journey, especially considering extra precautions that needed to be taken along the way to avoid calling attention to themselves, or worse, being captured. They needed to be in position within a week.

The group was led by Alexandria Aquino. A young woman with a calm yet gritty personality, she had proven herself to leadership when she cunningly misdirected Reso forces who were about to ambush a *Molon Labe* cell gathering near Ottumwa, Iowa. She called attention to herself whereby Reso commandoes began tracking her. They thought she would lead them directly to the cell. Instead, she led the Reso forces across the Des Moines River from where the cell was actually meeting. By so doing, *Molon Labe* scouts observed the Reso's river crossing and alerted the gathered cell. Aquino's calm head and wits saved the lives of over fifty *Molon Labe* patriots.

Zim was with their group as well. Klein discovered that Zim's real name was Klaus Markus Zimmer. As a kid, Zim was called Markus by his parent. Klaus was a family name on his mother's side. As a traditional German family, that name finding its way onto his birth certificate was a certainty. What was also a certainty for young Markus Zimmer was that once kids found out about his first name they'd call him Santa at every opportunity. Young Markus learned very quickly the power of humor to diffuse any tense or awkward situation. When kids would tease him by calling him Santa Klaus, he'd remind them that he was keeping the naughty and nice list. He was an expert at the well-timed joke or pun. Along with helping with morale, Zim had another benefit. He grew up in Lincoln Square, the German heart of Chicago.

The group's trek would take them across northern Nebraska through or close to Valentine, central Iowa (Sioux City, Fort Dodge, Waterloo, Dubuque), and northern Illinois by way of Rockford and into Chicagoland. Their plan was to follow as much of Old Highway 20 as was safe. Aquino's regional knowledge was also a plus. She knew all of Iowa very well. She also had substantial experience and friendly contacts in and around good portions of Nebraska, South Dakota, Minnesota, Missouri, Illinois, and Wisconsin. She was a true Midwesterner.

They set out from Chadron, reminiscent in destination only of the so-called Great 1,000-mile Race from Chadron to Chicago of 1893. The late nineteenth-century race was started as a joke. This group's start, and potential finish, was no joke at all. Lives were at stake, and not just theirs.

They would travel by whatever means was available. They were hosted by cell members. They used whatever mode of transport the cells had at their disposal. They'd travel day or night, as well as day and night, depending.

It was a tough journey. Although the terrain was mostly flat with rolling hills, the weather made for some difficult stretches. Yet, nobody complained. Except while traveling in a small convoy of old vintage pickup trucks just outside of Cedar Falls as they were nearing an old high school campus, they spotted a tornado approaching them from the southwest. They took cover in a ditch as the tornado passed them to the south.

"Whew, we almost met our Waterloo here!" Zim quipped. Less than twenty miles away was Waterloo, Iowa.

Chapter XLIV

"Oh, thank you so much. So very kind. Please, come in" Anjali said as she invited Jeannie and her girls inside. "We don't get out much. Okay, we never get out. I've made dinner for all five of you. If your girls aren't big fans of chicken tikka masala, I've got plenty of mac and cheese too."

Jeannie chuckled, "They'll be just fine. That wasn't necessary. Although I appreciate a home-cooked meal, especially when I'm not the one doing the home cooking."

"Right, exactly," Anjali agreed. "Before Stefan gets here, can we chat about something?"

"Girls, why don't you go see what Bhavi and Nyra are up to?"

"My goodness, how rude of me. Girls, please come with me. Bhavi and NyNy are playing their interactive math game. You probably know it already. You can all play together. This way, girls." Anjali escorted the youngsters down the hall to a room toward the back.

Jeannie looked around. There were plenty of family pictures, all full of joy. Also, some souvenirs from travels; looked like international travel. *Must've been prior days. Nobody travels much anymore,* thought Jeannie.

She then looked at a bookcase, which was stocked full of mathematics, computer, Artificial Intelligence, and other technical books. There was also a strong presence of what looked to be romance novels. *Romance novels?* she thought. They seemed so out of place. Intrigued, Jeannie picked one up.

Anjali reentered the room. "Okay, I think the girls are set now, at least for the next five minutes."

"Stefan's?" Jeannie said as she held up *Wife by Wednesday*.

"Oh goodness, no," replied Anjali. "He's more of a fan of Bybee's 'Not Quite' series. You know, *Not Quite Dating, Not Quite Mine*, and, of course, his favorite, *Not Quite Enough*!" Anjali said with emphasis as she rolled her eyes. They both had a nice laugh.

"So, what'd you want to talk about?"

"Thanks. Please sit down." They both sat on a plush white sofa with a nice view across the courtyard to another similar building.

Anjali looked concerned. "Jeannie, I thought you might be able to help me make sense of something. In your job, you regularly work with Legacy Coins."

Interesting opener, thought Jeannie. "Yes, I do."

"Right, you gave me two," Anjali acknowledged. "You might've seen this when you were looking at books. See, our Legacy Coin holders there? They're empty."

"Right. You turned them in. I expect you'll get your replacements soon."

"Here's the thing. Before the announcement came out, you know, requiring their return, they were already gone. I noticed it while Stefan was . . ." Anjali paused. Her eyes started to tear up. "I'm so sorry to bother you with this. It's probably nothing. And I shouldn't involve you if it is something." Anjali paused again to dab her eyes. "Naan?"

"What?"

"Naan? I made fresh homemade naan; would you like some?"

"Anjali, what's going on?"

"I, uh, I, I shouldn't have even brought this up."

"Anjali, I haven't known you too long, but you have quickly become dear to me and my girls. If there's something I can do to help you, I want to. As a doctor, I'm good at keeping confidentiality—particularly if it isn't otherwise captured in a digital record and reviewed by *them*."

Anjali smiled. "Okay," she shook her hands. "I'll just say it fast. If you don't want to know more, or if it's too much, let's just enjoy some naan together, deal?"

"Deal."

"I think our Legacy Coins were stolen. I noticed it when Stefan was gone from us. He was taken at night by the Reso. After two days, they released him."

Jeannie's mind was working overtime. She reminded herself to just listen and listen very carefully.

Anjali continued, "And here's the question I have for you if you know and can share with me. Shortly after Stefan was released, *they* issued an order requiring the return of all Legacy Coins. Do you know why they did that? I thought maybe being in the profession that you are, you might know or have a sense of what's going on. Something. Anything. There, that's it. Thanks for listening. I feel better just sharing with you." Anjali reached out and touched Jeannie's hand.

The first thing that popped into Jeannie's mind was hearing two voices she loved speaking in synchronicity, "Fork in the road, Jeannie, fork in the road." It was soothing to think of Double and Pop in this moment.

"I don't know, not for certain anyway. But I'm suspicious, Anjali, and I'm not the suspicious type. My husband, he was definitely the suspicious type. Lawyer. Writer. They have that gene. Me, no. But now, given what I've been seeing and with what you just said, I think there may be something happening here."

"Yes, me too," said Anjali soberly.

There were two quick beeps at the door. Stefan walked in, hurriedly. Anjali and Jeannie stood. Anjali started in Stefan's direction. "So sorry. Sorry I'm late. Had to wrap up a few final things so we can enjoy tonight uninterrupted." They kissed on the cheek.

"Speaking of uninterrupted, Jeannie, thank you for watching our girls," Stefan said as he extended a hand to her. "If they get out of line, just threaten to report their bad behavior for social credit withdrawals. That usually does the trick for me."

"I'm sure that won't be necessary. Happy to do it. And Anji made us a delicious meal, so I'm looking forward to that. And, of course, getting started on one of the 'Not Quite' books."

"Sorry," said a confused Stefan.

"Never mind, love. After you quickly wash up, why don't you say hello and goodbye to the girls? We need to leave soon. Big night out on the town."

"*Ja*, will do. Back *gleich*."

After Stefan made his way down the hall, entered the master bedroom, and closed the door, Anjali spoke, "There's more. I'm concerned about what they may've done to Stefan while he was being held. He hasn't been himself," Anjali was speaking very quickly. It was difficult for Jeannie to follow each word given the rapid speech coupled with hushed tones. "I looked at him, and he looked back at me as if he was apologizing for what they did to him. I can't say for certain, but I'm scared Jeannie. So scared."

Jeannie embraced Anjali and held her tight while whispering, "We'll figure this out. We will. Together. Okay?"

"Okay, we will. Together," Anjali whispered back. They continued to hold each other tightly.

"Ah ha, caught you!" Stefan shouted from just inside the room. "You two talking about me, no doubt."

Anjali and Jeannie broke their embrace. Anjali shot Stefan a look, which would have dropped a rhino midstride. Stefan got the message.

"Jeannie," Stefan said, changing his tone and energy, "if there is anything I can do to help, please do let me know. We want to be supportive of you and your girls." Stefan glanced quickly at Anjali as if asking if he made up for his earlier insensitive interruption.

"Thank you, Stefan, that'd be nice," Jeannie replied. Stefan smiled. Jeannie went on, "In fact, there is one thing."

"Name it. Please."

"Well, I'm *not quite* sure how to ask you this," Jeannie said as she glanced at Anjali, "Here goes. In your learned opinion," Jeannie asked, completely deadpan, "Should I start with mine, forever, perfect, or crazy? Dating and enough are out of the picture."

Anjali giggled. Stefan was confused. Jeannie had hope. She came to a fork in the road . . . and took it.

Chapter XLV

Mitchell Iron Falcon had always been at least one step ahead of others. As one of five children, the second oldest overall and oldest boy, he had a keen sense of observation to go with incredible intellect. When he was a kid growing up on the Pine Ridge Reservation, he and others lacked hope. The hopelessness was born of a thoughtful understanding of the environment in which he and others on the reservation lived. It wasn't hard to see why.

The Pine Ridge Reservation was located on more than 2.8 million acres in Oglala Lakota County in southwestern South Dakota. This county had been perennially the poorest or second poorest in the entire United States, with an average per capita income of less than $10,000 for years upon years. With unemployment close to 90 percent, it was no surprise why income levels were so low. Alcoholism (notwithstanding the reservation being dry), diabetes leading to amputations and death at three to four times the national rate, high levels of suicide (especially teen suicide at four times the national average), infant mortality rates at five times greater than the national average, heart disease, obesity, poor quality healthcare, and extremely low life expectancy (twenty years below neighboring counties and akin to numbers found in the former countries of India, Iraq, and Sudan) all led to systemic challenges that had not been adequately addressed . . . ever. Hope was a luxury the residents on the Pine Ridge Indian Reservation lands could not afford.

However, juxtaposed against this background and circumstance, Mitch's upbringing brought him great joy. There was plenty of love in his home. He was surrounded by his four siblings and over a dozen or so cousins who lived close by. There were ready playmates at any time. His father worked for the US Department of the Interior in the Badlands National Park as a senior maintenance mechanic. His mother, descended from the well-known Lakota spiritual leader, Knowing Fire Eyes, worked part-time as the church secretary for the Catholic Church on the reservation. His parents were devout Catholics who routinely shared what they had with others. Rare was the time when there weren't cousins or neighbor kids eating supper at the table with him and his family. There never seemed to be a lack of delicious and nutritious food or sweet fellowship.

Mitch excelled in the classroom and athletic courts and fields while attending Red Cloud High School. He was also very involved with volunteer activities at his church and service projects at his high school. Mitch was proud to attend school founded by Chief Red Cloud along with Catholic Jesuits. He didn't view it as a burden. Rather, Mitch considered it an honor and obligation to lead and give back to his people as his ancestors did over a century and a half earlier.

Although he received numerous offers to continue his studies at universities as geographically diverse as James Madison University, University of Florida, and San Diego State University, Mitch decided to attend Chadron State College. This allowed him to study close to home to help his family while also allowing them to see him participate in cross country along with track and field. Mitch ran like the wind.

Many sports commentators noted that he was the fastest Native American runner since the late, great Billy Mills. Mills was Mitch's inspiration. Mills, who was born in Pine Ridge and was Oglala Lakota, served in the United States Marine Corps and won an Olympic Gold medal in the 10,000-meter run while competing in the 1964 Tokyo Olympics. More than that, Mitch admired Mills for his post-running career dedicated to helping Native American people fulfill their basic needs, gain self-sufficiency and self-esteem, and empower Native youth to follow their dreams.

Mitchell Iron Falcon graduated from Chadron State College with a double degree in geoscience and business administration with an emphasis in finance. Although he considered attending law school with an eye toward advocating on behalf of his tribe and tribal members in court, he found his real passion was being outdoors. So, instead of law school, he took a page out of Billy Mills' book and joined the United States Army.

His geoscience experience served him very well in the Army. His finance degree, not so much. It wasn't long until he was invited to participate in the Ranger Assessment and Selection Program, which he passed. Then he took on the sixty-one-day arduous rite of passage known as Ranger School. All those years of hunting, fishing, working outdoors, camping, running, and more helped Mitch to pass without being recycled back into that grueling training.

Mitch served with distinction. He became a trusted tactician in his Regiment. Once The Legacy disbanded or incorporated the former US military into the Resolution Department, Mitch knew that it was time to opt for retirement . . . at thirty-five years of age. He quickly stepped out of his so-called retirement and joined *Molon Labe* in the fight to regain the country.

The sum of all of his educational and life experiences led him to this critical point in time. Mitch believed that it was divine direction, coupled with his ancestral visions, which allowed him the opportunity to draw up the plans of attack. He spent days and nights fine-tuning the details. He knew that the element of surprise would be key.

Mitch, under the leadership of Shontae Lewis, was headed with a small *Molon Labe* group to the Front Range. Their goal was simple. Draw attention to themselves and away from other potential target sites. The Lewis Band would engage The Legacy and hit it hard. That would draw additional resources, including Reso personnel, to the area and beyond. That would make Phase II easier. Phase II involved twelve *Molon Labe* groups, including the Aquino Band, who would execute repatriation missions in the locales of the former United States Federal Reserve Banks.

The Lewis Band would hit the Hyperloop heading into The Legacy's Great Divide Tunnel on the east side. Once the Reso redeployed its assets in a search-and-destroy mission, the other twelve bands would carry out their repatriation missions. Although nobody was exactly clear on the *why* part of the mission, the *what* was crystal clear. Liberate or destroy as many Legacy Coins being held in the Fed vaults as possible and hide them in secure sites.

Mitch didn't *hope* that the plan he devised would work. He was fond of routinely saying, "Hope is not a plan." He had a plan. He had experience. He had acumen. He also had faith, faith in his problem-solving skills (which he called playing three-dimensional chess), his ability to tap into his ancestors' collective wisdom, and God. He had strong faith in all three, but his faith in God was strongest of all. As an adult, Mitch better understood the value of hope, hope for the future. He clearly and deeply understood the value of faith. And he most clearly recalled the words of the apostle Paul, that even greater than hope and faith was love. Mitch had an abundance of love for his birth country and its people—all of its people.

Chapter XLVI

"Right this way, *Señor y Señora* Ertz." The hostess motioned for Stefan and Anjali to follow her. What a place. Neither Stefan nor Anjali had been in a restaurant like this since their days in West Europe Province. They saved their money for a night on the town to celebrate their first anniversary when they still lived in Zürich. They had a lovely, romantic dinner at *Weisses Rössli*. But even that amazing French-Mediterranean restaurant had nothing on *Casa de Flor*.

While they were being escorted to their table, they heard a voice say, "*Disculpe Señor y Señora* Ertz. I am so sorry to not greet you upon arrival. Apologies. I am Martín. *Por favor,* allow me to escort you to your seats." Martín turned to the hostess, "*Gracias, Xochitl*, I'll take it from here." She smiled and handed him the menus. "*Disfruten*. Enjoy," Xochitl said pleasantly to the guests as she headed back to the front.

Martín showed them to their table, a booth toward the back. The candlelight illuminated a colorful and bright bouquet of flowers on the table. There were hanging baskets with flowers. Flower portraits hung on the walls. Martín had a fresh white carnation on his jacket's lapel. There were flowers everywhere. Of course, it was *Casa de Flor*—Flower House.

"*Señor* Berko has informed me that you are his guests this evening," Martín offered as he passed along the menus, including the wine menu. "Have you dined with us before?"

"No, we haven't." Stefan answered.

"Well, welcome to *Casa de Flor*. We hope your dining experience will exceed your expectations. Most of our food is locally sourced, fresh, organic. Some items, like some of our fish, are flown in on ice and have been caught no more than twenty-four hours ago. In addition, some of our Spanish menu items are flown in twice per week from South Europe Province to maintain freshness and quality."

Anjali was looking very closely at the menu. It was as if she was looking for something in particular. "*Señora*, you will notice there are no prices on the menu. That will encourage you, hopefully, to order whatever you wish. Wine included. So please do not be bashful. If you have any questions about the menu, your server is Carlos, and he can assist. Your *sommelier* is María, who will be here momentarily. Might you have any questions?"

Both Stefan and Anjali gently shook their heads no. "No, thank you, I think we've got it," said Stefan confidently.

"This looks wonderful. Thank you, *Señor Martín*," Anjali said with a hint of a Spanish accent when saying his name. Martín was impressed.

"*¿Habla usted español?*" he asked Anjali.

"*No, solamente dos palabras*," she responded.

Martín laughed. "Ah, only two words in Spanish. By my count, that was more than two, *Señora. Muy bien. Disfruten, por favor!* Enjoy!"

Martín excused himself. He spoke briefly with their service team. They all paid close attention and nodded affirmatively when he was done speaking with them. As Berko's guests,

Martín didn't want to have their complete satisfaction left to chance.

After having started with *ensalada mixta*, *jamón Ibérico de Bellota*, *queso Manchego viejo*, *aceitunas*, and a bottle of *Remírez de Ganuza Gran Reserva*, Stefan and Anjali prepared themselves for the main course. They were both bordering on full, but the food was so delicious that they vowed to keep "disfruting" as Stefan said, butchering the language.

While they awaited the main course, Anjali couldn't help but to notice all the care and special touches that went into making this restaurant the very best in the province. The woodwork, paintings, frescos, all tastefully done. And the flowers and related accents, it was a dream.

It was said that only regime leaders and their invited guests ever dined at *Casa de Flor*. It took so many social credits to gain entrance that it had become a symbol for The Legacy and its hypocrisy—although no one dared say it or even think it too strongly. If The Legacy was about the people and liberalism, Anjali wondered how a restaurant like this could exist that was exclusively for the elites? Even so, Anjali determined to enjoy this once-in-a-lifetime experience—which she was. Then, something else beyond the décor caught her eye. At the bar, there was a man who appeared to be looking at her. *Oh, that's silly,* she thought. It was low light and over fifty meters away. She looked away, enjoying some of the additional décor items. When her eyes circled back across the room, she again saw this man. He was looking at her and doing so quite intently and intensely. She wondered if she knew him. He didn't seem familiar to her.

"*Señora*, for you, the *paella de marisco*, the seafood paella," Carlos said as he set Anjali's plate in front of her. It smelled beyond this world. "And for you, *Señor,*" Carlos said, while Anjali's attention was drawn away. She received a light tap on her PCD. She caught a quick glimpse of her message while Carlos was discussing the finer points of *cochinillo asado* from Spain's Segovia region and the strict standards used in identifying and preparing suckling pig. It was Jeannie.

After Carlos excused himself, Stefan turned his attention to his wife. "Everything okay?"

"Yes, everything's fine. Jeannie just sent a quick update. The girls have had dinner. Even the Garcia girls ate my food. Looks like plenty of leftover mac and cheese for you, *meine Liebe*."

"Oh, that'd usually sound great, but I'm not sure that I'll ever need to eat again. Just look at this pig!"

"I see it. That's some pig alright. Good thing we didn't move back to my hometown. Not sure your *cochinillo* would be on the menu."

Stefan engrossed himself in his meal. Good thing because Anjali hated to deceive him, especially if he asked a direct question. But after she told him about the girls eating dinner, he seemed satisfied enough about the update from home. Truth is that Jeannie did report on the dinner. She also added four important words. "I have an idea."

After the main course, Anjali sipped on a *café con leche* while Stefan enjoyed a Dow Vintage Port. They somehow managed to share a *Tarta de Santiago* as well.

"Stefan, this has been such a special evening. Just sharing time with you, this beautiful restaurant, wonderful food, wine, everything. But having you to myself, talking about whatever we wanted, it has been a night to always remember." Anjali said as she reached her hand out to hold Stefan's.

"Thank you, *maay jaan*. It has been a special night out here with you, my beautiful wife."

A man approached their table. Stefan started to skootch himself out from the booth.

"No, no, please, sit," the man said. "You are a better man than I, Stefan. I wouldn't dare try to get out from a booth after devouring cochinillo. They'd have to wheel me out of here."

Stefan smiled. He immediately extended his hand in greeting. "*Herr* Berko, this is my wife, Anjali. Anjali, this is Mr. Berko, our host."

"Such a pleasure," Berko bowed slightly. "I trust you two have been enjoying your evening out?"

"Yes, we have, thank you, Mr. Berko," said Anjali, deferentially. It was the man who was staring at her from the bar. Anjali started to feel a bit uneasy.

"Oh, yes, sir, indeed we have. Very generous of you. Exceptionally generous. Thank you again, sir."

Berko turned to Stefan, "Think nothing of it. My pleasure. Stefan, let's meet briefly on Monday afternoon. Nothing urgent. I just wanted to have a short conversation about something I want to get your opinion on regarding ratios," Berko paused. He slowly turned toward Anjali while he was still talking with Stefan, "I have an idea."

Anjali immediately felt cold, the kind of cold you feel when you step into cold mountain air on a dark, clear winter night. She had the goosebumps to show for it.

Stefan began hearing the synchronous mantra building in his brain. It was getting louder and louder. Faster and faster. *Comply or die. Comply or die. Comply or die.* Although it took a moment for Stefan to respond, when he did, it was as eager as a child being told that they will get ice cream . . . for breakfast.

"That sounds very good. Monday afternoon. I'll be there whenever you wish. What a special evening, thanks to you. Again, our thanks, *Herr* Berko."

Berko responded in what seemed to be a deliberately slow pace, "And, again, the pleasure was truly all mine." Berko smiled and left.

She looked at her husband. He seemed a bit off. Actually, more than a bit. She didn't think it was the alcohol. He wasn't like this ten minutes ago. Something was in his eyes. They had a faraway look, something vacuous. There was something wrong. He caught her looking at him. Instead of a knowing and sympathetic look, it was taciturn, dark, and detached.

Anjali immediately broke into a cold sweat.

CHAPTER XLVII

Flying at Mach 5 was something people only dreamed of earlier in the twenty-first century. Hypersonic flight was a challenge that Hank Hatua met with enthusiasm and skill. He hired the best aeronautical, structural, and mechanical engineers. The foremost materials scientists were also engaged. These engineers and scientists were tasked to solve the most critical challenge to flying at speeds at or above 3,800 miles per hour. That challenge was heat. At hypersonic speeds, the buildup of heat would be so extreme that it could melt metal. Without being properly and consistently cooled, the result would be disastrous. And for those who tried to solve the challenge before Hatua, it was indeed disastrous.

Hatua's engineers solved the challenge. By pre-cooling the engine with special cooling tubes and utilizing heat-resistant and ultra-sensitive sensors, the cooling tubes engaged as needed throughout the flight. Design and prototype success propelled Hatua Aeronautical Company in moving forward with the manufacturing and selling of hypersonic passenger and cargo planes. It was a disruptive shock to air travel. Although initially produced at the former Boeing facility near Seattle, as well at the former Airbus facilities in the North, West, and South Europe Provinces, Hatua Aeronautical Company entered into an agreement to share its technology with the CCP. Thereafter, all hypersonic planes in the world were manufactured in the Pudong District, Shanghai, China. It was a financially lucrative deal for Hatua and a strategic advance for China's continued world dominance in both significant civilian and military uses.

The CCP permitted hypersonic travel for The Legacy's use, as well as the other leadership regimes installed by the CCP throughout the other twenty-one provinces. The concept was to provide a way for province leaders to travel to Beijing quickly, especially when summoned for important in-person meetings. Hypersonic travel was not generally available to the public unless they had sufficient social credits to travel and, more particularly, travel great distances to other provinces with the required transit paperwork. There weren't many who qualified for such a perk.

Less than 2 percent of the public worldwide qualified with sufficient credits to travel by air. Most of that travel was intraprovince. Of the 2 percent, approximately 5 percent regularly maintained sufficient credits for interprovince travel. And, of that, only 3 percent could potentially travel between provinces using hypersonic aircraft. That still amounted to approximately 150,000 people in an ever-shrinking world population of 5 billion.

Most of those fortunate enough to travel via hypersonic plane were provincial leaders, provincial bureaucrats, and associated *friends* of the respective regimes, and military troops. Plenty of military troops were transported to global hot spots as needed. In the case of an uprising, local troops were deemed unreliable. The CCP, who made these deployment decisions, called upon troops from faraway provinces, or historical enemies, to quash any rebellion quickly, decisively, and brutally. Fear was a great way to keep potential treasonous activities repressed.

And Hank Hatua's aeronautical company supplied the means by which these troops and their equipment traveled swiftly.

Hatua was flying in his private eighteen-person hypersonic plane over the Bering Sea at 96,000 feet. The thinner air at the higher altitude allowed for a balancing of air pressure. If the plane were to go hypersonic in the 30,000-foot flight range, his aircraft would likely disintegrate. Given the substantial pressure and stress considerations, Hatua Aeronautical's engineers designed hypersonic planes without windows. Hatua sat back comfortably for the routine three- and one-half-hour journey from Legacy City to Beijing.

As he was reviewing data on the proposed Stage II of the new Legacy Coin rollout campaign, including a quality sampling report, his PCD tapped his wrist. He looked down. It was Cassie.

"Go incoming, Cassie, view," Hatua said, instructing his PCD to connect him to Cassie while displaying her live on a small screen in front of him. "Hello, my love. Miss me already?"

"Of course, I do, " Cassie replied pleasantly. "How's your flight?"

"Easy. I'm not the captain."

Cassie offered a faint laugh. "May I speak with you privately, Hank?"

Hatua commanded his seating suite to switch to "private mode." His suite was immediately enclosed by an opaque material. The others in his travel party, who sat behind him, could no longer see into his suite, nor could they hear anything blocked by the sound-absorbing barrier.

"Done," Hatua said. "All private now, Cass."

"Thanks," Cassie said as her demeanor switched from pleasant to pensive. "Hank, I wanted to talk with you about our engagement. There's something that you need to know. Something important . . . about family."

Hank looked at Cassie calmly, "Is this about your father?"

"Yes, it is." Cassie looked a bit surprised.

"And his new wife?"

"Yes." She cocked her head sideways, as if trying to communicate, "How? What?"

"Cass, I know all about him, about them. It's okay. I wouldn't have asked you to marry me if that was a problem."

"You mean you wouldn't have asked me to marry you without having done a comprehensive background check on my family . . . and me."

"Yes, true, that too." Hatua smiled, trying to bring a little levity. Cassie was still concerned. "It's fine Cass. Really, not a problem."

"You know how this may look for you," Cassie said. Deep down, she was trying to protect her father while also offering up the idea of protecting her fiancé too.

"Yes, I do. I do also appreciate your concern for my welfare and reputation," Hatua said. Based on his tone, Cassie wasn't sure if he was being straight with her or a bit facetious. "I think I can handle it."

"My love," Cassie paused, letting those words sink in, "How can we best protect my father and Dianne? You know he's not doing well health-wise."

"Yes. I understand. I've given it thought. My apologies, Cass, but I took a few steps to protect them already."

"What? What did you do? I mean, thanks. But Hank, what'd you do?" Cassie felt a bit of her anxiety diminishing, but not completely.

"Your father and stepmother will be receiving a transfer shortly. It's all arranged and approved by the Department of Wellbeing, and others." Cassie knew what he meant by others. The Legacy had to have been involved. It was no simple transfer. Even Hank Hatua couldn't pull off a transfer like this without The Legacy's review and approval.

Hatua continued, "He'll receive care in Legacy City, near us. He will have the best doctors available. They'll also have a suitable living unit assigned to them, a very nice unit, I might add. I think they'll like it. I hope you'll like it too."

"I'm sure I will. Thanks. It'll be nice to have my father very close. It's been a very long time since I've seen him in person, hugged him." Cassie was starting to feel much better. She started to tear up. She thought of her father, how much they'd been through together, his sacrificial love for her, and she thought of Hank. Maybe she misjudged Hank. Maybe he did have her best interests top of mind. Maybe, just maybe, he did love her more than his companies, fame, and special status. Maybe her happiness was put above pleasing The Legacy and CCP.

"Where do you think they'll be assigned to live? What area? You said you think they'll like it. That I'll like it."

"I expect they will be assigned your unit."

"What?" Cassie blurted out without thinking. She quickly gathered herself. "My unit? Why would they be assigned my unit?"

"That's a good question, Cass. I think it's time for us to talk about our wedding date."

Chapter XLVIII

Anjali looked at the words scribbled on a piece of paper. They made no sense to her. Jeannie was peering over Anjali's shoulder as if doing so would expedite solving the letters and symbols puzzle. Anjali was oblivious to Jeannie's space invasion.

"You know, I used to do these types of puzzles when I was younger. I couldn't rest until I unscrambled the hidden words or phrases. I'll tell you what . . ." Anjali turned a bit toward her space-invading friend.

"What?" responded Jeannie.

"These are not simple. Not at all."

"For example, look at this one," Anjali pointed to the letters handwritten by Jeannie on the paper. "Golre!!a. Gorillla perhaps? Three l's with that having a special meaning. Three l's mean anything to you? Those two exclamation points there, maybe they are l's?"

"Nope. I checked them out very carefully. They are most definitely exclamation points."

"Okay, I thought maybe it had something to do with gorillas or three l's. Don't know what he'd be doing with gorillas, but it's not it, so moving on."

"Good idea. And Anjali, thanks." Jeannie gave Anjali a squeeze on the shoulder.

"Don't mention it. Let's keep trying." Anjali sounded out many potential word combinations, but none of them fit. Then she got excited, "Go! Real! Go Real! Something like that. What would Rolando mean by Go Real? With exclamation marks?"

"Hmmm," Jeannie said aloud while thinking. "I think there was a soccer team in Spain a long time ago with that name. He was a soccer fan. Maybe he pulled up old games from prior days. Not sure where he'd get them now. Most of that has been destroyed. Too *petite bourgeoise* for these days, I imagine."

"Maybe its Eral. That's Indian. A little town in the *Tamil Nadu* region. Did Rolando ever travel to India? Have any Indian friends, except for me?"

"I don't think he ever traveled to India. Pretty sure he didn't. I don't know about other Indian friends. Might be a colleague? Never heard him use that name or word."

Oh, silly me!" Anjali took the heel of her right hand and hit her forehead. "Earl. What about Earl? Go Earl, with exclamation points either together or separated after each word. Who did he know named Earl?"

"I'm trying, Anjali, really, I am," Jeannie said, beginning to get flustered. She felt as if she should have been able to solve these puzzles as she called them on her own. But Anjali was a walking computer. Who better to help her solve? Plus, she trusted Anjali more than she trusted any computer. "I can't think of an Earl that we know, or he ever mentioned." Jeannie buried her head in her hands.

"Let's change this up a little. I noticed the Chinese characters. You speak and write Chinese? It is Chinese, right?" Anjali asked.

"Oh, heavens no, "Jeannie scoffed. "I barely get English right. That's why I went into medicine. I think the characters are Chinese. Not sure though. I just copied them as best as I could."

"I think it's Chinese. Clearly, the Chinese will need someone else to decipher unless I can use my PCD to scan the characters and then run an unscramble program."

"As much as I'd like to say yes, we can't use PCDs. Who knows who or what may be monitoring our PCDs or the programs? We don't want to do anything to trigger attention within the regime. And clearly not the Reso."

"True. Guess we'll go back to where we were then. No Eral. No Earl."

"This. Is. So. Frustrating. *Conjo!*" Jeannie exclaimed.

"What? What was that last word you said?"

"Sorry. Sorry. I didn't mean to say that. Sorry. It's just so frustrating." Jeannie said apologetically. "You know that word, right?"

"I think so. It means rabbit in English." Anjali said in a disarmingly innocent way.

"No, that's *conejo*. The word I said is something altogether different."

"No? Not rabbit. Okay, what did you say again?"

"Well, I learned it from Rolando. It's Spanish. It's a bad word. Very bad. I used to hear from him so many times when he was frustrated—or stubbed a toe—that I learned it myself. I'm not exactly sure what it means, but I sure feel better after I say it a few times. I have to be careful not to say it with the girls around. I think it's the Spanish equivalent of the F word or something like that."

"Jeannie, that's great! Oh, my goodness, that's just great! You just figured it out!"

"What?" Jeannie gave it more emphasis, "You mean it all comes back to *Conjo!!!*"

"No, not that part, although I'm glad saying it so enthusiastically is making you feel better. Jeannie, tell me, what languages did Rolando speak?"

"English, of course. Fluent or close to fluent in Spanish. Some Mandarin Chinese. And," Jeannie rolled her eyes, "a few words in Swahili. Don't ask."

"Got it. Let's try Spanish. I know a little Spanish. How about you?"

"Un poco, gracias. Very little poco, though," Jeannie responded, in *Spanglish*.

"In Spanish, I seem to recall that exclamation marks, if used, are at both the front and back of a word or sentence. So, let's take them out and place them aside for that purpose."

"Yes, that's right. You're right. Keep going, Anji!" Jeannie said, encouraging her friend.

"What we have left is golrea. Golrea. Goalre." Anjali kept working combinations. Gerloa. Not starting with a 'g.' Let's go to 'l.' Logear. Ear log? That's English again. Makes no sense to me. You?"

"Nope. I think you're on the right track with Spanish."

"Jeannie, once we figure his system, then we should be able to solve other puzzles. Legrao. Let's move on to 'r.' Rolgea."

"I got it! Regalo. It's regalo. That's Spanish for gift." Jeannie was thrilled. "Rolando made this entry several times on his calendar, leading up to our tenth anniversary. It must've been his reminders about the gift he gave me."

"That's fantastic, Jeannie! Well done! Now, let's try out this theory, assuming it's our cypher."

"The next one looks tough. Maybe its multiple words?"

"You may be right. That's a long word for Spanish," Anjali said as she started to break up the letters and reassemble them in what were likely combinations. "Wish I could use a program. I could probably write a program to decode faster than decoding these by hand . . . and foggy brain."

"I understand. Neither of us can risk it. We're making progress, though."

Anjali slowly spelled out the letters to yoenloocred. "Let's assume the 'y' is for and. We may have two other words here." Anjali's eyes were moving at a rapid pace, back and forth and back and forth they went. "*Leon y cordero. Leon* is lion, no? Is that something? Wait, will you please grab my old Spanish language book on the bookshelf?"

"*Cordero*," said Jeannie as she flipped pages, "Here it is. Cordero is lamb. Leon is lion. *Leon y cordero*. Lion and lamb."

"Sounds biblical. Something Christian?"

"In for a penny, in for a pound." Jeanne said aloud to herself but loud enough for Anjali to hear.

"Is that something related to *leon y cordero*?"

"Somewhat. Anji, Rolando was a Christian. He grew up that way. He continued believing till his dying day. I didn't know about it. At least not that he was still a practicing Christian while we were together. He was faithful . . . to me, to our family. He didn't want his religious beliefs to cause trouble or worse for us. I'll give him that."

"He loved you. That's what matters most."

"Okay," Jeannie refocused. "We have gift. We have lion and lamb. What about this one?" Jeannie pointed to nicogelclay.

"Let's see," Anjali refocused as well. "If we take the 'y' out like we did with the last puzzle, what are we left with here? Maybe double l's like in *ella*? Woman or girl. She or it. *Ella y noccig*? *Ella y gnocci*?"

"Dumpling woman? Better not be in the context of *regalo*, or I'll chase him down in the afterlife." Anjali looked at Jeannie, not knowing whether to be amused or horrified. "If there's an afterlife," Jeannie added.

"Hmm, I don't think this is right. Let me ask you. In his calendar and notes, were all the words scrambled?"

"Not all. Some. Some notes were in English. Some in Spanish. And some just a mess, like these."

"Let's try English again," Anjali offered. She started working at warp speed. "It's not Spanish. It's English. The answer is Legacy . . ."

"Coins," Jeannie interrupted. "Legacy Coins. That makes sense to me. He was concerned about Legacy Coins. The return of the coins. You are a walking computer, Anji."

"You too. You sure you didn't study math or computer science in school?"

"Nope, just enough to graduate. But my teachers said I was really good at science. My math teachers said that." They both chuckled. Even with the heavy and dangerous nature of their work, there was a sense of ease between them as if they had been good friends for decades.

"Our next one," Anjali said as she pointed to unhakthaa. "Another way to look at these is how they might be related. We have gift, lion and lamb, Legacy Coins. Not sure I see a connection yet. You?"

"No, not yet. Three a's and two h's." Jeannie was mesmerized by effort. Her lips moved, but no words were coming out.

"Hank Hatua!" Anjali shrieked. "Let's see if it fits. Yep, all letters accounted for; that's it, Hank Hatua."

"Makes sense again because Hank Hatua's company designed and manufactured Legacy Coins. They still do."

"Great. Two more. Let's do this one next." Anjali pointed at sciengue.

"Segue. Nice. Science. Hmm" Jeannie kept mumbling options, this time aloud.

"Eugenics," Anjali said confidently. "Eugenics. Checks out."

Jeannie shook Anjali's shoulders. "Superstar! Okay, last one."

"Last one on the sheet for today, you mean?"

"Isn't that what I said?" Jeannie gave a sideways glance and a grin to match.

"Could be English or Spanish."

"Or a name."

"Let's do this."

They both concentrated on the final handwritten scrambled up letters and symbol—osso?korrebbrie.

"This is a tough one. Let's talk this one out. What do we have?" Anjali said.

"We have a bear who likes cheese?" Jeannie offered. "A running bear who likes cheese?"

"Maybe so. Maybe no."

"Probably no," Jeannie said without hesitation. "Perhaps take the question mark out. That likely goes at the end."

"Yes. Definitely."

"Looks like there's a Reso in there too. What if we take that out for now? Might line up. What are we left with?" Jeannie asked.

"Ten letters. Two o's. Two b's . . . and a k." Anjali stopped. She didn't move. She barely breathed.

"What? Did you solve it? What's the answer?"

"At dinner last night, I met a man. He was staring at me from the bar. At first, I was annoyed, then unsettled. He came over to our table. He was as frightening of a person that I've ever met. He acted like he knew me, really knew me."

"That sounds scary," Jeannie said empathetically.

"That's not all. Remember what you sent me last night? The exact words you used?"

"I have an idea."

"Right. As he was wrapping up with our table, he was talking with Stefan suggesting that they get together Monday to meet. His words at the end were, 'I have an idea.'"

"Could've been a coincidence," Jeannie said in a pleading sort of questioning way.

"I don't think so. He was looking right at me when he said it. I think he was trying to actually look in me, looking for any tell I might show to give something away."

"Okay, so this creepy guy was staring at you, came over, and maybe he has exceptional vision or he's a mind reader or . . ."

"Jeannie, that man was our host, the man who paid for our meal, the man who gave Stefan a bonus of several hundred social credits, plus the dinner, the wine, the whole regime-level dining experience."

"How does this relate to our puzzle?" Jeannie asked anxiously.

"I think your husband was trying to make a connection between this man and the Reso. Odds are that it had to do with Hank Hatua, Legacy Coins, and eugenics. I don't think your anniversary gift is related. The rest, I believe, is connected. And if this man is Reso, that explains how he might've intercepted your message to me, how he was toying with me."

"Why would he be toying with you?"

"I don't know."

"Tell me, does this puzzle solve for someone's name?"

"Yes, it does. The man's name is Boris Berko. I think he's Reso . . . and as evil as evil can be."

Chapter XLIX

"Good. It's all set then. Start moving now. We need to get resources in place as soon as we can, no later than by Legacy Day. They must be in place by then. Send your best and most inspired, as I'm sure you understand what I mean. We'll need the extra support. Yes. If not for Legacy Day, then for our plans afterward. Comms? Use mixed comms chatter to decoy plans. Do not, under any circumstances, use my comms team as lead. We'll respond to chatter on our end as needed under my direction. Keep it highest security level. We'll coordinate your plans with ours. How about your plans? All set on your end? Good. Anything else? Nothing here. *Xiè xiè. Zài jiàn.*"

Berko was pleased, as pleased as he could be. His plans were taking shape. He had a substantial number of additional security forces on the way to protect against potential *Molon Labe* attacks throughout the province on Legacy Day. That seemed to be a favorite day for them to be disruptive. Even more significantly, Berko would have access to a supreme fighting force, unrelated to the province's people, to root out the nasty thorn in his side.

Molon Labe, and especially those who referred to themselves as the Siouxlanders, had occupied his attention for too long. Although they were a pain and a distraction, Berko was cunning enough to use the excuse of fighting *Molon Labe* to increase his power base.

As a result of *Molon Labe's* activities—actual, attributed to them, or created out of whole cloth—more draconian measures had been implemented, all with The Legacy's approval. The Legacy Credits system was created and tightened. Food, energy, and potable water shortages were created. Travel was severely curtailed. The Reso was given extraordinary powers without any meaningful limitations. And who was to blame? Who would earn the loathing and distrust of the masses for these measures and shortages? *Molon Labe*. They had proven to be a convenient foil to advance Berko's lust for control, ultimate control. Almost two hundred years prior, Lord Acton penned a phrase Berko embraced as a badge of honor.

> Power tends to corrupt and
>
> Absolute power corrupts absolutely.
>
> Great men are almost always bad men.

Berko viewed himself a great man, a very great man. He wanted people to know how great he was. Berko's esteem and ultimate fulfillment was predicated on being considered great.

As to whether he was bad or not, he'd let history decide. His focus was on the present, a present focus to achieve future goals, to achieve his own personal legacy.

Chapter L

Klein considered his options. He dropped his pen and picked up arms. He never felt stronger, more alive, and scared. He was scared not for himself but for the country he once knew, for the world, but especially for his granddaughter.

Hannah had always been his favorite grandchild. He even preferred her over her parents. From the time she was a toddler, they were inseparable. They would play. She would sing. He loved hearing her sing loudly without a care in the world. He would ask her opinion about local, national, and world events. Even when she was too young to understand the complexities involved, sometimes that was a benefit . . . for her, and him.

Sometimes her opinions would simplify a disturbingly complex set of events and put them in context. Klein loved sharing the story when she was seven years old and the world was going through yet another seismic upheaval. The CCP was in the process of implementing its social credit system. The rollout was taking place worldwide but with different results. Some provinces were accepting of the new program. They acted with great deference to China, like a child would to a parent . . . before the tween years. That was not the case in North America Province. Klein had explained the basics of the credits system, how it worked, and what the rules were. He also explained the penalties for not following the rules. There were many rules.

They were extremely detailed. Some seemed contradictory—mind your business, report on your neighbors.

Hannah asked some pointed questions like why are these rules being implemented? How were people to know how to act and what to do? And, finally, what were the benefits of following these rules? After she was satisfied with all she was told, she came up with this assessment. "Grandpa, I can follow rules I know. I can't follow rules I don't know or that change without me knowing. It's that simple."

Therein lay the straightforwardness of a child. As Klein summarized it in one of his columns, "If you know the rules, you can play the game. If not, you can't." The challenge for those older than seven was the rules were, in fact, constantly changing. The ground beneath the people trying to comply and co-exist in the new world was constantly shifting. At times, the rules were being made up as the regime went along. The twenty-two provincial leadership teams adjusted rules as they needed to accommodate the results required by the CCP. And the CCP changed the results it wanted at times too. The devil was, in fact, in the details. And the devil was also personified in those making and carrying out myriad horrendous orders.

The older Hannah got the more details Klein would share with her. By the time she was thirteen, Klein communicated with her in a completely transparent and unfiltered way. He respected her intellect and intuition. Most of all, he respected her values. She had strong values. She knew to the essence of her being the difference between right and wrong. And, she knew how to figure out the rules so she could survive.

Hannah grew up during a particularly difficult time, "The Mad Max Years," as Klein frequently called them. Nobody was safe. Roving bands of thugs were stealing and destroying what seemed to be everything in their path. In their wake, the thugs left fear, destruction, need, emptiness, injury, and death. Gangs of thugs battled each other, leaving even more carnage. There was no answer to this problem because the vile outcomes were exactly part of the CCP's plan; disruption, constant chaos, extreme fear, scarcity, and death, all of this to create a need, a need for a better today and tomorrow, a need for stability and safety.

Hannah was a sweet little girl. Along with hanging out with her grandfather, she enjoyed playing with her dolls and painting pictures. Klein had at least one hundred paintings that she gave him over the years. He kept every last one of them. And she sang and danced around as if she lived in a music box without the need to turn it on. Singing and dancing. Dancing and singing. Mad Max biosphere outside. Unabashed happiness inside. That was little Hannah. Spreading her gift of music, art, cheerfulness, and joy everywhere she went.

From sweet and innocent little girl, Hannah developed into a streetwise and strong young woman. She dropped out of the university to join *Molon Labe*. Knowing everything that she did, all the history and current events she learned at the feet of her grandfather, to fail to fight would be akin to killing off a huge part of herself. She couldn't do otherwise; she had to right the wrongs. For her, it was duty. For her grandfather, he could have predicted it. After all, as a precocious and insightful child, she once said that she could only follow rules she knew. Rules were constantly changing in her lifetime; she could not live under those circumstances. It stole her *joie de vivre*.

As their group approached Chicago, they were taken in by several *Molon Labe* families. Everyone was undercover. Nobody broadcasted the fact that they were part of the rebellion. Some high-ranking officials in the regime were *Molon Labe* or *Molon Labe* sympathizers. They were either undiscovered or were being watched and planned to be used at a more opportune time to the regime.

Klein, Hannah, Zim, and a young man simply known as Zach were put up at a small family dairy farm about sixty kilometers outside Chicago. Others were similarly housed in small groups of four in areas within a fifty-kilometer radius of Naperville, including Schaumberg, Joliet, and Aurora, where Klein and his crew were housed nearby.

It was not uncommon for travelers to stay with families. In the age of social credits determining most everything, if people had little to no credits, they would have to travel by any means necessary and likewise stay with friends, family, or even be put up by strangers. Strangers would normally require something of value for the stay. It might include manual labor. An underground barter system emerged, predominantly within those on the lower rungs of society. It was an effective way to live, travel, and survive. There were risks involved, risks on both sides in the unsanctioned barter economy. Everything in society had risks.

Zim led the team. Although a bit of a cut-up, Zim could focus seriously when circumstances required. Zach was a young man in his late teens or early twenties. A tall, muscular man, he was an excellent listener and dutiful in his approach. He didn't speak much except when spoken to and, in that case, with very limited responses. It was as if he had served in the military, which was highly unlikely at his young age, and where he found himself with this *Molon Labe* group.

Zim met with their *Molon Labe* hosts, and it was determined that their cover was Zach and Hannah were engaged to be married. Zim was Zach's uncle. Hannah's grandfather was still her grandfather. They were on their way to meet with family near Buffalo in East Seneca. Given limited resources, they bartered for food and lodging for a few days of dairy farm labor. That was their story, and they planned to stick with it.

Their hosts were the Cruickshank family—Marvin, Betty, and their dogs, Bailey, a yellow Labrador retriever, and Annie, a Chesapeake Bay retriever. For Hannah, it was especially nice to have dogs around as she missed her Australian Shepherd, Gwennie, who passed the year she left for the university.

Marvin tended the livestock. Betty tended the kitchen. And the four guests worked hard feeding, cleaning, milking, maintaining equipment, and more. Marv taught them what they needed to know, and off they went. They enjoyed the experience. It was a nice distraction from what they were facing. They also knew this wasn't likely to be their full-time profession. Finally, there were some life-affirming moments like when they got to assist Marv with birthing two calves.

Betty fed them very well. Had they stayed more than a few days, they might have needed to go clothes shopping. From eggs to pies, coffee to lemonade, everything tasted farm fresh. They all slept well after working outside all day. The men were in one room, each with a small twin, and Hannah in her own room, which was the Cruickshank's now-grown daughter's room when she was growing up and before she left home. It was decorated in such a simple and warm way. Pastels colors, family pictures, and handsewn quilts adorned the room. Hannah wanted this to last. She knew it couldn't.

It was quiet in the middle of their third night at the Cruickshank's except for an occasional dark barking in the distance and Zach snoring in their shared room. Klein had been sleeping on and off. His mind was spinning. He was having some dreadful dreams, including one in which he was feeding the cows, when off in the distance, he spied an army approaching in their direction. It was a huge army, marching in unison and perfect rows, wave after wave of soldiers. He waited to see what they were doing. In his dream, he turned for a brief moment, then turned back to see that the soldiers were now upon them. They were being overrun. He called for Hannah. No response. He ran as fast as he could, dodging the soldiers, hiding behind whatever he could. He called for Hannah when he could. Still no response. Then, he heard her voice yelling for him. "Grandpa! Opa! Help me! Please! Oooopaaaa!" Her voice trailed off. He never saw her. When he went looking for her in the direction of her voice, a menacing face appeared less than a foot in front of his. The face was angry, yelling and spitting at him in a language he did not understand. The soldier looked Asian. He was large, fit, and intense. Then, he saw the soldier's arms and torso move. He immediately felt a stabbing pain in his belly, where his tissue was still tender from his recent surgery. He looked down. There was blood flowing out of him, all over; it was a bloody mess. He had been stabbed. He started to feel lightheaded. Then, in front of him was Hannah's face, telling him that everything will be alright. "Opa, just relax. You'll be fine. Trust me, Opa." Her face morphed into the angry, screaming soldier's face. The soldier stopped screaming. He started laughing. Klein, in his dream, was surrounded by laughing soldiers. He heard Hannah scream in the background. He saw her being carried away, tears running down her face. "Opa, Opa, Oooopaaaa!"

Marv was standing above him about two feet from his face. Marv was shaking Klein's body and saying something quickly.

"Wake up! Ed, wake up!" Marv said excitedly. When Marv saw that Klein's eyes were open, he moved over to Zim, "Wake up, Zim! Wake up!" Marv shook Zim's body while he was encouraging Zim to wake up.

"Wait, what?" was Zim's groggy reply.

Marv started to move toward Zach, but Zach beat him to it. Zach moved quickly out of bed and was almost finished getting dressed.

"Get dressed, all of you!" Marv commanded. "There's been an incident. Down in Joliet. You're going to have to leave right away!"

"What's going on, Marv? Calmly, please tell us," said Klein as he, too, dressed quickly while trying to convey a sense of calm to Marv, who was clearly not having it.

"The team in Joliet, including the hosts, the Johansen family, the Reso has them. The Reso has them all. You must leave . . . now! Betty's made provisions for you. Hustle! Now!"

"Hannah?"

"She's up. Go!"

Klein knew that this moment might come but prayed it wouldn't. War was filled with terror. He saw it in his dreams. He saw it in Marv's eyes too.

Chapter LI

Global Genomics had never been busier. With the Legacy Coin return program, the need for proper categorization and cross-referencing of Legacy Coins to their designated person was a Herculean task. All returned coins were first collected at the satellite sites. Each day, they were gathered and deposited consistent with strict security measures at one of twelve secure sites scattered throughout the North America Province. Instead of adding another travel step in the process, and for heightened security reasons, Global Genomics deployed a squad of its most trusted senior team technicians to each of the twelve secure locations to engage in the tedious 2C process. Insiders called it 2C to refer to the categorization and cross-referencing work. Some jokingly called it the 3C program. The third C stood for comatose because the work would either make you feel comatose due to its mind-numbing nature, or you'd rather be comatose than doing this job, again because of its mind-numbing nature.

Using an automated separator, Legacy Coins would be grouped together in one thousand-coin batches. The next step took years to design and test to the accuracy level required, 99.9999998 percent. Matching people to their unique Legacy Coin was part of what made this program so valuable for The Legacy. Another was the science and technology behind the implant. Being able to abort a fetus on demand was critical in the battle against global overpopulation. The ability to deploy the requisite chemicals only if commanded to do so, without error or risk of mistake, was a program imperative. Global Genomics had a stellar record in that regard. Not a perfect record, but a stellar one.

When the United Nations sanctioned the implantable birth control device trial in East Africa many years back, it did so with the full knowledge that the technology had not yet been fully developed. The UN and Global Genomics posited that this trial was safe. Perhaps better said, they thought it was safe enough. Notwithstanding protestations to the contrary, neither the UN nor Global Genomics cared about the women involved with the test. It was all about the "scientific process, the gathering of data, and the benefits to humanity."

They claimed that the injections were safe. They weren't. At least they weren't for all test subjects. Many women of childbearing years had adverse reactions to the implant. The data reported close to 15 percent of the subjects had some form of a negative reaction, from headaches and nausea all the way to infertility and death. The study results were never officially published. The adverse effects were deemed too high, so Hatua and his team went back to the lab to sketch out a new plan.

Round two wasn't much better. The UN again gave Global Genomics *carte blanche* to conduct round two, again in East Africa. The local population objected. There were riots and death threats against the UN and Global Genomics personnel. No matter, they proceeded anyway, this time with ample security. The results were much better this time. As Hatua put it in a presentation to the United Nations General Assembly, "We had less than a 1-percent negative reaction rate. That could have been caused by many factors, not the least of which was apparent host rejection. It was impossible to determine if those women had a particularized allergic reaction to the substances used in the implant. The rate of infertility was still a solid one-half of 1 percent, while the death rate dropped dramatically to under one in every 850.

It was back to the lab for further work based on the data. Global Genomics finally hit the desired goal of reducing infertility and death rates by half again. Once the United Nations was satisfied, it began deploying the implantable birth control and abortion on demand device, along with the corresponding coin, throughout most of the impoverished and developing world. At that point, Global Genomics was off and running, never looking back at the trail of infertility and death they wrought in East African communities. Global Genomics, Hank Hatua, and the United Nations were never held to account for their criminal indifference.

Hank Hatua paid a personal visit to the 2C taking place near Legacy City. He wanted to see for himself how the work was coming along. After successfully passing through three security checkpoints, he took a lift down to the subterranean vault area. He passed through one more security screening. There were over two dozen individual vaults with a large anteroom just outside them. In addition, there looked to be about six private offices that could be used for confidential meetings. Approximately twenty-four Global Genomics employees were working alongside the same number of personnel from The Legacy, one from each organization assigned to one specific vault. They were working in the anteroom while focused on their tasks with steely determination. Made sense. These workers were guaranteed social credits and Hawai'i travel vouchers for a perfect—not good, but perfect—outcome. Perfection was imperative.

Hatua knew the systems well. He should. After all, he designed them. He went to a windowless private room located between vaults 7 and 8. He closed the door. He looked into a camera inside.

"Hatua, Henry. 4285553025."

"Access granted," said a cheery computer-generated voice. With a ten-number access code that allowed for any particular number to be chosen and replaced again throughout the sequence, the number of potential combinations amounted to ten billion. Hatua believed that was a sufficient additional security step.

"Legacy Coin status, Cassandra Bowles."

"Checking. Bowles, Cassandra. Status. Legacy City. Vault 16."

"Legacy Coin status, Simon Bowles."

"Checking. Bowles, Simon. Status. Legacy City. Vault 16."

Legacy Coin status, Dianne Bowles."

"Checking. Bowles, Dianne. Legacy City. Vault 16."

"Check out Legacy Coins for Cassandra Bowles, Simon Bowles, and Dianne Bowles."

"Authorization required."

Hatua knew the multiple layers of security he designed would protect against thievery or worse. He placed his right hand above a scanner located on a table to his immediate right. He also looked at the retinal scanner directly adjacent to the monitoring screen in front of him.

"Authorization code 1014796606."

"Authorization verified. Delivery pending."

A ten-digit personal authorization number plus a ten-digit authorization code would lead to almost sixty-nine billion discrete combinations. Even for a privacy aficionado like Hatua, that seemed sufficiently secure.

Hatua watched on the screen in front of him as the automated retrieval system went to work. In less than two minutes, there was an audible ping.

The computer announced, "Retrievals successful for Bowles, Cassandra; Bowles, Simon; Bowles, Dianne."

Hatua opened a hatch above the table to his right. Inside, cradled in protective covering, were three Legacy Coins. They had no identifying markers on the outside to determine which coin corresponded to Cassandra, Simon, or Dianne. He had the only PCD scanner equipped to link coin to person. He scanned the coins to confirm that he had the exact Legacy Colins requested. The scan confirmed he did. He placed the coins in a small velvet precious gem carrier. He stood and placed the coins in his front left pocket and started to head for the door.

Hatua paused for a moment. Then he sat back down.

"Legacy Coin status. Boris Berko."

"Checking. Berko, Boris."

Hatua waited. It seemed odd to Hatua that this request was taking so long. Finally, the computer responded.

"Legacy Coin status, Berko, Boris. Access denied."

Denied? What was going on? It must be a glitch. Hatua asked again.

"Legacy Coin status. Boris Berko."

"Checking. Berko, Boris."

This time the wait was very short.

"Legacy Coin status, Berko, Boris. Access denied."

Must be something wrong, he thought. Hank Hatua designed the Legacy Coin systems. His team at Global Genomics built the systems. He oversaw all aspects of the design, build, and roll-out of the systems associated with Legacy Coins. He had the highest access level allowed, which granted him unfettered access to all data in the system. He would have to have been involved in downgrading his access. It could not be done without his express approval through multiple security layers. How could his access be denied then?

"Run systems check."

"Running systems check."

Hatua mind started thinking of potential scenarios where someone could have manipulated the system. It just couldn't be, he thought, not possible.

"Systems check complete. All systems functioning. Status green."

"Requests complete. Shut down."

"Access terminal closed," the computer responded. "Have a nice day, Mr. Hatua."

Hatua mumbled to himself, "Have a nice day indeed."

Chapter LII

Jeannie's PCD tapped her twice. She had a direct communication request pending. It was a private undisclosed request. No identifiable person. No identifiable location. She would normally reject these types of requests, but given everything going on and what she was learning, she decided to take a different approach.

"Accept communication request."

"Thank you for accepting my request," said a man's voice with a very proper British accent. "Dr. Garcia, my name is Disung. Your late husband gave me your contact information in the event we needed to communicate. Dr. Garcia, please let me begin by saying how sorry I am to hear about your husband's passing. He was a great man."

"Thank you," Jeannie replied warily. "What did you say your name was again?"

"Disung."

"Disung, how did you know my husband?"

"Dr. Garcia, I am connected to you on a top-level secure line, so I will speak plainly. I will also have to speak quickly."

"Okay. I understand. Again, how did you know my husband?"

"He and I were working together to discover connections between what was happening in the North America Province and the CCP, specifically, questions we had about the potential reasons why The Legacy and certain elements within CCP leadership were collecting Legacy Coins: why they wanted them, what their plans are with them, who was involved, and when these plans are set to be implemented."

"I see. Tell me, Mr. Disung, why are you calling me about this?"

"Because, Dr. Garcia, I don't believe your husband drowned. I believe he was murdered. I also believe that it is connected to his search for answers. Someone found out. And they killed him."

Jeannie was stunned. She had considered the real possibility that her husband was killed, but to have a complete stranger call her to make that point, and in the context of Legacy Coins, she could feel her heart beating faster.

"Tell me, Mr. Disung," Jeannie started.

Disung interrupted her, "Doctor, please pardon my interruption. My first name is Disung. My family name is Lee. Please call me Disung."

"Thank you. Tell me, Disung, what makes you think that my husband did not drown or die of natural causes?"

"Dr. Garcia, because your husband asked a lot of questions to people who had reason to report his activities. He made enemies, enemies he never met or perhaps didn't even know. Powerful enemies. Very powerful."

"Like whom?"

"For starters, top leadership within the CCP in China, especially those who would like to see much harm come to the North America Province. The hardliners, as we refer to them, these are brutal people who will do brutal things all in the name of China first, second, and always. They see no room for other races or peoples. If these others cannot serve them, their view is that they are expendable. If anyone threatens their power, authority, or plans, they are expendable too. Your husband trusted some of the wrong people. He paid his life for that."

"How do I know that you are not one of those people?"

"Because, your husband trusted me. Like a brother, if you know what I mean."

"I think I do."

"Your husband was a very smart man. He knew if this time ever came, you'd be skeptical if I reached out to you. He gave me a code word to use if you were guarded"

"I am guarded. You would be too, I suspect. Go ahead. What's the code word?"

"Double."

Jeannie offered a slight laugh. "Well, that wouldn't be too hard to find elsewhere. That's not enough. How do I know I can *really* trust you?"

"He said you'd respond that way. He really knew you. And loved you."

"Go ahead, Disung, convince me that I can trust you."

"Alright, "Disung said. "He told me to tell you, and I think I have the quote right, 'Come on DC, take the fork in the road.'"

It was as if Rolando was there, speaking to her directly. It was exactly as he would have put it, just not with the British accent. At that moment, she knew. Rolando had prepared so well for this. He sent Disung to her. Now, she needed to know why.

"Disung."

"Yes, Dr. Garcia."

"You've convinced me. I'll take that fork in the road. I hope that I won't regret trusting you."

"I pray neither of us will, Dr. Garcia"

"I'm Jeannie. Please call me Jeannie," Jeannie's tone had changed. "What do I need to know?"

"Thank you, Jeannie. In brief, here's what you should know. I've been asked to compile reports on two important initiatives. First, to cross-reference certain foreign groups with DNA matches. Another pandemic is about to be unleashed on the world. Chinese peoples, for the most part, will be immune to the virus. Second, and equally if not more important, the CCP is working with The Legacy to identify certain disfavored groups and to have their Legacy Coins combined. When requested, and I don't know the timing of this, but I believe soon. Those coins will be activated, and members of disfavored groups will be neutralized."

"Neutralized?"

"Killed."

"Help me to understand. As a physician who works with pregnancies and deliveries every day, I am as familiar as anyone regarding Legacy Coins, implants, and deactivation upon birth."

"With respect, they are not deactivated. They never have been. They were never intended to be. They are active."

"Okay, assuming that's true, Legacy Coins have only been distributed for about twenty years, and as far as full-scale adoption, maybe fifteen or sixteen years. That doesn't cover everyone. Adults would be immune to being neutralized, right?"

"No. For those who were born before widespread adoption, the implant was injected as part of a routine inoculation, be it influenza, tetanus, or some other jab. People don't know they have it. There was no Legacy Coin distributed. Yet they do exist, in secure vaults, and they are painstakingly categorized to avoid mishandling."

Jeannie covered her mouth with both hands. She was speechless. Was this true? It seemed so farfetched. Who would do such a thing?

"Hatua!" she blurted out. "Hatua did this. He knew, didn't he?"

"Global Genomics and Mr. Henry Hatua designed and manufactured Legacy Coins as you know. We suspect he knew. There is no evidence of that yet."

"Rolando's notes mentioned Hatua."

"What did he say about Hatua?"

"Not much. His notes were in code."

"Code, yes. That was smart. How did you break the code if I may ask?"

"I had a smart husband. I have an equally smart best friend."

"Well, your best friend is in danger. Just like you. There is no way to know who knows what about who."

"Disung, this is a lot to process. A lot."

"I understand. It is."

"Who's at risk?"

"Good question. For starters, *Molon Labe*, Siouxlanders, if they aren't already part of the *Molon Labe* dataset, any counterrevolutionaries of any kind, anyone who has spoken ill of the regime, China, or the CCP, and their families, friends, plus known associates or sympathizers. A wide net will be cast. China doesn't care if they get it wrong by involving too many people. China does care to ensure that they get it right."

Jeannie listened quietly. This was a horror she could never imagine.

"That's just the start. Intellectuals, educators, the educated, professionals—with some limited exceptions—known or suspected criminals, their families, friends, and associates will be next."

Jeannie was afraid to ask the follow-up question, "children?"

"Yes, included. No matter the age."

It was as if Jeannie could not get any breath. Her world was crashing down around her. Her husband, gone; her daughters, at risk as family of someone already considered an enemy of the state; all those families who she helped over the years; those innocent babies; children; young people; and unsuspecting adults.

"What kind of evil is this?"

"The worst kind. Evil for power's sake."

"Disung, how do you know all of this is true? Please tell me this is some kind of sick joke or a bad dream."

"I know this because I direct China's Global Population Longevity Center. I also know all of what I told you is true because of my special position."

"Special position?"

"Yes. You see, I serve as one of twenty-five members on the CCP's Central Committee."

As if her mind could not have been blown any more than it already had been, this was yet another reason to explode.

"I understand what you're saying, but I don't really understand why. Why would you work with my husband? Why would you risk your life like you do? Why would you call me? *Why* keeps coming to mind. Why?"

"Because," Disung paused, and for the first time, he seemed a bit distant. "Because, I owe it to my parents."

Jeannie was silent. She had nothing to say. Her husband was dead. Her girls no longer had a father. She got a call out of the blue informing her that fresh atrocities were about to be unleashed on an unsuspecting public. Her life of trying to help and heal was apparently a sham as she was an unwitting accomplice to a dreadfully evil scheme. And she was speaking with a member of the CCP's Central Committee, a Chinese Central Committee member who was trying to help *her*?

"Jeannie, please hear me. I have to go quickly. They'll be looking for me soon, if not already doing so. Rolando mentioned a Mr. Gies to you, yes?"

"Yes," Jeannie said weakly.

"Did Rolando ask you to await news of a coup before going to Mr. Gies?"

"Yes," Jeannie spoke again very softly.

"You must go see him now. And bring the girls. Analia and Julieta are in as much danger as you are. You have your province's Legacy Day holiday coming up. If anyone asks, just say you and the girls are heading out for a long holiday weekend to get fresh air and clear your minds given your family's recent tragedy."

"Okay."

"You know how to reach Mr. Gies?"

"Yes."

"He'll be suspicious that you are there before news of the coup. Tell him I sent you. If he's still hesitant, tell him 'leon y cordero,' that should convince him."

"Lion and lamb."

"Yes, you know it?"

"It was written in code many times in Rolando's PCD. We deciphered it."

"Speaking of that, and quickly if you can, what did Rolando write about Hatua? I must know if there is anything more there."

Jeannie did her best to snap out of her fog. "Hatua, yes, I meant to tell you earlier. Not much, except Hatua's name came up along with Legacy Coins, eugenics, and a man named Berko."

"I see. Boris Berko, no doubt."

"That's him. Boris Berko. And Berko's name came up with Reso."

"Of course. That makes perfect sense. Thanks, Jeannie, this is very helpful."

"Let me ask you again, Disung. Why are you helping us?"

"As I mentioned, I owe it to my parents," Disung then paused briefly. "And I owe it to your husband. He saved me. Truly. Saved my life . . . and my soul. Please trust me and do what I am suggesting. I must go now."

"How do I reach you?"

"You can't. I will reach out to you again soon. I give you my word."

"Disung?"

"Yes."

"Thank you. And thank you for honoring my husband with your bravery."

"I'm glad to do it. He was the brave one. God bless you and your family, Jeannie . . . and Godspeed."

Chapter LIII

The views were stunning. The Front Range of the Rocky Mountains had always inspired Mitch. Being in nature with diverse wildlife and flora was home to him, always had been.

Time was ticking. Shontae's leadership had got them to this point. He needed to finish the job. The other teams spread throughout the province were counting on this team to successfully divert attention and resources to protecting the Hyperloop system. Disabling and disrupting the Hyperloop was the goal. If it led to regime troops being destroyed in their exertions, even better.

Most Hyperloop tubes were constructed with composite materials. Doing so allowed for a lighter yet thicker tube. It also reduced risks associated with climate factors like expansion during hot weather and contraction during the cold.

There were some portions of the Hyperloop track that used older tubes made out of steel. The steel tubes were initially lauded as being puncture proof. Being "puncture proof" was a significant claim, a claim which didn't exactly prove true.

As a result, next-generation composites were employed. They were labeled 4GC. Newly constructed tubes made of 4GC composites replaced the older steel, at great cost. As Hatua's company methodically replaced older-styled steel with next-gen composites, some of the connectors were deemed vulnerable. Hatua's engineers called for increasing the thickness of both steel and composite materials at the joining sites. The problem was time. The Legacy demanded that Hatua have the Hyperloop fully operational with complete composite coverage throughout the entire system by Legacy Day.

Hatua stretched and pushed as far as his team would allow. Sourcing sufficient materials became a challenge. Replacing some stretches, especially in rough terrain, was another challenge. Refabricating the connecting joint areas became a bridge too far for his team. Meeting the Legacy Day schedule was difficult enough; and they were behind in making that goal. But reconnecting joints where connections included steel on one side and composite on the other, with newly fabricated thicker connects, was impossible. Hatua knew it. He kept his team working to their capacity. He'd have to risk that the joints would hold as currently constructed. There was no time, or appetite, for delay.

Mitch observed the construction activity going on near the entrance to The Legacy's Great Divide Tunnel on the west side. There was something that caught his attention. A glint of sunshine reflected and cascaded across one of the segments, which came to an abrupt halt when it met the adjoining segment. Given the angle of the sun and his location, the reflection should have continued for at least another thirty to forty meters. It didn't.

Mitch moved swiftly through the dense forest. He trekked in parallel with the Hyperloop track, staying far enough in the forest to avoid detection. What he noticed shocked yet pleased him very much. There were several stretches of track in very remote areas which had the same metal to some other substance connection. He figured that it must have been some type of composite material. Composites would explain the dissimilarity in sunlight reflection. It looked like composites were used to replace the old steel tubes except where the terrain became too difficult. The effort to replace steel with composite would require substantial effort, equipment, and time.

No matter. Mitch's keen observations were rewarded. During his trek back to the team, his mind was busily revising their plan. *They cut corners,* he thought, *and we caught a big break.*

CHAPTER LIV

They were on the run, not knowing if they were running away from or directly into danger. Their original plan was still intact, as far as they knew anyway. They were on foot, keeping off the main roads, and doing their best to stay out of sight. They weren't to be meeting up with the other teams—at least whoever wasn't captured or dead—for another two days. In the meantime, they needed to concoct a plan to hide out without being discovered.

Zim knew the area well. Having grown up in Chicagoland, Zim had relatives of some form or nature all over the zone. That included Naperville. The problem was, he didn't know if they were dead or alive, or worse, part of the regime. They had no additional *Molon Labe* contacts. Marv didn't have anyone to send them to or decided they were worth sacrificing to keep the cells safe.

They decided to hide out in a run-down park on the north side of Four Lakes. They didn't want to get too close to the meet-up point for two reasons. One, if Reso had the meet-up location, they'd be waiting for them there. And, two, if they were being followed, they didn't want to lead the Reso there. Either way, staying put for now until a better plan arose was the best course.

"Are you sure? We're already down at least a team. What if they find you?" Klein queried Zim.

"Listen, it's not like I want to leave you three behind. If I get caught, I'll joke around with the Reso so much they'll just straight away kill me rather than torture me. A fate worse than death? My quips!" Zim put on a brave face, but he was unnerved.

"I'll go with you then," added Zach.

"Hey, he speaks!" said Zim. "Hey, buddy, thanks but no thanks. We need you here. Three is better than two, if you get my math."

"Here," Hannah extended her hands. "Take them, I have plenty left." In her hands were a roll and muffin Betty gave her earlier.

"You sure?"

"Yep. Take them."

"Thanks, Hannah," said Zim thankfully.

Klein looked at his granddaughter. Without either of them saying a word, she nodded her head in the affirmative. Klein then turned to Zimmer. "Okay, Zim, you *will* make it back safely. You will," Klein stated firmly as if by saying it that way, it would guarantee Zim's safe return.

"If I'm not back by sundown, hunker down as best as you can. I'll try to be back beforehand. If I don't make it then, then I'll try again at first light. If that doesn't work out, I'll hope to make the rendezvous in two days."

"You will make it back," Hannah said firmly, just like her grandfather did.

"Okay, you three stay safe. Stay out of sight. And, one more thing."

"What's that?" asked Klein.

"Welcome to Chicagoland!" Zim extended his arms and then immediately broke into song with his best Sinatra impersonation, "*My kind of town, Chicago is!*"

"Go, please, go!" Klein said as they all shared a nervous chuckle. Even Zach was amused.

Zim headed back in the direction from which they came. It didn't take him long to blend in. He looked natural in these surroundings.

"Let's take a quick inventory of food supplies. We ran out of there fast. I have what looks to be a blackberry muffin and some water. I nibbled on a roll about an hour ago. Zach?"

"I have a roll and a muffin. Plus, water."

"Have you eaten?" inquired Klein.

"No sir. Thought I'd wait to see how things played out. I'm fine though, sir."

"Very well then. Hannah?"

"I'm fine, thanks Opa."

"Hannah?"

"What? I'm fine. Now, let's start evaluating next steps in case we need to move."

"Hannah, what supplies do you have?"

"Just this."

Klein and Zach looked at her as she pulled a water container out of her bag.

Klein looked at his granddaughter. He was both perturbed and proud, perturbed that she likely hadn't eaten and gave her food away, proud for the exact same reasons.

* * *

Zim made good time. He remembered his cousin, his father's youngest sister's oldest daughter lived near the river. At least she used to live there with her family, a husband and two kids. Twins. He used to call them Hansel and Gretel, even though they were both boys. It always made him popular, with at least one of the boys but not their father.

His cousin Katrina was about three years older than he. Even though age differences like that seemed like more with young kids, he and Katrina hung together as often as they could. She was a tomboy through and through. They'd wisecrack and pull pranks on one another. They'd roughhouse, get in trouble, and fish. They loved going fishing together. She was an expert angler, at least in his eyes. In fact, she could never do anything wrong in his eyes. He looked up to her with love and admiration. He was thankful to have her in his life. In some ways, she was both the brother and sister he never had.

Zim was raised an only child. He had older siblings, boy and girl, but they perished in a home fire before he was born. Zim was an accident. His parents were so distraught over the loss of their two older children they never recovered. Zim was loved but cautiously so. Understandably, the older Zimmers were fearful of getting too close to their new son as another loss would be too great to bear. His sense of humor was definitely an outgrowth of seeking attention and personal protection.

Zim remembered the neighborhood. It was as if he stepped into a time warp just as he recalled it from over a decade or more ago. Two boys were throwing a football in the front yard. *Must be the twins,* he thought. Talk about time warp, no one had played organized football for decades either. Then he remembered. Katrina's husband, Chuck, was a football player of sorts. Actually. He was a kicker. Zim would never give him credit for being a *real* football player, at least not until Chuck broke his clavicle while attempting to tackle a player on a kickoff return. Zim reminded Chuck that he was not on the football team to use his body, just his feet. As such, next time, "try tripping the guy," Zim suggested.

Chuck kicked for the nearby college, which was then called North Central College. That's where Chuck and Katrina met. As with most schools, colleges and universities included, names were changed when The Legacy took control. Usually the multi-directional universities and colleges survived the renaming game. But the North Central Cardinals became the People's Free University of Aurora. The cost of attendance was clearly set forth in its new name.

After renaming the college Zim used to tease Chuck, who joined the faculty at North Central shortly before the name change, that he went from being a *Cardinal* to a *Sitting Duck*. Zim even went so far as to boldly proclaim that they were going to rename the college again, this time to the *Legacy College Special Little Snowflakes of Aurora near Chicago*. Needless to say, Chuck was not fond of his wife's cousin. Safe to say that was one thing the two men shared in common. Zim wasn't fond of Chuck either. Although, as he spied his cousin's home, he couldn't help but to feel that he should have been nicer to Chuck, and one of the twins.

Zim thought engaging Katrina at home might be too dicey after all. He tried to remember where she worked. Post-Legacy jobs were a funny thing. Unless you had a real professional specialty, everyone was considered fungible. As people were paid a static "living wage," workers jumped from job to job quasi-freely or by regime assignment. There was a requirement to work. Just how hard was another question altogether.

The last he knew, Katrina worked as a dentist. "Top of my license" as Katrina would say gleefully. She wasn't a dentist as that term was formerly known. She learned on the job. That's how many people across the province survived, even thrived in some odd ways.

Zim crossed over the river and headed south down Bernie Sanders Memorial Drive, in former days, named South Washington Street. He was walking on autopilot. Some buildings had changed, but for the most part, it looked as he recalled. There it was. Katrina's dental office, or as the sign read, People's Free Dentistry. He decided to just walk in.

"Hi there," Zim said with enthusiasm to the less than energetic teen at the reception counter. "I'm here for my appointment, with *Doctor Wisniewski!*" Zim said, that last bit with exceptional emphasis and at a high decibel level.

"Name?"

"Octavius Baracuda," said Zim. "Baracuda, one r."

"I don't see any patient named . . ."

A woman bolted out from behind the door marked *Appointments Only*. "Oh, Mr. Baracuda, one r, please, come on in. You're late. I've been waiting for you."

Zim walked through the door. The woman at reception seemed unfazed.

"Zimmy!" Katrina shrieked while she made her body wiggle. Arms extended, she grabbed Zim in a bear hug worthy of Chicago's namesake former football team. "I can't believe it!"

"Katrina, I've missed you!"

"Me too, so much! Zimmy, what in the h-e-double Blackhawk sticks are you doing here?"

"Yeah, 'bout that. Do you have an office here or someplace we can talk?"

"Sure. Down the hall. Last door on the left. I'll be down in about two shakes. Gotta finish an extraction."

Poor unfortunate soul, Zim thought. He walked into her office. Small, yet tidy, it was replete with many family pictures in multiple collages. Katrina's family looked so happy—blissfully ignorant of what was happening all around them. *Twins will probably do that to a person,* he mused. And there they were, a collage just devoted to cousins. They had more than a dozen cousins, more than half grew up in the greater Chicago region. Such fun times. Innocent times, mostly.

Katrina entered quickly. "That wasn't long," Zim said.

"It was a 'yank and thank' procedure. Funny thing, I don't usually get too many thanks. Go figure. Maybe," she said as she cocked her head to the side, placed her left hand under her chin, and her left index finger over her mouth, "I ought to give them an anesthetic?" Her intonation rose at the last word to deliver that final punch.

Zim laughed out loud. He loved his cousin's sense of humor. As much as he wanted to engage in dueling puns with her, there wasn't time. His face turned serious on a dime.

"Kat, here's the thing. I may have made a mistake coming here to see you. I'm so sorry. If you need me to go, I'll do it. Just say the word."

"Huh? What's this crazy talk? And why so glum all of a sudden?"

"Once I share, there's no going back for you. You'll know. Are you sure you want to take that risk?"

"My goodness, you are serious. Zimmy, if you need me, I'm there for you. Anything. You know that. That's why you're here. You know I'd do anything for you." Katrina paused and looked at her cousin. She studied him closely. He looked older, a bit haggard, and anxious, not the youthful devil-may-care Zimmy she kept in her mind's eye—and in the collage pictures. "You're *Molon Labe*. I know that. I have at least suspected. Is that it?"

"Yes."

"That's okay. I know several. At least I suspect they are. No problem, Zimmy."

"That's not the whole story, Kat."

There was a knock at the closed door. A voice said, "Mr. Chesterfield is waiting in room 2."

"Be there in five. In the meantime, please give him a sedative."

"Excuse me?" said the voice.

"I'll be there in five. Thank you."

Katrina turned to her cousin. She grabbed both of his upper arms. "Whatever it is, just say it quickly. It will be easier that way."

"I, um, *we* need a place to stay for two nights, a safe place. Just two nights. When I say safe place, I mean a place where we—there are four of us—won't be noticed or reported if you understand."

"Yes. I think I do understand." Katrina was thinking. "Okay, here's one option. You could stay here after we close down at night. Would that work?"

"Too busy. Too risky."

"There's a shed out back of the house. Nobody goes in there anymore. The lawn proves it."

"What if Chuckles sees me or us. He's one of *them*. Nothing would make him happier than to see the Reso haul me away."

"True that." Katrina was straining to think of another option.

Another knock at the door. "Mr. Chesterfield wants to know if you plan on working today."

Katrina whispered to Zim, "Sorry, pain in the you-know-what. Precinct leader, social credits accumulator, and regime climber. You know the type. Wait here."

Katrina left. Zim started thinking being here wasn't a great idea. He was putting the person he loved most in the world, and her kids, at risk. As for Chuck, he'd prefer to feed him to the Reso, if he could.

Zim heard a door open and Katrina's voice down the hall. "Okay, Mr. Chesterfield, the Novocain will set in in about ten minutes. And so sorry about that first poke."

Katrina reentered her office. Zim said, "I shouldn't do this. I'm going to go. It was nice . . ."

"Oh no you don't. You don't just show up here, in trouble, and not let me help you. Sit down."

Zim sat down in the corner. She sat too and leaned in close. She had something in her hand. "This is the key to my storage unit. Down by Pioneer Park. I use it to store extra dental supplies. I don't have enough room here, and supplies can be hard to get sometimes. You and your friends can use it. There's no bathroom, so use the park, or the river, whatever, you have options."

"Aren't these units monitored?"

"No, don't think so. Haven't been for years. There are cameras not connected to anything. Owner is too cheap. Pretty sure there's illegal stuff going on in there. No one seems to mind, at least not the Reso. They seem to have other people to harass," Katrina said as she raised one eyebrow.

A knock at the door. "Mr. Chesterfield says that he's not feeling anything."

"Be right there, thanks. Tell him I may have to give him more."

Katrina whispered, "I gave him saline. Just wanted to poke him a few times. Love my job."

They both stood and embraced. It was a long, strong one. She patted him hard on the back. He patted her harder. It continued back and forth a few times. It was a cousin thing.

"I'll bring you food and water to last you all a few days. And TP. Will be later, though, after the boys go to sleep. Can you make it until then?"

"Yes, we can. Thanks. That'd be great."

"No more White Castle, though. You-know-who shut them down. Don't cry. I have plenty of stale bread to make your favorite peanut butter and hard-boiled egg sandwich," she quipped. "I can see your mouth watering already—it's a dentist thing."

Zim managed a little chuckle. "Thanks, Kat. You'll never know how much this means to me."

"I better someday know all about it when you come back and stay with us, next time," she said, her voice cracking "in the house. Okay?"

"Okay," Zim said forcing a smile. He started to open her office door to leave.

"Hey," she said in a stern mom voice, "don't you even think about peeing on the floor! I got tired of wiping up after you when you were little. Bad aim, kid, bad aim."

"My aim's better now. At least a little bit. I love you, cuz."

"Love you too, cuz. Stay safe," she said with moist eyes as she blew him a kiss.

Zim walked down the hall and didn't look back. He couldn't. As he walked through the waiting room door, he heard Katrina's voice.

"You don't say, Mr. Chesterfield. Well, I want you completely satisfied. Let's do this again, shall we? Just a little pinch . . ."

Chapter LV

"We're going with you."

Anjali had heard every word from Jeannie with laser-like intensity. Jeannie laid out everything she knew as well as everything she suspected. Anjali had no questions. She had no equivocation. She was earnest in her decision for herself and her two girls. She knew their time was fast approaching. She couldn't wait for events to overtake her. Anjali needed strength, found it, and shared it with her dearest friend.

"We, you and I, can do this. We have to do this."

"You know what this means?" asked Jeannie.

"Yes," said Anjali solemnly. "I do."

"You sure?"

"Yes. Positive."

"Okay then, when can you be ready?"

"Give me two hours. That's all I need."

"Okay, then meet me at the kid's playground three blocks north of Che Bakery. Let's say two and a half hours from now. I will have my girls with me. My mother-in-law has already agreed to join us at the park. She can watch all four girls when we head over to meet Frank. We'll tell her we're going to the bakery and ask if she wants anything that we can bring back for her. Only one school backpack for each child. For the two of us, nothing. Whatever you need put in their packs. Nothing to raise suspicions, especially for my mother-in-law. Sound like a plan?"

"Yes. Got it."

"You won't be going back once you shut that door," Jeannie said as she pointed to the front door of Anjali's unit. "You understand?"

"Yes. Clearly. I wish it could be different, but we've got to act now. I'm convinced of it."

"Okay, I'm going to go now. See you in two and a half."

"See you."

They embraced before Jeannie left.

Anjali slumped against the front door. She looked all around her. The walls and tables were ornamented with memories of happier times that filled her senses, pictures and souvenirs from travels with Stefan before the girls, wedding pictures, so many pictures of the girls, individual shots, two-girl shots, and full family shots. So many smiles. So many laughs. So many tender moments.

Her gaze turned to the bookshelf. Her eyes immediately caught the empty Legacy Coin holders. She took a deep breath. She knew she was making the right choice . . . for all four of them.

Chapter LVI

"Dad! Oh, Daddy!" Cassandra was shedding tears like a steep roof in a summer rain as she ran into the hospital room.

"My baby girl," said an emotional Simon Bowles as he embraced his daughter for the first time in what seemed to be forever. "My little Sandy, let me take a good look at you." He barely pulled away from their embrace to take a quick look at her. Then he grabbed her even tighter. He winced, but she didn't see it. Simon laid back down in bed.

"Sandy, this is my wife, Dianne. Dianne, this is Cassandra."

"Nice to meet you Dianne," Cassandra gave her a polite hug.

"You too, my dear," said Dianne. "And what shall I call you? I've heard so many nicknames for you."

"Whatever you wish. My Dad likes to call me Sandy. Our family called me Sandy." She paused to think a moment. She never got used to referring to her family in the past tense. "My professional colleagues call me Cassandra. Or, the boss lady!" She giggled in a cute, awkward way. "And, this guy here, he calls me Cass." Cassandra wrapped her arm around Hatua's.

"I'm Hank. Nice to meet you both. Sir," Hatua extended his hand to Simon, "the pleasure is completely mine." They shook hands firmly, although Simon felt as if Hatua could crush his hand if he wished to do so. Simon's fragile health had taken away much of his strength. "Ma'am, likewise." Hatua extended his hand, but Dianne embraced him before he knew what hit him.

Simon grinned, "Dianne's never met a stranger in her life."

"I see that," Hatua said as he grinned.

"Hank, I want you to know as a father, I love my little girl with everything I have." Simon's blue eyes pierced Hatua while he said, "Treat her well. Always, always, treat her well."

Hatua wasn't used to people speaking to him like that, but something about Simon and the way he said it didn't offend him at all. In fact, Hatua respected him for what he said and how he said it.

"Yes, sir. I will."

"Okay, now that we got that out of the way, we wanted to thank you, Hank, for arranging for us to be here in Legacy City. Being near you two is a," Simon had a short hiccup in his speech, "wish come true."

"It's *our* pleasure," responded Hatua as he smiled and looked at Cassandra. "We both wanted you close. And we certainly look forward to a day soon that you won't have to be in here." Hatua gestured around him. "Legacy City Recovery Center is the best care center in the entire province. Best physicians, staff, and equipment."

"I sure like the name of the hospital," offered Simon.

"Legacy City?" asked Hatua curiously.

"No," Simon said with a gleam in his eyes, "recovery!"

They all shared a laugh. Cassandra was so pleased to see her father joking again. It had been a long time since she had seen him, even longer since she saw him smile so much and joke around. Life had been hard on her father, exceptionally hard.

Perhaps now, she thought, *he could live out his final years in peace and happiness.*

"Speaking of that," Hank said, "and I hope you don't mind, I have spoken with the Center's Chief of Staff Dr. Wang. He is a fantastic leader as well as physician and surgeon. He has arranged for a comprehensive workup for you. No offense to your previous doctors, the folks here are truly the best of the best. Let's try to achieve that *recovery* sooner rather than later. Agreed?"

"My yes, thank you, Hank. That'd be wonderful. I'm afraid that we've had a bumpy go of it in recent times."

"Very sweet of you, my dear," Dianne chimed in looking adoringly at Hank.

"And, ma'am, you are welcome to stay in the suites associated with the Care Center. In that way, you'll be very close. When Mr. Bowles is ready to be discharged, we'll have other very nice accommodations for you."

"It's Simon. Or Dad. Whatever you prefer."

"Thank you, sir. Simon."

"Sir Simon, I rather like the ring to that," Simon responded using an over-the-top Cockney accent while hinting at days long since gone.

"Oh, Daddy!" Cassandra was beaming from ear to ear. "We do have some other news to share with you two."

"Go ahead, dear." Dianne clearly defaulted to calling everyone dear.

"Well, given you two are here now, we decided to share our wedding date with you. No need to wait."

"That's wonderful. Do tell. You've set a date then?" asked Simon.

"Daddy, we have." Cassandra squeezed Hatua's arm tight while looking at him, then back at her father. "Today. Here. Now. We're getting married right here and right now. How's that for a surprise?"

"Oh, my goodness honey. I, I, I just don't know what to say!"

"Well that's just wonderful, you dears!"

"Please excuse me," Hatua said respectfully. "I'll let them know we're ready."

Cassandra bent over again to embrace her father. His voice was getting weaker the longer they were in the room. She could tell he was tired. He'd never admit it, of course. He seemed energized and happy. Hopefully this wasn't taking too much out of him, she worried. She kissed him on the cheek and whispered, "I love you so much, Daddy."

He responded while whispering back in her ear, "I love you too, my precious not-so-little anymore girl. Tell me one thing."

"Yes, anything."

"Is he a good man?"

"I believe so, Daddy," Cassandra said, trying to convince not only her father, but herself. "I believe so."

Chapter LVII

"Sir, they've arrived," reported his chief of staff.

"Thank you, Everett. Please see to it that I speak immediately with the commanding officer. That is all."

"Yes, sir." Edward left almost as soon as he appeared. Nobody, not even his trusted COS dared tempt fate.

Berko was in the zone. Nothing could or should disturb him now. His sole focus was on executing his plan. His whole life had been building to this moment.

Boris Berko was raised in the small northern Ukrainian city of Slavutych. The city was built for the express purpose of housing personnel after the Chernobyl nuclear plant disaster of 1986. Both sets of Berko's grandparents were mere toddlers when they were uprooted from Pripyat and taken some forty-five kilometers away from the birth home they never knew. His grandparents and parents made their lives in Slavutych. They all had some form of employment related to the infamous power plant, either in remediation, monitoring, scientific endeavors, or tourism. They would regularly board a train for the forty-five-minute trip to Chernobyl, passing the adjacent border with Belarus twice each way in the process.

Young Boris, or Bo, as he was called, was the oldest of five children. As a youngster, he was sickly. His family believed that he was a *grandchild of Chernobyl.* His frequent illness and slow physical development was blamed on the deleterious effects of his family's radiation exposure. Mutated DNA was common among those surviving families. And, ultimately, children of Chernobyl gave way to grandchildren of Chernobyl. The negative impacts, such as thyroid cancer, leukemia, and children being born with heart defects as well as other disabilities, were effects still being passed on.

Bo did very well in school. He struggled making friends and was frequently bullied being so much smaller than other children his age. Instead of having real friends, he invented them. Although he had siblings at home, he was four years older than his nearest sibling in age, so he did most of his entertaining by himself. He read a lot, including reading books in other languages. He taught himself several foreign languages, including English, German, and Spanish, although his pronunciation was off until he attended the university in Kiev.

He first attended *Kyiv* National University of Construction and Architecture, a fairly low-level university. However, he excelled in all of his classes. After two years, and with the special recommendation of the university's senior leadership, he was offered a place at Ukraine's preeminent university, National Taras Shevchenko University of *Kyiv.* Bo Berko's facility with languages and sharp problem-solving skills led to his being noticed by the then-Ukrainian government. Upon graduation, he was offered a job in foreign service. He began as a low-level analyst. He was promoted to field work and then special assistant at the Ukrainian Embassy in Madrid, Spain. He would transport diplomatic letters between Kiev and Madrid as well as other European capitals.

The post-war shake-up changed everything. As a tremendous political operative, he found himself firmly ensconced in the Central Europe Province's Department of Provincial Security. The DPS was a combination of national and international security apparatuses. It also housed all prisoners and enemies of the province, including traditional and political prisoners. It was there that he honed his interrogation techniques. It was also there that his sub-surface hard edge was brought above the surface. He was encouraged to sharpen his personal brand of intimidation. It proved helpful to him as he ascended into the most senior leadership position in his department. At a comparatively young age, he became the most feared person in all of the Central Europe Province.

Berko succeeded at most everything he put his mind to except for love. His romantic pursuits were routinely rebuffed. His small stature, pock-marked face, deep-set features, extraordinary intensity, and extreme social unawareness made him a wholly unattractive love candidate save for the most desperate. His consistent rejection led to an internal jealousy and rage, which rose to a level of disdain and even wishing harm to come to those whose happiness in coupledom was visible. In essence, he learned to hate people and love.

If people were not his source of happiness, acquisition of power firmly stood in its place. He attended a meeting of provincial security leaders in Buenos Aires. It was there that he first met with leaders from The Legacy in North America. He had always wanted to live in America. World events initially dashed that dream. However, he built trust in this new relationship and was eventually offered the position of Provincial Director of Justice and Reform for North America Province. He received the blessing of the Central Europe regime to join The Legacy. His former colleagues were overjoyed to see him go and slept better because of it.

Berko proved himself a worthy addition. Under his leadership, the former United States Supreme Court was disbanded, and The Legacy's Equity Appeals Division substituted in its place. There was nothing equitable about it. It was tasked to uphold the regime's goals over all else. As far as reform went, he *reformed* by combining all law enforcement and military under one umbrella, The Legacy's Resolution Department. Berko was, in fact, the brainchild of the notorious Reso. As such, he became the Reso's first general.

With his continued successes and brilliant execution of plans—no matter how despicable—Berko became the most indispensable member of The Legacy's senior team. He ascended to an unnamed direct advisory position because his work touched every aspect of society. He had unfettered access to The Legacy. And the regime listened to Berko and most often adopted his recommendations.

Even after his move to North America Province, his hate grew stronger, deeper, and ate away any part of his soul that remained. His loneliness and self-imposed isolation from feelings of compassion or love made him stronger, so he thought. He had one weakness. That was Cassandra Bowles. He loved her, at least he loved her insofar as he understood that term. Yet, he tormented her. And her him, although her torment of Berko was unintentional. At times, Berko tormented her without intent, and other times fully cognizant of what he was doing. He had a twisted and perverse attraction to her. He was in a power relationship over her. He took every advantage of that power at every opportunity possible.

"Sir, General Zhang is ready on a secure channel."

"Thank you. You're excused." Berko waited for Everett to close the door. Berko gave an audio command, "max security."

His office became completely soundproof. Nobody could tap into the audio or see in. He had absolute privacy.

"General Zhang, welcome back to our humble North America Province."

"Thank you, General Berko. We're here with great pleasure and full of anticipation."

"No doubt, General. I was happily surprised to hear that you were personally coming. I thought you might assign a colonel to command in theater of operations and oversee from afar."

"This mission is critical to the CCP in ways you understand. There is no room for any mistake."

"Very well. Are we agreed on deployment plans?"

"Yes. We are readying our troops to deploy throughout the province. We are using both Hyperloop and traditional transport aircraft. They are currently mustering supplies, confirming that we will maintain a healthy, yet as subtle as possible, presence near Legacy City ready at your disposal."

"Good. Thank you. Is there anything you need at this time?"

"Action. I promised my troops that they will see plenty of action with live rounds. They are anxious to begin 'Operation Cleanup' as I believe you named it."

"As am I, General."

Chapter LVIII

The entry door had an old-fashioned bell that sounded with each opening. The bell served as notice of a customer's entry as well as a warm welcome to the bakery. Jeannie and Anjali entered.

"Welcome!" said the three employees in unison. None of them bothered to look up. They had enough sense of movement in their shop to know that someone was entering as opposed to leaving. The bakery had several customers enjoying coffee and pastries at small tables near the window. That vantage point had a view directly across *Avenida de la Victoria* to Province House. Che Bakery was well-known to be the preferred stopping spot for regime leaders and their support staff for a quick coffee and perhaps some sweet treat.

Jeannie and Anjali were both trying their best to hide their nerves. This was a huge step for them, a step into an unknown next chapter.

"Next." A woman in her mid-fifties was at the counter and looking directly at the two friends awaiting their turn to order. Jeannie and Anjali stepped forward as Jeannie said something inaudible to Anjali, who nodded.

"Yes," Jeannie said politely, but not too much so. "We'd both like a coffee. I'll take mine with double cream and quadruple sugar."

Anjali quickly added, "I'll have the same."

The woman, who had been wiping the counter between them, perked up.

"And . . ." Jeannie surveyed the display case full of delicious-looking baked goods, "Are those almond-filled?" Jeannie inquired while pointing at a rack filled with croissants.

"Yes," the woman looked closely at Jeannie and Anjali. "Yes, they are."

"Okay, two of those please."

"Very well," the woman said a bit louder, "Two coffees, double cream, and quad sugar, and two almond croissants. Is that correct?"

Looking through the open partition between the front area and the baking prep and cook area in the back, an older man turned his head slightly to see who was at the counter.

"Yes, one more thing please. May I have a dozen mixed cookies to go? That's all. Thank you."

The bell went off, and all three employees said in unison, "Thank you!" Someone had left.

"Payment, please."

Jeannie extended her PCD over a scanner at waist height on the counter. She then looked at the amount showing on her PCD and said, "Approve payment."

The woman looked at her screen. It showed 'Dr. Jeanette W Washington. L5. PA.' Jeannie's social credits status with The Legacy was Level 5. It allowed her special perks like purchasing items in a store like Che Bakery. Her purchase was approved.

"Here are your coffees and croissants."

"Thank you," said Jeannie. Anjali smiled and nodded.

"Please have a seat. You might prefer over there," the woman moved her head to the left, indicating the back corner. "I'll have Frank bring you the cookies."

"Very well, thank you again," said Jeannie as she and Anjali took items to the suggested area. They sat down in the booth.

As they sat down, a non-descript bureaucratic-looking man, who was probably much younger than he appeared, walked with his small coffee to the booth directly in front of theirs. He looked at Jeannie blankly. As he took his seat, he looked at her again, this time, with more interest. His back was to Anjali. Jeannie whispered to Anjali, "small talk."

The two sipped on their coffees while Jeannie kept a wary eye out for the comings and goings of customers. The man near them rose to leave. He started toward the door, then made a 180-degree turn and headed for their booth. He stood above the seated ladies.

"Dr. Garcia?"

"Yes," said Jeannie cautiously.

"I'm so sorry to hear about your husband. Our condolences."

"Thank you. Do I know you?"

"Yes," said the man who seemed a slight bit hurt. "You no doubt have many families you have worked with." He paused a moment. "You delivered our baby girl not long ago, Rebecca."

"Ah, of course," Jeannie said, her protective demeanor now loosening a bit, "David, right?"

"Yes," his spirits quickly lifted.

"Audrey's husband. How are they doing now? I haven't seen them since shortly after delivery."

"They are doing great. Both of them. Thanks again, Doc, for all you did. You saved them." He turned to Anjali, "She's the very best doc out there. If you're going to ever have children, Doc Garcia is the best."

"Yes, she is, thank you." Anjali said softly as the thought of what she had just done stung her heart greatly.

Their uninvited guest was not taking any social cues that it was time for his visit to come to an end. After a few more minutes of banal chatter, Jeannie noticed a man standing behind Audrey's chattering husband.

"Well, David," said Jeannie as she stood to shake his hand to better move him along, "It was nice seeing you again. Thanks for saying hello, and please extend my very best to Audrey. Okay? Thanks, and goodbye David." She touched his left shoulder and gently guided him away.

"Your cookies, ma'am."

Jeannie took the box. "Thank you." She looked around. The bakery was empty save for a couple of men arguing up front near the window. They seemed to be having a disagreement about social credits and whether that granted access to a particular store. Jeannie asked, "Are you Frank?"

"Yes."

"Frank Gies?"

"Yes."

"My husband was Rolando Garcia. Did you know him?"

"Yes."

The man just stood there directly in front of Jeannie. Anjali was still seated as she couldn't really stand at this point given the man's location right up against her right side. Jeannie thought that it was strange that the man said as little as possible yet just stood there.

"Mr. Gies, my husband was fond of you. He told me to come see you."

"He did," said Gies flatly.

"Yes, he did. He said to come," Jeannie was trying to find a way to phrase it so Gies would have confidence that she was who she claimed to be while also not saying too much directly, just in case. "Disung said to come now."

"Who?"

"Disung."

"Sorry, that name is not familiar to me."

Disung mentioned that he'd be suspicious. Given his bakery's location and clientele, he had to be, Jeannie surmised. She looked as deep into his eyes as she could. She said softly, yet strongly, "leon y cordero."

"Did your husband recently give you any jewelry?" Gies inquired in a firm yet polite way.

"Excuse me?"

"Did your husband recently give you any jewelry?"

"Yes."

"What was it?"

"A necklace."

"The necklace that your husband gave you. Describe it."

"It has interlocking . . ." Jeannie began to say. "Here, take a look." She pulled the necklace out from under her top and showed him.

"Thank you, Doctor Garcia." Gies looked around the bakery. Still just the two men arguing, this time about how fast the Hyperloop would be able to travel at top speeds.

Gies increased the volume of his voice, "A quick tour of the bakery? But of course. We'd be honored to show you. Right this way if you please."

The two men stopped their arguing to catch a glimpse of who the VIPs were, probably a couple of newly promoted managers from a subregion. *Silly,* they thought, *these bakers may be close to Province House, but they can't help you get ahead. Go ahead and waste your time.* They went back to arguing.

Gies gave an outward show of a quick tour in case they were being observed. They ended the tour in the office area in the back. The three entered. Gies shut the door.

"One moment," Gies said as he followed up with, "Privacy sequence. Start." He waited for a count of three. A voice said, "Privacy protocols active."

"Very well, we are free to speak plainly now. Doctor Garcia, I apologize for out there. Our necessity to be discreet is a matter of life and death for many, including my family."

"I understand." Jeannie turned to her friend. "This is Anjali Gowda. She's with me. She's with us, I should say."

"Yes," as Gies turned to Anjali. "A pleasure."

"Pleasure is mine, sir," Anjali responded.

"Sorry for coming early," offered Jeannie. "Disung said to come as soon as possible."

"I understand. He would know best. Where are your children?"

"Three blocks away with Rolando's mother. Anjali's two girls too."

"At the playground?"

"Yes."

"Good. We need to get you all to a safe place. How soon are you ready to go?"

"Now." Jeannie and Anjali said together.

"Very good." Gies busied himself pulling together what looked to be official transportation documents.

"May I ask a quick question?" Jeannie queried.

"Yes," replied Gies, still working on his tasks, "by all means."

"How did you know about the jewelry? The necklace?"

"Because," Gies stopped briefly to look at Jeannie, "my dear Doctor, I made it."

"What?"

"Made it to Rolando's specifications. He designed it. I first removed small diamonds from two rings. Then he had me melt down the gold bands. What were once wedding rings belonging to his mother and grandmother became your anniversary present."

Jeannie clutched at the necklace. She pulled it out again.

"He designed it to be uniquely yours. The Double DC. The cross."

Jeannie interrupted as she said, "There's no cross."

"Look again, carefully."

She pulled it out and unclasped it. She looked at it carefully. There, for the first time, she saw it. Her husband's design had diamonds vertically along the D spine, with diamonds horizontally along the bottom of the top DC and along the top of the bottom backwards DC. It made a perfect cross, a beautiful diamond cross shining brightly in the light.

"See it now?"

"Yes."

"He wanted to protect you. If he couldn't be there to do it, he wanted someone greater to do so."

"But I'm not a believer."

Gies just smiled and carried on with his work. "And, take a look at the back. Turn it over. Do you see the etching?"

"I don't see anything. Wait. The small etching in the middle. Very small. And very beautiful. Is that?"

"Yes," said Gies, still focused on gathering what they needed to move on. "It's a small etching in the middle of the gold. It's a lion with a lamb . . . laying peacefully together."

"*Leon y cordero.*"

"Yes. Use it only as you must. Be extremely careful before you show it to anyone."

"Use it for what?"

"It's your pass to those who are with us—the brothers and sisters of *Leon y Cordero.*"

"I understand why Rolando referred to you as brother," Jeannie offered. "He was so fond—"

There were quick two knocks followed by the door opening. The woman from the front counter entered excitedly.

"Sorry to intrude. Frank, something urgent."

"This is my wife, Margot. She's safe."

"It's China. The coup has begun. Two lower-level members of The Legacy's communications team were talking about it while they waited in line to order. They're gone now."

Gies turned to Jeannie. "Your timing seems to be on point, Doctor. Everything is in motion now."

"What is *everything*?"

"Not exactly sure. That's what your husband was trying to figure out. He was close. I know he was close." Gies turned back to his wife, "Thank you, my love."

"Frank, there's one more thing."

"Yes?"

"He's here. Drinking his coffee. Slowly. Very slowly."

Gies' face turned ashen. "Okay, " Gies said in a distracted way as he looked down, as if searching for something. "Thinking."

"What's wrong? Who's here?" asked Jeannie.

Gies took a moment. He looked at the two guests in a concerned way and said gravely, "We call him *The Angel of Death Incarnate*. Others call him Boris Berko."

Chapter LIX

They ate as if they hadn't eaten for days, which, in their case, happened to be true. Katrina brought plenty of peanut butter and fresh blackberry preserve sandwiches, cheese sandwiches, fresh apples and pears, a mixture of assorted veggies, and some sweet crackers. She also brought water, two smallish cantaloupes, and a special treat: a box full of assorted chocolates.

"Didn't I tell you," Zim said with his mouth full of sandwich, "my cuz is the best ever."

"Agreed," Klein said in concert with others nodding their heads in approval. They couldn't talk for fear of spraying the others with food from their full mouths. "You were absolutely right, Zim. Very thoughtful of you, young lady. Thank you for the food and this shelter. We will be leaving in the morning before daylight. Hope we haven't been too much of an imposition. Now, not to be rude, but in the interest of your safety, I suggest you leave us to your graciously sponsored gluttony."

Zim belched. "He's probably right, cuz. No need taking any more risks here. If we get busted, we'll just say we picked the lock looking for valuables, like your vintage Pez dispenser collection!"

"Funny. Is there anything else you want or need? I'm happy to get it for you."

"I can't stress enough how grateful we are. Truly grateful," Klein said. "This is serious business we are involved with. I understand that you have a family."

"She has two boys, and a dork-for-brains husband. Does he count?"

"In any event," continued Klein without being distracted by Zim. "We'll be fine the rest of the way. You brought us so much food. There's nothing else. You've done so much already. We owe you a major debt of thanks, Katrina."

"Okay. If anything changes or you need to reach me, Zim knows the drill."

Zim wiped his mouth and got up. He hugged his cousin tight. "Better than any stinkin' ole belly bombs, cuz. So much better. I love you."

"I love you too. Stay safe." Katrina accepted thanks and hugs from the others except Zach, who shook her hand. "Hey, please watch out for this guy, okay?" She said pointing at her cousin. "If he bugs you too much, though, you have my permission to turn him into the Reso yourselves. He can get annoying, right?"

"Right!" the three said together.

"Hey, not so loud." Zim said, putting his index finger over his lips. "Shhhhh. You'll wake the neighbors."

"I think the *neighbors* in the storage units behind us are having a bender, so don't worry, cuz." Katrina joked.

"Anyway, good luck and stay safe, all of you." Katrina blew Zim a kiss and left.

"Really nice of her. Super woman," Hannah said.

"A class act," chimed in Klein.

They heard a quick knock, and the door to the unit slowly opened.

"Come on, cuz, you've seriously got more for us?"

As soon as he finished saying the last word, the top of a head which was just appearing swiftly moved back, and the door shut hard. They heard someone running outside.

Zach bolted off the floor, through the door, and gave chase. Zim was also in hot pursuit but not as fast as Zach. Zim rounded two corners and saw Zach on top of someone. A man.

"Who are you? What are you doing here?" Zach asked angrily. "Huh? Who are you?"

The man started screaming, "Help! Get off me!"

Zach slammed the man's head against the pavement. "Shut up. Shut up, or I'll kill you."

"Help!" the man said, this time weakly.

Zach again slammed the man's head down hard. Zim heard a thump like the man's head was a watermelon. The man stopped talking. Blood oozed from his mouth, nose, and right ear. Zach took the man's pulse and listened for his breathing.

"He's still alive." Zach turned to Zim, "help me move him to the unit."

Zim looked at the man lying injured on the ground. He stood there. Frozen.

"Quickly. Come on, Zim. Let's do this, now."

Zim snapped out of it and grabbed the man's legs. He and Zach moved quickly while they carried the man to the storage unit. They hustled inside, and Klein shut the door.

"What happened?" asked Hannah, anxiously.

"This man," Zach tried to talk, but he was still breathing hard. "This man, he saw us. This man . . ."

"This man," said Zim soberly, "is my cousin's husband."

"Oh my," said Klein with great concern.

* * *

"Just let me go, Zim. If you let me go, there won't be any trouble. I'll keep quiet. You know I will."

Zim was deep in thought. He loved his cousin. Why did Chuck come to the unit? He was obviously following Katrina. Why? Why did he have to stick his nose in her business? In their business? Zim loathed Chuck, but he was Katrina's husband and the twins' father. And now Zim and the others needed to agree on what to do with him. If they let him go, Zim was confident that Chuck would rat them out. He might even hurt Katrina. That's how little Zim thought of Chuck. On the other hand, if they killed Chuck, it would be like killing a piece of his cousin Katrina too.

"Look, Zim, I promise, if you let me go, I'll never breathe a word of this to anyone, not even Kat. I swear."

"Swear? Swear? Swear on what? A textbook? That's rich, Chuck, really rich! What the hell were you doing following your wife? Huh? What the hell, Chuck?" Zim was getting into Chuck's face. The overspray from his words coating Chuck's face. "What's wrong with you? Dammit Chuck, you did this to yourself! And to your family!"

"Zim. Zim," said Klein as he lightly touched Zim's shoulder in an attempt to stop him from further escalation. "Come on, let's go for a walk. It's late, probably nobody around, so we'll be safe. What do you say?"

Zim relented. He spat on the floor near Chuck, looked at him, and walked away with Klein.

"Listen, this is a tough situation, especially for you. And for us." Klein started. "I have heard you talk about Chuck. That he's likely to rat us out, if given a chance. Did you really mean it, Zim? Or was that just bluster because you've had a long running history with him?"

"Ed, I admit that's it's hard to tell sometimes with me. Trust me when I tell you, straight up, he will report us. He might," Zim stopped to make sure his words were precise, "He might also report Katrina for aiding and abetting us. Things have been strained between them. He's more interested in his career and social credits than her. Always has been. Just getting worse over the years. And, his affair, that's another thing too. They've reconciled, at least enough to keep the twins out of it, but he's a louse. A rat. A scoundrel."

"But . . .?"

"But," Zim sighed, "Yeah, you're good, Ed. But, she loves him. And isn't that rich too? Ain't that the thing?"

"Sometimes we humans try to justify away reality. We make up a narrative to fit what we wished would be rather than what is. You understand?"

"Yes." Zim was listening, yet he seemed so far away. He was layers deep into his internal turmoil. There was not a clear right or acceptable answer, only two bad answers.

"You're our team's leader, Zim. We respect you. We'll accept whatever you decide. The simple question seems to be whether this is an acceptable risk. If it is, we'll take steps to further minimize the risk and move on. If it isn't, then we'll do what's needed there too. Nobody's in a better position to make this decision. Got it?"

"Yep. Got it. Let's go back. I know what we need to do."

Zim and Klein entered the storage unit. They were the only ones there. Chuck was gone. Zach and Hannah were gone too.

"What the hell? Where are they?"

The door opened. Zach and Hannah entered.

Zim grabbed Zach, "Where is he? Where's Chuck? What'd you do with him? Huh? Huh?" Zach looked at Zim, expressionless.

"He's gone," said Zach.

"Gone? Gone? What the hell does *he's gone* mean?" Zim, although much smaller than Zach, was right up into Zach's grill.

"Dead."

In an instant Zim took a swing at Zach. Zach avoided the punch and backed up. Zim tried again, this time, he caught a glancing blow. Zach was uninjured and spun around to restrain Zim from behind.

"I'm going to kill you! You had no right! That was Katrina's husband. I'm going to kill you!"

"Then kill me," said Hannah flatly. Her words stopped Zim from struggling. Zach still held on, just in case.

"What?"

"Then kill me, Zim." Hannah moved toward Zim. "I ordered it. That's right. I ordered it. It's done. It's for the best. We gagged him, took him to the river, and killed him. Dumped him in the river. By the time he's found, we'll be long gone. We'll clean up here and move out. We'll find another place to hunker down until it's go time. Zim, look at me."

Zim couldn't. How could she? How could they? It was his call. His call.

"Zim, you were conflicted here. We saw it. We're down a team already. He was one of *them*. He would've reported us *and* your cousin, you know that."

Zim was still looking down. Hannah approached and gently touched his chin to lift it. Tears were streaming down Zim's face.

"I know this is hard. Very hard. We did it for the mission, sure. We did it for Katrina too. We had to; you know that."

Zim struggled a bit. "Let him go," directed Hannah.

Zach let go. Zim stumbled and fell to his knees, hands covering his face. Hannah got on the floor very close to him. She hugged his shoulder. Zim turned into her and embraced her while sobbing.

"Zim," she whispered in his ear, "I did this for you. You have a clean conscience. You are clean. I know what you would've done. You have a clean conscience, Zim."

Zim wiped his face. "Okay, what's done is done. Let's get ready to move out. Clean up in here first. I'm going to get some fresh air. Be back shortly."

Zim stepped outside. He took several deep breaths while he walked around the corner. He dropped to his knees and proceeded to retch his guts out.

Chapter LX

Shontae Lewis studied the plan over and over again. Her eyes were bloodshot. She hadn't slept but a few hours over the past several days. How could she? She tried to consider every possible *what if* scenario, and how she and her team would or could overcome each challenge. She felt a weighty responsibility for her forces, not only in the Front Range but spread throughout the province.

The pain associated with the massacre at Pryor, Oklahoma, was still fresh. She led twenty-two patriots to their death, right into a trap. She should've seen it coming, she thought. The Reso was awaiting them. The Legacy used Shontae's zeal and ambition against her. Shontae and her team were itching for a fight. What they got was a slaughter. She swore never to suffer that kind of carnage or anguish ever again. So, she prepared.

While Shontae studied quietly, Mitch sat silent as well. He thought about some of the same things she did. In addition, he thought about how brave she was and how much he admired her. She showed exceptional bravery for having pulled three injured warriors from the Pryor ambush to safety. Two ultimately didn't survive. He did. He owed her his life.

Mitch had an additional thought. If, somehow, if, they survived, and the world could somehow change for the better, how he would love nothing more than to settle down back at Pine

Ridge and grow a family with Shontae. There was a long list of things he wanted to do as a husband, father, and community advocate; to coach the kids, especially at basketball, to teach his native language to their children and others who were interested, to share their passion for their respective cultural backgrounds while also instilling in their children a profound love for this once great country—a country that they could make exceptional once more, and to preach, preach the Word. He had it all mapped out. He just hadn't shared his other plans with Shontae yet.

Shontae caught Mitch looking at her. "What?" she said softly.

"Later," he responded.

That response was good enough for them both. They were interrupted by a young member of their squad.

"Ma'am. Sir."

"Yes, go ahead, Gorostiza."

"Both Legacy and CCP comms suggest troop movement into this region. They are mustering now. In Legacy City."

"CCP comms too?" asked Shontae.

"Ma'am, yes. Apparently Chinese troops have arrived in Legacy City. Unsure about numbers."

"Anything else?" asked Shontae.

"Yes, one thing. We have intercepted Reso chatter indicating that they neutralized one of our cells in Illinois. Four dead. No survivors. No way to confirm this news quickly on our end without risking our location and other cells."

"Anything else?"

"No, ma'am."

"Thank you, Gorostiza. You're excused."

"Ma'am. Sir." Gorostiza left the two to consider the impact of the news.

Shontae turned to Mitch. "Assessment?"

Mitch thought for a moment before speaking. "The Chinese troops are here to neutralize us. The Legacy won't use Reso forces to engage in political genocide. The CCP has a history of this. The Legacy is serious about wiping us out. They've had enough. They want to crush dissent entirely, once and for all."

"Does that change our plans?"

"No. We go forward. Our plans are solid. We planned for some redundancies in case of losses. Our timing could've been better if we were at go-time now. We'll hold tight for the next," he looked at his PCD, "fourteen hours, per plans."

"Agreed. I'm concerned about the Chicago team. If they lost Aquino, we've got Zim as next in command."

"Yes. Zim's got a strong team with him. Hannah, Zach, and Ed. They'll help Zim pull it together. We don't know if any team has been lost and, if so, whether Aquino was involved."

"My intuition is telling me that we'll need Zim and his team to come up strong."

Mitch nodded in agreement. He knew to trust Shontae's intuition. After all, it was her intuition to reshuffle teams to surround Zim with those three.

Chapter LXI

Three stories above Che Bakery, the apartment had an impressive view of *Avenida de la Victoria* and the gargantuan regime buildings across the street. The flat was clean and tidy. One bedroom with an en suite bathroom, shared living area with kitchenette, and a half bathroom, which was a luxurious extra. The girls thought it was a cool adventure to have a sleepover together.

Jeannie, Anjali, and their girls were to stay in the flat until other plans could be made to get them safely out of Legacy City and placed in a new environment. The Gies family possessed all four floors straight up from their bakery. The second floor was devoted to storage. The third floor was the Gies' family living space. The fourth floor was developed into four separate flats, all like the one occupied by Jeannie and the group. All four flats were occupied. The flats were not designed for a long-term stay. They were organized for very short-term way stations as people were processed out throughout the province.

The rules were simple. Occupants on the fourth floor were to stay put and stay quiet. Also, stay away from windows and absolutely no lights at night. The Gies family would visit twice per day to deliver food and see if anything else was needed. Any slip-up could cause serious trouble. Children were a wildcard. Young children even more so.

The windows were adorned with semi-sheer honeycomb blinds allowing for daylight. As the sun was setting, occupants were required to pull down the blackout shades. The only light that could be on at night was a small light used in the en suite. It was almost impossible for any light to get from the en suite, through the bedroom, and out past the blackout shades.

There were plenty of books for young and old readers. Lots of paper, pens, and crayons too. Other than that, resting, sleeping, and talking at a low volume were the norm. Jeannie and Anjali made it a game for the girls to see who could be the quietest each hour. The winner would receive some treat or other special surprise.

"I've been thinking," said Anjali. The girls were in the bedroom having a picture-drawing contest, so the adults finally had a few minutes to themselves.

"About what?" Jeannie asked as she looked out the partially shaded window.

"The CCP officer said that Legacy Coins were not deactivated and that they were never intended to be. Right?"

"Yep, that's what he said. I don't know if it's true, though."

"Let's assume for the sake of argument that it is true; doesn't it all fit together then? Having control of Legacy Coins gives ultimate power to whomever has them?"

"It does."

"When you presented Legacy Coins, did you have some type of registration procedure you'd have to follow?"

"Sort of, we'd scan in a coin before we presented it. We'd also scan in the mother's fingerprints. It was described to us in training as an activation process as each coin was unique to each fetus."

"So, it was unique to each fetus, and the mother or parents controlled the fate of that fetus until birth, correct?"

"Yes."

"I know about the collection points. The Legacy Coin depositories throughout the province. What I don't know is what the steps are if a Legacy Coin was deposited, what happened next, if you know?"

"Here's what we were taught. When a Legacy Coin was deposited, it was collected and then forwarded to the master coin collection center for that subregion. Depositories, I think that's what they're called. There are, or were, eleven or twelve as my memory recalls. The coins were then scanned and cross-referenced against the fetus. It was then catalogued and mechanically filed in the appropriate place. Cataloguing was key. It helped to guarantee that all coins could be properly traced. There was also a cooling off period of three days to allow for recovery of a coin in the event of theft or mistaken deposit."

"How did they, I'm guessing trainers from Global Genomics, describe the deactivation process?"

"Once the baby was delivered, the mother would give the attending physician her Legacy Coin, and it would be deactivated once a scanner on the bottom of the Legacy Coin box read and confirmed the mother's fingerprint. The coin would illuminate, thereby indicating that the coin was deactivated. The family could keep the coin and box as a token, or they could leave it with us. Apparently, the deactivation would be done at the computer level. Not sure who kept those records, The Legacy or Global Genomics."

"Ever hear of or know of anyone who put a Legacy Coin in a deposit box for a person who was already born?"

"Never. That's why what Disung said was so confusing to me. You'd think we'd know about that kind of glitch in the system if there was a glitch like that. You'd think that even some teenagers horsing around would've figured it out . . . maybe at their peril or death."

"Either way, there is a connection between the implant, the Legacy Coin, and data. See where I'm going?" Anjali smiled. She could've been a lawyer, Jeannie thought, given how her friend took her each step through the process.

"Brilliant! Yes! I see what you did there. Great thinking, A!"

"Thanks. Now, let's think about how we invite ourselves to the computer party."

There was a quick knock and the sound of beep unlocking the door. It was Margot Gies.

"How about some soothing chicken soup and fresh bread tonight. Good?"

"Wonderful, and thank you, Mrs. Gies."

"Call me Margot, please. And need anything else?"

Jeannie looked at Anjali, then back at Margot, "Well, Margot, as a matter of fact, if it isn't *too* much trouble . . ."

Chapter LXII

Some days are better than others, he thought. After a successive string of bad ones, Stefan was in an exceptionally good mood. Today was a good day, mostly because he was left alone to crunch his numbers without interference. There were no political lenses demanded to be placed atop his mathematics and analyses. Stefan understood how his work was being bastardized by the powers above him. He had concerns about the fudged numbers presented to The Legacy. Given the .93 submission, the only way to hit the required 1.0 ratio was to make an adjustment to the denominator, meaning there needed to be fewer people. Yet, every time he started to think about these ratios, the mantra would grow and grow inside his brain. He learned that the only way to turn it off was to think of something he loved and gave him joy—his family.

Stefan thought to make a quick stop on his walk home to pick up something special for his girls, all three of them. He enjoyed surprising them. He'd been so distant and difficult lately. He couldn't explain it. It would just come over him. It was as if he was under the control of something or someone. He tried to communicate with Anjali about how distressed he was without using words. He had concerns. When he was being held in B5, he gave himself a 99.98 percent probability of not returning home. Yet, he did. He beat the odds, but did he?

He couldn't recall every moment he spent in B5. He was sleep-deprived, questioned, and not tortured, at least not that he recalled. He did receive at least two injections. He lost track of time. He lost track of his senses. He lost hope. But, there he was, still enjoying life and appreciating just how precious and fragile life can be.

He opened the door. A bell announced his arrival. "Welcome," said the man at the counter.

"Good evening, Frank. How are you this evening?"

"Good evening, Doctor Ertz. What can I get for you this evening?"

"How about one piece of *Apfelstrudel*, one cherry strudel," Stefan paused as he looked at what was left in the display case after a long day of customers stopping at the bakery, "Oh my goodness, you have plum cake, yes, that last piece of *Pflaumenkuchen*. My wife absolutely loves plum cake. We used to save our money to splurge and buy one piece to share together when we were young and poor living in Zürich. Those were wonderful times."

Frank smiled gently. His eyes were kind. "Will there be anything else?" Frank asked.

"No, I think not. Although I'm half-tempted to get a few of those croissants there. They go great with coffee. Is it marzipan? Oh, never mind, that's enough. I'll just share a little bit of all three with my three lovely ladies at home. That'll be all, thank you, Frank."

Frank wrapped the desserts while Stefan scanned his PCD for payment. Frank handed the box to Stefan. "Here you are, Dr. Ertz."

"Thank you, Frank. Have a nice evening. And give my best to Margot, please."

Frank just smiled and bowed ever so slightly. He couldn't do anything more than that. He knew what this man was going to encounter that evening. Frank's heart hurt but not as much as his customer's heart would be hurting when he arrived home. Frank prepared to close the store for the night. He locked the door, then leaned back against it, and closed his eyes. As he did, he said a silent prayer.

Chapter LXIII

The battery of tests were familiar. Nothing invasive, save for several blood draws. Although taking actual blood had been replaced in many healthcare facilities by scanning, the doctors at the Legacy City Recovery Center preferred actual blood draws to run tests. "Much more accurate," they would say before having their patients stuck with needles.

Simon Bowles was delighted and relieved to be closer to his daughter. It buoyed his spirits. His health had been poor for several years. He suffered from many ailments: hypertension, heart arrhythmia, diabetes, stomach pains, and most perplexing of all, infrequent, sudden onset of mild paralysis. He also suffered from chronic muscle pain. His previous physicians had ruled out several diseases as the cause of his afflictions, including muscular dystrophy, Guillain-Barré syndrome, multiple sclerosis, and amyotrophic lateral sclerosis. There was no evidence of his having suffered a stroke. Simon Bowles was a puzzling case study.

When he was in London, Simon noticed a real need for the "extraordinary people," as he called them, to have pastoral care. These were the downtrodden, working class, and families who had lost loved ones in WWIII or from the multiple purges that were directed by the North Europe Province's ruling regime. It was on his heart to care for them. In so doing, he simultaneously neglected to care for himself and allowed his health to deteriorate.

His love for others and abundantly positive personality was like a warm blanket enveloping the frozen and broken. His brand of caring for those who needed someone to appreciate them, smile at them, laugh and cry with them, and love them without judgment caught on. It was like a whirlwind that started in London and then swept over the province as word of his ministry spread throughout the European provinces and beyond.

North Europe Province's regime, named The Guardians, had a problem. Simon's ministry gave the people something that their rulers wanted to remove from their beings, hope. The Guardians considered neutralizing Simon. They consulted with other provincial regimes and, of course, the CCP. To kill Simon would lead to potential uprisings and unrest at a global level. That would not do. So, they devised another plan.

Simon and his new bride, Dianne Hutchinson, whom he met while visiting extended family in Cheshire, were *released* into the custody of The Legacy. The planned regime-created narrative was the Bowles wanted to be closer to Simon's daughter in North America Province. However, there was no intent to ever make that happen. Nor was there any intent to solve or resolve Simon's many health problems. Simon and Dianne were sent to Sunny Days Sanitarium in the Coachella Valley. It was less sanitarium than prison. There they lived under strict control, with some marginal medical care. The plan was to make him weaker, more feeble, and begin the process of reprogramming him. If they could turn him, his movement might dissipate, perhaps even cease to exist. It grew through the power of his personality, strength of his words, and depth of his compassion.

The CCP was most concerned about his invoking the words of Mother Teresa, including, "Small things done with great love will change the world." The Chinese had no interest in changing the world the way Simon and his devotees desired. It was a danger to their global hegemony.

The CCP and provincial leaders had reason to be fearful. Individually, neither Simon nor any of his followers could accomplish much of anything. But, as Mother Teresa reminded her devotees, "together we can do great things." And that concerned all regimes, near and far.

Simon never spoke ill of any regime. Simon never spoke ill of the CCP. He focused on human potential, something shared and something greater than the person's day-to-day existence, something immortal. The CCP needed to make Simon impotent in the eyes of his followers. In that way, his message of hope would be made a lie. That was the plan until Hank Hatua got involved.

Hatua's relationship with Cassandra Bowles disrupted the CCP's plan for the time being. Hatua was too powerful with too many resources, as well as future important plans to advance the CCP's stranglehold on the globe, that they could play the waiting game. The Chinese had always taken that approach. Take the long view. That's how they ascended into the preeminent global power position. Patience indeed was a virtue. They planned to be virtuous with one of their best allies—at least for now.

Each day, regime leaders came and went to Legacy City Recovery Center for treatment. Medical care at the center was rationed for elites with the highest level of social credits. Yet,

Simon was different. They had never treated someone like him before, not because he wasn't in regime leadership or had no social standing or credits to speak of. That wasn't it. It was something unique. Simon Bowles was someone who smiled constantly, inspired *them*, and radiated goodness, hope, and love, no matter the discomfort and pain he was experiencing.

Simon Bowles was an extraordinary patient. Word spread among the Recovery Center staff that he was being treated there. Soon, his room became a must-see experience. He'd invite people to join him in his room for a chat if they felt brave enough to do so without having a specific care task to accomplish. There were risks involved, but that didn't seem to stop the parade of people. It was as if the strongest magnet possible was stashed in his room. And it turned out he was that magnet.

They came to see him. They came to hear him. They came to be touched by him. They came to be cured by him. They came to be loved by him. They came for Simon Bowles, founder, and spiritual leader of *Leon y Cordero*.

Chapter LXIV

A vintage KC-46 Pegasus refueling tanker plane was taken from the aircraft graveyard in the Mojave Desert years earlier. It was no ordinary Pegasus. This version was the first generation to include an autonomous flight option. No pilot needed. *Molon Labe* kept its prized possession hidden in the desert outside Las Vegas while its engineers worked to reconfigure the onboard tech systems to provide better operations and security. The Pegasus was also rehabilitated, restored to its proud heritage. The work was a labor of patriotism. *Molon Labe* would likely have only one shot at using this bird, and it knew it had better make that shot count.

Mitch had studied terrain, angles, obstructions, and weak points. Between the sparsely populated town of Dillon and The Legacy's Great Divide Tunnel's west entrance, Mitch picked what he thought was the perfect spot for targeting. Approximately two miles west from the tunnel's west entrance were a series of connections between steel and composite materials. These were the weakest joinder spots and more easily breached. It posed some challenges, most especially a narrow gorge running along the river adjacent to the Hyperloop track. Mitch had imagined the assault over and over. He used visual imagery to ready himself. He also practiced calming breathing techniques. A shaky hand or unsteady mind could doom the mission.

Shontae and Mitch spied their target from atop one of the nearby mountain ridges. Even given advanced technology, Mitch did not want the mountains to obstruct his signal controlling the giant plane loaded with over 100,000 kilos of fuel. The Pegasus had an ignition payload installed, which was also synched with Mitch's master controller. His plan considered the potential that the fuel available to them might include carbon polymer additives, making the fuel less likely to mist and ignite. Nothing was left to chance, so the plan included a pre-crash detonation and explosion designed to create sufficient mist and fireball immediately before impact.

Chinese troops were transiting via Hyperloop pods from Legacy City to Denver, one pod after another full of foreign troops and gear. In all, over five hundred of the CCP's most specialized and well-trained were onboard pods of thirty to thirty-five crammed in without seats. The seats were removed to accommodate more troops and gear.

Mitch had no trouble managing Pegasus' takeoff from a very long private airstrip in the desert near Mesquite. The flight plan called for a heading along the north rim of the Grand Canyon, then a left turn above Mesa Verde, heading north until taking a gradual right turn, maintaining its position south of Grand Junction, Glenwood Springs, and Vail. Pegasus would begin its descent and glide north of the Dillon Reservoir before winding its way into a final target position while aligning quasi-parallel with Straight Creek.

Pegasus was outfitted with stealth technology to limit its aerial footprint as much as possible. *Molon Labe* team members also flooded The Legacy's air control system with false positives and scrambling interference techniques. It was hoped that by the time Pegasus' flight was found out, if it was found out, it'd be too late.

Mitch maneuvered the aircraft expertly. It was a good day for flying with little wind and good visibility. He saw a reflection in the sky. With the sun about to set, he tried his best to keep Pegasus in the sun as much as possible. In that way, he could gain an additional element of surprise for those looking in that direction.

"Take cover!" Mitch shouted to Shontae. She immediately ran behind the tree line as he slowly made his way in this same direction while trying to keep steady to not affect Pegasus' course. Mitch noticed several reflections in the sky not far from Pegasus. At the same time, he heard rumblings from the Hyperloop as pods went screaming by at over 500 miles per hour. As the reflections got closer, he adjusted his goggles to provide better vision into the glare as well as increase the distance.

He could see Pegasus trailing behind multiple Airborne Assist Remotes, or AARs. There were easily a dozen of them. AARs were unmanned drones assigned to cover troop transports and other special missions. They were outfitted with weapons systems and special cameras. One operator flew one AAR. Mitch was surprised to see that the AARs seemed to be providing cover for the Hyperloop transport but had not yet detected the flying fuel can behind them. The sun's relative location, combined with stealth protection, seemed to be working. Mitch just needed a few more minutes.

The sound of the pods mixed with the AARs made for a surreal acoustic background to Mitch's work. Both he and Shontae had taken cover and put a heat protective covering over them in case the AARs were equipped with heat sensors—which they likely were. Mitch was flying exclusively via his instruments. He'd have to fly the last few miles that way. All of his training and visualization work now kicked in at its highest level. He calmed himself, decreased his heart rate, and focused on just one thing, hitting the target.

One minute until impact. Pegasus was on final approach to the target. The sound from the KC-46 in the canyon was deafening. Mitch got out from under the cover. He needed and wanted to see the exact moment of impact. He readied the detonator.

"Spotted! Pegs has been spotted!" shouted Shontae.

A handful of AARs had broken off from their line and were now headed toward Pegasus. There wasn't much room in the canyon for taking evasive measures. Pegasus was in the zone of no return. *Just keep the heading,* Mitch said to himself. *Stay steady. Steady.* It was only a brief moment until they would fire, or would they? Pegasus was already so low and so close to target that they could do *Molon Labe*'s work for them. It was too late. The AARs, with CCP markings, froze for a moment. They then set off as fast as they could, away from the imminent impact. There was nothing the pods below could do. Mitch had a clear shot at the target. Detonation in three, two, one.

Both Shontae and Mitch had been in war. They had heard munitions exploding. There was nothing even close to what they experienced when Pegasus exploded five seconds before impacting the targeted Hyperloop connections. They saw the blindingly bright fireball. A split second later, a deafening explosion rocked their ears and knocked them down. Another burst of light and further explosion followed it. Neither one could hear the other. They both had protective eyewear and noise reduction headsets on anticipating the blast. They weren't prepared for the force of it all. There was nowhere for the energy to go other than through the tunnel and up the canyon and through their bodies.

What was left at the impact site was akin to what damage a series of bunker busters would leave behind. The force destroyed all signs of the Hyperloop for several miles. The entrance to the tunnel was obliterated. The west side tunnel was covered in debris. No doubt the east side was significantly damaged as well. Shontae deployed a series of spotters and drones throughout the region along the Hyperloop track to conduct damage assessments and collect intel on enemy movements post-attack. They were also to be used as decoys, if needed.

Smoke billowed from the Hyperloop track. Shrapnel and debris were everywhere. Bodies too. Mitch's plan led by Shontae and her team looked like a complete success.

Shontae and Mitch ran as fast as they could through the dense forest at altitude. Their escape route was pre-planned, yet in the fog of war, even the best laid plans could become a bit scrambled.

Soldiers streamed out of the Hyperloop, further to the west and miles before the impact zone. They kept coming and coming, like ants running out of an ant hill. Some ablaze. Some missing limbs. Others in a stupor. The few who weren't gravely injured spread out in all directions in search of something, anything that could have visited this devastating harm on them.

Chapter LXV

"That's impossible! They don't have that kind of capability! What? No. No, I haven't. Compile the preliminary assessment immediately. No, I don't care. Do it! Now!"

Berko was enraged. How could *Molon Labe* pull off something of this magnitude? It just couldn't be.

Everett interrupted his thought. "Sir, live video of the site is available now, and prelim damage report coming through forthwith." Everett left as soon as he said the last word.

Berko couldn't believe his eyes. He was watching live shots from several drones showing the destruction around the tunnel's west side. There was nothing left to identify the location as a tunnel, Hyperloop track, or anything else for that matter. He switched camera options to review the east side. There was extensive damage but not as severe as on the west side. There were no cameras available inside the tunnel. It didn't matter. Nothing could have survived inside. The tunnel likely collapsed throughout.

"Sir, confidential early assessment." As soon as Berko took the report, Everett left. He knew better than to stay one second longer than was absolutely needed. Berko reviewed the report. Hyperloop, out of commission indefinitely. Over 200 CCP troops dead, another 50 plus missing, and over 60 injured. Most killed at the impact site. Some killed in tunnel collapse. Others killed due to Hyperloop pressure breach. Rescue and recovery operation underway.

"Get me Hatua!"

Berko was so angry he didn't even know where to start. Where was his intel team? Where were his Reso undercover agents? Why was this allowed to happen? It clearly took many people, resources, and time. How was this plot not discovered?

"Sir, Mr. Hatua is waiting."

"What the hell, Hank? What do *you* mean what do I mean. The terrorist attack on the Hyperloop. I don't care if you are celebrating your wedding. You told me the Hyperloop was impenetrable. Impenetrable. Guess what, Hank? Not true. You failed, Hank. You failed The Legacy. You failed me!" Berko disconnected the communication.

"Get me Bowles!"

How could Hatua be so stupid, Berko thought. His mind was shrieking at him. He had no way at this point to calm down. This was bad. Very bad. Bad for The Legacy and its relations with China. Bad for him and his relations with China . . . and his greater plans.

"Sir, Bowles is waiting."

"Cassandra, I understand you are celebrating your wedding. The Legacy needs you and your team in here as soon as possible. Yes, it's about the attack near Denver. See you soon."

How could she marry that clown? He screwed up everything. Everything. Incompetent daddy's boy.

"Get me Reso."

Of all the things that could happen, the timing couldn't be worse. Who tipped them off? Who knew?

"Sir, Reso is waiting."

"This is Berko. Redeploy as many assets as possible to the Rocky Mountain region. Set up a grid and comb the area for *Molon Labe* members and sympathizers. When in doubt, consider them hostile. They must still be in the area. Get them, alive preferably, and bring them to B5. Yes, whatever it takes. You have The Legacy's full authority and support. All available personnel and materials. I want them, and I want them here. Got it?"

"Sir, General Zhang is waiting."

"Everett, can't you see I'm busy!" Berko was losing his cool. "Tell the general that I'll get back when I can."

"Um, sir, the General's right here."

General Zhang entered Berko's office. She closed the door behind her.

Chapter LXVI

Klein and the others were scrambling to put on technical uniforms and related gear provided to them as they jumped into the back of a secure transport. It looked like a typical Reso transport. There was one small light to help them see. The uniforms were *exact* replicas of current Reso uniforms. They were manufactured by the same company that made Reso uniforms. The company apparently had a shrinkage problem recently, Klein mused to himself.

They had heard about the successful *Molon Labe* attack west of Denver, a significant number of Chinese troops killed, missing, and wounded. The western Hyperloop was all but destroyed. *Wow,* thought Klein, *they really did it. They pulled it off.* And Chinese troops. If it wasn't a full-on war before, it was surely on at this point.

They met up with the other groups and were now consolidated as one. Aquino's group didn't make it, as they suspected. They had a brief remembrance of her and the others on her team, then boarded their transport to Chicago's financial district.

With Aquino gone, Zim assumed command. He reviewed their orders, which were clear to all. Use their cover as supplemental Reso forces assigned to the Chicago Legacy Coin Depository as a result of the recent terrorist attack to gain access to the former Federal Reserve Bank of Chicago. Once inside, they were to use whatever means necessary to repatriate or destroy the Legacy Coins contained in the subterranean vaults. Timing was critical. *Molon Labe* forces were staged and ready to act on the same orders at the same time throughout the province, descending upon all twelve former Fed Districts and their secure vaults.

"Any questions?" asked Zim of the group.

One hand went up. It was Cory from Huntsville. "Sir, will we ever be authorized to use our arms?"

"Yes," Zim replied followed by a brief pause. "And your legs. Brains would be a good idea too," said Zim. He had at least a portion of his sense of humor back. Klein thought it was an excellent sign that Zim was back in the battle. People chuckled. They needed a light moment to cut the tension. Zim continued, "Look, you all know the rules of engagement here. Unless completely backed into a corner from which there is no other way out, stand down. We are here to provide supplemental security to the base security apparatus already in place. We are *with them* in this case, not against them. Unless. You know the rest."

"Thank you, sir," said Cory.

"Good question, Cory. Any other questions?"

"Yes, I have a question." It was Hannah. She and Zim had not spoken since the events of two nights prior. "After we are successful," she paused to let that point sink in, "may we go for a few rounds of Old Style?"

Zim looked at her. He knew he had to let it go. She was with him. For him. For their mission. Zim responded flatly, "No. That's not acceptable, Hannah." She wasn't sure she should've engaged him like that. It might've been a bad call. Zim continued, "Team, look at that patriot there." He pointed to Hannah. "She's got things all wrong," Zim said as a twinkle appeared in his eyes, and a smile started to crack his face. "A few will not do. It'll be four or more rounds. Four or more!" Zim looked at Hannah, and she at him. They were good to go. The team broke into a chant of "Four or more!"

Zim held up his hand to stop the chanting. "We're crossing over the river and approaching our target. We're trained. We're briefed. We're ready. Cover up." They all pulled down their face coverings. Reso technical teams used face coverings to avoid identification by those in the communities in which they served. It allowed anonymity for the dirty work they did for The Legacy.

The transport came to a halt. Zim quickly said, "Remember the meet-up point. Let's get this done."

The troops piled out, looking exactly like any other Reso squad. They immediately formed a perimeter as Zim marched straight up to the security checkpoint booth. Zim barked out an order to have four of his charges rotate from security booth to outside security. "Show force to anyone who might get ideas," he said gruffly. Zim approached the two security guards at the booth.

"As requested, we're here now. Who's your commanding officer?"

"That'd be Sergeant Arnaud. He's inside."

Zim turned to his team, "Let's go then. You four, stay here with the private. I want boots moving around the block. Change up timing and rotate. But movement is key. Eyes peeled. Got it?"

"Sir, yes, sir!" the four said in unison.

"Sir, I beg your pardon, may I please see your ID and orders?" the private asked.

"Well done, private. Here." Zim handed what he requested. Everything was in order. The private waved them in, including their transport.

Zim and seven others proceeded down the ramp and inside the building. Zim was saluted as they passed another checkpoint. "Stairs, split up!" Zim commanded as they broke into two groups of four and headed down stairways on the north and south side to the subbasement level. The two groups arrived there at about the same time.

"Where's Sergeant Arnaud?" Zim said gruffly.

"I'm Arnaud."

"Sir, I'm Arnaud, sir." Zim said as he got up into Arnaud's face.

"Sir, I'm Arnaud, sir."

"Better. Sergeant, as you know, there's been an attack against The Legacy outside of Denver. Terrorist scum have killed some of our Chinese brothers. We're under orders to help secure critical regime facilities. This is one of them. I'm in command now. How many personnel do I have at my disposal?"

Zim is extraordinary, thought Klein. *My goodness, in another day, he could've been an actor.*

Arnaud was caught off guard. Zim was aggressive and kept the sergeant's mind occupied. Arnaud responded, "Sir, there are a total of eight of us."

"Eight? Eight? No wonder they sent us here. What's your current deployment of those assets and protection strategy?"

Arnaud was clearly on the defensive, yet he mustered enough courage to push back. "Major, with respect, I wasn't informed of your team's arrival. I'd like to confirm with my commanding officer that we should receive your support."

"The order came directly from General Berko himself. I have the orders here," Zim flashed the orders so Arnaud could see them, but Zim did not hand them over. "If you have any questions, Sergeant, I suggest you perhaps might like to contact General Berko himself. I'm sure he'd be very pleased to hear from you at this hour given what we're facing. Please, go right ahead. I'll wait."

"The papers look in order, Sir." The sergeant blinked, exactly as Zim planned for and could have predicted. Just the mention of Berko's name had the same reaction in most anyone. "We're very pleased to accept your assistance in securing this facility. We have a pair each located on the rooftop, at the security gate, at the main level, and down here."

"And protection strategy?"

"Take incremental steps to avoid a breach. Call in reinforcements as needed."

"Open up comms to your team, I want to address them directly."

"Yes, Sir. Comms line open, Sir."

"Brothers and Sisters, this is Major Vonk. I expect you saw me and my team upon arrival. We have orders to provide supplemental protective force to guarantee this building and its contents are secure, especially against any terrorist activity. You all know of the tragedy—the *fugazi*—outside Denver. Be assured, the terrorist scum will pay. Oh, yes, they will pay. In the meantime, we are adding my team to the existing protection force. My team will be relieving you from your posts shortly so I may personally meet with you and review our enhanced security plan. The balloon has gone up. Don't know where. But we, WE, will be prepared for anything. I will conduct this briefing once. When relieved, get down to the subbasement level ASAP. Post-briefing, you will receive your new assignments and issued additional gear. Thanks be to The Legacy. That is all."

Arnaud closed the open comms line. "Sir, comms closed."

"Thank you, Sergeant." Zim turned to his team, pointing as he went down the line. "You two, roof. You two, main level.

Relieve and establish comms on new secure channel. Go." The four moved quickly and left.

Klein, Hannah, and Zach were still with Zim. Zim pointed to Klein and Zach, "You two, sitrep this level. Go." Klein and Zach left immediately.

Arnaud's team arrived within five minutes after having been relieved of their posts. They gathered around Zim.

Zim addressed the group. "Lieutenant Olsen here," Zim said, referring to Hannah, "will be trading out your comms pieces for our new secure ones. We have intel that the ML pukewads have access to our comms and are monitoring at will." Hannah went through the group, took their existing comms unit and earpieces, and exchanged them out for the new ones.

"Next, the lieutenant will give you a new bang-bang. You'll love it!" Zim said with emphasis. "Lieutenant Olsen will secure your old pieces, so you don't get dinged." Hannah exchanged their weapons for the new ones.

"Saweeeet!" exclaimed one of Arnaud's team as he looked at his new sidearm.

"Now, about our new enhanced security plan," Zim said as he looked at Klein and Zach who had quietly returned and were stationed at forty-five-degree angles from Arnaud's assembled team of eight.

"Hands up and against the wall!" yelled Zach in a frightening deep baritone. It was always a bit unnerving when Zach spoke, as he did it so infrequently. Zach and Klein had their weapons trained on Arnaud's team.

Zim pivoted away to his left to move out of the way. Once he did, there was a clear path to the wall.

"Against. The. Wall. Now!" Zach ordered again.

"Do it," Arnaud said.

The man who was admiring his new sidearm drew it and pointed it at Hannah. "I'll shoot her. I swear, I will."

Zim looked at him and started walking toward him with his hand out, as if requesting the handgun.

"Stop right there, Major, or I'll shoot." Zim smirked. *He still thinks I'm a Major, that's cute,* Zim thought.

"Go ahead. Shoot. Shoot her now," Zim said as he continued his walk toward the man.

"Last warning. Stop! Stop! I'll shoot, I swear I'll shoot!"

"You keep saying that. Well, we're waiting."

Sweat was pouring down the man's face. The man pulled the trigger. Nothing. He pulled it again. Nothing.

Hannah, who had not broken a sweat the entire time, took the sidearm from the man. "Dummy," she said calmly.

"Dummy, dummy," said Zim gleefully. He turned to the others who were facing the wall with their hands up. "Now, if any of you move, we'll just shoot you all. Got it?"

With weapons trained on the eight, Zim and Hannah made fast work of securing their captives' hands behind them with zip ties. They blindfolded each of them, gagged them, and locked them in four separate vaults, two apiece.

The four pulled their hoods off. Klein looked at Zim, "I must say, very impressive young man. Very impressive."

"Thanks, but wait," replied Zim, who started to talk in a sing-song sort of way. "You just ain't seen nothin' yet!" He unzipped two bags filled with plastic explosives. "Here's something you're never gonna forget. Guaranteed to blow your mind . . . anytime!"

Klein looked at the time. "We have exactly fifty-seven minutes."

CHAPTER LXVII

Anjali was focused. She had the skills. She hoped that the hardware Margot Gies provided her would do the trick. The computer she was given was old. Margot insisted that it was untraceable and that she and others had routinely used this computer to access data sets of all kinds, just not the kind that Anjali and Jeannie were after.

"Mommy," said a sleepy voice coming out from the bedroom. It was Juli. "I can't sleep."

"Oh, honey," said Jeannie softly and sweetly, "come here."

Juli walked toward her mother's outstretched arms with her little eyes almost fully shut. Jeannie picked her up and took her to the small sofa away from Anjali so as not to disturb her work.

"Honey, just lie here with Mommy. I'll tell you a story, okay?"

Juli burrowed into her mother like she was a little joey trying to find its way into its kangaroo mama's pouch. Jeannie rubbed her daughter's back and then slowly and lightly caressed the area between her eyes and across her forehead. Juli laid peacefully with her eyes closed.

"Mommy," Juli said faintly, "tell me a story about Daddy."

Jeannie understood. She was feeling it too. It was surprising to her that all four girls weren't on her lap. Anji too, she thought. They were all going through some heady and heartbreaking changes.

Jeannie said softly, "Okay, I'll tell you a story about your Daddy. When you were still in Mommy's belly, you kept kicking and punching me. Your Daddy would be so amused to see Mommy's belly move around and the skin extend out when you were fighting for more room or just exercising. Anyway, your Daddy was so amused because you were so active. Your sister punched and kicked too when she was in Mommy's belly, but nothing like you. Not even close. You were such a little warrior. A fighter. That's why Daddy liked to call you, *mi pequeña peleona*, my little scrapper. Daddy was always so proud of you. Always fighting to learn, to help others, to make right what was wrong, even fighting to defend your big sister. You are and will always be loved, *pequeña peleona*." Juli was breathing deeply. She had a contented look on her face. She was fast asleep.

Anjali carefully walked over to the sofa to avoid disturbing the little one. She stood looking at the two of them, especially Juli. "She's so adorable. And, yes, a scrapper too. I hope you don't mind; I heard your story. So sweet."

"Thanks. We're all going through a lot. How are you holding up?" Jeannie extended her hand as Juli slept without disruption. Anjali grabbed Jeannie's hand with hers.

"Okay, it's hard. I try not to think too much about it. I'm sure Stefan has read my letter by now. I can't imagine what he thinks of me. Hates me at the very least." Anjali had her head down, looking at the floor.

"He could never hate you." Jeannie squeezed Anjali's hand as she said, "He loves you. He always will."

"Thanks," Anjali took a deep breath then exhaled. "Okay, changing the subject. I was able to get in, but only so far."

"Tell me."

"The Legacy Coin system has a number of sophisticated security firewalls and authentication requirements built in. The bottom line is I can't get where I need to go without getting deeper into the system."

"How far do you need to get?"

"In simple terms, I need to have an all-access pass. Make sense?"

"I think so. Do you know what you need to get that pass?"

"Well, I found a pathway in. So that's good. But they have a top-level multi-pronged authentication process set-up. So, what I need is to get past the ten-digit verification, followed by an alpha-numeric symbols code, and, finally, a biometric scanner. There are techniques to crack the first two. I've even developed tools to do it using brute force, rainbow, cataclysm, and other forms of attack. When I was a grad assistant, I even taught a course on ethical hacking and counter-hacking measures. The real challenge is the retinal scanning. I can't hack that, at least not anymore. I used to be able to, but they've tightened the system."

"So, what now? What can we do?"

"It depends. If the system is locked down by The Legacy, we'll need someone in the regime with that security access. However, if the system is Global Genomics-based, we'll likewise need someone there with that level of security access."

"Sounds like a flip of the coin, either regime or GG, although we don't use coins anymore. I don't know why I used that phrase."

"You're brilliant. You just solved it!"

"I did? Of course, I did. What did I do again?"

"Flip of a coin. A Legacy Coin. Global Genomics created it, designed it, sold it, and maintains it. It must be Global Genomics. Now, who at Global Genomics can help us?"

"I have no idea. But I bet we both know someone who does." Jeannie looked at her daughter sleeping so soundly. It made her relax somewhat too. They were making progress. They just needed to move quickly. All of their lives depended on it.

"Frank said to contact him, day or night, if we needed anything. I think this is one of those times."

"Let me lay her down. I'll go downstairs and see if he's still up."

"I'll watch the kids and keep probing the system and see if anything else pops up."

Jeannie laid Juli on the bed with the other three girls. They were just a jumble of arms and legs all over, like a pile of puppies or kittens, blissfully unaware of what was going on, at least not the details and risks.

Jeannie walked down the stairs and tapped lightly on the third-floor door. Margot opened the door and invited Jeannie in.

"So sorry to disturb you. I was hoping to talk with you and Frank about something important."

"Sure, Frank's in the study. Quite the news tonight."

"What news?"

"You haven't heard? Oh, my goodness!"

They entered the study. "Jeannie, come in please. Have a seat."

Jeannie sat down. Margot said to Frank, "Frank, tell Jeannie what happened out by Denver. She hasn't heard."

Frank proceeded to fill Jeannie in on what happened at a very basic level. She was shocked.

"Something tells me this is the beginning. This was a huge masterstroke by *Molon Labe*. Given what happened to the Chinese, there will be retribution the size of which we can't even contemplate. Plus, it looks like the hardliners have been successful in their takeover of China. Everyone in North

America Province is at great risk. And it will spread from here throughout the world."

Jeannie let his words sink in. "Then our work is even more important. Let me fill you two in on what we've been doing." Jeannie explained about Anjali's hacking progress and the obstacles they've encountered.

"Hmmm," Frank said. "We're in a very tough situation. I have to give this some additional thought. If I make a connection for you, it could compromise our most helpful asset. If not, we all could be very dead very soon." He looked at his wife. "Guess it wasn't such a tough decision after all once I heard myself say it that way."

Frank said, "Contact *Baker*, confidential security."

A woman's voice was connected, "Safe for two minutes."

"I'm sending you a job applicant tomorrow morning."

"Good, I need one."

"How about two?"

"Even better, but no more. Seven a.m. sharp."

"They'll be there then."

"Good. Bye."

The communication ended. Frank turned to Jeannie. "Margot, would you mind watching the kids in the morning?"

"Would I mind? I'd be delighted. I love those girls already."

"Thanks, hon." Frank looked directly at Jeannie. "Are you sure you want to do this? Are you and Anjali up to this?"

"Yes, of course. Why are you saying it that way?"

"Because, once you cross that threshold tomorrow morning, there's no going back. I won't be able to help you."

"Frank, stop it. You're scaring the poor girl," Margot implored.

Frank responded to his wife, "She should be scared." Margot shot him a look. "Well, at least on high alert. Cautious. Very cautious." Frank turned back to Jeannie, looking at her intensely. "Because tomorrow morning, you'll be walking directly into the belly of the beast."

Chapter LXVIII

General Zhang left an indelible mark on Berko. She also left a sting. It was clear to Berko he needed to act quickly and decisively. General Zhang needed to be satisfied. China needed to be satisfied. It was a tall order to satisfy the sole global power who suffered a wholly unacceptable loss. The numbers kept trickling in. The most recent tally showed 227 dead, 32 missing, and 37 injured. Of the injured, over half were in critical condition. Of the missing, they were all presumed dead.

It was the middle of the night or middle of the morning, Berko lost track. He didn't care about the time; he knew it was dark. He hadn't left Province House. He was racing against time. He would not sleep nor rest until he had answers. He wanted those terrorists who were responsible for the carnage brought to him for his special brand of justice. He wanted the perpetrators. He wanted the accomplices. He wanted vengeance.

Province House was a hub of activity. Unlike most nights when just a handful of staff were present overnight, not including security, this night was an all-hands-on-deck situation. Even those who were not part of the security apparatus were present, if only to show support to those who had to be there.

Information kept pouring in. Double and triple-checking that information for accuracy became imperative. Berko assembled data for The Legacy's review. The last thing he needed was inaccurate data that later needed to be retracted or amended.

And he kept thinking about General Zhang. The general was direct. Operation Cleanup needed to move forward expeditiously. The first priority was to neutralize *Molon Labe* members and sympathizers. This would be the first step to regaining the trust of the CCP, especially the hardliners who were now in complete control.

Berko stood in Cassandra's doorway, staring. She felt a cold presence and looked up. She waited to a count of three before saying anything. As she looked at him, she saw a different kind of stare. Berko's well-known stare had a piercing quality to it. This time, for the first time, his stare gave her the feeling of a wounded animal. Berko was as dangerous as he had ever been.

"Send out comms on behalf of The Legacy to all channels. Make it short and plain. It should read, record this."

Cassandra said, "Record to text."

Berko continued, "The Legacy is appalled by and mourns with all of you the loss of life of our noble and brave Chinese friends. The death, injury, and destruction caused by terrorists who threaten our way of life and peaceful co-existence with our brothers and sisters will not, and cannot, stand. The Legacy is offering social credits of up to 10,000 for the capture of any terrorist or terrorist collaborator, sympathizer, or organizer, and up to 50,000 for the capture of anyone directly involved in the attack near Denver. Contact your local Resolution Department with information. Long live and thanks be to The Legacy!"

Cassandra asked, "All channels?"

"All channels, immediately. What are you waiting for? Do it, *Bowles*."

His emphasis on her name was an attack. She knew it. He knew that she knew it.

She wanted him to leave as soon as humanly possible. Yet, she had to engage him for one quick item. "Sir, we're acquiring information and providing comms province-wide support for you and the regime. We're at risk of falling behind. I'd like your permission to call in additional support."

"Done."

"Sir?" It was Everett. "Classified intel communique for your eyes only."

Berko turned and left. Cassandra went to work dispatching the new comms. For a bounty like that, she thought, parents, siblings, spouses, and lovers were all at risk of being turned in. No one would be spared. No one was safe.

Berko reviewed the intel report. It simply said, *Suspicious activity Legacy Coin Depositories NY Dallas*.

"Everett, get me Reso."

"Sir, anything else?"

"Is General Zhang still in the building?"

"I believe so, yes, Sir. In the PLA section."

"I'll head over there after speaking with Reso."

"Sir, Reso is waiting."

"Berko here. I want additional forces deployed immediately to Legacy Coin Depositories in New York and Dallas," Berko paused. "On second thought, deploy additional forces to all twelve depositories. What? I don't care. I know we have sent all available extra resources to the Denver area. Call up reserves, retirees, and even reprobates, for all I care. I need forces in those twelve locations. Now!"

Berko had a hunch. He learned long ago to trust his hunches. He had another hunch. Another misstep, and his plan to become The Legacy leader would be dead . . . as would he.

Chapter LXIX

"We've got visitors. Looks like Reso."

Zim heard the words he was hoping to avoid. The rooftop team alerted him to what could be additional support or their demise. Zim instructed his team to hasten the pace of setting the C-4 explosives in their pre-planned locations.

"Klein!"

Klein stopped working on laying explosives. He came over to Zim as quickly as he could.

"Here," Zim said as he handed Klein a small bag and unzipped it. "Take the syringes and jab the prisoners. One syringe, one person. Got it?"

Klein looked horrified. He had never killed anyone before.

Zim read Klein's face. "It won't kill them; it'll knock them out for hours. Can you do it?"

"Yes."

"Good, thanks. And pull their coverings over their faces."

"Understood."

Zim studied the explosives and made a few cosmetic adjustments. The benefit they had was the moldable plastic explosive material was similar in color to the vault areas. An additional benefit was it was odorless.

"Attention brothers and sisters," Zim said calmly while addressing his team on the all comms channel. "We're expecting

Reso members any moment. Keep cool. They are with us, and we with them. Remember our convo in transit. *We* are the assigned security detail. Remember that. We have held the building. Direct all inquiries to me. We're holding terrorist scum who unsuccessfully tried to breach the building for reasons unknown to us. We're holding them in the vault for processing and transit for interrogation. Keep your faces visible except those of you on the exterior perimeter. We've got nothing to hide. Quick questions? None. Good. It *can* be done, and *we* can do this. Out."

Within seconds, Cory reported to Zim, "Reso approaching the gate."

"Roger."

In a matter of minutes, they heard footsteps coming from both stairwells.

"Who's in command?" shouted an impressive stocky man. He looked like he was built without a neck. Although older, perhaps in his fifties, he was fit and serious. He was accompanied by three others.

"Sir, I am, Sir."

"Major, what's our sitrep?"

"Colonel, these eight," Zim said, pointing to the bodies lying in the vaults near the doors, "attempted to breach our security. They posed as Reso forces. We neutralized the threat and are awaiting further orders for transit and interrogation."

"Anything else?"

"Sir, yes, Sir. We believe they may be *Molon Labe* scum. Sorry, Sir, terrorists."

"Any arms fired?"

"No Sir. We were able to secure them here at this level without fire. They've been injected, so they're out for now and for at least another hour."

"Excellent work, Major. Bravo Zulu to you and your team."

The colonel communicated with his superiors, explaining what he had been told. He turned to Zim, "My team will take the prisoners to be interrogated. We'll load them up in the lift. Do you need any additional resources?"

"Sir, negative. We've got this," Zim said in a professionally confident manner.

"Very well. I'll be requesting that you and your team receive The Legacy Cross for exemplary service. As you are aware, if granted, that will come with a sizable social credit award as well."

"Thank you, Sir. It was the team that performed exemplary service. I just drank coffee."

"That's why you are successful major. I'll be requesting a promotion for you. The Legacy needs more like you, son."

"Thank you, Sir. Thanks be to The Legacy."

The colonel and his team, with the assistance of Zim and his team, moved the drugged security members to the elevator and took them away. They were loaded into the colonel's transit. They all left almost as soon as they came, likely to take more credit than what they deserved, Zim thought. He smiled, thinking of the credit they would ultimately receive.

"No time for a grab and go. Let's get those detonators placed!"

Zim, Klein, Hannah, and Zach made quick work of readying the building for explosion. Zim double-checked their work. It looked like everything was set.

"Prepare to depart, everyone."

Zim and his team entered their transport. He turned on his remote detonation device and waited for them to leave the blast zone. Although they were twenty minutes past the planned coordinated detonation time, "Better late than never" said Zim to his team.

The colonel had his prize. He'd be feted and receive accolades for his team and, even better, for himself. Bringing in eight *Molon Labe* terrorists would be a crowning achievement for him. He'd likely receive a promotion. He and his family would be set for life with the social credits they would earn. He'd generously share credit with his team. They needed to play along. After all, it was the colonel's keen sense of something being amiss that led to the detection and apprehension of these terrorists. Their mission was thwarted. He'd become a provincial hero. A small smile cracked his face.

His thoughts were interrupted by a loud sound, followed by another, and yet another. Shock waves hit their transit as it skidded and swerved to stay on the road. He looked back. Smoke was billowing from the area they just left as debris slowly made its way back to *terra firma*.

In the blink of an eye, the colonel went from hero to zero—never to be heard from again.

Chapter LXX

They were on the run. Shots were being fired at them from below and above. Drones were everywhere. Troops had been airlifted into the sector for the hunt. Shontae and Mitch were zigzagging their way across the mountains.

Their team had taken up strategic points along their escape route to assist. They were woefully outnumbered and out-re-sourced. *Molon Labe* had a reserve of drones to use in an emergency. A few had been sent airborne already to provide cover. They were summarily shot down.

Molon Labe fighters were being picked off by Chinese drones. The preplanned escape route was no longer a viable option. There was no support left. Shontae and Mitch were on their own. If anyone could survive this onslaught, it was these two. After all, they had done it before in Oklahoma.

The terrain became particularly steep and rugged. Only experienced mountaineers could survive. It would be slow-moving. The problem was once spotted by a drone, they would be easy targets. Mitch had an idea. Instead of trying to escape, he went into hunting mode. Before long, Mitch had tracked a herd of Rocky Mountain Elk. He killed two. Mitch and Shontae each took one and set themselves about 300 yards apart, between boulders in a rugged, rocky area. They then gutted the elk, stripped down, and hid their clothes and weapons. They wanted to have dry clothes and workable weapons in the event they survived. Naked, they climbed inside. It was their only chance to live. They cut a hole in the elk's trachea to help with airflow. In that way, they were able to secure themselves with a tighter seal.

They hoped heat sensors on the drones wouldn't distinguish their heat from the elk's. The elk were still plenty warm. It took hours to cool down after gutting. With the tough terrain, ground forces would most probably look for an easier pathway and use scopes to check for movement or anything suspicious. That was their plan. The plan was not perfect, but it gave them their best chance of survival.

They heard the whizzing sound of drones as they flew by one after another. Shontae and Mitch were completely covered by their respective elk carcass so there was no way to know how many drones there were. It could have been a few drones, which circled back, or many operating in a grid or patterned formation.

They heard voices in the distance that became louder. They were experienced to know better than to think they had the all-clear if they simply didn't hear anymore chatter. They had to be patient.

It had been over an hour since they last heard a sound. Mitch gave a birdcall signaling he was going to check the area. He slowly moved out from under his carcass. He didn't hear anything except for the wind, which was whipping up out of the west. He crawled out more. With each inch, he was able to see more and more. There was nothing of concern. Mitch gave another birdcall indicating the all-clear. Shontae came out from under her carcass.

They both were covered in elk blood and fluids. Neither was ashamed of being naked in front of the other, probably because they didn't look naked, especially not at 300 yards. They looked painted. They smiled at each other briefly, then, without a word, did their best to clean up and get dressed.

They gathered together and hugged tightly. Mitch thanked the elk for their sacrifice in saving them. They both took a quiet moment.

Shontae broke the silence. "What do you think about heading back to the south, then staying along the tree line to the west? We might be able to get to the alternate safe house in Silverthorne that way."

"I like the plan. Let's take it slow and steady. Eyes and ears."

"Got it. I'll take point for now."

They set off. They were double backing to almost where they started. There were still plenty of Chinese troops and probably Reso mixed in too, down in the valley near the crash site. However, there was no activity up the mountain or the ridgeline, at least for the time being.

They were making good time. As dangerous their situation was, Mitch had never felt more alive. He loved having a purpose, being with Shontae, and sharing the outdoors with her. The extra adrenaline he could do without.

A single shot rang out. It sounded like it was behind them even higher up the mountain. Mitch turned toward the sound. He couldn't see anything. No movement. No activity. No further noise. He took cover behind some trees. He turned and looked up ahead for Shontae on point. She was down.

Mitch rushed to her. Another shot rang out. He felt a sting in his leg. He'd been hit. He quickly pulled Shontae out of the open spot to gain tree cover. She was unconscious and bleeding from her chest. Mitch applied pressure to her wound. He let his rucksack fall off behind him. He then kept one hand on her chest as direct pressure and reached into his backpack. He grabbed a small towel and used it to help quell the flow of blood. Once the bleeding had stopped, he rinsed the wound with water. He rummaged around through his bag, grabbed an antibiotic cream, and applied some to the wound.

Shontae was periodically coming in and out of consciousness. She looked at Mitch. She tried talking, but nothing came out.

"Shhhh. I've got you."

She tried speaking again. Mitch leaned in with his ear close to her lips. "I'm here."

In a faint voice and with her eyes closed, Shontae said, "Sniper. No fear." She choked and then opened her eyes as he leaned in further, "I love you." She slipped back into unconsciousness.

Mitch quickly donned his rucksack, checking the area for the sniper or anyone else, and lifted Shontae over his shoulder. He ran carrying her as best as he could. He kept within cover. He knew he had to move fast.

After carrying Shontae for miles, they descended into Silverthorne. He heard the whirling of drones getting closer. He located their safe house on the upper east side of the mountain in the Lake View area. He unlocked the back door using voice code activation. Inside were two of their squad who had survived the drone attacks along the ridge. They rushed to his aid and helped lay Shontae on the couch.

"She's lost a lot of blood." Mitch went back to applying direct pressure. "We need to transfuse. What's your blood type?" Mitch asked the two without looking.

"Universal," said one.

"Good, let's prepare for Valkyrie transfusion."

"Sir," said the other who was checking her vitals. He looked at Mitch sympathetically, "I'm sorry."

Chapter LXXI

"Your plans seem to be falling apart, General Berko. Looks like you could use my help." General Zhang was a shrewd negotiator. A brilliant military strategist, she was even better at politics.

"Really, General?" Berko countered. He, too, was a supreme-level strategist, brutal tactician, and effective enough at politics . . . the way suffering blunt force trauma was effective at having someone forget about hang nail pain. "The way I see it, *Molon Labe* severely miscalculated. They've given us even more reason to crack down harder and faster than previously planned."

"Perhaps, yet I sense you're losing control. Let me help you, my longtime friend."

The way Zhang offered help was not helpful at all, as Berko saw it. Zhang would want something in return, something big. Berko had it all mapped out. Sure, there were a few minor glitches—and one major one—but as he learned many years ago in a land far from Legacy City, don't let a good crisis go to waste. And Berko wasn't going to let this one go without putting his own special spin on it.

"*Molon Labe* has declared war on The Legacy and our people," began Berko, as he shared aloud how his version of events would be cast. "The terrorists unsuccessfully tried to drive a wedge between the great peoples of our province and our dearest friends in China. No such bond will ever be broken. It is simply too strong. What is broken is any hope *Molon Labe* and their terrorist sympathizers will ever have in gaining trust with our wise people. For they have stood for war against peace. They have stood for destruction instead of building something to benefit our generation and generations to come. They have attempted to divide us as we come together as one. And they have stood with devaluing life over honoring the sanctity of each person's right to live, love, and be a part of our great province. The terrorists have repeatedly shown that they stand for fascism, totalitarianism, death, and destruction. The Legacy stands for and with you, our people, guided by the principles of Liberalism, Loyalty, and Legacy. Our greatest gift to our communal future and what we leave for those after us is created by our current decisions and actions as we create the perfect legacy."

General Zhang clapped slowly. "Bravo! You forgot to mention comrade and five-year plans. Other than that, very good."

Berko knew he was being played. No matter. General Zhang and her troops would help Berko achieve his ultimate goal. And that time was fast approaching.

"Sir," interrupted Everett.

"Yes, Everett."

"A communique. From Chicago."

Berko read stoically.

"So?" questioned General Zhang.

"Let's contact Hatua. Together. We need him to get moving right now, full speed ahead. Operation Cleanup shall be merged with Operation Activate to form a combined initiative—Operation New Day."

Chapter LXXII

It was early morning. Jeannie and Anjali were walking across *Avenida de la Victoria* toward Province House when Jeannie felt two taps from her PCD. She had a direct communication request pending. It was a private undisclosed request.

"Let's turn back. I have a private communication request pending. It might be Disung. He said he'd reach out to me again soon."

They both headed back. "Accept communication request," Jeannie said. It was, in fact, Disung.

"Jeannie," Disung said in a breathless way, as if he had been running. "Not much time. The Legacy is working with CCP special forces. It's called Operation Cleanup. The operation has been expedited and expanded. Hardliners coup is successful. They're in full control. The moderates are out. Hardliners have demanded full scale Legacy Coin activation. One hundred percent. All. Indiscriminate. You understand what this means?"

"I do."

"They want to send an unmistakable message to the world. Terrorism, loss of Chinese life, will be met with the harshest measures and outcomes imaginable. CCP contacted Hatua, who says his team can activate approximately 700,000 Legacy Coins per a twenty-four-hour period."

"When are they starting?"

"They already have. Must go. Bye."

Both Jeannie and Anjali stood there. It was 6:56 a.m. There was no time to discuss what Disung said. They needed to be on time. They rushed back across the street and walked into Province House. Once through security, they were escorted to the waiting area. Bodies were moving quickly from room to room, down hallway after hallway, crossing in front of them like the combination of the overcaffeinated meeting the zombie apocalypse. Clearly, everyone had been working overnight.

"Ladies, follow me please." A young man, who really looked more like a boy, led them down a maze of hallways to a suite of offices. "Wait here please," he said before heading into an office further down and to the right.

They heard someone yelling from the direction of their escort. "Do not interrupt me ever again! Do. You. Understand?! Well, do you?!" The voice was male and harsh. "Now, get out!"

Their young escort stepped out of an office. He looked away from the guests. He stood there. Still. Just waiting. Seconds later, a man walked out of the office, stood in front of the boy, and stared at him. Neither said anything. The man turned to his right and proceeded down the suite of offices and entered one at the end. The young man walked toward the door again and slipped his head in. He pulled his head out and walked toward Jeannie and Anjali. He looked as though nothing had happened.

"Ladies, please follow me." He escorted them to the office further down on the right.

"Hi, I'm Cassandra Bowles, I mean Cassandra Bowles Hatua," Cassandra said as she extended her hand to greet the guests.

Both Jeannie and Anjali had the same thought at the same time. Cassie Hatua? Why would Frank send us to Cassie Hatua? Why didn't he tell us ahead of time?

"Hi, Donna Williams," said Jeannie, meeting Cassandra's hand.

"Pavani," Anjali said as she, too, shook Cassandra's hand. "Pavani Patel."

"Nice meeting you both. Please have a seat." Cassandra went behind the ladies and mostly shut her door; she left a small crack open. She didn't want to raise any unnecessary suspicions.

"Thank you for meeting with us," Jeannie offered.

"Yes," Cassandra said somewhat loudly, "We're quite swamped and are in desperate need of additional, experienced comms help. I understand you both are experienced, is that true?" Cassandra nodded her head slightly up and down.

"Yes, we are," said Anjali confidently.

"Good. Good. Listen, I don't have a lot of time to supervise every aspect of your work. Are you independent workers? Capable of taking direction? Even what might be considered harsh critique? Nobody around here means anything personal. You need to get the job done—perfectly—and under stressful conditions. Understood?"

They both said yes.

Cassandra lowered her voice. "Forgive me, but how do I know you can be trusted?"

"Because Frank referred us," Anjali responded.

Jeannie kept thinking to herself, *Both sides are feeling each other out. This might take a while. It might not end well.*

"Well, that's nice, but—"

"Because of this." Jeannie reached under her collar and pulled out her necklace. "This." She held the pendant out directly to Cassandra.

"That's a beautiful pendant. I don't quite understand how this has anything to do with what we were dis—"

"Look closely," interrupted Jeannie. She was showing Cassandra the front side. She turned it over, showing the back. "Sorry, wrong way. Now look closely. Here." Jeannie unclasped the necklace and handed it to Cassandra. "In the middle. The etching."

Cassandra studied the pendant. There it was. The lion and the lamb. *Leon y cordero*.

"We're good. Now, how can I help you?"

Anjali started to explain the details of her hack into the Legacy Coin program and the authentication problem that she could not solve—the biometric retinal eye scanner. She was interrupted by a finger tap behind her.

Everett opened the door ever so slightly, popping his head in. "Apologies for the interruption. He wants to see you in five."

"Thank you, Everett."

Cassandra thought for a moment. She had an idea. "I will put you both in an interior office, no windows. If anyone asks, you've been brought on as extra comms support given recent events. You have to pass a quals test. Don't worry. It's your cover. You'll have access to the system, although it's not secure. Your every move is subject to being watched, including online. I'll need more time to think about retinal scan and how to get you secure access. In the meantime, I'll escort you to your office."

Cassandra, Jeannie, and Anjali made their way out of Cassandra's office and were heading back towards the main hallway when someone shouted, "Stop! Where are you going? We're meeting now." It was Berko.

Cassandra turned to address Berko while Jeannie and Anjali continued looking straight ahead. "Yes. We are. I was escorting my new comms help to qualifications testing. I need to get them through that so they can help support our efforts. We do need to get them going straight away, right, Sir?"

"Yes. I see." Berko approached the guests from behind. "And who do we have here?"

There was nothing they could do except turn around. As they did, Cassandra made the introductions, "Donna Williams, Pavani Patel, this is my boss, Boris Berko."

"A pleasure, ladies." Berko smiled awkwardly. He looked closely at both, especially so at Anjali. "I know you."

"Sir?"

"I've met you, haven't I?"

"I don't believe so, Sir," Anjali said as she increased the strength of her accent.

Berko asked, "*Casa de Flor*?" Anjali looked blankly at him, still smiling, though. Berko continued, "Your husband, Stefan, should be here shortly for a meeting. Perhaps you might like to say hello. Certainly, he'd enjoy that."

"Aw, Sir, you are referring to my older sister. I have been mistaken for her back home in India, never here." Anjali giggled. "She is quite the beauty, thank you for the compliment, Sir."

"Ah, I see." Berko was still not totally convinced. He turned his gaze upon Cassandra. "Bowles, once you deliver these two, I want to discuss something very important with you." He alternated looking at Jeannie and Anjali. "I have an idea." Neither of them blinked. No reaction. Same charming earnest faces.

"We'd better go so we can meet. Back in two to meet." Cassandra escorted the two away.

As they walked away, Berko said, "Enjoy your testing. Welcome aboard, and thanks be to The Legacy."

The three turned as if rehearsed, saying in unison, "Thanks be to The Legacy."

Once they reached the interior office and the door was shut, Cassandra said, "I'll be back as soon as I can. In the meantime, start working on these." Cassandra handed them each a set of documents. "This is your quals test. Do your best. Work on these in case anyone comes in. Be back soon." With that, Cassandra left.

Once the door was shut, Jeannie turned to Anjali and said, "Good call wearing glasses and your hair pulled back in a bun."

Anjali took her glasses off, smiling. "Can't see a thing with these on."

Chapter LXXIII

The machinery was working at maximum output. Every 1.5 seconds or less, a new input was read into the system. The error rate at that pace was negligible, although errors occurred. It was the price of speed and survival, not life survival. Rather, it was a *way of life* type of survival.

At a reading rate of forty per minute, and with eleven readers working at full capacity day and night, the daily output would exceed 630,000. With Chicago being offline, that was less than the approximately 700,000 predicted. Beginning in less than three days, over 630,000 North America Province residents would perish each day. The initial order called for a minimum of thirty days. That would be over 19,000,000 deaths at the command of the ultimate foreign power and its provincial puppet by way of technology sold to an unsuspecting public as *reproductive health* yet morphed into the most ghoulish form of genocide ever known. And he built it. He promoted it. He profited by it.

At some level, Hank Hatua was conflicted. The numbers were hauntingly hefty. These were real lives and real people, people with hopes and dreams, who had those they loved and loved them in return, old, middle-aged, and young, Black, brown, and white. It was indiscriminate. And it was final. Once the machine read a particular Legacy Coin, the seventy-two-hour clock started ticking. After that time expired, the implant would receive a message to release the toxin.

Succinylcholine, also known as Suxamethonium chloride, had been used for decades for its anesthetic properties. Unless administered under tightly controlled circumstances, *Sux*, as it was called, would lead to paralysis throughout the entire body. Arms and legs would cease working. The respiratory function would fail too, leading to suffocation or, in medical terms, asphyxia.

Hatua had cornered the market on Sux, and his scientific researchers developed Sux II, an even more lethal form. Sux II caused the paralytic outcomes much more quickly and with less quantity needed to do the job. In his view, it was the perfect agent for his abortion-on-demand implant. And it was the toxin loaded into Global Genomics' implant awaiting a coded release direction.

Hatua wondered deeply, who was more of a monster? Berko and his allies for wanting to use it on an unprecedented widespread scale? Or, him, for having thought of it and distributing it in the first place? In the end, he surmised, he and Berko would both go down in history alongside some of the world's most notorious and vile villains to ever take a breath on the planet.

Hatua was snapped back to reality when his PCD tapped his wrist twice. It was his wife. How he longed for a different outcome, that he was a different man, a better man, a man that a woman like her deserved. She radiated goodness and caring. She was also intelligent and beautiful. *What did she see in me?* he asked himself. *The real me?* His wrist felt the tapping again.

"Connect, Cass." He said plainly. He changed his energy in hopes of shaking off his dreadful thoughts. "Hi Cass! Nice surprise to hear from you."

"Hi Hank, things are crazy, as you know," she said, getting straight to the reason for her call. "I'm under a lot of pressure here. Can you help me?"

"Anything, what?"

"Berko is demanding that I develop a comms strategy to gather the remaining Legacy Coins that haven't yet been deposited. The problem is that the data is unclear, and I need to have a specific plan to him as soon as possible."

"The data we've been providing The Legacy should be accurate."

"Apparently, it isn't. And he's about ready to lose it . . . and I'm the targeted scapegoat, apparently."

"I see. Would you like to review the original source data? You can come here to do it. You won't have him looking over your shoulder that way."

"Yes, that'd be perfect. Thanks so much, Hank."

"As I said, anything. I'll get you set up in a confidential room with top-level access to all source materials. We can run a comparison to what you have on your end to see if anything's out of the ordinary or didn't translate properly. Plan?"

"Yes, perfect plan."

"See you shortly then, Cass. Bye—"

"One more thing. I have two trusted associates who are working in tandem with me. It's too much for just one person. I'll be bringing them with me if that's not a problem on your end."

"Let me check with the person who's in charge," he paused one beat, "No problem!"

"Ha," Cassandra managed a laugh, "It's amazing you can have a sense of humor at a time like this."

"You know what I like to say, you can laugh, or you can cry, I prefer to laugh. Love you, bye."

"Love you too, bye."

Cassandra got what they needed. Moving to the next step; lives were on the line. There was no other choice. She couldn't trust him completely, at least she didn't think she could. He was too close with the regime. He was particularly too close with the Chinese.

But lying to her husband? She hated doing that. He had been nothing but kind and loving to her and her family, especially her father. He didn't have to do that. It probably cost him some trust with both The Legacy and the CCP. He did it anyway. For her. And she rewarded him by lying to him. It didn't sit well with her, not at all.

No matter his history, Hank Hatua was now her husband. She promised to love and cherish him, under all circumstances. She fell short, way short of that. And how far was she willing to fall short? Under the regime's laws, she was a traitor. Under God's laws, she might be one as well, she thought. She failed in many ways. Her failures might cost her life. Worse yet, her failures might cost her soul.

Chapter LXXIV

The CCP's elite of the elite were staged in position. General Zhang always relied on this team of special operators when rapid response was imperative under unique conditions. A well-trained force, the *Ready Dragon Force* was founded after multiple limited conflicts in the 2020s and 2030s, including in Taiwan, the South China Sea, and India. CCP military leadership saw the need for a more robust and flexible elite force to deploy on a moment's notice under high-tech settings. The RDF's mission was to be the first on the ground in limited regional engagements. In addition, this group was specially trained for commando, counterterrorism, and intelligence gathering operations.

General Zhang placed her team in ready mode awaiting The Legacy's formal request for assistance. Given the terrorists' attack on the Hyperloop, assistance would be needed to not only root out the terrorists but also secure the safety and continued operation of other critical infrastructures, such as airports, Hyperloop and traditional rail, hospitals, power grids, water systems, fuel storage, power generation plants, dams, and communications networks. The latter was of critical importance to Berko. Without full comms control, his plans to remake The Legacy in his image and under his sole direction would likely fail.

Berko had what he wanted. The Legacy made a formal request for assistance. The request was two-fold. One, secure all critical provincial infrastructure. And, two, aid in the effort to capture or kill terrorists throughout the province. In turn, General Zhang gave the order. Her troops moved quickly and had secured all mission infrastructure objectives within the hour.

General Zhang kept close watch on Berko and his Reso forces. She didn't fully trust Berko. It was Berko who insisted on using the Hyperloop for transporting troops to the mid-province region. General Zhang wondered if somehow Berko didn't instigate or at least allow for *Molon Labe* to successfully carry out its deadly mission. General Zhang lost some face with her fellow hardliners back in Beijing when news of the massacre reached them. Yet, the general had plenty of goodwill with CCP leadership built up over time for her successful and brutal crackdowns both within China and in other provinces.

The general ascended to senior command after forces under her direction put down uprisings in both the Southeast and South Asia Provinces. In Southeast Asia, there were disputes between former Lao and Thai peoples. Their dispute devolved into battles near and at the ironically named Lao-Thai Friendship Bridge spanning across the Mekong River near Vientiane. The hand-to-hand combat between the Lao and Thai peoples was becoming so disruptive the CCP ordered then-Colonel Zhang to lead a team to restore peace in the region. Zhang's plan to do so was simple. Round up and dispose of all potential troublemakers on both sides. The area had been quiet ever since.

In South Asia, the newly minted general invoked a similar yet importantly different strategy. Punjabi independence activists engaged in a series of explosions, disrupting important trade infrastructure along with targeted killings of ethnic Chinese living in what was formerly northern India. Given the need to maintain order, as well as the sheer size of the population involved, General Zhang decided the best course was to imprison the offending activists far away. After time spent in captivity in northwest China, and taking a page out of China's prior treatment of its own Uyghur Muslim minority, she released the Punjabis back to their native general population—as mere shadows of their former selves after forced labor, brainwashing, sterilization, and torture. That seemed to have the desired impact. There were no more problems of note in that region or from that group.

"Ah, yes, General Berko. Yes. Yes, I saw the request, and my order followed immediately thereafter. Yes. RDF is in place. Operation New Day is now officially under way."

Chapter LXXV

"Nice seeing you, Alberto. Any news to share?" asked Cassandra cheerfully as she and her two colleagues approached two security officers.

"No ma'am, not yet. Still waiting. I think my wife is ready. Not so sure about me."

Cassandra offered a light laugh. "Don't worry. That's why we women are here, to take care of all the babies in our lives." She flashed a bright smile at the expectant father. "They're on my team," she said, nodding at Jeannie and Anjali. Jeannie tried to stay off to the side. She knew Alberto's wife, Ella. They'd been trying to get pregnant for years. They finally had success with a little scientific help. Ella was due any day. She met Alberto once. She hoped he wouldn't recognize her.

Alberto looked at both Jeannie and Anjali, then looked at a screen near him. "Ladies, one moment please. Our PCD ID reader is a bit slow. My apologies. Lots of activity."

Cassandra shook her head. "I'm not surprised. All this horrible news. Simply horrible. Security must be tight everywhere."

"It is," responded Alberto. "I was supposed to have today and the next several days off. All leave has been revoked until further notice."

Jeannie started to get nervous. *What if their cover backgrounds were discovered to be false? Didn't match up with their*

PCDs? *What if there was a malfunction in the synchronization they ran at Frank's?* She started to feel her heart rate increase as her palms became sweaty.

"Hmmm," murmured Alberto. "I don't get it."

"Is there a problem, Al?" said Cassandra, with the proper amount of concern based on timing as opposed to outcome.

"Well, the PCD reader at the main door didn't find your guests. There's no record of them at all. That can't be right. I see them right here in front of me, clear as day."

"Can I vouch for them and get going? He's expecting us. Perhaps you can grab us on the way out and whatever is wrong with the system will be resolved by then?"

"Yes, he informed us," replied the security guard. "I have an idea. One moment."

Anjali's mind was working as fast as it could, thinking about what could have gone wrong with the PCD synchronization protocol in the morning. She was certain that it took fine because she tested it and confirmed that both of their borrowed identities were in The Legacy's system.

"Officer, is your system aligned with The Legacy's PCD database?"

"Ma'am, with respect, I can't answer that other than to say we maintain enhanced security here at this location."

Anjali suspected that Frank's cover IDs were good for The Legacy's base level system. It may not have been updated or uploaded into anything requiring a higher level of scrutiny.

"We'll have to go old school." With that, Alberto took out an old wand. "Let's see if I can power this up. Here we go. How about that? Still works. My apologies, ladies please stand here and spread your arms out and maintain your legs at least shoulder distance apart."

"I've seen these on old movies," said Cassandra, making light of the situation. She wanted to get out of there as fast as the other two. Maybe more, as she had plenty to lose.

The officer started with Anjali. "Clear," he said.

He turned to Jeannie. "Ma'am," he said politely as he started waving the wand. Jeannie thought if this was a blood pressure reader or heartrate monitor, she'd be flagged, they'd dig deeper, and they would be taken into custody or worse. She thought about her girls who had gone through so much. *Calm yourself,* she reminded herself.

A loud beep occurred. Alberto tapped the wand. "Might be a false positive." He ran it over her again. Once more, a loud beep. Jeannie was trying to avoid a flight scenario as she positively knew she couldn't win in a fight.

He looked at Jeannie for a moment, which seemed like minutes to her. She tried to hide within herself, which, to her, seemed silly. Unlike Anjali, she didn't consider the need for a disguise of any type. Now she wished she would've done something to alter her looks. He'd recognized her, she thought. *Please God, no, please let me pass.*

"Ma'am, looks like the wand is picking up something below your neck."

Jeannie could barely hear him. Her head and ears were full of blood, and her knees about ready to give out.

"Ma'am," he said, a bit more businesslike this time. "Are you carrying anything metal on you?"

Cassandra interrupted, "Alberto, could a necklace or a pendant cause the beep?"

Alberto still eyed Jeannie while responding to Cassandra, "Perhaps."

Jeannie let out some air while she gave a nervous laugh, "Oh, yes, that must be it. My necklace." She reached along her neck and pulled out the necklace and pendant. She was initially holding it back side forward. She noticed and turned it around.

"Please hold the necklace as you are ma'am. I'll wand the area one more time." Nothing. No beep.

"Clear. All good here."

Jeannie started to put the necklace away when the guard said, "Ma'am, one moment please." Jeannie stopped. She felt a slight bit of perspiration forming on her forehead. "Mind if I look at that pendant again?"

"No," Jeannie said as she was trying desperately to maintain her composure, "not at all." This time, Jeannie displayed the front side of the pendant to the guard while trying not to have her hand visibly shake.

"That's beautiful. Gorgeous really. Who made it if you don't mind me asking?"

"I'm not sure. It was a gift."

"Perhaps they engraved the back with the artisan's name or logo?"

Cassandra jumped in, "Al, I'll try to find out who made it. We've got to go." She started walking away to give him the cue that they were done, "You know," she said as she mildly moved her eyes in the direction of the elevator, signaling she needed to meet up with her husband.

"Thanks. Oh yes. It just gave me an idea for my wife. She'd love a gift like that." Jeannie smiled and tried to get her legs moving toward Cassandra. She went slow so she wouldn't fall.

"She'd love it, no doubt," Cassandra said. "Let's move ladies, we're late."

Anjali got very close to Jeannie in case her friend buckled. Anjali was dying inside for her yet was impressed that her friend didn't panic.

"Okay. Thank you, ladies," said Alberto pleasantly. He turned to Cassandra, "My sincere apologies for the delay, ma'am."

"Not a problem, and congratulations in advance," she said as she walked away. With her back turned, she said loudly, "and say goodbye to a good night's sleep . . . forever!"

She then turned and winked at the guard. He took an over-emphasized deep breath, nodded his head, and slightly rolled his eyes. *Nice man,* she thought, *just doing his job. Aren't we all?*

Chapter LXXVI

Legacy City International Airport served a dual role. One, as a traditional passenger airport. And, two, as a joint civilian/military airfield. The civilian side activity had dropped off recurrently for decades and particularly so after The Legacy instituted the social credits system. However, the military side was the focal point of investment and expansion.

This was no more true than within the past twenty-four hours. Planeload after planeload of Chinese special forces and support personnel, along with their gear and supplies, were offloaded. They mustered up and were then given their orders. Some stayed in the Legacy City area. Others shipped out to other strategic areas within North America Province. To a person, the Chinese were looking forward to this deployment—not necessarily for the same reasons.

Some of the Chinese personnel wanted to see a land they had heard so much about. Notwithstanding the recent years of fundamental change, there was still something about America that stirred their senses. The ideas supporting America's history were so foreign to them in terms of daily life but intriguing, nonetheless; they hoped to encounter a taste of what that might be. For others, their enthusiasm for the deployment was much simpler. They were promised the chance to kill their sworn enemy.

These additional forces were requested to supplement the initial deployment of troops already well-positioned throughout the province. General Zhang made the request given the fatal attack on her forces in the Rockies. Among other things, her goal was to show an overwhelming force to those who might seek to cause more trouble. She also wanted to have another card to play in the off-chance that Reso troops decided to go "soft" on the locals.

Berko received reports of additional Chinese support streaming into Legacy City International. He was caught unaware of these additional incoming resources. He decided to visit General Zhang in the PLA wing of Province House. He ran into General Zhang in the corridor.

"General Zhang."

"General Berko."

Berko looked to see if anyone was in earshot. Nobody was. "General, what do you know of additional RDF personnel and supplies arriving at the airfield here?"

"I don't understand your question, General Berko. You want our operation to be successful, yes?"

"Of course."

"Well, given recent tragic events and the depletion of my team, I ordered additional support to backfill those losses and make sure we don't suffer that type of loss again."

"I wasn't consulted, General Zhang. This is *my* operation."

"Ah, I see your point," General Zhang smiled. "You've been busy, very busy with all the death and damage. Plus, no doubt, constant questions about the advisability of your strategy to move personnel as you did. I'm sure The Legacy has been questioning you plenty. I took the initiative to assist you. 'Lighten the load,' isn't that what *you* say here?"

"Yes, that's one thing *they* say here," Berko said as a not-so-subtle reminder that he was not from North America Province and earned his way through brutality to get there. "'*Do not engage an enemy more powerful than you.*' Isn't that what *you* say there?" The tone and message was clear as Berko quoted Sun Tzu.

General Zhang paused, then looked at Berko, matching stare for stare. General Zhang finally broke the silence. "Would you like for me to send the additional support back to China?"

"No, they're here already. No more though, General, unless they're requested by me." Berko leaned in and said softly, "Do we understand one another?"

"Yes, General Berko, I believe we do."

Berko turned and left. General Zhang smiled as she thought of another Sun Tzu quote applicable to this moment, *Never interrupt your enemy when he is making a mistake.*

Chapter LXXVII

The basement level was eerily quiet. When Cassandra, Jeannie, and Anjali stepped out of the elevator, they saw plenty of people scurrying about at a frenzied pace. Yet, it was if someone hit the mute button. Their shoes made no noise. Even the machinery was quiet. Jeannie looked to her right and saw shiny objects moving at breakneck speed through a series of scanners and sorters. She knew what those shiny objects were. Disung was right. She also knew that they needed to work quickly too.

Cassandra moved swiftly and deftly through the workers, smiling, and nodding as she did so. Everyone was curious about her. The woman who "boated the marlin," they said. Anjali and Jeannie followed close behind her, trying to keep up while also looking around to see what was happening in case a helpful clue might present itself.

Cassandra stopped in front of a small office encased in glass. Hatua motioned her forward while pointing to his right ear.

"I understand and agree. Yes. We're working on it. Yes. Working on that too. Should have the first sped up 20 percent. I'm afraid that's the best we can do." Hatua mouthed to Cassandra, *Berko*. "As for the second, after the CCP has finished with its investigation, we'll be begin repairs. Could be weeks. I'll have a better sense once my team has full access." Hatua motioned for the three to have a seat. "Right. Huh? That's interesting. How many? Sure, that'd be fine. Happy to help as we can. Okay. Bye."

Hatua was thinking. He looked a bit perplexed. He then focused on his wife and guests. "Hi Cass." Cassandra stood to greet him. He gave her a quick peck on the cheek, which she reciprocated.

"Everything alright?" asked Cassandra.

"Yes. Fine, just fine." Hatua wasn't convincing anyone, much less Cassandra.

"These are the two I mentioned," Cassandra said as the ladies stood. "Pavani Patel, Donna Williams, this is Hank Hatua."

Hatua extended his hand to them both. "My pleasure, indeed. I understand that there is some issue with the datasets provided to The Legacy in recent reporting. Is that correct?"

"Yes," responded Anjali. "It could be as simple as transposition issues or perhaps something contained in the chain, which corrupted the sets. In any event, if we can evaluate original data, we should be able to quickly discover what is causing the discrepancies, and we'll be out of your hair and on our way."

"No problem at all. Glad to have you all here. We certainly want to be absolutely certain that the data we're providing The Legacy is 100-percent accurate."

"That's wonderful, thanks Hank," Cassandra said. "Where can we get set up then? We'll need access to the system and original data, of course. I'm sure you have a backup set?"

"Yes, we do, of course. Although the original is the driver, the others are ghost sets. We can't run anything off them."

"Oh, are you still okay with us probing around then?"

"Sure, as long as you are overseeing the operation, Cass, that'd be fine. I'll be here for any needs or questions unless I'm summoned away."

"I understand that," Cassandra said while talking out of one side of her mouth for emphasis.

Hatua escorted the three to another glass-encased room with a table and six chairs. It had one computer set up on the conference room table. Let me get you started so we can make best use of your time."

Anjali looked at Jeannie, widening her eyes. Was Hatua going to assist them? All the way to the retinal scanner perhaps?

"Here you go. Should be all set for your review."

After the three thanked him, Cassandra turned on the opaque feature and closed the door. "Go!"

Anjali didn't need any encouragement. She was already off and running. She tested several pathways to get to the master dataset. She knew not more than thirty feet away, Legacy Coins were being read, and people's lives were about ready to change. She recognized prior pathways she had previously explored, all relating back to the same dead end. She needed access to the master set. Hatua had bluffed them. They were operating off a copy, a dummy set.

"We're stuck in the same place. Even here they have the exact same security protocols in place. Without retinal scan approval, we won't get in." Anjali was clearly frustrated.

"The scanner is all set?"

"Yes."

"Let me try something." Cassandra pulled up a hologram of Hatua. It was of the two of them on the Hyperloop. "Maybe this will work." Cassandra aligned the retinal scanner with

Hatua's left eye. She enlarged the eye and increased the focus of the scanner. "Anything?"

"Wait! There's something happening."

The three stood over the monitor looking. There was definitely something happening. A digital mix of squares was popping in different colors and patterns. Then, it changed. The pace of movement slowed down. The tiles were coming into focus, slowly. The picture was becoming clearer and clearer. It looked like it was forming into someone's face. A man's face.

It was the face of Hank Hatua. It just looked at them while they looked at it, as if they were expecting it to confirm that they were indeed into the master files within the system.

The face began to move. Then the lips parted. The eyes looked a bit sad, then blinked. A face of sadness slowly turned to anger and intensity. The lips moved.

"Cass, Cass, Cass. Why? Why would you do this to me? Have I not been good to you? Your family? Given you everything and more? With unlimited dreams for our future. And this? Why?"

Cassandra looked down. It was Hank. Not a digitized version. It was him.

"How could *I*, you ask? How about *you*? How could you, Hank? Do *his* bidding? *Their* bidding? How could *you*?! I wanted to believe in you. That you weren't *them*. But, I was wrong. You're just like them. Like, like Berko!"

Jeannie and Anjali were stunned. Jeannie reached for the door. Locked. Not that there was any chance of escaping, but she had to do something.

"Berko? Like Berko, you say! No. Not a chance. Berko chooses to be evil. That's how he lives to his core. As for me, I wanted a better world, a world that could support and sustain itself, a world where people could have lives, futures, love. Yes Cass, love. Just like I have for you." He paused. "I thought I had for you."

"How does slaughtering hundreds of thousands of innocent people equate to a better world as you put it? You're fooling yourself. And you set this up ahead of time. You lied to everyone, everyone, about Legacy Coins. They weren't for reproductive health or a women's right to control her body; it was a way—a sick and evil way—to commit genocide. Genocide. It was always about genocide. Now it's just on a grander scale. Genocide. Let that word sink in. Inside or outside the womb, it was genocide. Did *they* brainwash you? I hope and pray that they did. Otherwise, you're no better; in fact, you're worse than the rest of them. For you, Hank, you, created this—what would you even call it—indiscriminate killing machine . . . and gave them the keys to run it."

Hatua looked at her, then down, then back at her. "In life, you have choices. Cass, you chose. And you didn't choose me." He paused while looking anguished. "Please forgive me. I'm sorry for what I must now do."

Cassandra looked at him. "I came to love you, Hank. You have a choice too. You always have a choice."

"I wish I did, Cass. I really do. But I don't." A tear dripped down his cheek. He lifted his PCD, "Comms three. Two-sided speech to dictate. Begin comms. Cassandra is here. Come get her and her two associates. Details to follow. End comms." He looked at his wife and started to say something. He couldn't. Hank Hatua looked away as the screen went dark.

Chapter LXXVIII

Molon Labe was on the run throughout the province. From Miami to Memphis, Seattle to San Diego, Augusta to Austin, Reso forces, supported by the Chinese RDF, were slicing through city after city, town after town, and shack after shack, searching for and destroying most everything in their path. It didn't matter if they were met unarmed and without any show of struggle, the combined Reso and RDF fighters were making quick work of eliminating any future terrorist activities—or even mild dissent—against the regime and its friends. At times, women and children were spared. That is, if the marauding troops even bothered to identify them as such.

In Memphis, they strafed Beale Street's music venues while also flattening the famous Peabody Hotel and everyone in it, ducks included. Miami's South Beach and Little Havana were reduced to rubble. For *fun*, they took target practice on Maine's iconic Portland Head Light until it toppled. They continued down to Boston, obliterating Faneuil Hall, the John F. Kennedy Presidential Library, and the entirety of Harvard University. Throughout the province, there was no exact rhyme or reason for their selected targets. Other than, perhaps, to take away the North America Province dwellers' shared history, heart, and hope.

Beyond destroying or damaging historical and other meaningful targets, people were killed in the most brazen and indiscriminate ways. In some cases, like in Minneapolis, people would be first questioned about who they were, their jobs, social credits, and allegiances. Depending on the answer, they might survive. In other places, like Dallas, they were all viewed as enemies of the state, so there was no pretense involved. *If you see something, shoot something* was the mantra. The CCP's RDF was getting what it wanted—plenty of action.

Interestingly, General Zhang had her RDF team dress in Reso tactical clothing. With hoods covering their faces, there was little way for anyone to tell the difference between a native North America Province Reso member and a Chinese RDF member. Except there was one important difference. Due to special gear carried by the Chinese team, Reso weapons would not work on their fellow RDF combatants.

General Zhang received the latest update from the field. She reached out immediately to Berko. "General Berko, our collective teams have secured all province-wide comms channels."

"Excellent. I will be prepared to address the province within the hour. Bye, General."

Berko was pleased. So far, so good. Within an hour or more, he'd become the new regime leader, his lifetime's pinnacling achievement.

While Berko was focused on making final preparations to his remarks he would soon give to the province, General Zhang was making her own final preparations. Moments after she spoke with Berko, General Zhang checked in with her field commanders. They and their teams were ready. Once Berko began his broadcasted speech, it would be go-time for the RDF. They planned extensively for this moment, years and years of extensive training of the most grueling variety, unparalleled technical savvy, and sophisticated weaponry—much of it thanks to an unwitting and greedy America. Add to those advantages one more, and perhaps the most important one of all, the element of surprise. It all worked in their favor. They just waited to hear Berko's voice, and that would be their signal to commence what just might be the greatest Chinese military achievement of all time.

Chapter LXXIX

"I'm sure Berko is on his way," Cassandra said with resignation. "He won. We lost. Hear the coins processing in the background? We all lost."

"What will they do with us?" asked Jeannie.

"Take us to B5, then . . ." Cassandra couldn't say the words.

Anjali thought about B5. She saw firsthand what happened to someone who survived B5. Stefan was never the same, not around her or their family, certainly not the same when it came to doing Berko's bidding. Death might be a better outcome. What about her girls? She longed to hold them one last time. Jeannie did as well. It was the only thing on her mind. How could she have done something differently to save her girls? She kept coming back to the same answer. This was the right choice. It was the only choice to really save them.

"I'm so sorry. I shouldn't have suggested we come here. It's all my fault." Cassandra put her head in her hands. She couldn't bear to look at the other two ladies. She felt responsible for them and their families.

Jeannie touched Cassandra's shoulder, saying to her, "No, Cassandra, it's not your fault. This moment was long coming. My husband knew it. He knew that something ominous was coming. And his death wasn't in vain. It brought us to this moment in time, this exact moment. So close, so close to saving lives, so close to exposing the big lie. Legacy Coins were never about helping. They were, and are, about power, control, and death."

Anjali chimed in, "Look, we're not dead yet."

"Right, we'll fight to the end. But how? We're trapped here," said Jeannie.

The door abruptly opened. "Let's go!" said a man's voice excitedly.

Cassandra raced to the door, "Daddy!" It was Simon along with Dianne. Cassandra embraced her father tightly. Simon said, "We've got to go, now."

"But, I don't understand, what? Why? How?"

"Hank sent me a message instructing us to come get you and your colleagues. I then spoke with him. He's made arrangements for all of us." Simon looked at the ladies, "And your families too. We've got to hurry, though." Simon stopped and handed a small bag to Cassandra. "He gave me this."

Cassandra opened the bag and pulled out its contents. Legacy Coins. She looked at her father with a puzzled face, looking for answers.

"He loves you, Cass. He provided for you, for us." Simon looked somberly to Jeannie and Anjali. "There are only three coins there." They knew what he meant, Legacy Coins for Cassandra, Dianne, and Simon. The others' Coins were still in the batch being processed.

Simon was clearly not well, yet he was pulling his daughter along. She looked for Hank, hoping to see him, hoping to thank him, and hoping to convince him to come with them. She never saw him.

Hank saw her, though. He kept an eye on her via the security camera on his PCD. He took one last look at Cassandra as she and the others exited the building.

He took a deep breath. Hatua entered the room that was just moments prior occupied by his wife and her colleagues. He shut the door and sat down. He looked at the computer they were using. They got as far into the system as they could without passing the biometric security.

Hatua sat there looking into nowhere, just thinking. He concluded that his whole life was a waste. He cared more about money, fame, and power than people. He didn't really care about the science or technology he and his companies help advance. He didn't care about the people his work benefitted. So long as it all circled back to benefitting him and his needs, it was sufficient.

The Legacy. The Legacy. *What an ironic name*, he thought. He worked for The Legacy, yet his own legacy would be shameful. He laughed at himself. Shameful? What a weak word. He helped to destroy potential legacies of others. He was personally responsible for the deaths of uncounted millions. His legacy? It kept coming back to one word in his mind, the word that Cassandra kept throwing at him in what were their final moments together. It was like poison darts hitting one bullseye after another on a dartboard. One precisely descriptive word kept going over and over in his mind. Thump. Thump. Thump. Bullseye, again and again. Each successive dart hurting more than the previous one. That word was on an infinite loop in his mind, the singular word that would be synonymous with his name for time and all eternity was not related to his creations, his discoveries, not even his revolutionary successes. The word for which Hank Hatua would forever be known was something more base, more vile, more despicable.

That word was *genocide*.

Chapter LXXX

"In five, four," the floor manager then went from audible countdown to fingers showing three, two, one and then pointed straight at Berko.

"My friends, brothers and sisters, fellow North America Provincers," Berko began as he looked directly into the camera.

General Zhang was in the studio with Berko. She quietly whispered, "*Gōng jī*. Go."

Berko continued, "I come to you at this critical moment in our province's history, a moment that will be defined by no one except us. And that's a good thing, as together, we can defeat any enemy, overcome any challenge, and set the course for a brighter future as we do so . . . together.

"As you know, *Molon Labe* has declared war on our people," Berko said, using similar words and style that he previously shared with General Zhang but with important differences. "The *Molon Labe* terrorists have one ultimate goal—to have us serve them, to be subservient to them. They will kill us, all of us, if it fits their needs and wants, for the terrorists care about only one thing. And that one thing is power."

Berko felt that he was hitting his stride. He continued. "Friends, it pains me to share that The Legacy has not been able to better protect us. Even with prior warning of potential terrorist activity, The Legacy made the choice to proceed as if the terrorists were not to be taken seriously or couldn't muster the resources necessary to pull off consequential destruction to our people and land."

Berko leaned in, as if having a confidential conversation with a friend, "*Molon Labe* has been engaged in a systematic death and destruction spree throughout the province. The loss of life and property has been as devasting as it has been deliberate. For, you see, *Molon Labe* terrorists care not for you, your families, or our future. They have conducted these disgraceful acts under cover of false identification. *Molon Labe* outfitted themselves to look like our peacekeeping Resolution Department protective forces. How they acquired the tactical uniforms and gear is under investigation. In the meantime, we are outfitting our Resolution Department protective forces with new tactical gear that will readily identify them as legitimate. Your PCD is now programmed so you will be able to confirm whether anyone wearing a Resolution Department uniform is friend or foe.

"Sisters and brothers, we find ourselves at a decision point. Will we allow this type of terror to consume us? Or will we fight for a just and peaceful existence, where we can live, love, and raise our families in relative peace and harmony?

"*Molon Labe* members and their associates have unsuccessfully tried to drive a wedge between the great people of our province and our brothers and sisters in China. That bond will never be broken. It is simply too strong. What is broken is any hope *Molon Labe* and its terrorist sympathizers will ever have in gaining trust with our people—our people are too wise to allow it, for the terrorists have stood for war against peace. They have stood for destruction instead of building something to benefit our generation and generations to come. They have attempted to divide us as we desire with all our collective hearts to come together as one. And they have stood for devaluing life. That's right, *Molon Labe* devalues life at the highest level. The terrorists have disdain for those who honor the sanctity of each person's right to live, love, and be a part of our great province's future.

"What's more, the terrorists stand for fascism, totalitarianism, death, and destruction. We, in contrast, eschew those notions. We stand firmly together, all of us who seek goodness, with the principles of the three Ls—Liberalism, Loyalty, and Legacy.

"In this case, my friends, the last L—Legacy—is a small 'l' legacy. We seek to create a legacy for our future, our families and future generations, to look at us at this moment in time, giving thanks for our steadfastness and fortitude to do what is right, and to create what we know is possible, a perfect small 'l' legacy.

"It is in this spirit that I announce to you that a new regime has formed. The Legacy has failed us. The unmitigated killings, injuries, destruction, and pain will come to an immediate end. That was the small *l* legacy the former regime leaves. But that legacy will only live on in historical accounts because I announce to you at this time, our new regime has already begun taking steps—doing what is necessary—to eradicate *Molon Labe* and its brethren.

"Brothers and sisters, we proudly stand in this moment as witness to the creation of a *new day*. Effective immediately, The Legacy has been disbanded, and our new regime, with sworn dedication and devotion to you in addition to your collective safety and security, has risen to meet the challenge.

"My friends, in this hour of our province's greatest need, I have humbly accepted the call to leadership. What we create today ensures our finest and brightest tomorrows. It ensures that together, we will bring light to the dark, hope to the hopeless, and prosperity to the forgotten.

"Together, we are creating the perfect new day. In fact, it's truly a new day in our province." Berko rose from his seat. The camera widened as he stood rigid, arms at his side, with his trademark stare.

"Long live and thanks be to *The New Day!*"

Chapter LXXXI

They got to Legacy City International Airport as quickly as they could. They hardly had a moment to say thanks and goodbye to Frank and Margot. The Gies family had taken extraordinary risks on their behalf. For that, and for so much more, they would be eternally grateful.

Jeannie finally felt like she could breathe. Both she and Anjali had very little with them except, of course, what mattered most—their girls. Without much convincing, Jeannie was able to persuade Rolando's mother to come along. She didn't need details, just an invitation. Jeannie suspected that Alondra knew all along what was happening. Or, at a minimum, had a sense of it all.

The girls were in good spirits. None of the four had ever been on an airplane before. There was a sense of excitement and a hint of levity as well. Jeannie and Anjali had escaped certain imprisonment and likely execution. Now, they were on their way to start a new adventure, a new chapter, one they hoped would provide for safety and opportunity for their respective families.

"Girls, quiet please," Jeannie admonished her little ones as they approached the airport. Anjali's girls looked at their mother for guidance. Anjali quickly put her index finger over her pursed mouth. "Please, not again," said Jeannie with her hands clasped together.

"*Dios mío*," said Alondra softly, crossing herself on her lap to not call attention to herself.

The airport and adjoining airfield was surrounded by what appeared to be thousands of troops. It looked as though these troops meant business. They were met at the private aircraft entrance by a cadre of armed personnel.

"Papers," growled the soldier.

"Papers?" said Jeannie.

"Yes, papers. You cannot enter without papers."

The soldier had a definite accent. Jeannie wasn't sure, although it sounded like a hint of British English spoken by a native Mandarin speaker.

"We were instructed to come here. We're meeting Cassandra Hatua."

The soldier turned and spoke to another armed soldier. The show of security was as impressive as it was disquieting. After receiving some information, she returned to address Jeannie.

"You may pass. Third plane, right side."

When they arrived close to the plane, Cassandra stepped down to greet them. "So glad you made it. We're grounded. Don't know how long this will last."

"What's happening? So many troops?" Anjali asked.

"A coup. There's been a coup."

"A coup? How could there be a coup?" Jeannie questioned, trying to remain calm for the girls . . . and herself.

"It's tough to get accurate information at this moment. Berko went on all comms channels claiming he was in charge of a new ruling regime."

"Berko? Boris Berko?" asked a stunned Anjali.

"That's what I understand. Everything's as dense as fog around here during summer. Please come aboard, and we'll wait here until we know more."

The seven ladies joined Cassandra, Simon, Dianne, and the flight crew onboard the latest Hatua Aeronautical Company Global Traveler duel-engine jet. It was not in the hypersonic class, but it did have plenty of range, cabin space, and power. All that mattered not, at least not to the adults. The children were making themselves at home, swinging around on the club seats, and jumping on and off the three-seat divan.

The pilot came back to talk with Cassandra. They did so privately. She returned to the cockpit.

"The pilot tells me that she's been instructed to stand down and kill the engines. All aircraft are grounded. Even those already airborne have been instructed to land at the nearest airport. We might be here awhile."

Dianne decided to engage the girls in teaching them a card game in the aft cabin. Hearing "Go fish!" was a welcome relief from the anxiety-ridden moments. At times, it was tough to distinguish cries of "Go fish!" from calls for more "Goldfish" crackers. All four girls seemed captivated by Dianne's sweet personality. The candy and cheesy crackers on the table didn't hurt either.

"Are we safe here?" Jeannie asked cautiously.

"I think so, at least as safe as anywhere else at this point. It's a mess out there right now."

Jeannie looked out the window. Troops were moving about the airport's perimeter. Additional weapons were placed at varying points. Although she wasn't sure what those weapons were, she knew what the outcome would be if their group forced the troops to engage their use.

After about fifteen minutes of waiting, Jeannie received a double tap on her wrist. She had a direct communication request pending. As it was a private undisclosed request with no identifiable person and no identifiable location, it was probably worth taking.

"I think I have an incoming private communication request," Jeannie said to the others.

Cassandra said, "Please go to the forward cabin and shut the connector for privacy."

"Thank you." Jeannie moved forward to the cabin space between the cockpit and where they were sitting mid-plane.

"Accept communication request."

"Jeannie, thanks for accepting my request. Are you and the girls safe?"

"Yes, thanks, Disung. I think so, at least. I have Rolando's mother with us too."

"Excellent. If I may ask, where are you?"

"On a plane. With Hank Hatua's wife, Cassandra."

"I don't understand."

"To make a long story short, we were found out while at the Legacy City Coin Depository. Hank Hatua found us out. We weren't able to complete our mission. I'm so sorry Disung."

"It's important you are safe. How did you escape?"

"We didn't. Hatua let us go. All of us, including his wife, who was helping us."

"I see."

"Hank Hatua arranged for us to depart using one of his planes. It's all so odd to me."

"Me too. Not like him at all. Where are you headed?"

"Out of here, that's for sure. Is there a safe place anywhere?"

"Good question. Getting out of Legacy City is your first priority. Anywhere is better than there. There's been a coup."

"Yes, we heard. Berko is in charge, is that right?"

"Yes, it is," Disung paused.

"You still there?"

"Yes, I am. Jeannie, there will be more changes coming. It's very important that you leave. Are you all prepared to depart?"

"I think so. We have pilots, our families—Anjali is with us along with her two girls—and Cassandra's parents too. Well, I mean her father and his wife."

"Simon Bowles is with you? That's very good. Very good indeed."

"I heard that all air travel has been halted. Not just here, but province-wide."

"Yes, that's true. Jeannie, I must go now. I will reach out again. Stay safe."

"Disung."

"Yes."

"You stay safe too."

"I intend to, thank you. Bye for now."

Jeannie sat there thinking. They had been in harm's way and had survived thus far. Why? What plan was there for her and her family? Who or what was helping them? And Disung. He was in the middle of it all with the CCP leadership. How was he surviving? Why had he not been caught? So many questions. Jeannie's internal dialogue was interrupted by voices in the cockpit. She then heard the roar of the engines starting up. The pilot exited the cockpit, excused herself as she passed Jeannie, and went directly to Cassandra.

"We've been cleared to taxi out to the runway."

"What happened? What changed?"

"Can't say exactly. A miracle, perhaps? We're the only ones cleared at this time as far as I know."

"Okay, we'll take a miracle then."

"Ma'am, we'll need to know where to head. You have time to let us know. We're set for fuel and have plenty of range. Our priority is to get airborne quickly."

"Thank you. We'll discuss our destination and let you know."

The pilot excused herself and went back to the cockpit.

"I have an idea," said Simon Bowles. "There's a place for us."

Chapter LXXXII

"They're airborne? Safely on their way? Good, good. No, that's all. Thank you."

Hatua had thought enough. It was time to feel, to embrace his heart over his mind. He had lived in his mind his entire life. There was so much expected from him ever since he was a small child, all based on his mind, his intellect, his capacity to take disjointed information and make sense of it. Building devices, infrastructure, and more, all thanks to his incredible mind.

No more! That's enough! Hank Hatua heard screaming in his mind, as if his very own brain was under attack. Because it was. He was feeling at a deeper level than ever before. Life became very simple for him now. What were previously agonizingly complex decisions were as simple as second-grade math. His heart and feelings were no longer buried. They had been unlocked, all thanks to Cass. She showed him a better way. She brought it out of him. It was, in fact, there. It just needed the right person to help him expose the nerves he capped off. They were now exposed. Raw. Yet satisfying.

He knew what to do. For his love, Cassandra. And for himself. To find a way to finally accept himself and find love within himself. And, ultimately, to love himself too.

Hatua was as calm as he had ever been. A sense of peace and warmth enveloped him.

Hatua placed his right eye in front of the retinal scanner. *Hank Hatua. Confirmed. Access granted.* In front of him was the active Legacy Coin master dataset. He looked at it, his eyes focusing on one name after another, some still living, others who had passed, even others who never had the chance to take a breath on this earth. He closed his eyes. He asked for forgiveness for sins committed over so many, many years.

He opened his eyes, took a deep breath, and with a firm resolve to change the world for the better, uttered three simple words.

"Disable. Delete. Destroy."

It was done.

Chapter LXXXIII

"No. No! There must be some mistake. This can't be! Run a system check and get back to me. Do it, now!"

On this first day of his crowning achievement, his long-awaited and long sought-after triumph, Berko would not allow for any hiccups, no disruptions, nothing to deviate from his plan. Nothing.

"General Berko." It was General Zhang. *Why is it that Zhang would appear at the most inopportune moments,* Berko thought to himself. No matter. Berko was in charge. He could handle General Zhang.

"General Zhang. As you know, it's no longer General Berko. It's Supreme Leader Berko or Dear Leader. Either is fine."

"Yes, but of course. Titles do make the person, don't they? Or, do they?"

Berko wasn't in the mood for General Zhang's verbal repartee.

"So, you've heard the latest, have you?" the general said with some hint of perverse pleasure.

"Yes. We're running a system check. I'm expecting the reporting was in error, and we'll be back to processing Legacy Coins promptly."

"Do you?"

Berko was contemplating whether he should call in his Reso protective services to escort the general out —out of his office and out of his province. "Yes," said Berko with his characteristic confidence, "I do."

"Hmmm," mused the general as she paced around Berko. "I don't. You see—"

General Zhang was interrupted by a communication. She spoke rapidly in Chinese to someone. She would periodically look at Berko while she spoke. Then, she changed to responding in English while the other person continued in Mandarin.

"Yes, he's here. I understand. Yes. Immediately? Yes, I understand completely, sir. *Shì de. Wéi, nǐ hǎo.*"

General Zhang turned to Berko. "Mr. Berko, you—"

"That's Supreme Lead—"

"Mister," General Zhang interrupted, saying mister slowly and intentionally, "Berko. You have failed."

Berko decided to stand down and listen.

General Zhang continued, "You failed in protecting the lives of China's most valiant sons and daughters. Your failure led to the deaths of 237 RDF members. You failed in maintaining order in the province. Your Reso forces have been a disgrace, and we believe they have been significantly infiltrated by terrorists."

Although it appeared that the general was not finished, Berko decided that he needed to defend himself straight away. "General, as you know, the deaths were not my fault nor due to any negligence on my part. In fact—"

"Mister Berko, I suggest you listen. It may prove beneficial to you later."

"You failed in the mission to activate Legacy Coins. In Chicago, you failed to protect Legacy Coins from destruction. In the province as a whole, you failed to protect Legacy Coins from being disabled from within. Yes, it's been confirmed. Your friend, Hank Hatua—"

"You know Hatua's not my friend."

"Your friend," again, General Zhang was enjoying emphasizing pain points for Berko, "Hank Hatua, accessed the Legacy Coin system, overrode security protocols and coin activation process, including those on the three-day hold, and deleted the entire master dataset. He had the coin readers run an internal disintegration progression. There is no more Legacy Coin program. It has been destroyed. Destroyed. You failed in that as well."

Berko had been around long enough to know exactly where this was headed. He didn't have many, if any, cards to play. "If that is the conclusion, and that I will be tarnished with these events, then I will offer my resignation to the CCP leadership."

"Ha! Well played." General Zhang was grinning. "That won't do. You knew that anyway. You will stand trial in China for your crimes against the Party. Oh, one more thing, along with everything else, you will be charged with having mounted a coup against one of the CCP's hand-picked regimes. You might know that crime is the same as if you engaged in sedition against Beijing itself."

"But," Berko pleaded, "you know the truth. You can help me. You were involved as well. You helped me. We were doing this together. Coordinated. Complementary. Reso and RDF working together well for our new beginnings here."

"Were we? Was I?" General Zhang ran her hand along Berko's desk and rubbed her fingers together as if she was removing dust. "You know, leadership is furious . . . at you. There's nothing I can do about that," she paused, "my friend."

Berko slumped in his chair. It was over. His life's work and ambition, for what? Not even two hours' worth of return. It was as if all of his blood and energy had just been extracted from him. He sat there, motionless.

"I don't want you to worry about the trial, Bo. It will be a quick affair." General Zhang was enjoying this much more than she thought she would. But there was more. "As we speak, my RDF team is engaged in a cleanup operation of Reso members that *you* should've done long ago. Yes. That's right. We're here. Here to stay.

"Jǐng wèi!"

Guards filled the room promptly. General Zhang nodded in their direction as they pulled Berko up out of his seat and started walking him toward the door.

"Tíng zhǐ!"

The guards stopped on the general's command. She looked at Berko as if she was mocking him and his infamous stare.

"Boris Berko, you will be transported to China now. Sorry that I won't be joining you," said the general as she walked around Berko's desk to take a seat in Berko's large leather chair. She leaned back and put her spotless boots up on the desk. "I have duties here that will prevent me from doing so. I'll just watch with great interest from afar. I'm sure you'll understand." Berko's face was regaining blood. He was enraged inside yet didn't want to give General Zhang the satisfaction of seeing it. It was then that Berko swore to himself that he'd find a way to survive and get his revenge against the general.

General Zhang pulled her boots off the desk and walked toward Berko. She leaned in close to Berko's face. "Tsk tsk tsk. You should've known better, Boris. You call yourself a disciple of Sun Tzu? Well, if true, you must be familiar with one of

Master Tzu's greatest lessons. You know it, Boris?" General Zhang was within inches of Berko's face. Berko didn't move or flinch. "Hmm? No?" General Zhang said the last words as slowly as she could, with steely eyes looking for the moment of Berko's recognition of what the words she was about to speak meant in their context. "All . . . war . . . is . . . deception."

The general commanded flatly, "*Bǎ tā dài zǒu.*" The guards took Berko away.

Chapter LXXXIV

Klein was finally alone. Just he and his thoughts. It had been some time in coming. Not being alone, that wasn't it. It had been some time in coming when forces aligned to take the first step in taking back a once great nation. He was convinced that he wouldn't see it in his lifetime. But then again, "it takes one spark" as he would often say. It appeared to Klein that more than one spark converged to create a conflagration that he hoped and prayed would consume a people. Consume them in their pursuit of freedom.

He thought of the surgeon who saved him; Shontae and Mitch's leadership, love, and loss; Zim's virtue and how he intended to make things as right as he could for his cousin and her family; and Zim's leadership, under trying circumstances, and the victory their unlikeliest of teams secured against all odds. He thought of the countless lives saved by their actions.

Most of all, he thought of his granddaughter, Hannah, how her world might change for the better. How she, and others like her, were the hope. He was so proud to call her granddaughter. And, even more so, to call her friend and fellow warrior.

* * *

Jeannie was doing her thinking at 35,000 feet. The kids were napping. She sat there, surrounded by people in a plane yet, like Klein—a person she heard of but never met—very alone with her thoughts as well.

She was still mourning her loss. It remained raw and real. Even with that pain, she was thankful for how she and her girls survived, thankful to have Rolando's mom with them, and thankful to have gained a best friend, someone she admired and loved.

She looked at Cassandra, who looked like she was also deep in her own thoughts. Earlier, they heard the news about Hank Hatua being arrested, along with Boris Berko, for crimes against the province. They also heard about the destruction of the entire Legacy Coin operation and that Hank had made that sacrifice for which he would pay dearly, most probably with his life.

Jeannie struggled with understanding how the people of decades prior didn't see the warning signs on the horizon. They permitted themselves to be fooled. She believed that they knew they were being deceived, that their country was being dismantled piece by piece, but they were too busy, distracted, or afraid to do anything about it. Sheep being led to slaughter or like lemmings to the sea seemed appropriate analogies to her.

And what about her role in all of this? Why didn't she question what she was doing? What was the real intent behind the Legacy Coin program? Why didn't she care more about the *why* she was asked to do certain things rather than focusing just on the *what* of it all?

Anjali. Her brilliant and dear friend. She looked at Anjali asleep, with her girls nestled up against her. They looked so peaceful. There would be hard times ahead for them. Those girls were so fortunate to have a mom like Anji.

Her gaze then moved over to Ana and Juli. Jeannie couldn't comprehend life without them. They brought so much wonder, laughter, and innocence to her life. Innocence. What a strange word during these times. How could she ever protect them and their childhood from the clutches of a society complacent in tyranny, a society that put a premium on differences as opposed to what bound people together, and a society that showed little to no care for the sanctity of life? Jeannie resolved that even if she was the last to do so, she would fill her children with love for others, no matter their condition, just like their father would have done.

Rolando. Her love. In an odd way, being above the clouds brought her closer to him. She knew it wasn't actually true, yet in her heart, it felt that way. She hoped he would be proud of her, proud of the girls as she was certainly proud of him. It was as if he knew that he wouldn't survive his quest for answers, for truth. He set things up for her and her alone—okay, with Anji's help—to finish the job. She started to mouth words to him. *Rolando Rafael Garcia,* ***you*** *did it. You saved lives, hundreds of thousands if not millions of lives. You helped stopped genocide on a scale previously unthinkable. You confronted evil. You won, my love. You won.*

She clutched her pendant. She thought of his goofy message to her. She laughed to herself. While doing so, she unconsciously pulled out the pendent and began looking at it—front and back, feeling their love. She looked very closely at the *Leon y Cordero*. Indeed, her husband was both lion and lamb. She whispered, "Thank you, Rolando. I'll always love you." With tears streaming down her cheeks, she said something she never thought she would, yet it seemed so natural and right at that moment, "Thanks be to God."

Her moment was interrupted by a serious pain. It was a familiar pain to her. Her baby kicked her hard, then kicked again. She smiled. It was an authentic smile and not a grimace from the pain, for at that moment, she knew. It was a boy. Rolando's son. "What are you doing in there, Junior?" Another kick. "Junior, you like that name?" Two hard kicks and a punch. *Yep,* she thought, *we have another scrapper on our hands.* That was a good thing. He'd have to join the fight for their collective future. Jeannie knew that Junior would be up for it. He was, after all, the product of both the lion and the lamb.

She reached into her pocket and pulled out Junior's Legacy Coin. How blessed, she thought, were they. She felt the coin against her fingers. She ran her index finger along the ridges ringing the coin's outside. That's it. That's how they did it. For the first time, after handling hundreds of Legacy Coins, she noticed something new. The ridges were the key. That's how they knew which coins belonged to which person. There were subtle differences in the coins. That's how the coin readers worked. It was like a fingerprint. Clever, she thought. Clever in a wicked way.

She held the Legacy Coin flat in her lap. She thought of how Rolando would be talking to their baby. He loved to talk, sing, and read to their babies. He would even tell them jokes. That was his thing. Then, something caught her attention, something that made her heart flutter. She began to panic. The Legacy Coin was illuminated brightly. What was happening? Her baby? Her boy? What did she or someone do? How could this be stopped?

As she began to turn to Anji to wake her up, she noticed something else. The coin wasn't illuminated anymore. She giggled. She couldn't stop giggling. She giggled like she was a preteen again. She covered her mouth so she wouldn't disturb anyone. The illumination wasn't from her baby's Legacy Coin being activated or deactivated. Stress might've been getting to her. It wasn't the type of illumination she would see when she was working with patients and delivering babies. Instead, it was life-affirming light. It was the sun's rays reflecting off the coin.

She did clearly disturb one person due to her outburst. Her baby kicked again and again. She considered those sympathy kicks for her giggling episode.

Jeannie considered the sun, her son, and the Son shining brightly on them all. Perhaps, just perhaps, it was a metaphor for where they and their province were headed, in a better direction, for a brighter future filled with more freedom, forgiveness, and perhaps even faith. Rolando taught her so many important life lessons. What was especially speaking to her heart was the truth that Rolando lived day in and day out. Nothing was more important than family and faith.

She spoke softly to her yet unborn baby. "Your sisters and I can't wait to meet you. The world is upside down now. But, little love, I promise you this. Everything's gonna be alright. I just know it. Your daddy is with us, with you, in you. He loves you and us so much. Know this, that he and I will do everything in our power to give you and your sisters a better life, a better future."

Jeannie closed her eyes and took a deep breath. She knew with a certainty that surpassed all understanding, and with a clarity and peace she had never previously felt, that with the impending turn of the calendar year, her world—their world—would change dramatically for the better.

She looked forward to the promise of renewed hope in 2085.

-The End-

Epilogue

"Hey, I found something. Come here!"

"What?" said the teenaged girl, sounding more annoyed than curious.

"Look at this," said a boy who looked like he was still a year or more short of a decade. His face full of wonder, he offered his outstretched hand to the girl. "It looks valuable. Like money."

The girl took the item from the boy.

"Well," inquired the boy with anticipation, "what is it?"

She quickly knew what she held in her hand. Her disposition changed as a sense of foreboding swept over her.

"We need to go. Now!"

"What? What is it? Hey, give it back!"

The girl reared back and threw the item as hard and as far as she could. Given their perch near the top of a mountain, the result of her throw belied her demure stature.

"What'd you do that for?"

"Randy, stop! Come back here."

She was too late. He couldn't hear her. Or didn't want to. The boy followed the trajectory of her throw down the steep slope. He skidded and tumbled downward. In a few moments, he would be catapulted off the side of the mountain to boulders located over one thousand feet below.

"Randy! Stop! Raaaandeeee!" The girl shrieked. She knew in an instant, the boy would head over the cliff to his certain and untimely death.

She heard a loud thud. Then silence.

She ran as fast as she could down the hill, grabbing at branches, and clawed at the ground to keep her balance.

Her worst fears were not realized. Lying still on the ground was her little brother. He was whimpering in a muted way. He was clearly hurt, yet still alive. He didn't go over the cliff as she dreaded. And she quickly discerned why he hadn't. While tumbling down the grade, he was saved by something that caused his body to come to an immediate halt just before the edge. In an instant, she recognized what saved him.

It was a chunk of an airplane's fuselage.

Acknowledgements

To my original editor extraordinaire, Joseph M. Earley, Jr., your wordsmithing prowess, and attention to the minutest of details, will always reign supreme. Just wish you were still with us to hold our final product in your hands. To Marina, may God bless and keep you. Thanks for your steadfast support along the way.

To my medical experts, Drs. Dan Blue and Chris Johansen, thank you for saving me from the embarrassment of observing a J.D. practicing medicine (on these pages, at least) without a license.

To my buddy and international relations/military expert, Chris Stewart, the Fishin' Magician has nothing on your helpful insights – except as to alligator gar fishing, perhaps. Mo'o!

To my dream team of readers – Alicia Garcia, Robin Zephier (Sungila Sapa), Larry LaHaye, Seth Mallios, and Jim Herrick – your precision questioning and suggestions made this novel better. They also made me a better writer.

To my Liberty Hill and Salem Author Services team, especially Toni Riggs, Robert McDougal, and Nina Sterling, working with you was such a blessing and pleasure. Here's to our next adventure!

Credit and thanks also to Christy Callahan and Rod Evans Photography for bringing your energy and talents to this project.

And, finally, to my spice girls. Life is better with a healthy serving of Ginger and Little Miss Nutmeg. I couldn't imagine life without you two. Thank you for the constant love, support, encouragement, and well-placed ideas. I love you bunches!

What They're Saying About *The Coin*

Reagan said, "Those who have known freedom, and then lost it, have never known it again." In case you are tempted to believe that W.T. Earley's dystopian world is pure fantasy, an examination of history will prove that folly. Look at all the damage our nation has suffered at the hands of the most unaccountable and incompetent regime in American history. Left unchecked, the woke mobs, progressive elites, and their tools of anarchy will eventually destroy the American experiment. The privileged "untouchables," who greatly miscalculate their power, won't decide how America will be remade -- Communist China will. *The Coin* isn't only a compelling thought piece. It's a warning for every freedom-loving patriot!

--Chris Salcedo, Host, The Chris Salcedo Show on Newsmax TV

The Coin is a poignant look at what all Americans and all the world should take to heart and be aware, as this is where our world is heading. A great novel brilliantly conceived, beautifully written, and smacks with the reality we all live in today. An excellent read.

--Larry LaHaye, son of the late Pastor Dr. Tim LaHaye, co-author of the *Left Behind* series

In a dystopian society where all power rests with the autocratic few, freedom is on life support. W.T. Earley answers the question: what may (or perhaps will) happen to our beloved country if China's ruthless leaders, woke mobs, leftist media, and greedy technocrats are allowed to rule with impunity? Ronald Reagan's iconic and prescient warning of the fragile nature of freedom comes to alarming life in the pages of *The Coin*. A must read, *The Coin* is a clarion call for free peoples the world over to stand against the rise of the left's unapologetic lies and tyranny!

--Brent Bozell, Founder and President, Media Research Center

CPSIA information can be obtained
at www.ICGtesting.com
Printed in the USA
BVHW070245201122
652313BV00001B/1

9 781662 863288